# THE UNDEFEATED

*"A blessed companion is a book"*—JERROLD

# THE
# UNDEFEATED

\*

## I. A. R. WYLIE

**THE COMPANION BOOK CLUB**
LONDON

*To*

NICOLAS AND MARGUERITE BENSA

*with affection and admiration*

*Made and Printed in Great Britain
for The Companion Book Club (Odhams Press Ltd.)
by Odhams (Watford) Limited
Watford, Herts*
S.1258.Z.RA.

# CONTENTS

# CONTENTS

# PART ONE

# ROCQUEDUR, SPRING 1953

# I

THE guidebooks call Rocquedur a "village perché". But in fact it is a walled citadel, once haughtily powerful, that has at last surrendered to forces against which neither boiling oil, arrows nor even guns prevail. In one place its high thick ramparts have crumbled, and through the breach tall ancient houses have seeped onto the open mountainside, to which they cling with tenacious fangs. The nerve-flaying mistral and the wild storms that in winter crash about the peaks of the Alpes-Maritimes should long since have dislodged a seemingly dying habitat and blown its rags and tatters of stubborn life to limbo. But stones and life seem to have attained a sort of permanence in ruin.

The Abbé, Thomas Clerissy, maintains that when the last atomic bomb has wiped out the last of sinful but, worst of all, idiot humanity (for one can cope with sin, but against idiocy God Himself is helpless), Rocquedur's roots, woven fast into the mountain's flanks, will send up fresh shoots. The tall, pale houses will rise again, stone by stone, out of utter desolation. Radiant human dust will silt onto the worn doorsteps and settle on the sightless windows. But then the Abbé, notoriously heterodox, was born in one of those houses and admits robustly that he has crazy notions. His church is built on the foundations of a Roman temple. It is a sort of poor relation of the parish church at Basdur, at the base of the mountain. (Basdur and Rocquedur despise each other. Basdur has become a town with a weekly cinema, a post-office and a railway station.) It guards the Grand' Place on the west and defies the vulgar modernity of the Café des Artistes on the east. Its south portals open on the Place de l'Eglise where is the Abbé's presbytery. The church is grim and ugly, only redeemed by a delicately wrought iron belfry whose cracked bell tolls the hour twice for the benefit of the inattentive. Inside, its vaulted ceiling flickers with gold stars. Its walls and pillars are washed with a faded Virgin's blue. Garish but rather shabby saints stand watch in their shallow niches, their feet hidden in faded wreaths, their haloes dustily askew. About them small marble plaques testify to their

11

miraculous intervention. ("Merci, St. Roche.") The last plaque is dated August, 1949. After that, it seems, the age of miracles came to an end. By the west door a tall crucifix hangs in shadow, the gaunt face of its blood-streaked burden downcast in perpetual agony. There are no wreaths about its nail-torn feet and no thank-offerings. It has the resigned sadness of someone once dearly loved and now almost forgotten. The tiny altar lamp glows in the grey chill like a warm, throbbing heart. The Abbé tends it himself. His sacristan is old, stupid and indifferent. Besides, the Abbé has another notion that if he tends it faithfully, the little light will one day burst into a great flame which will consume the faithless indifference of his people.

At Easter and other great festivals, Monsieur le Curé of Basdur drives up in his Renault to celebrate High Mass, and his Vicaire, the Abbé Clerissy serves him with becoming if unusual humility. He is passionately ashamed of his congregation, which consists mainly of old women who come from habit and children who can't help themselves. The old women are a race apart. In the daytime they live silently behind closed shutters, or, if they emerge briefly, it is to walk with a slow but inexorable tread which permits no loitering. On summer evenings they sit close to each other on the communal benches and knit or watch the goings-on at the Café des Artistes with sharp enigmatic eyes. Tomorrow, perhaps, the bell will toll for one of them. But another will take her place. She will wear the same rusty black. Her face will be the same grey, deeply scored mask which betrays nothing of what its wearer has learned from hard joyless living. The old women of Rocquedur are formidable. Death may attack them, but they close ranks.

The old men, and such of their sons and daughters as remain to them, go down before daybreak to their vineyards, whose steep terraces girdle the mountain flank. Their wine is poor and sells poorly. So the young people are drifting away, lured by the glittering illusion of the cities. Those who remain are taciturn and brooding, as though they find themselves tangled in a web from which there is no escape. There are children, too, who have a gnome-like look of agelessness. In the morning they crowd silently into the bleak schoolroom on the rue François and recite the départements and préfectures of France like a litany. Monsieur Boutton conducts their sing-song with a wooden baton. He is a withered stalk of an old man. He came to Rocquedur years ago, but no one remembers that he was ever young. The authorities, apparently, forgot him altogether. At least they never offered him a better post. He has one pleasure, to play chess with the Abbé, one ambition, to drag his small-fry, by hook or crook, through their *certificat des études*, one hope, to attain the tiny pension that will see him to the end of his puzzling little life.

At nightfall the children, barefoot, chase each other, silent as bats, through the ill-lit, fugitive streets, up and down the steep worn steps that lead from one level to another, and under the great oak-beam across the rue des Princes. The oldest among them remembers a man dangling from it, like a huge black candle with a twisted wick. He hung there for three days. He would have hung there longer if the Americans hadn't cut him down.

Years ago foreigners came to Rocquedur. Except for La Baronne and Mlle Milly, they fled in 1940—no one knew or cared where. But they came back. They live in wildly cluttered rooms in the old houses. They wear strange clothes and believe that they have "gone native". The real natives tolerate them. At the end of the month when presumably thankfully distant relatives pay them off, they dine heartily at the Auberge des Alouettes, which forms a triangle between the Place de l'Eglise and the rue François. For the rest of the month they eat mysteriously and alone.

La Baronne, when she is sober, paints bad water-colours. Sometimes tourists buy them, and then she enjoys a bout of hilarious, furious Russian drunkenness. Mlle Milly rents her an attic in the two-storied old house she owns next to the presbytery. The rent is never paid. But Mlle Milly has a small, steady income accruing from War Bonds, and an understanding affection for the lost. Her house is overrun by cats that from hunted and starving strays have become sleek, insolent tyrants. Mlle Milly speaks French fluently with a determined English accent. She manages to be exquisitely clean and hopelessly untidy. Like La Baronne, she is an artist. She has her own kiln in her cellar and bakes horrible painted plates and ash-trays. Bewildered tourists buy them too.

For the travel agencies have developed Rocquedur into a cultural "must"—a sort of hair-shirt atonement for the facile frivolities of Nice and Cannes. The road thither boasts of

twenty hairpin bends which the bus drivers negotiate with
blood-curdling nonchalance. Suddenly, in a cleft of the great
valley of the Var, the travellers see Rocquedur high above
them, on a thrust-out bastion like the prow of a fantastic
ship. It looks madly inaccessible. But eventually the road,
which seems to have some far-off purpose of its own, reaches
it and passes behind it to a clearing where the buses, like
panting dragons, disgorge their victims. The latter pass
under a broken arch and by way of a steep and narrow
cobbled street attain the Grand' Place and its church ("two-
starred fifteenth century and not to be missed") with its
worn, wide flight of steps. They cast grateful eyes at the
Café des Artistes (once a down-at-heel *bistro*) which offers
them refreshment under gay umbrellas that are as incon-
gruous as butterflies on a prison wall. There is a charming
fountain whose ancient dolphins toss up streams of crystal-
clear, sweet tinkling water into the sunlight. A medieval page
stands in the midst of them, carrying a stone standard on
which are carved the armorial bearings of the Counts de
Fouqué-Basdur, the citadel's one-time masters. The present
Count, the last one of his race, is a fat, white-faced old man
who still lives in the chateau on the rue des Princes, whose
outer wall is that of the rampart itself. The street door is
iron-studded and has an air of being closed irrevocably. In
fact since that night in August, 1944, when the old Count
guarded it with two old-fashioned but effective pistols, he has
not crossed the threshold. His housekeeper, Madame Julie,
creeps out at dusk and scurries from one shop to another as
though her own shadow might overtake and destroy her. She
is very stupid and very faithful. The shopkeepers treat her
as someone of no substance. They barely acknowledge her.

The guide mentions the Fouqué-Basdurs, but not their
present representative. He avoids him, as he avoids the little
burying ground lying on a grassy plateau just to the right of
the main gateway. It is not the communal cemetery whose
granite and marble mausoleums and tin wreaths and faded
glass portraits of the grim-faced departed cling to the mountainside outside the walls. It is a place sadly set apart for the
eight men and two women who lie neatly side by side,
headed by small wooden crosses on which are painted their
names and a common date—August 25, 1944. Well, that is all
of nine years ago. Better forgotten.

At the ramparts the tourists gape obediently at what they

14

are told is one of the most impressive views in Europe. It oppresses them. Far beneath, out of sight, is a turbulent little river whose glacial waters, centuries ago, cleft the mountain range and now pour through to join the sprawling Var on their common journey to the sea. Opposite are range upon range of purple-shadowed hills that, since they rise from sea-level, are considered mountains and appear majestic. Wherever there is a foothold their flanks are criss-crossed with vineyards or patched with the soft green of olive groves or aflame, in springtime, with roses and carnations. In the far distance loom the ghostly sentinels of the Bas-Alpes.

Having done their duty, the tourists turn thankfully—for it is all too much for them, too remote from their experience—to the Café des Artistes, which proffers relief to their thirsty exhaustion, and to the village vendors who lurk behind their temporary wooden booths like spiders. La Baronne, if she happens to be sober, has erected a sort of wooden screen on which she has festooned examples of her art. At all prices and in all shapes and sizes she exhibits her version of Rocquedur in flaming sunsets, thunderstorms and moonlight. There are even portraits of the natives in their Provençal dress, which they no longer wear. Her huge swollen body draped in scarves and layers of moth-eaten cardigans—for even in the height of summer she is cold—the wild peroxide hair and drink- and disease-raddled face, made up as in a nightmare, terrify customers into an obsequious buying. (They do not notice her eyes, which under their hooded lids are shrewd and kindly, still tragically beautiful.)

The tourists move on thankfully. They buy postcards with which to annoy friends at home, lavender bags which they will lose, and even honey, which they will never eat, from the man with his two-wheeled donkey cart and a black shaggy dog that in more sophisticated canine circles might have been a poodle. The donkey is a salesman in himself. He has polished hoofs and a plump well-being not usual in Provençal donkeys. The man is blind. However, the visitors do not buy from him out of pity but because, in spite of the dark glasses and the scar that zig-zags from his right temple across a sun-browned cheek, he has battered good looks and a warm, gay friendliness. His hand, holding out awkwardly a painted pot of honey, is deformed as though in some bad accident. The tourists inquire discreetly. La Baronne, who is never discreet, tells them that he is Pascal Guis, a man

15

highly honoured in these parts. But a man selling honey and wearing a peasant's faded jeans does not accord with the tourists' notion of an important man. He is too obviously poor.

In response to the bored admonitions of their guide, they trail back to the waiting buses and roll down the horrifying road to the coast and the white glittering cities which they understand, which do not trouble them.

The wooden booths are then folded up and hidden out of sight. Men come up from the vineyards to play *boule* on the Grand' Place. They play in silence, their movements prescribed as by some ancient ritual. The *cochonet* tossed expertly sends up a tiny cloud of dust. The light fades. The games are over. The Place empties. The whole village sinks into an immemorial silence, broken only by the sad-voiced bell which is so much a part of life that no one hears it any more.

But in late spring and the height of summer other invaders storm the citadel. Young women cling to young men on screeching and snorting Vespas, huge foreign cars laden with opulent seekers of relief from the coastal heat, negotiate as best they can the hair-pin bends. Their lights flash like fire-flies and throw yellow streamers over the mountainside. The Café des Artistes springs into full life. Waitresses in white blouses and Provençal skirts hurry from the modern kitchen to the crowded tables. Behind his bar the bartender and general manager, Pierre Donadet, juggles his gay bottles with increasing speed. Paper lanterns throw kaleidoscope colours on the couples who dance languidly on the small paved dance floor to brassy music tossed down to them from the loud-speaker hidden in the solitary plane tree. Children and village dogs chase one another round the fountain and even among the dancers, who do not seem aware of them. They are shadows with their own secretive and silent life.

Outside the circle of light the old women sit close-packed on their benches and watch with stolid patience. Perhaps they take obscure pleasure in the music and flamboyant life. No one knows. The men perch on the ramparts or lean against them, their faded shirts open to the waist, their arms folded. Their cigarettes, like tiny pulses, throb against the dark. Sometimes one of them will turn and look down into the lightless valley as though in expectation of some event, long awaited, long overdue.

Freddi Waldkirch, the café's patron, clad exquisitely in cream-coloured shirt and slacks, saunters among his guests. He has a good host's way with him. Where he stops to chat, somehow champagne is ordered. The gaiety reaches a crescendo before it sags slowly to grey lassitude.

At two o'clock punctually the lights go out. The waitresses and cooks trail, sore-footed, to the bus that awaits them outside the gate. Freddi Waldkirch drives a closed Jaguar. A favoured guest drives with him. This is a privilege, for Freddi is a superb driver, at once smooth, fast and cautious.

By dawn the last of the invaders has fled. The citadel resumes its enigmatic reality. It watches over the slowly emerging valley as for an ancient enemy who never comes.

This is Rocquedur in the spring of 1953. It is as the driver of a dark green Volkswagen gliding toward Nice by way of the Grande Corniche remembers it. Such changes as have taken place in his eight years of waiting will not astonish or disconcert him. He has foreseen them. He has prepared himself to meet them.

## II

THE Domaine Guis lies at a kilometre's distance from Rocquedur and is reached from the citadel by a rough dirt road guarded on its outer flank from a precipice by tall, closely ranked cypresses. On its way it passes a wine-press, a stable and a deep cellar, both carved out of the cliff's face, squeezes behind the Mas and straggles haphazard down into the valley. It is good enough for wine-laden ox-carts. But motorists, trapped by curiosity, have been known to lose their nerve. Nina Guis, who knows every rut and curve like the features of a rugged old friend, has had to reassure them and manoeuvre them into safety.

Close to the kitchen door a goat track twists up the face of the cliff, eventually to the summit, but first to a deep cave which long ago served as a look-out for the beleaguered city, and recently as a desperate way of escape for hunted men. It is now overgrown with weeds, wild flowers, and broom, and half-blocked by fallen stones. Sometimes Pascal Guis pulls Suzon, his dog, to a halt and caught in a web of remembrance lifts his blank eyes to the great height and feels his forehead damp with sweat.

17

Cedars, orange and olive groves encircle the Domaine like a defending army. Its vineyards descend the mountainside in steep terraces. They are small, but their soil has a stony porous quality and enjoys the sunlight of the great Burgundies. So it has been the dream of the Guis people that one year they will produce a truly noble wine. Where the descent is less precipitous, a plateau of lavender, with bee-hives in its midst, breathes out a ghostly mist of sweetness.

The Mas is two storied. It straggles along the face of the cliff that, because its ochre-hue is faintly rose-streaked, is called the Baue Rouge. Since the Mas is built of the same stone, it melts into its towering background. The rooms are low-ceilinged and dark and furnished with pleasant indifference to comfort. Hard, high-backed chairs, great hard beds where generations have been born, have loved, have died. Water is still raised from an ancient well. There is no sanitation that sophisticated town-dwellers would recognize as such. It has remained through the years, and even in its resurrection, implacably austere. Yet it has a quality of warmth, of hearty and hardy human endeavour. Two orange trees guard the patio, open on one side to the valley, and at dusk their fruit glows like golden lanterns. The patio itself, sheltered in spring and summer by a giant vine whose gnarled fist holds fast to the stones, is a pleasant place, the Abbé Clerissy thinks, for friends to get together, to watch the clouds, rosy with sunset, throw drifting shadows over the beloved country, to breathe the scent of roses, full-blown already and pouring in fiery tumult over pale walls, eat Grand'mère Guis's rich Provençal stew and help empty the carafe of the 1947 vintage.

The Abbé scrubs his plate clean with a last crust which he pops into a cheerful, capacious mouth.

"The worst of all heresies," he booms, "is the belief that the pleasures of the flesh are evil. God provided them for our spiritual good. To deny them is to play into the hands of the devil, who wants nothing better than that we should be bored, miserable, and therefore sinful." He fumbles in the pockets of his green-hued soutane for a battered packet of Gaulois. "Monsieur le Curé, not to mention my Bishop, does not approve of me. I have not only been a trouble-maker; I am considered a gross fellow. But it is my conviction that I am a man after God's own heart."

The man and woman smile at him across the table. They

18

sit close to each other, as though from deeply familiar custom, so that the man has only to move slightly to touch the woman's shoulder. The vine, still wearing its young green, throws a delicate pattern on their faces and on the table with its red cloth and clutter of plates and glasses.

"At Mass," the Abbé continues—for he is a great talker when he finds anyone to listen to him—"God and I are together, but on formal terms. We are, so to speak, *en frac*. Here, in this good company, after this good meal, He and I are in shirtsleeves. We *tutoye* each other like old friends." He chuckles. "Do not denounce me."

He frowns at himself. The word "denounce" has a sorry quality. It is like a dangerous outcropping of rock in a smooth-flowing river. Not so long ago it had sounded a death-knell.

The Abbé sits back, stretching his huge shoulders so that the seams of his soutane crack in protest. He goes on, rather too fast and a little confusedly, covering a social *gaffe*. "Well, I must be on my way. I promised to look in on Mlle Milly to discuss the problem of another litter. It is strange that she doesn't become crazier or saner or even older." He breaks off to accept a lighted match from the woman's fingers. He blows a vigorous cloud of smoke into the still air and watches it dissolve with brown, slightly viscous eyes. Being elderly himself, he is an easy prey to memory. Since, as he says, he hasn't much to look forward to, except purgatory, about which he has unorthodox doubts, and a heaven about which he admits he has little knowledge, he is driven back into the substantial past. He is remembering, for instance, the Mas when it had been a tragic ruin. The French Milice had taken it apart, dynamiting the old stones that stubbornly defied them. Theirs had been the viciousness of guilt-hounded men— unlike the shooting of those ten village hostages by the Occupation Forces—an act of sheer revengeful savagery. (Things hadn't been going well with the Thousand Years' Reich. It was numbering its days.) Actually, Captain Ulrich von Freytag had expressed formal regrets. He had been, throughout, quite charmingly correct.

"You too have been a soldier, Abbé. You know how even disciplined soldiers, if they are angry, lose their heads."

The Abbé heaves a sigh.

"My God, but I gave her up for lost," he says out of his crowding thoughts. "There she was—an Englishwoman with an expired passport and a 'permis de séjour' as useful as a scrap of toiletpaper—indeed much less useful. I explained to the Captain, I said, 'She's crazy. She wouldn't go with the other English on account of her damned cats. She wouldn't desert them.' I must say he was quite decent. He said all the English were crazy and he liked cats. A lot of people thought he just commandeered her place (God knows it wasn't much better than a lying-in hospital for every feline female in the village. It stank!), but actually he made a bargain with her: her best room and its care against immunity and tidbits. They seem to have taken a queer liking to each other. He might have been another 'lost and strayed' about whose paternity and qualifications for kindness she asked no questions. She mothered him. She cleaned and even cooked for him—her abominable English cooking—and when she stole from his rations to keep La Baronne alive and reasonably drunk, he closed both military eyes. He used to kiss her hand, as I remember—a rather dirty claw in those soapless days. She was quite girlishly pleased." The Abbé helps himself to the dregs of the carafe. "Well, there she still is, and where he is the devil only knows."

He tosses his wine expertly down a wide-open gullet, his massive head thrown back to hide embarrassment. It's all old stuff. To recall it is like digging up bones that still have a few tatters of flesh clinging to them and give off a faint odour of putrefaction.

But the man's face opposite remains tranquil. A handsome face, except for the long white scar, smoothly bronzed and with a Roman quality of blunt-featured forcefulness. His eyes, behind their dark glasses, might be still grey and beautiful. The long mobile mouth has acquired, the Abbé reflects, a proud control over its capacity for fear, wild wrath and passion. It has become serene with a boyish gaiety lurking in its corners. (The Abbé remembers a child's face, asleep in a Provençal crib, and how he had looked down at it as at the embodiment of an official sin. Later the ragged, black browed, black-haired boy, skulking about the streets in savage loneliness, had driven out guilt so that compassion and tenderness had found place in his priest's tormented heart. He had held out a paternal hand. It had been fiercely rejected, until that day when, overwhelmed by a common grief, they had wept and prayed together.)

How long ago! Another life. His own self of those days

has become strange to him. Wounds have healed. A scar or two aches in certain weathers. Nina and Pascal may suffer sometimes. They may dream nightmares. The Abbé does. But at least they have this present and a future. The man turns to the woman, smiling mischievously, as though reminding her of dear intimacies, and with an unerring hand, confident that it will always find her, ruffles her short ruddy hair, cut to the fringe of a medieval page and almost reaching the dark arched brows. Her beauty, which to the Abbé had once seemed brittle and even vicious, has matured and stabilized to dignity. When she is an old woman the long line of her jaw, the fine straight nose, the unconscious pride of the small head will come into their own. She laughs and pulls away out of reach of a boy's impertinence. Her eyes, the colour of a fawn's hide, meet the Abbé's with whimsical appeal, and the Abbé grins back, tolerant and affectionate.

But against his will, he calculates and remembers.

It must be all of ten years since the gala night when Freddi Waldkirch had opened the Cafés des Artistes to the Big Brass of the Wehrmacht and S.S. For the occasion he had imported a four-piece orchestra and two of the finest surviving chefs from Nice. The upper rooms of the café were reserved for the heavy, stamping, sweating, perfumed officers and the girls they had brought with them in their high-powered cars. The house, in fact, served as a gilt-edged brothel. It all went to show, as Freddi had pointed out, how harmonious Franco-German relations could be. All women were women. All men were men under their uniforms, which were themselves those of an international trades union. Victor de Fouqué-Basdur, for instance, the scion of one of France's noblest families and captain of a disintegrated regiment of Chasseurs, had become Wehrmacht Captain Ulrich von Freytag's intimate friend. Yet he and his fat, bewildered mother and fat, white-faced angry father had fled Paris before the threat of occupation. Really, as it proved, so foolish and unnecessary. For there they all were, drinking to the Third Reich, to the dear Marshal, to each other, and to the damnation of the trouble-makers.

The Abbé sighs again, from a replete stomach and a momentarily troubled heart. Memory, he reflects, is like a dangerous monster coiled in the dark of a man's consciousness, which, when he is off guard, rises to the surface to disturb his peace. He wishes grimly that he need never remember the woman opposite him, as he had just seen her. But also the memory reaffirms one of the constant observations of his stormy life. The fool things that man does are often the foundations of his happiness. Pull them out from under and the whole edifice—otherwise secured with good sense and virtue—crumbles. Everyone knew that Pascal had been a madman to marry Nina Gifford. But out of his madness had grown this lovely, tranquil life. God knows his business. His course may seem wayward, but in the end, it leads home.

The Abbé stands up, stretching his powerful shoulders as though to relieve them of a burden. Pascal walks beside him down the flagged path, his arm over his wife's shoulder, a shaggy black dog at his heels, trailing its lead. The Abbé has a hard fight with his Vespa, propped against the stable-door —a second-hand affair which Freddi sold him at a knock-down price. It snorts resentfully like a fat pig aroused from sleep. After a succession of admonitory kicks, however, it breaks into a resigned splutter. Nina straddles the rear seat and clasps her arms about the Abbé's considerable waist.

"Another scandal!" he chuckles. "One day, Nina, you will surely get me unfrocked."

"Take care of her!" Pascal tells him. "You are still a reckless fellow."

"If I am halfway sober," the Abbé tosses over his shoulder, "it is no thanks to you, my son."

He and his passenger vanish in a cloud of evil-smelling smoke and dust, spiralling up the deep-shadowed road between the cypresses and the mountain flank. Pascal stands for a while and listens. When the Vespa's last snort and rattle have faded in the distance, he stoops and gropes for the dog's lead and the two of them make their way back, in companionable understanding, to the patio. There they come to a brief halt. The man draws a deep contented breath of the clear, warm air. Beneath the dying sweetness of the roses lies a scent more subtle and more dear to him—that of his budding lavender. In those days when he had wondered, in an agony of loneliness and self-distrust, what manner of man he really was, its fragrance had encompassed him with ghostly reassurance. It had even overpowered the stench of man's brutality.

All gone. All healed. All well. He is at last deep-rooted in a soil that has become his. The vines on the steeply descending terraces are sending out their first fruit. He can see them, against his darkness, like small smouldering torches, row upon row, ready to burst into green flame, and the pines and orange and olive trees that enclose the Domaine in their old and strong embrace. He speaks softly to his companion, and they move on slowly along the front of the Mas to the goat track that peters out close to the kitchen door. A tangle of yellow broom veils its straggling dangerous ascent. But he sees it as he had seen it that last time. He remembers the cave that had been a refuge for a frightened, unhappy child and that later had been another sort of refuge to be reached even on moonless stormy nights by hunted, desperate men. His face, which for all its virility has retained a boyish roundness, falls into bleak lines. On the olive skin the scar shows more sharply. But then the corners of the long mouth relax to a wry smile. He bends down to caress his companion's head.

"We couldn't do that now, my old friend. Or could we—if we were frightened enough? Well, we won't ever be frightened like that again." He becomes suddenly alert and still. He cannot have heard the old woman who has emerged suddenly against the dark of the open kitchen doorway. She has made no sound. She stands there motionless too except for her toothless mouth which she sucks in and out in a queer rhythmic grimace and for her eyes, deep-sunken in that skull-like lair and which dart out at the man in furtive question. Her dress is old and dirty, as she is, and seems too heavy for the stooped and scarecrow body. She stares at the man standing by the goat track as though she sees him for the first time and deeply fears him.

He says quietly, "What are you doing, Grand'mère?"

She flinches. So, after all her caution, he is aware of her. She cannot hide from him.

"What should I be doing? Washing dishes. Though the good God knows there is little need. You and your Abbé lick them clean."

"You feed us too well. You should have eaten with us."

"I did not choose to."

"Because you hate us? That's a lot of hate to carry all these years, Grand'mère." He adds softly, casually, "Or are you afraid? There's no need—not any more."

23

She turns sharply. But before she creeps back into the shadow she spits over her shoulder. "How do you know of what I should be frightened? I'm old. The old have nothing left to fear."

"Only themselves perhaps—like all of us."

At which she laughs. He hears her laughing to herself in the dark cave of her kitchen. It's a rusty, whirring sound like that of an old clock whose springs, suddenly, have broken.

## III

THE bar of the Café des Artistes is a pleasantly cool refuge in the heat of summer, and on winter days when the mistral hunts fugitives through the narrow streets, Pierre Donadet, bartender and general manager, puts a match to the logs in the great stone fireplace, and such of the foreign population as can afford an apéritif or a beer discuss art, death and the hereafter within the circle of their warmth. They expand with well-being and illusions. Great pictures will be painted, rat holes become studios and Meccas for the big dealers and well-heeled collectors eager to pick the first crop of a new Renoir, a young Picasso. Pierre Donadet, white-jacketed and monolithic against the shelves of proudly labelled bottles, listens, summer or winter, with cynical indifference. He has listened for so many years that he could act as prompter—if anyone should need a prompter.

At the host's round table Mayor Toussan has gathered the members of his Council. So long as it doesn't cost too much he likes to play the open-handed good fellow. Besides, with the elections close at hand, it behooves him to make sure of his friends and hamstring, if possible, his opponents. He has nothing to fear from pallid little Dr. Chinot except an incapacity to say "no" to anyone and a good deal to hope from Emile Royat, whose fruit stall backs out from his wife's general store onto the Place de l'Eglise and who, as a *Résistance* man, imprisoned and tortured, can be played off against Lucien Sauvan. The Mayor fears and detests Sauvan. Even in far-off Nice he has made a name for himself as a trouble-maker of unbounded ambition—a tall, well-built fellow, whose harsh good looks fascinate the women. And it is the

24

women who feel most sharply the pinch of rising prices against which Sauvan rails with such well-calculated passion. As to the men, whatever their own record, they are impressed by Sauvan's claim that he and his P.F.T.F. were the only real patriots. (Of course the *Résistance* is old stuff. It should be buried and forgotten. But at election time the sins of one's great-grandmothers are dug up and trailed indecently around the market-place.)

The postman, Georges Robert, sits next to Sauvan and watches and listens to him like a devoted dog, hoping to understand and give loyal satisfaction. He earns 900 francs a day and has an invalid wife and ailing baby and doesn't know how he is going to pay the rent of their one room, a share in a cluttered kitchen, and a stinking outdoor privy. He is a sturdy little fellow whose dense black hair, cut *en brosse*, thatches a round weathered face expressing chronic bewilderment and an innocent good-will. Sometimes he feels like a juggler he'd seen once in a travelling circus and whose cunning hands kept a dozen balls flying in the air. If one of them had dropped, he would have been a laughing stock and have lost his job, just as, if Georges's swollen varicose veins give out, he will lose his. But Lucien Sauvan says that long before that happens everything will be different. And Georges believes him as simply and humbly as his mother had believed in saints and miracles.

Eugène Ribout, tax-collector, sits on the Mayor's right. Like the Mayor and Dr. Chinot, he wears city clothes that are neat but twenty years out of date. If no one likes his rather furtive meagreness, he is not hated as was his predecessor, Félix Millo, who stuck his nose into affairs that were none of his and who for his pains hung for three days from that oak-beam on the rue des Princes. He is treated, if not with cordiality, with respect and consideration. He can pick out Emile Royat's best basket of strawberries and payment will be waved off with a well-understood "For your good wife, with our compliments, Monsieur Ribout." Butcher François Dieudonné keeps the best cuts for him. His "additions" at the café are politely sidetracked. "What is a Pernod between friends?" Donadet says with a cynical flash of humour.

Freddi Waldkirch himself is not a Council member. He just happens to be present and, as he has ordered a round of drinks on the house, is invited to sit in. Though Rocquedur dislikes foreigners and even the inhabitants of the next village, they take a slinking pride in this exotic bird whose bright expensive plumage does them obscure credit. He wears, as usual, light gabardine slacks and a summer sports coat that falls loose over hip pockets from which, at need, he can produce wads of 10,000 franc notes and for which, as far as Monsieur Ribout is concerned, the Café des Artistes is a sufficient official explanation. But tourists, wishing to exchange their currency to the best advantage, have only to ring a certain Niçois number and announce the arrival of Aunt So-and-so, and Freddi will drive over in his Jaguar and with a gold pencil and a sheet of paper prove to his relative that he is doing her or him a closely calculated service. Subsequent transactions are known only to mysterious associates in Switzerland, London, and New York. Monsieur Ribout, of course, remains determinedly unaware of them. He has no liking for oak-beams.

Discussions between these men centres on two items—that of a memorial to those ten lying in half-forgotten loneliness outside the walls and the approaching fête of St. Roche. The former is an old bone of contention. Lucien Sauvan still makes the worst of it. He emphasizes the well-known fact that memorials cost money. And after all, the dead are dead. One should consider the living, who fight daily for a mere existence against the forces of greed and corruption. (To Georges Robert, Sauvan's promises of a better life and revenge on a ruthless, greedy society sound like a tocsin, calling him to hope. He doesn't really want to cut anyone's throat. He only wants to know that he can pay his rent and feed his wife and baby so that they will live.) The Mayor, as usual, has nothing to offer except compromise. He has always compromised— even with the Germans. That ten-year-old sore has healed over. But Sauvan, when and if he chooses, rubs it open till it bleeds. The Mayor shifts his well-fed bulk uneasily and mops himself. He knows that he can't hope for quarter.

"Why a monument to mere hostages?" Sauvan demands scornfully. "They died because they damn well had to. They didn't even deserve to die. They never lifted a hand to fight anyone. You insult men, like mine, who gave their lives as patriots."

"But they too died bravely," Dr. Chinot murmurs. He has grown very pale. The hand with which he smooths down his thin grey hair trembles. "I was with them. I know."

26

"You mean that they had enough sense to take it quietly. Kicking and screaming would only have made it worse for them. We all die. Few of us make a fuss about it."

"But most of us get a memorial of sorts," Freddi interposes smoothly. "If I agree with you, Sauvan, it is on other grounds. Why rub noses in old dirt? Those wayside crosses—'Here the barbarian Nazis murdered So-and-so'—are natural expressions of indignation. But they aren't good for international relations, and to be frank they are damn bad for business." His plump, well-kept hands make a delicate gesture of dismissal. "Sooner or later they will be ploughed under or simply allowed to disintegrate. It's inevitable."

The Mayor clears his throat.

"Pascal Guis has offered to erect a cross at his own expense."

Whereat Lucien Sauvan tilts back his chair and laughs. It is a singularly mirthless sound. It grates down the Mayor's spine. He is convinced the fellow has never laughed at a real joke in his life.

"The good Pascal may well," Sauvan says. "If it hadn't been for his futile trouble-making, those ten might be alive today. Or if his precious *Alliance* hadn't been too intent on saving their own skins." He brings his chair down with the crack of a pistol shot. "It's clever to be blind. You can't forget a blind man. He sticks out like a sore thumb. I have a scar from my thigh to my knee. It aches like a bad tooth. But I can't take down my pants every five minutes to prove it. But Pascal Guis has only to follow his damn dog across the Place and you all genuflect. And what was he anyhow? A coward who ran away from himself."

"Shut up!"

Sauvan turns, furious and incredulous, as on a harmless garter snake turned into a hissing rattler.

"What did you say?"

"I said 'Shut up', Comrade," Georges Robert repeats. But fear at his own temerity has sent the blood to the roots of his black hair. "Pascal is a decent fellow. He has been kind to me."

"Kind! A sop to stuff a silly bourgeois mouth!" Sauvan slaps Robert on the shoulder with a contemptuous patronage. "I'm afraid, Comrade Robert, you will be a bourgeois to the end."

Freddi intervenes again. He has seen tears in the little postman's eyes. He has a mild dislike for seeing men frightened and humiliated. Against his custom he signals Pierre Donadet for a second round of drinks.

"Anyway, it's all water under the bridge, isn't it? Perhaps a cross with just 'In memory of our citizens' without comment would satisfy everybody. And if Monsieur Guis wants to foot the bill, who are we to raise objections?"

Everybody laughs. Sauvan shrugs, and there the matter is allowed to rest. The fête of St. Roche sails on relatively smooth waters. No one, Sauvan says, except a lot of old women, believe that St. Roche so much as existed. But as his fête is an established custom, Sauvan and his comrades are prepared to go along. Freddi offers a four-piece orchestra. Perhaps Nina Guis will sing for them. (Sauvan observes, grinning, that St. Roche deserves a whore, whereat Robert winces as though he had been slapped.) The music, carried by an amplifier, will serve not only Freddi's gilded clientèle but the village dancers too.

"Who can dance in the dust," Sauvan adds viciously.

Then there will be a merry-go-round for the children, a shooting-gallery and a *boule* competition with prizes for the men. The old women, as usual, will sit on the sidelines, watch, criticize and presumably enjoy themselves.

"And who pays for all this?" Sauvan demands. "I can tell you. The people pay. They buy their own rotten prizes. And who pockets the money? You do, Monsieur Waldkirch."

"I provide it, too," Freddi retorts, unruffled. "You know as well as I do, Sauvan, that without me Rocquedur would be just another decaying rat's nest."

The Mayor stands up. He doesn't like his village to be called a rat's nest. Besides he has heard the chug-chug of a Vespa break the afternoon's peace of the Grand' Place. He recognizes it with apprehension.

"Our friend, the Abbé, may want a finger in the pie."

"Not a finger," Sauvan corrects, "but a whole damn clerical fist."


IV


THE Abbé keeps to the deeply rutted dirt road by a great effort of faith, muscle and determination. At the worst moments, when his rattling and snorting Vespa threatens to come to a final and resentful standstill, he and Nina put their feet down and push in unison. But once through the gateway, the worst is over. Finally they slither to a full stop by the fountain on the Grand' Place. The Abbé, still astride, mops his face and listens gratefully to the cool tinkle of the water which the dolphins toss up into the last afternoon sunlight.

"Well, we've made it," he says over his shoulder. "Every time I'm sure is the last and resolve to wring our Freddi's abominable neck."

Nina Guis swings herself lightly to the ground. But she stays close to him, and he gives her a wondering, sidelong glance. It is difficult for an old man to remember how the young think about the past, or whether they think about it at all. Having a future, they can probably close the door on it, and all this psychological stuff about wounded childish egos is just another exploitation of man's gullibility and his frantic urge to find a solution to himself.

But then the past which the Abbé shares with Nina Guis is still so close. It seems to the Abbé both yesterday and another lifetime. He can never lift his eyes to the church tower without seeing a black-clad figure—himself with a better wind—racing up the steep worn steps to the belfry to ring a tocsin against the enemy twisting like a black serpent up the main road from the valley. A foolish gesture, expressive of the passionate, impulsive man he was—and still is, God forgive him. What had he hoped? That the long dead men and women who as a last gesture of defiance had poured boiling pitch on the heads of the besiegers, whose dust still blew with the mistral down the dark, remembering streets, would rise in answer? If so, he had been disillusioned. Their descendants had blinked up, scowling and resentful, and taken to their houses with the smug air of good citizens going in all innocence about their lawful business. If physical survival is, after all, the main concern of man, they had been right. The enemy had behaved impeccably. The dusty Wehrmacht had stood at ease, grinning and amiable. Captain Ulrich von Freytag had paid his respects to the Mayor, wearing his badge of office. They had stood together like men of the world who were determined to make the best of the situation. The whole Occupation had been carried out by the Germans with a decorum which, as the Mayor pointed out with a little bow, almost but not quite obsequious, contrasted most agreeably with their Italian predecessors.

"So very unpredictable, if I may say so, Captain."

"We shall not be unpredictable," Ulrich von Freytag had assured him, smiling faintly.

The orderliness of the occasion was a bitter contrast to that night, August 4, 1944, to be exact, when the men and women of Rocquedur had celebrated the departure of the last of their field-grey masters. Then the Grand' Place had witnessed the outbreak of man's vicious inhumanity, the release of long-shackled, venomous hatreds. But because of what had seemed a well-established order, a deep-rooted conception of man's relation to his neighbour, the scene had been horrible beyond belief, a rift in the seemingly solid earth spewing out unimaginable filth. The Abbé had fought his way to the steps of his church and with his arms frantically out-flung had shouted to God to bring reason to His mad children. God had not chosen to intervene. A woman's frantic, half-strangled scream, rising above the animal roar of bloody triumph had been the only answer.

The Abbé wonders if Nina is remembering too. She draws closer to him. The five men who stroll out of the Café des Artistes advance with the cautious deliberation of a hostile deputation come to parley. Georges Robert, indeed, touches his official kepi and smiles shyly. Lucien Sauvan had called Madame Guis a whore. Robert knows nothing personally about whores. On 900 francs a day a man is lucky to have a wife—even an ailing one. But he remembers that when he cycles down to the Domaine, as he does sometimes, outside his prescribed route, she always has coffee and a *fine* for him and something good to take home. Whore or no whore, she too is kind. But he shoots Sauvan an anxious, apologetic glance. Has his politeness been bourgeois and disloyal?

The Abbé greets them with a bluff "Good day, my children," partly because he feels paternal, but mainly because he knows that form of address infuriates Sauvan to speechlessness. The Mayor in response touches a beret which he wears atop his city clothes to signify to the natives that he is, in spite of his office, still one of them. His brown eyes blink, as though against the light, but actually to avoid the Abbé's direct regard. He does not believe in God. He detests the Church. But he insists on his wife's punctual attendance. Having successfully walked the tightrope of War and Occupation, he isn't going to slip now, and in these restless, uncertain days one never knows.

"You're just in time, Monsieur l'Abbé," he says. "We were discussing the fête of St. Roche. You may have ideas. Monsieur Waldkirch has promised a gala soirée with a real orchestra and a champagne supper—"

"—for which his damned capitalists will be soaked and scalped," Sauvan interjects. "He has my Party blessing."

There is laughter. Their rancours, which have been floating perilously near the surface, sink out of sight. Up to a point they have to live and let live. Even Sauvan has known through the last years of impatient waiting that men must be given time to get their breath. Wounds must be allowed a superficial healing before they are rubbed open again, into suppurating infection. The Abbé thinks he smells them—a faint but sickening odour.

He and Freddi shake hands. Freddi is a great handshaker. He is still, in spite of a layer of fat which good living has spread over a well-groomed body, a rather handsome fellow who carries himself with feline grace. The dark eyes have a child's friendliness and a guttersnipe's shrewdness. The Abbé has to like him. He has, of course, no accepted principles. But he has his own. He is honestly dishonest. And besides, the Abbé reflects, who does have principles these days? Only a precious few who are as disconcerting as rocks thrust up out of a dirty but smooth-running tide. And it is an ugly fact that in overstrained bureaucracy a few drops of illicit oil prevent the detested and cumbersome machine from grinding to a complete standstill. It is hard to think of Freddi as a public benefactor. He certainly does not consider himself as one. But the ways of God are mysterious. Even Lucien Sauvan may serve them.

"At a 200 per cent profit," the Abbé suggests solemnly, "Monsieur Waldkirch could well dedicate, let us say 10 per cent to my deserving and undeserving poor."

"Didn't I tell you? St. Roche is about to receive a new halo. And the presbytery will be warm next winter."

"Sometimes, Sauvan," the Abbé interposes, "I am almost irresistibly tempted to unfrock myself in order to knock your teeth down your foul throat."

"Try it!"

"I prefer to be unfrocked in a better cause." He has his volcanic temper in hand again. He rummages in his soutane pocket and produces a rag and dipping it in the fountain washes a smear of dust from his Vespa's mirror. "You owe me something, Freddi, if only as compensation for this precious bargain."

"It goes, doesn't it?"

"When I kick it hard enough."

"You should pray over it."

"It's the work of the devil—beyond prayer."

Freddi chuckles a rich amusement. But the atmosphere is still uneasy. Georges Robert, in spite of Sauvan, likes to be friendly. He has, besides, the little fellow's need to count for something. On his routine journey to Basdur's post-office he collects scraps of gossip and news of the big world which he hands out like tidbits to the hungry villagers who wait in their doorways for him to pass. Now he pushes back his kepi with a casual gesture that discards a petty officialdom. He is a man among men. He becomes a focal point of attention.

"Perhaps you gentlemen have already heard . . . It came over the radio. A military tribunal has released Captain von Freytag—a month ago. They say it was all a mistake. He was not responsible for"—he jerks his thumb over his shoulder—"them."

Nothing, apparently, has changed. Yet there is a change. The silence is tense like that of hunters close to their quarry, or of the hunted who listen for the first ominous footfall of pursuit. The five men look up instinctively, as though at a sudden clouding of the sun. But there are no clouds. The evening sky is tranquil.

"Well, time passes," Freddi observes easily. (But his lazy brown eyes have become alert.) "Even, no doubt, in prison. I'm not sorry. He wasn't a bad fellow."

The Mayor thrusts his pudgy hands in his pockets. He might be hiding them. He says, rather loudly, as though addressing a public meeting, "He was always correct. If we were left relatively in peace, we owe it to him."

"And to you, my dear Mayor."

Toussan stares at Sauvan. His round face with the small bunched-up features has become red and swollen-looking.

"I did my duty as I saw it."

"As you saw it, no doubt," Sauvan agrees maliciously.

Throughout, Nina Guis has stood apart from the uneasy group of men. With her face upturned, her hands loosely clasped behind her, like an attentive child, she watches the swallows wheel about the belfry and swoop out of sight behind the steep dark roofs. There is a belief that when swallows fly high they presage good weather. But there has been too much good weather. A relentless sun has parched the earth to dust. The groves of cypress and olive and the encircling pine forest are scorched. A careless spark could kindle them to a furnace.

"So please fly low!" she tells the swallows out of her smiling thought. But she shares their exultant, life-loving flight, their freedom of the sky and sunlight. They have fought for survival as she has. Only those who have known peril can know safety. Only those who have been unhappy can know happiness. She is happy. She is safe.

And then, suddenly, a man's name . . .

A minute later, when the Abbé turns, remembering her, he finds her gone.

## V

A BROAD, cobbled passage leads out of the Grand' Place to what the inhabitants call in affectionate abbreviation "La Petite". It is actually more a widening of the rue des Flèches than a Place. There Madame Bernard sits outside her scabrous little house, beside her husband Paul, whose wooden stumps she keeps covered with a blanket, even in this heat. She knows how bitterly he hates the sight of them. She sews swiftly at the little muslin bags that later will be filled with the Guis lavender and sold to tourists. She has an oval Madonna face that was beautiful before hardship and grief had etched it with deep lines. Her dark eyes have the serenity of those who have fronted the worst of life and remained unbroken. They are not like her husband's eyes that are sombre with unforgotten torment.

She looks up with a friendly pleasure.

"Good day, Madame."

"Good day, Madame."

Nina is in haste—almost in flight. But she has to stop. These two are dear to Pascal, who has never forgotten that Paul had stripped off the security of his gendarme's uniform to fight at his side and suffer brutal mutilation. The man's eyes seek hers with an appeal she does not understand. "Help me! Help me!" How can she help him? She cannot help herself. As though in answer to an unspoken question, his wife pats the man's arm, gently reproving.

"Paul is troubled. He will listen to Madam Royat's radio. She plays it full blast. It seems that they have released that German captain. I tell him he was never anything to us. He isn't now. Besides he will not come back."

"Why should he?" Nina asks.

She asks it, not knowing why, of the cripple, who shakes his head at her like a baited, bewildered animal. His hands are knotted in the blanket as though in an effort to keep them still.

"That's what I say. It's all in the past. It is our business to forget."

But forgetfulness is not so easy.

The younger woman fights down a physical nausea. She says steadily, "Pascal sends his greetings. He will be coming to see you soon. He will tell you there is no need to be afraid."

"Of course not. It's absurd. We're at peace."

But peace is just a word.

Next door is Madame Royat's dark little shop where the foreigners can buy the *cœurs sucrés* which are *la spécialité de la maison,* and sugar candies in tall glass bottles. The villagers buy cheese and butter, sausages and ham and even pots and pans and brooms. Madame Royat likes to boast that she and her husband Emile sell everything a reasonable person needs. Her shop has a back entrance on the Place de l'Eglise where Emile has his covered stall of vegetables and fruit and flowers. Madame Royat looms up behind her laden counter. She has turned off her radio. Her shop is full of a hot, breathless silence. Her upturned nose gives her round rosy face a look of good humour. But her eyes are a fox's eyes, sharp, hard and vigilant. Usually she is complaisant and even patronizing. Her eldest son Louis is a croupier at the Cannes Casino—an honourable position—and her second, Claude, is married to an industrialist's daughter in Lyons whose *dot* has set him up in business as a retail wine merchant. She has reason to be self-satisfied, especially in regard to this foreign woman who, whatever she is now, was worse than nothing. But for once she is almost aggressive in her friendliness.

"All this fuss! Who cares? I tell myself, Madame Guis,

34

why should we concern ourselves? After eight years in prison the fellow will be glad to let well enough alone." She wraps up half a dozen *cœurs sucrés* (which Pascal loves like a greedy boy) in a neat firm package as though she were wrapping up a mere annoyance to be done with it. "Your husband is well, I hope?"

"Yes—" Nina draws a deep breath. It is as though she had been running too fast. Her breast hurts her. "But he worries about the vines. If only we could have a little rain!"

"Yes, indeed. Let us hope none of those wretched foreigners toss out a lighted cigarette. We want no more trouble."

La Petite plunges down hill and by way of the rue des Flèches reaches the rue des Princes and the ramparts. At a junction of narrow streets that are like rivulets flowing down from the main source of the Grand' Place, the Auberge des Alouettes forms a triangle. Its apex is a small paved patio whose wrought-iron tables are shaded by a dusty plane tree. It is a sad place. Thanks to the tree, the tables are never out of shadow. Madame Drouet, in hopes of evening custom, spreads them with gay red-chequered tablecloths.

In a way the Drouets have been lucky. A direct hit by an American bomb shattered the old Auberge so that when they came back from those two lost years, it was to a pile of rubble. So they were spared the refugees who settled on deserted houses like locusts to whom the world owed an unlimited debt. Men and women who had given the best of their lives to their country found themselves homeless and the Law cynically indifferent. The Drouets, at least, possessed a ruin. They rebuilt it. No one had helped them. They were Normans by birth and had been trouble-makers. If they had been shot, Mayor Toussan had once declared peevishly, they would have got no more than their deserts.

Raymonde Drouet had been a pretty, vivacious woman. She still has a pretty woman's vanity. Her blonde hair, silvered by those two years, is arranged artfully to cover the scar on her right temple. She dresses with a fastidiousness that makes a simple frock elegant. A touch of discreet colour warms the high cheekbones. Her worn hands are carefully manicured, the nails painted to match the scarlet of a proud, stern mouth. She looks up and smiles almost gratefully. For the Drouets are lonely people.

"Good day, Madame Guis."

"Good day, Madame Drouet."

For after years of friendship the Frenchwoman still imposes on the Englishwoman her stiff formality.

Nina sees Monsieur Richard standing behind the empty bar—waiting. In the first years English and American flyers had crowded it with their gratitude. It had been a place of pilgrimage to which later they had brought their wives. But then children had come. Life flowed over an old debt. Letters dwindled to Christmas cards. The stream of gratitude ran dry. If the Auberge survives, it is thanks to the rag-and-bobtail foreigners and Madame's superb 500-franc dinner—a good Norman potage, veal cutlet with vegetables, fruit and excellent coffee, over which they can sit and talk about themselves till daybreak. Often the Abbé strolls round in the evening for a *fine* and listens to the dark-skinned stocky man's bitterness. In the end he is apt to say, half sternly, half in affection, "My poor friend, you suffered for your honour's sake. You must not ask for gratitude."

Now Nina Guis stands and looks up into the heavy foliage of the plane tree. She says abruptly, like someone goaded by an inner compulsion, "Perhaps you have heard. Ulrich von Freytag has been released."

The worn old-young face stiffens as though against a sudden taste of foulness.

"He never concerned us. He does not concern us now."

But in the twilit room behind them both women hear the shrill tinkle of a broken glass.

Jean Barberis runs up the worn steps that lead from the rue des Princes to the Place de l'Eglise. As he passes her, Nina catches only a glimpse of his dark, gaunt face. He makes her a furtive gesture of greeting, as though no one must know that they are friends.

In the morning he carries his father's long, crisp loaves in a cone-shaped basket on his back. He goes from house to house and forgets no one. In the daytime he works with Guis in the vineyards. He has become Pascal's eyes. He weeds and grafts like an expert. But he is as silent as though he were dumb and deaf. Something more than ordinary prison ill-treatment has shattered him. It is hard to remember that he was once a mischievous, happy boy.

36

He is gone—like a shadow.

His father's bakery occupies a corner of the Place de l'Eglise. At night it flames like the mouth of a small volcano. Especially in winter, the children gather on the steps to warm themselves in the red glow and watch Antoine Barberis knead the great piles of dough with his big hairy hands.

Now he stands with his back to his cold, dark ovens, his soiled white coat unbuttoned, grey stubble on his heavy jowls. He says almost threateningly, "I saw my son awhile back. He flits about like a bat. Where does he keep himself these days?"

Nina answers, "He still works for us."

"Fine work. He's crazy. He remembers my customers, otherwise I should have him locked up. One day he will do someone an injury, and I shall be responsible."

Nina shakes her head.

"He is gentle and compassionate. He would never hurt anyone."

The old man rubs his hand over his thick, white-powdered eyebrows. He might be hiding his eyes from her. The idea of compassion means nothing to him. He has no compassion, even for himself. He cares only for his good bread and for the hoard which he keeps hidden, no one knows where, least of all the Banque de France and Monsieur Ribout.

He growls sullenly, "Well, so they've let that captain fellow loose. And why not? War is war. You can't fight war with kid gloves. He kept his promises. He did his best to be correct, as the saying goes."

Nina, in her blind haste, stumbles over a loose cobble. So everyone knows. Even Mlle Milly. Two cats sun themselves smugly on the window sill of her tall narrow house next the presbytery. Between them the small wrinkled face smiles down cheerfully. She speaks in English. After all, French is the language of foreigners. You spoke it only when you had to and then as badly as possible.

"What a lovely day, dear Nina. It must be wonderful to be free after all these years. The captain and I were quite friends, you know. He thought I was crazy—on account of my cats. I thought him quite an engaging fellow. And so lonely that he liked to talk to me." She gives a merry, high-pitched laugh. "Such interesting talk. If ever he comes back, I shall have to tell him. He will be so amused."

If he comes back . . .

37

La Baronne is giving one of her famous cocktail parties to which her guests, from long experience of proper convention, bring the drinks. Already someone is singing—a bellowing man's voice that shatters the drowsy tranquillity of the place like a fist blow.

La Baronne peers out of her attic window. The two strange faces, posed one above the other, make Nina remember a Russian opera whose chief character was a mad broken puppet jiggling in his box. All the other characters had seemed mad too.

La Baronne's flushed and swollen face is at the moment benign. Later on she will become violent and, with the best intentions, dangerous.

"Come up and join us, darling. We are drinking the health of my old friend."

To La Baronne, no doubt, he had been a friend. At least they had had enemies in common—the men who some thirty years before had massacred her people and turned a lovely, cherished girl into a hunted vagabond and finally to a drink-sodden old hellion.

You couldn't even be angry with her.

"Thanks," Nina calls back. "I must go home."

"Ah, you have a home and a man." La Baronne chuckles. "Hurry, my child."

Nina walks fast. The early dusk fills the narrow streets but not till dawn will a cool breath from the mountains relieve their lifeless, stifling heat. Once outside the gateway, suddenly she begins to run, headlong, as she had done that other night. Only now the pursuers are phantoms, and at the end of the black tunnel of cypresses Pascal will be waiting for her. She will be safe.

## VI

THE Abbè comes down the steps of the church's south porch and crosses the Place to his presbytery. He is accustomed to La Baronne's celebrations and their inevitable uproar. All that bothers him is the probability that he will have to persuade the gendarmerie (summoned from Basdur by an indignant Mayor) that though violent she is harmless. And he is so damn tired. Dr. Chinot has warned him that he should ease off burdens that his heart can no longer carry. Typical medical advice. Burdens are not so easily discarded.

His old housekeeper, Madeleine, peers out of a disorderly cockroach-infested kitchen.

"A gentleman, Father, is waiting for you."

The Abbé sighs. All he needs is a gentleman lying in wait for him.

His study is a big shabby room lined with dusty books that he no longer reads. His desk is littered with the draft of a sermon no one will listen to. The old women will drowse, the children fidget. As soon as the latter have acquired their first Communion clothes, they will slough off God like a shabby old-fashioned coat. Another, newer faith lies like a wolf in ambush, waiting for them and the emptiness of their hearts.

There is enough light seeping through the tall dirty window for him to recognize the man seated in the one easy chair and who, arrogantly, does not rise. The Abbé groans softly, trying to ease the clutch of that merciless hand on his breast.

"This is an unexpected visit, Monsieur le Comte.

"But not, I am sure, a welcome one."

The voice is rusty, as though from long disuse. The squat, obese figure is like that of a *revenant,* something that has struggled up from under the stone of an old grave, dressed in the habiliments of another world by a half-forgotten generation. The stiff double collar supports the folds of a heavy chin. The narrow trousers are hitched up and show the small feet in their buttoned boots. The white soft hands are folded precisely on the gold top of an ebony cane. Yet the grotesque figure is not ridiculous, any more than the pale, disease-raddled face is wholly hideous and detestable. The unblinking eyes, under their hooded lids, have their own tragic integrity and courage.

"I am surprised, Monsieur le Comte. It is many years . . ."

"If I have stayed behind my walls," his visitor interrupts impatiently, "it is not you or your like who has constrained me. I have merely retreated from a world I detest and a people I despise. If I have emerged briefly, it is to do something that does not come easy to me—to ask your co-operation, Monsieur l'Abbé."

Clerissy raises heavy interrogatory eyebrows.

"In what way can I be of service?"

39

"I wish you to preach a sermon—on the subject of reconciliation."

"With whom—the devil?"

"You please to be facetious."

"No—just curious."

"You may have heard," the Count persists with cold patience, "Captain von Freytag has been exonerated and released. I have had a letter from him. He is coming here."

"Why?"

"To resume old friendships." The Count stares at the Abbé as though to stare him to his knees. "Captain von Freytag is a gentleman. I am one myself."

"Your ancestors, Monsieur le Comte, were Frenchmen."

The white face lightens with ironic amusement.

"Your history is typically tendentious, Monsieur l'Abbé. Otherwise you would know that we are Fouqué-Basdurs in the first instance, Lords of Provence in the second. We thought very little of the Capets, less of the Bourbons, and less than nothing of these foul republics."

"And France?"

"France is a geographical term. It is a place where men live. It is what they make of it."

"And what would you make of it?"

"A place fit for gentlemen to live in."

The Abbé bursts into a big laugh.

"Since my people and I are merely French, that rules me out."

"By no means. We have usually supported the Church and the Church has usually supported us. I am requesting that it support me now. I wish Captain von Freytag's visit to be without incident—to be, in fact, amicable."

The Abbé thrusts his fists into his soutane pockets. He stands with his big feet apart as though he were riding a ship in a high sea.

"I have been a violent fellow in my time," he says. "But I do not preach violence or vengeance. You can rely on me for that much. And what else?"

"I wish my property to be freed of vermin."

"You ask the impossible, Monsieur le Comte. I can't manage my own cockroaches."

The Count passes over the jest with haughty contempt.

"I am speaking of human vermin. The house on the Place de l'Eglise is mine. It has been in my family for generations.

I have a right to determine its occupants. It may not be a legal right. In these days the Law is corrupt, as is all else in this unhappy country. I claim it as a moral right." His hands fold more tightly on the cane between his heavy thighs. "You have influence with the mad Englishwoman. Convince her that she and that Russian sot are not wanted here. Let us be cleansed of these intruders who degrade us."

"Degrade—in what way?"

The Count frees one hand to make a gesture towards the uproar pouring across the square through the open window.

"Do you approve of such scandal?"

"There are worse scandals."

"They disgust me. My son is coming home. He is married. He will need a place of his own. Besides, I want those women out of my village—out of my country. They are contaminating."

"I believe that our despised Law is against you, Monsieur le Comte. No one can be dispossessed these days."

"I am not invoking the Law. I look to you, Monsieur l'Abbé."

"Mlle Milly has her cats," the Abbé points out. "The English have some sort of quarantine. She would have to desert them. She won't. She refused once before, if you remember."

The toad-like figure heaves itself to its inadequate feet.

"You please to make fun of me, Monsieur l'Abbé."

"No, indeed. I am merely reminding you."

Monsieur de Fouqué-Basdur moves painfully to the door. He is not without dignity. He might be marshalling an invisible army.

"So you refuse?"

"Yes."

"Then I shall appeal to the Mayor. He needs my influence if he is to stay Mayor."

"It would not be the first time, Monsieur le Comte, that you and he have collaborated."

In the heavy silence the Abbé feels the man's hate of him like a corporeal threatening presence.

"Let me tell you something, Monsieur l'Abbe. You pose as a patriot and a man of God. I regard you as an embodiment of evil—of the cancer that is eating the heart of this unhappy country. I suspect that your Curé and your Bishop agree with me."

"It need not be a suspicion, Monsieur le Comte. It is a fact."

The door closes sharply. The Abbé switches on his desk lamp. Somehow La Baronne's voice booming incomprehensibly in Russian comforts him. He wishes he could join her and those other dispossessed and get obliviously, gloriously, gloriously drunk with them.

# VII

MADAME Marcel Passano stands on the threshold of her little Niçois shop "Mille Choses" on the rue Meyerbeer. She looks over her shoulder at her little shop-assistant, Jeanne. They smile knowingly at each other.

*"Un tout petit gouter!* In ten minutes I shall be back."

It is a familiar ritual. Really she should not take even ten minutes, much less that *gouter.* The late afternoon is the most lucrative period of the Nice day. The tourists come out of their "déjeuner" stupor and saunter among the shops and spend like children with too much pocket-money and no sense. Jeanne can't speak English, much less German. The French don't count, of course. Even on vacation they squeeze the sous. The English, it is true, don't count much either. They are too worried as to how they are to get home on what the French hoteliers have left them. But there are the Americans. And of course the Germans. Well, God knows where they get their money. But they have it. And after their offensive fashion they spend it. ("We poor Germans! We lost the War. So we have to travel.") No one watching them swagger down the Promenade des Anglais could imagine them scurrying out of Nice as fast as high-powered cars, caissons and camions could carry them. Not that, even then, they had their tails between their legs. They'd snarled at the spectators on the pavements, holding in their yells of hate and derision until the last field-grey was well out of sight, "We'll be back!" Or they'd laughed and waved good-naturedly, as at children who believe in a fairy story of victory over an unconquerable people.

Yes, they are big, brutal and stupid, but if you flatter them they can be managed. And there she is, leaving her bewildered Jeanne to cope with them. But she simply can't help herself. Every morning she makes the same firm resolutions and every afternoon round five o'clock her flesh clamours and her will weakens. Ah, those flaky *mille feuilles*, that cup of coffee at Queenie's, music coming over gaily from the near-by casino, the comic, motley crowd of strollers, half-dressed women waddling on spike-heels, fat bald men in awful sports shirts and shorts stretched to bursting over thick thighs (you can see how young and irresistible they think themselves), donkey-carts packed with awe-struck children, a stout woman in slacks running alongside, flourishing a whip, fiacres whose striped awnings shade sleek American women who look down on the show as though they'd bought and paid for it! What fun it all is! It makes little Francine Passano feel gay all over. And she adores gaiety as she adores good food. She has never been able to resist either.

She stops for a moment to look into the window of her shop. A printed notice announces "Man spricht Deutsch" and "English spoken". Such a successful little shop! Souvenirs at all prices—hand-bags, lighters, flags for the car with "Nice" emblazoned on them, toys for the children, jewel-studded collars for the poodles. The money she rakes in helps to pad out Marcel's miserly salary as official in the *Bureau de Poste et Télégraphe*. She adores him. It makes her glow with happiness to surround him with little luxuries and to make up to him for those four cruel, terrifying years. (But she never understands how he could have been so stupid. After all, he was born in Menton and from time to time his people had been Italians. There was no sense in his feeling for France the way he did.) Anyhow he helps her too. As an official he knows other officials. He and Monsieur Bonnet, the tax-assessor, are good friends, Monsieur Bonnet dines quite often at the little apartment on the Boulevard du Cimiez, and after a cup of good coffee they go over the accounts of "Mille Choses" and everything arranges itself. After all, everyone knows the taxes are unjust. It's almost a civic duty to dodge them.

She chuckles softly. How delightfully easy life can be if you know how to give and take, and above all if you are not stiff-necked about things that don't matter a sou to anyone.

There is a mirror in the shop window. She stoops to catch a glimpse of herself, to touch her curly red-brown hair to a casual neatness. A charming woman still not fat, just warm and plump—like a partridge, as Marcel says tenderly. All the same, she must watch her weight. She'll begin working on it tomorrow.

Her high heels make a gallant, provocative rat-a-tat-tat on the pavement. The *brouhaha* of the Promenade des Anglais drowns the cheerful little sound. Alas, the poor English! The Promenade and its memories are about all that is left them. But when you think about it seriously, you realize that they have only themselves to blame. How much pleasanter for everyone if they had accepted the *fait accompli* and followed the poor dear Marshal's guidance. Then everybody would have settled down in peace and quiet to mind their own business. Some people say even now that it is the English, even more than the Americans, who are to blame for everything.

She hums a lively little tune. She is happy. But then, somehow—and even in the worst times—she has always managed to be happy. It is as though happiness is part of her and never fails to answer the smallest provocation. For instance, that day when she said good-bye to poor weeping Marcel in his scrubby uniform she had walked back from the station to their empty apartment, humming as she does now, and just because the sun was shining. She loves the sunlight and the red umbrellas that at dusk will be folded away but which now string themselves around the sapphire and emerald sea like the beads of a gay necklace. She adores the huge foreign cars, and even the little fellows, drawn up against the crowded pavement. She stops to take a closer look at one of them—a dark green Volkswagen with its big white "D" over the rear licence plate. It interests her because Freddi Waldkirch has told her that he can get her one cheap and that she can pay for it in instalments. (What fun to drive Marcel over the Corniches which, for all that he is now a Niçois, he has never seen.) Freddi always has a way to manage things—especially during the Occupation, when he became so prosperous, so well-dressed and sleek. He is not the kind to forget old friends.

Well, the War and Occupation are *tempi passati,* as Marcel says in his Italian moods. The thing to do is to keep one's mind on today, take care of Marcel, and make the most of the sunshine. In spite of what the Curé at St. Vincent's tells her, she suspects that one is a long time dead.

Abruptly she turns away from the car. She is almost sure someone had called her by name. A man is seated at a round table close to the sidewalk. He has taken off his grey soft hat which lies on the chair next him, and the sunlight polishes his short grey-black hair so that it gleams like a steel casque. For a minute she cannot, will not, believe her eyes. She is sure that she is asleep and dreaming one of her rare nightmares and that soon she will wake up and find Marcel breathing peacefully beside her. Or perhaps it is just that the little German car has conjured up the past—the submerged memory of a long tightly folded mouth and stone-grey, hooded eyes. (Under the left eye had been a half-circle of flesh on which the eye-glass rested so firmly that it had seemed ingrown. Without it—as in moments of intimacy—the lean, hard-featured, handsome face had looked almost indecently naked. It is naked now.)

He bows to her, smiling. She walks on. She stumbles against people, who look at her indignantly as though she were drunk. Then, slowly, as though caught on a relentless, invisible hook, she turns and comes back. He rises and shifts the grey hat so that she can sit beside him. (He had always been, even in his most ruthless moments, punctiliously polite.)

"What a happy chance, Mitzi!"

After all those years he still speaks perfect French. The nickname makes her so sick that she waves off the waiter with his tray of delicious pâtisseries as though he had insulted her. She feels as though she will never eat again. The man beside her murmurs teasingly, "What! Not even a *mille feuilles*, Mitzi? You disappoint me!"

# PART TWO

# THE PAST

# I

## OF THE ABBÉ THOMAS CLERISSY

I was born lucky. Enough brains to keep my head above water. A fine appetite. A good digestion. A wonderful, preposterous mother. No father to speak of—at least Maman never mentioned him. A love of life. Love of my fellows. The love of God. What more could a man ask?

I believe that God and I were together from the start, that He took me as a child to Himself because perhaps He knew I needed Him more than most children, or perhaps because He had a little weakness for me. (I have always imagined that He likes big, hearty fellows.) But my awareness of Him came gradually, like daybreak, at first a pale brightness dispelling the confusion of my childhood, then spreading in a golden flood through my whole being, as the sun, emerging from behind our mountains, flows over the vineyards and fills our deepest valleys. I shall remember the moment of full realization in the hour of my death as the most lovely moment of my life.

My mother, Rose-Thérèse, and my ostensible father, Alois, lived in a gone-to-seed farmhouse just outside the village walls. Alois was himself a feckless derelict who when he cultivated bees was stung almost to death by them and whose small vineyard, as sickly and untended as himself, had never yielded more than a rough country wine. As he could not sell it, he and his few friends periodically soaked in it. Probably the old house with its three filthy and cluttered rooms would have fallen apart altogether if it hadn't been for my mother, who was, as we say, another pair of shoes. Why she had bothered to marry Alois Clerissy was one of the village's perennial subjects for argument. She told me herself in an expansive mood that since she was going to have me anyway —and indeed wanted me—she thought it was only fair to make me legitimate. And no doubt she calculated that Alois would be more manageable than most husbands. So I was born to her in her eighteenth year, and thereafter she made a home for me by her own industry.

She was as beautiful as an earthy Italian Madonna and so lustily and gaily immoral that when most women of her calling were worn-out drabs she could still pick her man and name her price. She was also shrewd and, in the midst of seeming disorder, orderly. Once a week she kissed me with more than usual ardour—I invariably howled at her desertion—and took the local bus to Nice. She was gone three nights and came back punctually with expensive toys and clothes for her little Thomas and enough supplies to keep our crazy household going through her next absence. She had, in fact, a permanent engagement at Madame Sautier's brothel on the Quai—an exclusive establishment recommended to foreign gentlemen by the concièrges of the best hotels. She and Madame Sautier were fast friends and honest business associates. At the conclusion of Maman's weekly assignment they celebrated together in Madame's red-and-gold draped salon. The best champagne brought Maman back to Rocquedur in a state of exuberant love for her anxiously waiting son and a good-humoured tolerance for Alois. By this time he had no morals either. He was a kept man and glad of it.

"Marry a pretty woman," he would hiccough to his cronies, "and make the best of her."

His cronies were the village no-goods. His crude hospitality couldn't have bribed the respectable menfolk to defy their women, who regarded Maman with indignation modified by a surreptitious envy. It was an offence to their bleak sobriety that this scandalous woman should dress like a queen and lord it over them with her abominable affluence. They did not, however, ostracize her. Her flamboyant assurance may have warned them against a head-on encounter; they treated her, in her whirlwind appearances, with a guarded politeness and an insatiable curiosity which she sometimes gratified. After the Occupation and in what, technically, were her declining years, she and La Baronne would sit together on a summer's evening at one of Freddi Waldkirch's tables and drink up a succession of *fines* whilst the villagers, like flies round honey, would edge in closer to share in the exchange of bawdy reminiscences. For La Baronne, during a prolonged stop-over in Istanbul, had been a prostitute.

"It was the only possible profession for an aristocrat like myself," La Baronne would explain, waving a long ebony cigarette-holder whose cigarette she had "borrowed" from

Maman's thin gold case. "I was beautiful. I was—*pour ainsi dire*—my own mistress. I had Russian dukes and Turkish caliphs. Never for too long. Men, en masse, are tolerable. But one, inevitably, becomes a bore."

"The English are the worst," Maman would say in her clear, carrying voice. (Even the *boule* players would forsake their games to listen, winking at each other.) "They are always so ashamed. When they put money on the mantelshelf, you would think they were stealing it. But I'm sorry for them. They have such awful wives. How they beget children is a mystery to me. But the Germans are the funniest. They are so ugly, and they want so much to be loved. I remember during the Occupation they would cry on my shoulder; they were grateful to me for being kind to them. And the next day they would shoot a few more hostages."

Both ladies would shake with laughter.

Among Maman's many qualities was one of a sort of indestructibility and an infinite capacity to trim her sails to any wind. She was at the height of her mature beauty in World War I, when Nice was crowded with convalescent, lonely, sex-starved officers of all the allied nations. She made a modest fortune during the subsequent boom and sailed through the depression with flying colours. With World War II and the succeeding Italian-German Occupation, she came into another and different heyday. By then she had reached her sixties—a magnificent matriarch who, having inherited Madame Sautier's happy family of girls, ran their home not only as a jolly brothel but as a sort of club where the Big Brass of the Wehrmacht and the S.S. could foregather without embarrassment or fear that an inebriated slip of the tongue might be betrayed. In fact Maman never betrayed anyone. From the beginning she had put herself firmly outside the Law, which shrugged its shoulders at her and even respected her as a useful outlaw who by keeping the enemy cheerful and sexually satisfied performed a public service.

Until I was twelve I went to school at Rocquedur and learned to recite the départements, préfectures, and sous-préfectures of France under the baton of young Monsieur Boutton, who was much more frightened of his pupils than they were of him. I was dressed so elegantly that periodically my schoolmates would set on me and tear my clothes to ribbons; they knew all their parents knew but were less

51

tolerant. So in my first years I was a hunted but not lonely child. I had Maman. All my warm over-flowing heart went out to the lovely, alarming woman who when she leapt down gracefully from the returning bus would gather me to an ample, sweet-scented bosom and smother me with kisses.

"My darling—wait and see what I have brought you!"

I pretended delight in the expensive, too elaborate presents that she unwrapped for me under Alois' bleary sardonic eyes. I knew instinctively what pleasure she had had in buying them and that a rejection would really wound her. I had no doubt that she was wicked. (Though she took me to church, she never went to Confession or Communion, thereby sparing our poor Curé much spiritual embarrassment.) Nonetheless it was from her I learned the fundamentals of my own faith. I learned—I hope—to understand and to be compassionate.

On my tenth birthday I took my first Communion. Father Benedict, whose place before the altar I would one day take, had prepared me with the other children and in the teeth of the villagers' sullen opposition. Especially to the women it seemed outrageous that the son of a notorious harlot should be received at God's table. The old Curé preached a sermon on "Christ does not visit the sins of the parents upon the children", but as so few of his congregations listened it did not help much. Only he, Maman and I knew of their private encounter—the Scarlet Woman and her blushing son facing him across his presbytery desk. Her arm was over my shoulder, her beautiful warm eyes were lifted to the silver crucifix on the wall behind the old man's head.

"Thomas is innocent," she declared firmly, "and so, for that matter, am I. God made me what I am. When we meet each other He will say, 'Well, my child, you made the best of what I gave you'."

"But you won't meet God," the Curé had warned her. "God is not to be found in Hell."

"How do you know?" she retorted. "Surely that is where He is needed most."

I knew that she was teasing him. (She had pinched my ear as she did when she wanted to call my attention to a good joke.) As a matter of fact, she didn't believe in Hell. She kept an open mind about God.

The Curé was old. Probably his half-empty church and the perfunctory faith of his few faithful had made him sick at heart. He blessed her sadly. "Go and sin no more, my daughter."

I remember how she smiled at him with a sort of good-humoured pity and what was more deplorable, a conspiratorial understanding of the official red-tape which made him talk such nonsense.

I associate my first Communion mainly with my new trousers, which pinched me in the crotch, and a stiff collar with a white flowing tie which half-choked me. I was puzzled by the whole business and rather frightened lest what was happening might come between me and the glowing, resplendent woman seated far back in the shadow of the church. It was a week later, on one of my lonely expeditions to the rim of the Baue Rouge that like a small Saul, I met God face to face. (That He had been lurking in wait for me I was subsequently sure.) I had been sad because the other children would not play with me and because for the next three days my home would be grey and desolate. With my arms locked about my knees, I sat on a high rock overlooking the wide valley of the Var. It was April. The whole world seemed to have burst into a tender flowering. Shadows of clouds drifted over the great river in full spate, and over the far-off mountains that were as mysterious as my dreams. And suddenly I awoke to beauty and thus to God. I loved this dear land, the flowers, the river, the budding vines, the grass under my hands, with a passion that swelled my boy's heart to overflowing and chocked my throat with tears.

I could explain what happened to me by saying that because I loved the world so greatly I knew that there was a God who loved it too—every speck of earth, every atom of its life, every dusty sparrow, even myself. It was all that. But it was much more—much less simple. It was a breaking through to another level of experience, into another world of which this was but a shadow. I might never see it again, but I would never forget that it was there. The knowledge would shield me all my life from total despair and fear and grief.

Afterwards I realized, of course, that this experience to the rationalist would have proved nothing, could have been explained by glands, hormones or complexes. It would have meant no more to him than music to the tone-deaf. This didn't bother me. I accepted illumination as an artist accepts inspiration, not questioning it, humbly counting myself most blessed.

Strangely enough, from that time on the barrier between other children and myself melted. I became one of them, the Curé chose me as a server, and I knelt at an altar which was to become my home, and swung the ancient silver censer so that clouds of grey sweetness should rise to God's nostrils. I accepted ritual as the Curé gave it to me to understand.

"When you are older, my son, you may be fretted and even shocked at what may seem to you vain repetition and unbelievable superstition. Remember, it is not God who prescribes our childish tributes, our blundering ways of seeking Him. Ritual is a man-made ladder. It helps us by its mystique to climb out of the fog of our daily life closer to heaven. Do not be, therefore, affronted or dismayed."

For which unorthodoxy, no doubt, he would have been unfrocked, but he was too old to be afraid. He loved me too much to lose me to ancient shibboleths or the barren rationalism of the age. Little Thomas Clerissy had to be saved for God.

So we sat together through long winter evenings in the presbytery study, and he taught me all he knew and believed. For it was tacitly accepted by both of us that in due course I should enter the priesthood and serve God to the utmost of my powers to my days' end.

When I was twelve and had acquired my *certificat des études,* Maman sent me to the Lycée at Avignon. I boarded with a grim old couple who in spite of Maman's lavish contributions to the household regarded me as an intruder and didn't feed me very well. But still upheld by my child's simple faith, I was not lonely or unhappy. During the holidays Maman would arrive to take me to the best pâtisseries and most expensive restaurants, and, when my unaccustomed stomach revolted under the strain, would sit beside my bed and lay a cool, lovely hand on my aching head— which was more to me than the best food in the world. The family accepted Maman for what she so decorously seemed: a decent bourgeois wife and mother. Even the men on the street gave her no more than an admiring glance, for she could not disguise her beauty. When one bold fellow actually drew alongside to murmur some scabrous invitation, she pulled herself to her full height and said witheringly, "Monsieur mistakes himself."

(It was lucky that the offender did not see what I suspected—the flash of laughter in those brilliant dark-brown Madonna eyes.)

She accepted my spiritual vocation as she would have accepted my determination to be a lion-tamer; she was amused and tolerant.

I was eighteen when the First World War woke me from my adolescence. I volunteered. I fought with my infantry regiment at Verdun, was wounded and decorated with the Croix de Guerre. I was not so much frightened during that hideous battle as bewildered. After all, faith wasn't so easy. It was difficult to see my best friend disembowelled at my side, to hear his scream and feel his hot blood splash my face, and believe in anything but an all-powerful Evil. But gradually my faith righted itself. I saw God and the Devil locked in a mortal struggle that would endure till our world melted into everlasting light. God needed me too. I ranged myself shoulder to shoulder with Him.

During my time in hospital Maman came north, bringing with her a load of illicit delicacies. In the overcrowded ward, drab and squalid with neglect (for the great ladies of France satisfied their patriotism with brilliant social charities), the ashen-faced, unwashed, unshaven men turned to her as starved plants turn to the sunlight. The dying took heart to laugh with her and exchange winks with each other. Her gorgeousness set fire to the grey stubble of their despair and pain. By one dying forsaken man she sat all night, holding his fevered hand in her strong woman's clasp until at dawn he smiled at her and let her go.

When she left she took me with her on a brief leave.

By this time Alois had drunk himself into a premature senility. In our derelict household he was no more than a dirty, snivelling ghost. Maman took time off from her profession to furnish our three rooms with such bits and pieces as she could pick up in those days of drastic shortages. They were, by consequence, a confusion of tawdry luxury and bleak discomfort. But it was the only home I knew, just as she was all I had—at least until the day I limped along the rough track to the high rocky plateau where I had first found God. This time I found a woman.

Much else had changed. I had killed men. I had been close to my own death. I had a fatalistic conviction that I was to die soon. I had witnessed man's incredible inhumanity. Only my faith had led me through a jungle whose vicious tentacles had tried to wind themselves about my heart and shut out the light of heaven. For the first time, I was aware of a desperate physical hunger and loneliness. God might suffice the bodies of saints. I was no saint.

The woman lay on her face. At first I thought she was asleep. But then, standing beside her motionless and perplexed, I knew that she was crying. I knelt and laid a shy hand on her shoulder. The sobbing ceased. Her slender young body seemed to be listening to me as a small hunted animal listens to some fateful, unidentified approach.

"Don't cry!" I begged. "Please don't cry."

For I had reached the limits of my own capacity to suffer. More grief was unendurable. She drew herself up slowly. All I realized of her then, or later, was a frail, fair prettiness. Only her eyes, though they were red and swollen with weeping, were beautiful—the grey of our skies with the sun behind them. She hiccoughed like an exhausted child.

"Who are you?"

"Thomas Clerissy."

"Madame Rose-Thérèse's son?"

I nodded. Perhaps she expected me to be ashamed. I wasn't. Indeed, I never was. I asked, "Who are you?"

"Roberta, Christophe Guis's wife."

I remembered what Maman had written me. The hunchback owner of the Domaine Guis had found a wife at last, a girl he had picked up in Nice, much younger than himself, whom he had brought home with a sort of defiant triumph. No one knew much about her, and no one cared. Christophe and his club-footed mother were half-feared, half-hated as people under a curse and who might, in turn, have the power to curse. The young wife came rarely to the village—a timid, pale little thing, Maman had described her, who because she didn't give Christophe what he wanted of her—a son to work beside him, to inherit the vineyards that were his life—was treated like an unsatisfactory servant.

"Does Monsieur Guis expect miracles?" Maman had asked enigmatically and evidently savouring her own private little joke.

I kept very still. A lizard, a small streak of life, shot into the long grass, almost under my hand. I wished that it had lingered, trusted me. I wanted this girl to trust me too.

"You were wounded, weren't you?"

"A little," I told her. "I'm almost all right now. In a few days I shall be going back."

After a moment she asked shyly, "May I talk to you? No one ever talks to me."

We moved closer to each other, like orphan children seeking consolation from each other. I could feel her warmth mingle with mine. And over me hovered a grey presence warning me that my time was almost over, that this golden hour might be all of life remaining to me.

"Why were you crying, Roberta?"

"I was unhappy."

I persisted. "Why?"

"Because everyone hates me." She let a handful of dust seep through her thin, work-worn fingers. "I don't know why. I don't know why Christophe wanted me."

"Why did you want him? He's ugly—inside and out."

"I didn't—I mean I was all alone. When you are all alone you are so frightened. My people are in Metz; I don't know if they're even alive. They'd sent me south because I'm not strong. I got work in a café where Christophe met me. I was sorry for him. He told me how sad he was because he couldn't fight—and—and about the Domaine where I should be safe with him."

"Aren't you?"

She shook her head, her eyes averted. I knew there was something in her life so terrible, so shameful, that she could never tell me.

"Now Christophe says that the war is all nonsense. He never wanted to fight. He never wanted me—not really."

She asked me to tell her about the war. But I couldn't. No one could. It was something monstrous, outside the range of words. But to please her I talked about myself, my childhood, even about Maman. I made her laugh. And all the time I had the feeling that I was climbing up to some high moment of experience in which loneliness and hunger would be resolved forever. I didn't forget God, but it was as though He had withdrawn a little, leaving me to find my own way.

She and I met each evening. How she escaped I did not know. We talked less and less. We held each other close, waiting with heavy beating hearts for the rising tide to sweep

57

us from our moorings to that unimaginable magic height. We reached it. We melted, in an anguish of expectation, into each other's flesh. Then it was all over. There was nothing. We were just ourselves.

When she left me—for we did not dare be seen together—I sat there for a long time, lost in infinite sadness. A light breeze came to me from the mountains. I felt as though God ruffled my hair with a compassionate hand. "You see, my son, one is still alone."

But He did not convict me of sin either then or nine months later, just before the Armistice, when Maman wrote me, "St. Roche has performed another miracle. Christophe Guis has a son." But then, it seemed, the Saint had lost interest, or he had his own ideas about miracles. For young Madame Guis had died in childbirth.

The war was over. Or so they said. I, Captain Thomas Clerissy, came home. Alois, having drifted into the village cemetery, the Clerissy farm was given over to the weeds. Maman had a charming little apartment in Nice, whence she paid her regular visits to her good friend, Madame Sautier, whose girls welcomed her with affectionate envy. She brought them little gifts and sometimes lavish clients. She listened to their griefs and when asked shared her professional wisdom with them. She was the ideal to which they all aspired, for the most part vainly: a sound business woman who sold her cheap goods at a profit and kept intact the important value of herself.

I spent my first night in the derelict house. The tawdry furnishings were rotted and mildewed. I shared my bed with mice. The next day I closed the rickety door for the last time. I took shelter with the old Curé and went to school with him again. At evening I would stroll down the cypress-shadowed road that led to the Domaine Guis and, standing under the close-ranked trees, look down on the terraced vineyards and the red-brown roof of the old Mas. Sometimes I imagined that I heard a child's voice. Instead, one evening, a man called up to me. "Welcome home, Captain."

It was Christophe, who looked up at me from the terrace immediately beneath—a grinning and scowling Christophe. "You have heard, no doubt. I have acquired a son and heir. Won't you drink his health with me?"

It was no act of good-will. It was a challenge and perhaps a threat. I scrambled down to the hunchback's side and measured my step to his dragging limp. "My wife died, you know," Christophe went on. "She was a good-for-nothing little thing."

He said it with such venom that my hands tightened to fists.

We crossed the courtyard to the patio, over which the giant vine hung its burden of purple grapes. A crib stood in the last patch of sunlight, guarded by a grey-haired, grey-faced woman who stared at me with narrowed, bitter eyes. Either, mysteriously, she knew, or she suspected. But I guessed that she would keep her silence. For after all, here was an inheritor, someone who one day would press the wine that would be called by a famous name and take its place alongside the great *crus* of Burgundy.

"Behold!" Christophe declaimed with a savage pride. "Pascal Guis—my son!"

He was a black-haired, olive-skinned baby, serious but good-humoured. His eyes, looking up at me straightly, were a clear grey. "His mother's eyes," Christophe said viciously. "The doctor says that they may change. Let us hope so. Otherwise he is pure Guis. Or don't you think so, Captain?"

"Yes," I said, "pure Guis."

I bent down and laid my hand on Pascal's forehead. The caress was my blessing and a sort of promise.

"They tell me you are going into the priesthood," Christophe went on. "Well, it's one way to be safe, though how an honest man can pretend to believe all that shabby nonsense is beyond me. What has God done for us? What has belief in Christ done for us except to plunge us into one another's blood? Thank God," and he grinned, sourly, at his own slip of the tongue, "my son will be freer even than I am of all that criminal superstition." He cast a dark cynical glance at me. "Will you drink a glass of good wine with a heretic, Captain?"

"I'm always ready to drink good wine," I said, suddenly and strangely light of heart, "with the devil himself."

Grand'mère Guis wheeled the crib indoors. I could hear her crooning some old Provençal lullaby. Christophe and I sat opposite each other at the round table, a carafe of purple wine between us. To avoid the hunchback's belligerent questioning stare, I kept my eyes on the well-tended, still sunlit terraces beneath us.

59

"Lucky that I'm a cripple," Christophe said. "My back kept me out of all that bloody folly. There isn't a vineyard in the whole country that hasn't suffered, except mine. When Pascal Guis comes of age, 'Chateau Guis' will be one of the great marques."

He went on boasting. I scarcely heard him. I was listening to a child's sleepy murmur sink into a contented silence. I remembered a woman who had clung to me in loneliness and sorrow, who had given me comfort. A sin? Perhaps. At least it would be the last.

Entering the Seminary at Avignon wasn't easy. Maman had paid her peculiar contribution to the war effort with notorious success. She was now in her early forties. She should have been raddled and ruined, but actually she was at the peak of her beauty and apparently inexhaustible enjoyment of the flesh. Her financial status brought her respectful greeting from the employees of her Niçois bank. The son of such a deplorable success was a dubious candidate for the priesthood. The Bishop, consulted by an uneasy Rector, sent for me. After all, a poilu who had earned a captaincy and the Croix de Guerre with palms deserved consideration. I was abashed, almost panic-stricken. I had never been in such a lovely place or confronted a man at once so fragile and so strong. From behind his vast episcopal desk he looked me over with grave, faded blue eyes.

"You have one clear duty, my son. Either rescue your mother from her infamous life or cut yourself loose from her. God's servants must have clean hands."

I was like one of our obstinate mountain mules. I dug my heels in.

"She wouldn't soil anyone, Monseigneur," I said. "She is kind. She has been good to me and to many others. I could not judge or abandon her."

The Bishop had a fair thin skin like the petal of a dying rose. It flushed faintly. For some reason, perhaps obscure even to himself, he yielded ground. He gave me his ring to kiss.

"Go in peace, my son. I shall not forget you."

I hope the subsequent record of the seminarian Thomas Clerissy justified him. I was reckoned a good student. My superiors described me, as I learned later, as a blameless if somewhat too passionate soul, destined for a high place in the ecclesiastical hierarchy. Instead I pleaded to be allowed to live out my days in my own village, serving the altar of my childhood.

"Humility can be a form of arrogance," the Bishop warned me. (He was a dying man. He made me feel like a great oaf, too full of life.) "What do you aspire to—sainthood?"

I could only shake my head. What I, the Abbé Thomas Clerissy, aspired to, was locked in my heart, known only to God.

It was ten years after my entry into the Church before I saw Pascal Guis again. Rocquedur's church of St. Roche was crowded to receive me, not by the faithful but by the curious who had come to see what the son of Rose-Thérèse and heaven knew whom had made of himself. I had no illusions. I felt, as I mounted the pulpit, the malice and cynicism of those watchful eyes. I had a hard, lonely road ahead of me. As I came out onto the Place de l'Eglise I saw a boy standing by the steps. I had no doubts. My heart thundered recognition of the dense black hair, the blunt, already passionate, virile features, but above all of the eyes. Though they were shadowed by heavy thunderous brows, they were her eyes— the clear grey of a clouded summer sky, transfused with struggling sunlight. What had brought him there, as though to greet me? Chance? Destiny? Had he been lured by the whine of the old organ, the crude singing of the choir, or by some mysterious instinct of the blood? We stood there, briefly motionless, considering each other. Even in our attitudes we had something in common. The boy's hands were thrust in the pockets of his black *tablier* as mine were thrust in the pockets of my soutane. I said quietly, "My son," as I had a priestly right to do, and he turned, like a startled lizard, and flashed down the steep steps that led to the rue des Princes. In the sleepy silence of mid-day I could hear the scuffle of his flying, naked feet.

Rocquedur's schoolmaster, Monsieur Boutton, on the verge of retirement, had one passion which made him accept me whom, as a priest, he would otherwise have avoided like the plague. He played chess, and having discovered that he could give me two pawns and still beat me, he would drift over, of an evening, to the presbytery and by the last light sit hunched, like an old general, over the small squared battle-field. With a triumphant "Check mate!" he would sit back, a Gaulois dangling from his starved lips, and be prepared to gossip.

"A queer youngster," he said one night in answer to my slyly careful question. "A savage. He does not play with the other children. He used to fight them. Now they're afraid of him and leave him alone. Well, what can you expect from the son of such a misshapen devil? Not even a good scholar. I said to him, 'You have a head on your shoulders, Pascal, but I doubt if even I can drag you through your *certificat des études.*' Do you know what he answered? 'I don't need a *certificat* to weed vineyards.' He said it as though he hated them. As you know, of course, he does not come to church. If it hadn't been for your mother, Monsieur l'Abbé" (the old eyes glinted with malice), "who was prepared to make a village scandal of an affair that was none of hers, he wouldn't have been baptized. Well, I distrust clerical influence. But I would not have you think I am responsible for the boy's godlessness."

"Pascal will decide himself," I said, resetting the chessmen, "whether God exists or not."

I took my daily walk, after vespers, along the dusty cypress-shaded road to the Mas. But once in sight of the red-brown roof I would turn and trudge slowly back. Thus it happened sometimes that I would meet Pascal on his way home from some village errand and would say, "Good evening, my son," and get no answer. Instead the boy would hasten his lagging steps, as though my voice frightened or angered him. At his heels hung a strange apparition—a shaggy little cur in which a dozen village mongrels had had their share. The two of them, in the tree's shadow, were gnome-like. The boy's satchel, strapped high on his shoulders, made him a small sinister replica of the hunchback who was not his father, who had, God be thanked, no part in him.

Once when I was belated and when, perhaps, he no longer feared to meet me, I found those two seated by the roadside, pressed close to each other in secret, sorrowful communion. As I loomed over them Pascal started to his feet as though caught in some shameful weakness. He and his companion fled together, but not before the boy had stammered some sort of acknowledgment of my greeting. That night I felt singularly light of heart; it was like one of those far-off future nights when I would crouch over a radio transmitter and listen in fearful hope and at last catch the faint tapping out of a friend's message: I was no longer quite alone.

I remember, as another crucial moment of my life, that early winter's afternoon when I heard pursuing footsteps and a panting, agonized boy's voice, when I felt a hand clutch at my sleeve. It was the first time that we had touched each other.

"I've lost her, Father. I've lost Suzon. No one has seen her since morning. She came to school with me, but she didn't come back for me. She always came." He shook my sleeve fiercely. "Have you seen her?"

"No, my son. But now we'll find her."

We hunted through the vineyards, either side by side, or with Pascal tagging at my heels, his high clear voice calling the absurd name in an agony of appeal to a dead silence. We worked our way from terrace to terrace, to the hill of fir trees, where we found the poor small body, broken and dying, its throat mangled, perhaps by some fierce village dog, perhaps by vicious human hatred. She had a last strength to lick gratefully the boy's brown, caressing hand. She died then, stretching out with a deep sigh of weariness, and Pascal flung himself on the earth beside her, digging his nails into its dust, clinging to it as to the breast of a last and only friend. I knelt and gathered the convulsed body in my arms.

"Be comforted. Not a sparrow falls without God's knowledge and compassion."

The boy struggled furiously to free himself.

"That's a damned lie. There isn't any God. Or if there is— he's a devil. He's cruel. He killed Suzon!"

"Cruelty is of the devil, my son. God fights it. It's an age-old battle. He can only win it if we fight with Him—sometimes against ourselves."

"But we've lost," the boy stammered in wild scorn and despair. "Suzon is dead."

"Perhaps not," I said. "We're an arrogant lot, we humans. We deny a hereafter to fellow creatures more innocent and deserving than we are. I do not know by what right."

I had spoken as one sorrowful and baffled adult to another. He listened. The fierce, shattering sobs eased a little. By unspoken consent we dug a grave among the pine-needles, a safe, deep grave, and I found a stone to mark it. When our task was finished, we stood close to each other, looking down on the smooth earth. I knew that I had laid hold of my son's heart. I would never let it go or fail it.

63

There was a last unsteady sigh.

"That's all, isn't it?"

"We could say a prayer."

"A prayer?"

"To God, for a friend. At least I could. You see, I believe in Him."

The boy muttered, "All right. What else is there, when one has lost someone?"

So I folded my hands. I made up a prayer of great simplicity.

"Dear Father in Heaven, have loving kindness on this, thy creature . . ."

Then with my hand firmly on Pascal's shoulder I turned about, and together we climbed back to the road. There I stopped and stood back a little, looking into the dark young face still smeared with grief. The eyes, lifted to mine, were those of a woman who had loved and trusted me.

"There's something more you can do for Suzon," I said. "You can make another dog as happy as she was."

He almost laughed at my innocence.

"But she wasn't happy. She had to hide in a cave at night. Father kicked her when he could reach her. She would have starved if Grand'mère hadn't given me scraps, I don't know why."

"But she was happy sometimes, when she was with you. None of us can hope to be more than happy sometimes." I bent and kissed his cheek, and he did not flinch away from me. "Believe me, another Suzon is waiting somewhere for you."

The next day happened to be Maman's day of rest, which was not necessarily a Sunday. I found her, opulently beautiful, enthroned in her salon, a place of stiff and awful bourgeois elegance. She had prepared déjeuner for me—escalopes de veau au Madère, a ripe Camembert, washed down by a Haut-Brion such as she knew I loved and could not possibly afford.

"Mama, perhaps you could help me. I want a puppy, a pedigree puppy who could be properly called Suzon."

"Since when, my dear, have you become a dog fancier? Or perhaps it is not for you—perhaps for some child?"

"A boy."

"By name of Pascal Guis?"

64

I managed to meet her dark Madonna eyes, alive with delighted wickedness.

"How did you know?"

"In my profession, Thomas, one becomes knowledgeable, above all where men are concerned. Christophe Guis was once a patron of ours. Not a successful one. He made trouble. He tried to beat one of our best girls. And it was not her fault." She chuckled richly. "I assure you, Christophe Guis never begot so much as a horned toad."

I stared down at my square-toed boots and hoped she would not see the blood rising in my face. If she could no longer shock me, she could still startle me. Now she stood up, billowing silk and sending out waves of a not too subtle perfume, and kissed me lightly on the head. "I should hate to think a son of mine was a eunuch," she said gaily. "And I have a friend who breeds poodles—a very valuable breed."

"Maman! I am a poor priest."

"But I have explained—he is a friend."

So shortly thereafter I paid my second visit in many years to the Mas Guis and laid a black ball of wriggling life in Pascal's arms. I had no doubt that the hunchback and his club-footed mother would have enjoyed murdering me.

"Thank you for nothing, Monsieur l'Abbé. We want no more stray curs around here."

"This is no cur, Monsieur," I assured him. "She is a *chienne de race*, most valuable. With due care her progeny should make money for you."

The shot went home. His fists relaxed. The small eyes, brown and hard as pebbles, became sly and calculating. They had not seen what I had seen—the boy's black stare of hatred and nascent defiance.

"Well, in that case, Monsieur l'Abbé, I suppose we should be grateful."

So another younger, prouder Suzon learned to love and to teach love. Because of her value she was allowed to sleep in Pascal's attic. She followed Pascal to school and waited on the schoolhouse steps, her black nose between her aristocratic paws, her eyes alert for the hour of deliverance. They played together on the way home. They greeted me as a trusted friend, and I would walk with them, casually, as though by chance, as far as the Guis courtyard. Usually we walked in silence, for Pascal was still cautious; he did not open his heart to anyone.

"A strange boy," Monsieur Boutton commented. Having just forced my poor deserted king to abject surrender, he could sit back and relax. "He draws rather remarkably. He must have stolen paper and some of my coloured crayons. Here is one result. He is a protégé of yours, isn't he? I thought you might be interested."

Boutton and I had treated ourselves to Madame Drouet's dinner at the Auberge des Alouettes and had fought out our battle on the table that Monsieur Drouet had cleared for us. By the light hanging from the plane tree I studied the soiled and crumpled picture that Boutton had unrolled for me. Its subject alone astonished me—Christ's entry into Jerusalem. The Christ was certainly unconventional, a big, dark, clean-shaven fellow. He rode into a Jerusalem that was our village, and familiar men and women spread vine-leaves under His donkey's hoofs. Angels perched like birds in the branches of the plane tree on the Grand' Place. There was even a hunchbacked devil lurking in its shadow.

The two Drouets looked over my shoulder. (They were such gay, charming people in those days, so happy with each other, so proud of their old Auberge.) I heard Madame Drouet's soft laugh.

"Don't you recognize yourself, Monsieur l'Abbé?"

"Assuredly," her husband murmured, "an amazing likeness."

Boutton tittered. His little bombshell had exploded with good effect.

"I thought you would see it. No offence, Monsieur l'Abbé. You are a good man. Still—as our Saviour! Well, the boy must think the world of you."

I felt my ears grow red and hot as they always do when I'm embarrassed.

"I gave him his dog," I explained gruffly. "Any man who gives a boy a dog becomes godlike." I re-rolled the picture and thrust it into the breast of my soutane. "You will permit me to keep this testimonial?"

"Of course. I'd never show it to his father, who would burst a blood vessel. As to our young artist, he has already forgotten it. He presses on from one thing to another as though time were snapping at his heels. He is, I may add, still at the bottom of his class."

66

I framed the picture and hung it in the sacristy beneath the medieval silver crucifix which Maman had given me on my ordination and which was my one sinfully cherished treasure. It did not occur to me that Pascal would ever see it. The boy, by the skin of his teeth, obtained his *certificat des études*, and then his schooling days were over. He became a peasant, working in the Domaine from dawn to sundown. So I walked alone, heavy-hearted, under the cypresses. One summer night, by chance, we met and stood side by side, listening to a nightingale's farewell and broken song. But Pascal was weighed down with physical weariness and a despair I could not reach or comfort. I blessed him, and he drew away from me, sharply, almost angrily, as though my blessing had been a mockery.

I remember another night, sultry with storm. I had conducted vespers in an almost empty church. As I locked the west door and one by one extinguished the few candles guttering at St. Roche's feet, I admitted my failure as a priest. No words of mine, nothing that I had tried to do, had roused my people from their cynical indifference. The church felt cold and dead as my hopes. Then one of the shadows under a pillar detached itself and came toward me. By the pale light of the altar lamp I recognized it, my heart thudding in my breast. I asked, barely above a whisper, "What are you doing here?"

"I want to confess to you."

"Confess—to me?"

The young voice was faintly ironical.

"That's what sinners do, isn't it?"

"But you, my son, you don't belong; you don't even believe. I could not give you absolution." I found myself stammering. I tried to meet irony with irony. "Besides, a youngster like you can't have any serious sins to boast of."

"I am not boasting. It is serious. I—I don't know how to carry it."

I led the way into the dim and shabby sacristy. The sacristan had gone. He was old and lazy and had left my vestments tossed carelessly on the altar, like a discarded body. There was enough daylight seeping through a dirty overhead window to illuminate the crucifix and the picture beneath it. The boy's sombre face lighted with recognition.

"Your schoolmaster gave it to me," I explained almost in apology.

He walked closer to it, sternly frowning.

"It's awful. Why did you keep it?"

I chuckled.

"Perhaps because I was flattered. Perhaps because it moved me—like an Italian primitive."

"What is an Italian primitive?"

"You know by instinct. You draw from the same source."

"What source."

"Faith."

"But I haven't—I don't believe in anything." He added chokingly, "Not even myself."

"That's the worst apostasy, my son. A man must believe in himself before he can believe in God."

"Is that what your Church teaches, Father?"

"No, my son, it is not. It happens to be one of my peculiar notions."

The boy stared at me. His round, still childish face looked almost old.

"I want to paint," he said. He made his picture a curt, dismissing gesture. "Not stuff like that. I must. But I never shall. I shall weed and graft until my hands are stiff, useless. I hate the vineyards. I hate my father."

"Is hate your sin?"

"No." The flat negative sounded haughty and contemptuous.

"Well, hate is a poor sort of sin anyway. One might call it a mere weakness, good for nothing." I began to pace back and forth as I do when I am deep in difficult thought. "You know, Pascal, I have a trick. You might call it a sort of spiritual trick. When I find myself hating some poor devil I tell myself that he is just another 'I'. He says, as I do, '*I* am angry. *I* am misunderstood. *I* am unhappy. *I* am lonely. One day, and all alone, *I* shall suffer and die.' When I walk in our cemetery those rows upon rows of dead men and women and children become myself. I am one with them, and they are one with me." I stopped short, knowing that I had described badly what was of great moment to me. "Think of Christophe Guis as an 'I' who is afflicted, cut off from normal life and love. You might find it too difficult to hate him."

"He hates me," the boy said stubbornly. (Perhaps he had not even listened.) "He and Grand'mère. I don't know why. I think they'd throw me out, except that I'm useful in the vineyards. They're all he loves."

"A man must love something. Why not tell him the truth?"

"He would beat me. He's still stronger than I am. And— and I'm afraid."

"You used to fight your schoolmates. You weren't afraid of them."

"But I was—I was. Terribly. I had to make them afraid of me, so that they wouldn't find out." He whispered, shame-faced and desperate, "I am a coward, Father."

"Of what are you afraid?"

"Pain—being hurt."

"We all are. Even the saints had to ask God's help. Cowardice may be a sort of sin, but it can be cast out. Besides, no one can be sure until he has been really tested. We may run away from small conflicts, whimper under small hurts, but when the supreme hour strikes for us we may stand our ground like men." I added, "It is not for me to forgive you. One day you will be able to forgive yourself."

It was poor consolation. I began to pace again, my hands clenched in my soutane pockets. "Pascal, how old are you?"

"Thirteen, Monsieur l'Abbé."

"Call me 'Father'. It is more friendly. Well, in a few years you will be a man and free to choose your own road. It may lead to Paris, to the studio of some great master."

He almost snarled at me.

"That's mean—that's cruel. There are no miracles, not any more."

My fists relaxed. I put my hands on Pascal's shoulders. Yielding to a great wave of tenderness, I drew the tense young body close to me.

"I'll do my damnedest to be a miracle. I promise you."

It was a hard promise to fulfil. A priest's stipend doesn't allow for much paring. I was a big, brawny fellow. I had to admit Madame Madeleine's accusation that I became a sickly looking wraith. There were no more dinners at the Auberge, no more *fines* drunk under the plane tree. Monsieur Boutton could give me a bishop and check-mate me in ten moves.

"You are too hard on yourself," Madame Drouet scolded in her clear Northern French.

Sometimes I was weak. I accepted kindness from them.

An anxious, indignant Maman offered to help me. I would not let her. In this matter I nursed one of my crazy notions—

69

perhaps no more than a superstition. The miracle had to be fashioned out of the suffering of my own flesh.

"The body is of God," Maman preached piously. "To starve it is to insult Him."

But if a man's heart is fed, he does not starve.

Pascal and I met rarely, and then like conspirators who exchange signals of reassurance. The boy's hands became hard with toil. They did not lose their secret cunning. From time to time I would find a drawing laid on my sacristy table, from which I knew that the purpose in him burned steadily and that his faith in miracles still remained unshaken.

There were moments of different consolation. A gangling, anxious youngster kneeling by my sickbed. "Don't die, Father. I love you. You are all I have."

"There's always Suzon," I teased him gaily, but with a proud and grateful heart.

So the years passed. One day a young man climbed into the Paris train that was to carry him to freedom. I stood on the Nice platform and waved to the last glimpse of that handsome, illuminated face. When I turned away I was alone, but deeply satisfied at last.

The Germans entered Paris. The flow of Pascal's proud, exuberant letters ceased. The French Milice, under Gestapo orders, arrested Christophe Guis, whose son was believed to be a *chef de résistance* and whose hideout he could not betray for the simple reason that he did not know it. The hunchback, raving and struggling, had been shot down in cold blood. They left the old woman, who seemed senile and of no account, to bury him as best she could.

God alone knows what fear I suffered in those years.

After the despised Italians, the Germans came to Rocquedur. A detachment of the Wehrmacht under the command of a spruce, monocled young officer, marched up the winding road and stood at ease, sweating and grinning, in the Grand' Place. The officer introduced himself to Mayor Toussan, who wore his full official regalia.

"Captain Ulrich von Freytag." His salute had the stylized grace of a ballet dancer. "As a loyal Frenchman, Monsieur le Maire, you will accept what is best for France. You and I should have no trouble."

70

"All we desire here," Toussan answered too quickly, "is to live in peace and go about our business."

"Then we understand each other."

I stood on the church steps. I had rung my futile tocsin. No one regarded me. I could have vomited with shame and rage.

The Captain and his men were scrupulously correct. When they went from house to house seeking no one knew what, it was with regretful courtesy. They brought Freddi Waldkirch in their train and the shabby old *bistro* on the Grand' Place became the gay, prosperous Café des Artistes. Monsieur le Comte de Fouqué-Basdur and his family had returned from Paris to the ancestral chateau and now kept open house to the invaders. There were no shortages. Captain von Freytag, who had peculiar powers, kept our little shops well supplied. Perhaps, like so many Germans, he really loved France. He became quite popular. Our villagers touched their berets to him. "Good day, my Captain." He saluted in turn. "Good day, my friend."

He spoke perfect French.

But underneath the prosperity and new order flowed a dark and ugly tide. Men and women who had been friends no longer stopped to exchange gossip. They passed each other with sullen averted eyes. The men forsook their *boule* and the benches on the Grand' Place were often empty, like the seats of a theatre whose play has failed. On the walls of my church were pasted notices in big, blood-red print:

"Frenchmen, co-operate with your true friends and allies. Do not be misled by traitors. The penalty for the misguided is death."

Men and women came to confession and Mass, many of them for the first time in years. Their eyes, hungry and fearful, followed me as I mounted the pulpit. I preached, "Those who live by the sword shall perish by the sword," and "What shall it profit a man if he gain the whole world and lose his own soul?"

A new and younger Bishop reproved me.

"You are rash and impolitic, Monsieur l'Abbé. One must bow to God's will."

Captain von Freytag paid a semi-official visit to my presbytery.

"You seem to have some influence, Monsieur l'Abbé. Do

not misuse it. Believe me, as a patriot I understand and respect patriotism. But you too are a man of the world and should accept the *fait accompli*. Unlike our predecessors, we Germans have behaved with correctness. We demand correctness in return."

"Of what do you complain, my Captain?"

"Of your sermons, for one thing. They are calculated to provoke disorder. We should suppress it reluctantly but ruthlessly. For another, it is known to us that the so-called *Résistance* have planted a radio transmitter somewhere in the neighbourhood. We track it down but hitherto it has been moved too fast for us. If any information should come your way, you would be well advised to pass it on to us."

"I am not a spy, my Captain."

"I hope," he retorted, his stone-grey eyes inimical, "that you are a wise shepherd."

Freddi Waldkirch organized "La Grande Ouverture" of the Café des Artistes. It was an expensive affair, everything of the best and plenty of it. Maman sent up a bus-load of her prettiest girls. If she did not come herself, as she explained to me, it was because she was too old for such capers. Captain von Freytag brought his special friend, a plump, golden-haired, brown-eyed little woman whom he called "Mitzi" and whom the Fouqué-Basdurs had to accept at their table, though she was obviously a petite bourgeoise and hopelessly ill-at-ease among the elegant Big Brass of the Wehrmacht and the S.S. It was a small price, no doubt, to pay for the Captain's friendship and which incidentally proved the folly of their flight from Paris. Monsieur le Comte often declared publicly that they should have stayed to welcome the saviours of the best traditions and families of France.

The villagers gathered round in a dark sullen circle just outside the range of the garish lights. Even I was drawn against my will and judgment to watch with them. I had never seen anything like it before—the long flower-decked tables, littered with discarded food that would have kept our people fed for a month, the noisy yet sensuous music, the scurrying, obsequious waiters, the loose-mouthed, loose-jointed civilians paying court to the officers whose hard, alert eyes belied the carelessly unbuttoned tunics. I hated all of it and all of them. My device for retaining compassionate

72

understanding for my fellow creatures for once failed me. It seemed to me that all the evil, all the treachery and foulness that for centuries had slept in the dust of our village had come to life to set out in this sinister danse macabre.

Most of all I hated young Victor de Fouqué-Basdur, still captain of a regiment that had long since disintegrated on some shameful battlefield. He looked like a diseased, inbred greyhound. La Baronne had told me about the girl he danced with—an English girl whom the Fouqué-Basdurs had rescued in Paris and brought south with them—ostensibly as Madame la Comtesse's nurse-companion. She did not look like a nurse-companion. She looked what La Baronne said she was—some sort of night-club singer who knew how to dance with a man as no decent woman should. But beautifully. And she was beautiful. Hating with all my heart, I had to admit her loveliness. The wide Provençal skirt swayed round her delicate feet and ankles. Her shoulders, rising out of the simple low-cut blouse, gleamed like polished ivory. She wore her russet hair as does the standard-bearer in our fountain, short-cut with a straight fringe almost to her brows. It gave her charming face, upturned provocatively to meet Victor de Fouqué-Basdur's little sensual grin, a disconcerting, troubling look of innocence. Of course I had known of her existence, but until the German Occupation none of the Fouqué-Basdurs had trusted themselves outside the chateau wall, among, what they still called with a perhaps unconscious insolence, their people.

So I saw Nina Gifford, who was to be Nina Guis, for the first time.

At the head of his table, Monsieur le Comte heaved his obese body onto its inadequate aristocratic feet and raised his glass.

"To our good German allies who have saved us from the Communist canaille!"

It was then that someone whispered to me, "Pascal Guis has been arrested." I caught the flash of a woman's red-gold hair and turned and followed Madame Drouet to the dark deserted Auberge. The brief walk was a nightmare of fear and rage. It seemed to me that I felt the clinging of a desperate child—that I heard in my heart that cry of pitiful self-incrimination, "Father, I am a coward."

Madame Drouet and her husband locked the Auberge

door and switched on a single light that showed me their grey but resolute faces.

"He warned us. He can't stand pain. If they torture him, he may betray us all."

"He promised that he would shoot himself. They did not give him time. They caught him asleep."

I asked, "How do you dare to trust me?"

"Because we know you. We know what Pascal means to you."

"What can I do?"

"If we are arrested, take our place."

We talked together for an hour, with speed and brevity. Then through the narrow, night-haunted street Madame Drouet led me out onto the Place de l'Eglise to the house next to my presbytery and where Captain von Freytag had his quarters. In response to a signal the door opened and a cat, like a small released demon, shot past me into the dark.

"There!" Mlle Milly said sadly, "when Alphonse is in love there's no holding him." She looked up into my face with a smile of childlike welcome. "So you have come to us at last, Father. We have been waiting for you. I was just about to send a message to London when you knocked. The poor dear Captain is so chatty sometimes. I think he's lonely."

So I met Mlle Milly really for the first time too. I became a soldier who wore his insignia under the sleeve of a soutane. In dark days of dread, uncertainty and fear I learned to know myself and the strange ambivalence of men's souls. I reached, on my journey, the final frontiers of their courage.

## II

### OF PASCAL GUIS

I WAS born to the knowledge of hatred, cruelty and fear.

My first memory, which is like a picture painted on darkness and suddenly revealed by a glaring searchlight, is of two faces, so close to mine, so terrifying in their unsmiling scrutiny, that I screamed. My screams filled my whole world, my whole consciousness. They were to haunt me to the verge of manhood. Instantly the faces vanished. I vanished. It is as though I crept back into some safe place and fell asleep.

When I awoke to myself again I was a little boy in a black *tablier*. I had a father and a grandmother who hated me. Since hatred was all I knew, I took it to be natural and inevitable. I hated them too.

When I discovered love it was in myself and for someone I had never seen, since, as Grand'mère told me, she had died giving me birth. (So I had killed her.) But I was sure that Grand'mère lied. I did not believe that my mother was dead. One evening in the mysterious hour between sunset and night, I saw her—a pale, luminous shadow hovering over the lavender field which lies at the foot of the vineyard terraces. I knew she was waiting for me, and I ran headlong. But when I reached the place where I had seen her, she was gone. There was nothing but the fragrant grey mist which rises from lavender at nightfall.

"One of these days you'll break your neck," Grand'mère snapped at me. "Why did you run like that?"

"I saw my mother," I said. "She isn't dead. I didn't kill her."

I didn't know whether I believed what I'd said or not. It was a sort of inspiration—a sudden awareness of an enemy's vulnerability. Grand'mère's small eyes seemed to recede into her skull as though they were trying to hide from mine. From that moment I knew she was afraid of me.

But neither she nor my father wanted me to break my neck. My father, who had a hump on his back, had some purpose with me stronger than his hatred. When I was five years old I fell very ill. They sent for the doctor and took turns sitting up with me at night. They gave me cooling drinks and put damp cloths to my hot forehead. When I was better they made a bed for me in the sun and answered my faintest call. But without love.

One night I sat, forgotten, on the steps of our patio and listened to the frogs croak to each other and the broken summer song of the nightingales. My father sat above me at the round table with a carafe of Guis wine between him and two peasants who worked in the vineyards with him. They were sullenly angry because of something called a war in which they had had to fight. Now their jobs were gone. They had, in return for wounds, a miserable pension which would not even buy them bread. But for the Guis vineyards they would have starved. My father folded his powerful arms over his pigeon chest and jeered at them. They should have been

75

deformed like himself, or they should have taken to the hills. Afterwards no one would have known or cared. A man had only one life, he insisted. Why should he toss it away to satisfy the greed of scoundrelly generals and politicians? Frenchmen and Germans were all alike—except that the Germans had more sense. They wouldn't crush a man with crazy taxes, and they knew how to keep order. It would have been better for everyone if they had won. Then men could give their lives to minding their own business.

I heard all this as a sort of dark accompaniment to my own vague thoughts. I did not understand war. I did not understand my father. I didn't love the vineyards. They were my father's business, not mine. I had some business of my own, as yet not clear to me. My mother would have understood it. She would have been able to see what I was trying to see and known what I should do about it. She had my eyes. Grand'mère spoke of them contemptuously. She called them "northern eyes".

I never knew why I was so sure that the lavender field had been dear to my mother and that she had entrusted it to me. I would hide in it and bury my face in a mauve tuft of aromatic sweetness as though it had been her breast. It was there that with a stolen pencil and a sheet of paper I drew my first picture of her.

Father, for all his crooked back and lameness, could move as fast and as quietly as a cat. He came up behind me and snatched the paper out of my hands and tore it across and across, his thick brown eyes almost black with rage.

"You never saw her," he yelled. "You must be bewitched."

He took my arm and twisted it behind my back. He was suddenly very quiet and deliberate. He was like a desperately hungry man in sight of a feast but who means to take time to savour it.

"Say after me, 'My mother was a whore'."

I wailed, "My mother was a whore."

"Say, 'I am a bastard'."

I whimpered in agony, "I am a bastard."

He released me then with a savage clout over the head so that for hours afterwards I was deaf and tottered as though my legs didn't belong to me. But worst of all was my knowledge of myself. Even if I hadn't known, Grand'mère took care to tell me.

"Like her—a little coward."

76

All the same I heard her speak sharply to my father, "You don't want to kill him, do you?"

I heard his answer—dark and sullen.

"Sometimes I do."

I learned trust and compassion in a strange way—from a mongrel puppy that someone had kicked half to death and tossed into a village gutter. When I picked it up, it did not snarl at me or try to bite me, but licked my hand, as though it had found in me something I did not know of myself. It trusted me. Its trust was like a warm flood pouring into my own untrusting heart. I carried it home and hid it in the cave halfway up the goat track that ran from our kitchen door up the face of the Baue Rouge. I stole scraps for it. One day, of course, it was discovered. My father wanted to kill it then and there, but to my astonishment Grand'mère said, "No, it does no harm. It may serve as watch-dog." At that time I was sure that she saw something in my scowling, desperate face that reminded her that she was afraid of me.

I called my puppy "Suzon". I don't know why. But since then, for love of her, there has always been a Suzon in my life.

When I was seven I was given a leather satchel and a new black *tablier* and sent up the road to the village school. Suzon tagged at my heels.

I had never played with children. I had been so rarely in the village that my future schoolmates stood around me in the street outside our classroom as though I were a strange animal trying to break into their herd. For a moment they didn't seem to know what to do with me. Then a boy picked up a stone and threw it. It hit Suzon instead, and she ran yelping with her tail between her legs. I was terrified of pain. I knew I couldn't bear it. But I couldn't bear Suzon's pain either. It was the worst pain of all. I threw myself like a mad bull-calf on the big lout who had thrown the stone and who, taken unawares, went down before my frantic assault with a bloody nose and a lost tooth. Thereafter I was left alone. Like Grand'mère, the children were afraid of me. But from a safe distance they would jeer, "Heathen! Heathen! Dirty little heathen!"

So I wasn't only a coward. I was a heathen too.

I didn't know what the word meant, but I did know that it had to do with the old grey church whose cracked bell rang out the hours and the big red-faced man in the long black frock who smiled at me when we met on the road home and said, "Good evening, my son", as though he too were alone and wanted to be friends. My father said he was a liar and a thief who squeezed money out of the poor with threats of a hell that didn't exist and promises of a heaven that didn't exist either. So I ran away from him.

It was one of our queer foreigners who helped me to understand heathens. She was the queerest of them all, her big face creased and puffy-looking and her untidy hair sometimes a bright, hard gold and sometimes a dirty grey. She wore strange clothes too, one tattered garment piled on another and festooned with bits and pieces of faded finery that, as I learned later, were the leftovers from another life. She was seated on the church steps, munching little cakes out of a paper bag, when she called to me.

"Come here, you funny little fellow. I've got something for you."

I came to her slowly and distrustfully, and she put a fat arm around me and drew me down beside her. She crammed a cake into my astonished mouth. She asked, "Does your little dog like cake?" and emptied crumbs on the step which Suzon licked up joyfully. From that moment the strange woman was our friend.

Little girls broke through the swing doors of the church and raced down the steps and seeing me shrieked out their favourite taunt, "Heathen! Dirty heathen!" The woman turned to me, fixing me with her bloodshot blue eyes.

"Why don't they like you, little one?"

"I don't know, Madame. I don't like them."

"An excellent reason. But you must call me 'La Baronne'. It reminds me of what I really am. Do you know who you are, by any chance?"

"My name is Pascal Guis, Madame." I added—"la Baronne," hastily, since it seemed to mean so much to her, and I did not want to hurt her feelings.

"What's in a name? Nothing. Just now one of those hussies called you a heathen. Are you a heathen, Monsieur Pascal?"

"I'm not sure, Madame la Baronne. What is a heathen?"

"Someone who does not believe in someone else's God."

"My father doesn't believe in any God. He says all that"—
I glanced over my shoulder—"is just a lot of lies."

"It may be. Or perhaps not. Life is dangerous enough. It is not wise to take unnecessary risks. If I were you, Monsieur Pascal, I should seek God. You may find Him, but even if He doesn't exist He will be a source of comfort to you."

"Have you found Him, Madame la Baronne?"

"Not permanently, Monsieur Pascal. From time to time He and I get together—usually when I am not quite sober. Which might seem like a black mark against us both. But in effect I do not think God cares much how we come to Him. Some of us choose one way, some another. Mine, I confess, is apt to weave." She stood up, lumberingly. "Come, Monsieur Pascal. I am sure you and your friend are still hungry. I happen to be in funds. We will visit Madame Royat and see what she can do for us."

I had never been in Madame Royat's shop before. Its many delicacies, the sweet-smelling warmth of a recent baking, made my mouth water. Madame Royat behind her counter looked like a benevolent fox. Her eyes were merry and hard and keen. She picked up a stale *palmier* from a big tin tray.

"There, my little one. I have two youngsters like you. And they are always hungry." And she began to talk of her Louis and Claude who were at the Lycée at Nice and so brilliant that certainly neither of them would come into the Royat business.

"But everything arranges itself," she said contentedly.

Madame la Baronne bought me a *cœur sucré* and half a sausage for Suzon.

That night Grand'mère shook crumbs out of my *tablier*. She was so angry that her black eyes were like smouldering coals.

"Since when does a Guis go begging?" she demanded fiercely. "Don't we feed you enough, little good-for-nothing?"

But she did not strike me. She did not tell my father. She was afraid of me.

In our free time Suzon and I would climb onto the shelf of rock outside our cave. We would sit close to each other and look out over the valley and evening-shadowed mountains and imagine, both of us perhaps, that we were safe and free. At least, for the first time we both knew that we were loved.

Suzon learned to follow me to school and to wait for me, safe while hidden outside the village gate. Or on one of the evenings when my father went to Nice on some mysterious errand, we two would step up to the Grand' Place and watch the men play their silent games. The women, like black crows, would sit close to each other on the wooden benches, watching too, or knitting and gossiping. The foreigners drifted up from the side streets to drink a *fine* or a cup of coffee at the shabby bistro. (If times were good, they dined at the Auberge des Alouettes.) But like Suzon and me, they were set apart. They did not belong. The villagers barely returned their salutations. Yet some of them had lived for years in their dusty attics that they called "ateliers". The little Englishwoman, Mlle Milly, whose untidy brown hair hung in wisps about her delicately featured face, actually owned one of the old houses on the Place de l'Eglise. It was a home for every stray village cat, and two sullen tabbies trailed invariably at her flat heels. If she had been a native she would have been considered crazy. Because she was a foreigner, no one bothered about her.

My father hated foreigners. He said they were good-for-nothings who were paid by relatives to keep out of their own countries. But to me they seemed gentle, harmless people. They smiled at me when we met and even spoke to me in their clumsy French, as though they sensed that Suzon and I were lonely too. Madame la Baronne gave me a sketchbook and coloured pencils which I hid in our cave. She taught me something she called "perspective". She made a sketch of Suzon and me which she sold to a tourist for enough francs to keep her mildly drunk for a week.

"What is a whore, Madame la Baronne?"

We were seated together on the church steps, which had become our meeting place. She was sober and therefore sad and seemed absorbed in tragically happy memories. At least she ignored my question and began to talk of her life in Russia—of the wonderful parties which went on for weeks, of the troikas that carried beautiful, laughing young people racing across the snow, of balls in Moscow, of hundreds of devoted servants, of so much of everything. Madame la Baronne waved her cigarette in its long ebony holder, tracing a circle of smoke in the quiet air. "Pouf! All gone! Like Cinderella's dreams at the hour of twelve."

I had never heard of Cinderella. Madame la Baronne glanced at my open sketchbook and observed that donkeys' ears didn't grow like that and that those odd-looking creatures perched in the plane tree would certainly fall down and break their necks.

"But they are angels, Madame la Baronne. They have wings."

"What do you know of angels? Besides, I am talking of time. One should never wait for twelve o'clock to strike. Then it is too late. We waited. And our world vanished." She broke off. "You asked a question, Monsieur Pascal?"

"What is a whore, Madame la Baronne?"

"A whore is a *femme de carrière*, as you might say; sometimes like other professionals, honest, sometimes dishonest. I was a whore, in my good days, and too honest for my own good." She considered her long rather dirty nails reflectingly. Her childlike blue eyes under their swollen lids smiled at my perplexity. "Ask me something more simple, Monsieur Pascal."

"What is a bastard?"

"Usually a whore's son."

"Doesn't it have a father?"

"Invariably. But not officially."

"Would it be possible for my father not to be my father?"

La Baronne gave a husky chuckle.

"From what I hear, quite possible." She took a handful of my unruly black hair and turned me about to look at me. "Whosesoever son you are, you are a sturdy, handsome fellow. Those eyes—that mouth . . . One day women will want to kiss it. Do little girls kiss you, Monsieur Pascal?"

I shuddered.

"No, indeed, Madame la Baronne. They don't like me."

"They will. And you will like them to kiss you. Very much."

And she kissed me herself, lightly, on both cheeks. Her breath smelt of wine and tobacco. But no one had ever kissed me before. It was true—I liked it. I felt quite strangely happy.

One day I was invited to take tea with her friend the Englishwoman, Mlle Milly. I had never tasted tea before. I had never been in such a strange room. It was so crowded with things and cats (I had left Suzon to wait for me outside). There seemed to be a litter of kittens in every corner. They smelt. But Mlle Milly had cakes for me, and she said she knew I was a kind little boy, and kindness was so important, wasn't it? I hadn't thought about it. I didn't even know I was kind.

But I was glad she liked me. After that we were friends. She smiled at me when we met, and I would touch my beret to her, as I had seen the foreign gentlemen do.

It was difficult to believe what my father said about Monsieur l'Abbé: that he was a scoundrel who cheated money out of the poor with threats and false promises. For one thing, he didn't look as though he had any money at all. The beret that he wore rather defiantly atop his big red face was as shabby and green-hued as his long black robe. It was difficult to ignore his friendly greetings. One gloomy winter's evening he came upon Suzon and me talking to each other by the roadside. He took me unawares, and I stammered, "Good evening, Father," before Suzon and I took to our heels. I felt that he was kind and that he knew I wasn't just a heathen and a cowardly bastard. So that when Suzon disappeared, when I knew something dreadful had happened to her, I ran after him and clung to him. And he came with me at once, as though it was natural that he should help me find her.

We did find her. The Abbé said gently that some savage dog must have set on her. But I knew. I didn't tell him; though he was a man and I was only a boy, I felt that he couldn't know how cruel people are, and that it would be a shame to hurt him. I let him say a prayer over Suzon's grave. It couldn't do any harm, and I remembered what La Baronne had said about not taking unnecessary risks. It was a fact that the Abbé's prayer did comfort me. So perhaps it had comforted Suzon too.

I didn't believe in miracles, but when the Abbé brought me another puppy and even persuaded Father to let me keep it, I wasn't so sure. It was a sort of miracle. It made it possible for me to trust his promise that one day I should be free and happy and paint my pictures.

In the midst of an arithmetic lesson Monsieur Boutton pounced on my sketchbook. I expected him to box my ears and ducked away from him. But he just set his spectacles more firmly on his thin red nose.

"And what, may I ask, is this supposed to represent?"

"Christ's entry into Jerusalem, Monsieur."

"Hem. I didn't know that the Guis family recognized our Saviour's existence. Monsieur l'Abbé should be interested.

But you will, in future, concentrate on the fact that two and two do not make five."

He tore out my picture and carried it to his own desk. I was utterly astonished, partly because he had not punished me, most of all because in spite of his sarcasm I knew that he had been astonished too.

I was just a boy. I was careless. One day much later Father came on me drawing when I should have been weeding. He beat me so that I howled like an animal. I cried all night from shame. But in the morning the shame was still there. It drove me into the church to find the only friend I had who would perhaps understand and help me to endure myself. He didn't seem to mind much that I was a coward. He took me into his sacristy, and there on the wall, under a crucifix, was my picture. I couldn't understand why he liked it. It was such a poor thing. I could do so much better. Only, of course, I wouldn't, because I'd never have the chance. The Abbé began to talk about the future. It was there, he said, waiting for me. I had only to be steady and stubborn enough. And trust him. In a few years, he said, I should be a man. I should be free and on my way. He promised.

Time can pass so slowly. Each day was like a heavy stone that I picked up and threw over my shoulder. I found that it was less heavy if I worked in the vineyards and the lavender field until I stumbled from exhaustion and fell into a bottomless sleep. I didn't grow tall, but I grew strong. My father didn't beat me any more. The three of us lived together in a watchful, brooding sort of silence.

Grand'mère's increasing lameness forced her to let me do some of her marketing. She had forgotten how fast a boy can run. So quite often I could steal an hour and sit on the church steps and draw my pictures of the village and its people and of my fancies that gave me no peace until they had found their way out of me. Then I could forget them. In sober states La Baronne would sit beside me and give advice. But I began to realize that crude and stupid as my efforts were, they had left her far behind. She knew it herself. She would laugh good-humouredly—"Monsieur Pascal, one day soon you will be showing *me*."

When a drawing was finished I would slink into the sacristy and lay it on the altar. It was my way of telling Monsieur l'Abbé that I was still stubborn and steady. Sometimes I would find him kneeling in prayer, and I would wait patiently until he and God had settled their mysterious affairs together. At length the Abbé would lumber to his feet and adjust his spectacles.

"Not bad, but it might be better. Remember, my son, we are aiming at the Prix de Rome."

And he would tear up my picture and toss it into his waste-paper basket. And somehow I felt reassured. I wasn't fooling myself or being fooled. I was on my way. Those clumsy efforts of mine were just milestones on a long road. I even gained a certain physical confidence. The young people who had been my schoolmates no longer taunted me. They were not my friends—I did not need them—but they were not enemies. The girls would nudge me teasingly and run off giggling, as though they knew something about me that I did not know myself. Once the oldest and prettiest of them kissed me—so quickly that I had no defence. I remembered what La Baronne had said: One day I would be pleased when a girl kissed me. That day had not arrived. I wiped my cheek with my always dirty handkerchief. I was disgusted.

I found the sacristy empty. The cross old sacristan told me that Monsieur l'Abbé had been taken ill. I haunted the steps of the presbytery and saw the new young Dr. Chinot step off his bicycle and with his black bag in hand push open the unlocked door. Like a thief I stole in after him. I hid in the dim passage and listened to the two men's voices and Madeleine, the Abbé's housekeeper, clucking indignantly. After a time she and the doctor came out together. She was still grumbling.

"He won't eat properly. He has been fasting for months. One would think he was trying to purge himself of a mortal sin. And he is a good man."

"If he doesn't mend his ways," the young doctor asserted briskly, "he will find himself where good men go—in heaven."

I edged past him into the sick-room. It was as poor and barren as my own attic—a chair, a table, an iron cot, and over it a cheap, awful wooden crucifix. I had never seen the Abbé without his soutane. He looked like a swarthy, black-jowled scarecrow that had been laid flat by a high wind. His brown eyes were almost black in their hollows. But he managed a grin of pleasure.

"Thank God you fooled that old witch! She wouldn't even

84

give you a message. Here—I've something for you." He fumbled under his pillow. "A savings-account book. It's in your name. When you are eighteen, you will be able to draw the money out. It won't be enough for what I'd planned. I haven't had the time. But if I die, my mother will help you. She is a kind and generous woman."

I crouched by his bedside.

"But you are not to die. You are not to starve yourself for me." I blurted out something that I had never acknowledged, even to myself. "I love you—I do love you."

A feeble arm held me close.

"My son—my dear son."

But then he called even old people his children. He was father to them all, whether they wanted him to be or not, so that to be his son was just to be one of many. Madeleine, discovering me, shooed me out, and I went across the Place and through the south door into the dark and gloomy church. It was empty. Only a few candles guttered at St. Roche's feet. There was a wooden box beneath a tray of new candles into which one was supposed to drop at least thirty francs. I hadn't any francs. But I picked out the biggest candle and lit it and thrust it onto an iron spike so that it stood straight and burned with a clear and steady flame. I knelt as Christians knelt the people whose marble plaques testified to miracles.

"Whoever you are, please don't let Monsieur l'Abbé die. I only ask, please make him well again."

I had no real faith in that pink-cheeked, blank-faced saint with his wooden halo, but I wasn't going to leave a stone unturned. And it seemed that St. Roche, or someone, was gratified by my theft, for a week later the Abbé, wrapped up in shawls, sat in a rickety armchair, outside the presbytery in a patch of sunlight.

"Madeleine's stuffing me like a Strasbourg goose," he complained gaily. Then he chuckled. "I'm rather glad, you know, to be alive."

The days passed, and the months, and even the years. I helped build a new terrace and set down the roots of a vine that would perhaps, long hence, make the Domaine Guis famous.

The day of the usual *vendange* came on my eighteenth birthday. The men and women of Rocquedur with their children trooped down the dusty road to help gather the harvest of black, swollen grapes. They disliked my father and Grand'mère as people malignant and accursed, but the *vendange* was part of their tradition—the one golden event in their sombre year. The young village gendarme, Paul Bernard, discarded his uniform for his "blues", trusting that no one in his absence would commit theft or murder. Madame la Baronne, at least, he could keep an eye on. Assured of plentiful food and drink, but too fat to walk, she had borrowed a donkey-cart and now sat, as became an aristocrat, on our patio steps and watched the workers pass the baskets from hand to hand along the terraces to where wheelbarrows waited to carry the lush, spilling contents to the wine-press in the mountainside. When the last grape had been gathered, they elbowed each other around the long living-room table for once set out generously with hams and sausages and long golden loaves and carafes of red wine. With their platters and mugs they settled themselves on the steps and along the terraces under a harvest moon. They ate and drank voraciously. It had been a stifling September day. Their tired bodies gave off a rank odour of stale sweat. The sun had got into their blood, waking the dark violence that lay usually dormant under their taciturnity. Old quarrels and resentments sputtered into flame and died into sullen mutterings or broke into rude malicious laughter. Young men and women, tight-leashed by village custom, broke loose and lay locked silently together in the shadows.

"Next year we shall see another sort of harvest," Emile Royat declared good-humouredly.

Madame la Baronne sang, first in Russian for her own pleasure and then in French for the benefit of the ignorant,

> *Ne me gronde pas, Maman,*
> *Que je l'aime tant.*
> *C'est triste, chère Maman,*
> *De vivre sans lui.*

Her voice was already thick and almost tuneless. She did not seem to care that no one listened to her.

I picked my way over the sprawling bodies. I refilled mugs from an earthenware jar. I had reached a frontier. In a little while I should have crossed over into freedom. This was my last *vendange*. Perhaps the last of most things is sad. As I came back into our living-room I saw my grave face in the old ghostly mirror lighted by candles in sconces on either side. It was still a round and boyish face, streaked with sweat and dirt and the juice of grapes. The unruly black hair hung almost to my eyes. With my blue shirt open to the waist, I looked a rough, hard-handed peasant. But I had taken care of my hands. I might be a Guis, but my mouth wasn't a Guis mouth, not small and tight but long and, I supposed, passionate—though until now I had only been conscious of a stubborn patience. My shoulders were wide and powerful. Deformity had skipped a generation.

The faces of the villagers gleamed in the moonlight like strange flowers. The eyes of the women sparkled as I once more passed among them. Someone plucked at me. A woman whispered to me, "You don't carry a pack on your back, Pascal," and there was a subdued sly laughter. Our butcher, François Dieudonné, stood up with a full glass and bellowed drunkenly, "To Pascal Guis, son and heir to the Domaine and the Grand Marque of 1950"—he hiccoughed—"perhaps."

I was drunk too with weariness, the new wine and the feeling that I was rushing headlong toward a violent crisis. Something too long contained exploded in me. I emptied my jar over the patio so that a dark stream flowed down the steps like a libation to an oath. I heard myself shouting, half in panic, half in triumph, "You're drinking to the wrong man. I'm not the heir. To hell with the Domaine! I'm on my way out, and, name of God, I am never coming back."

They were stricken motionless and silent like spectators of a drama whose unfolding they had watched for years. Only La Baronne went on abstractedly singing to herself,

> Qu'est qu'il peut bien y avoir?
> C'est venu si vite.
> Mon cœur est plein de tristesse . . .

I felt my sudden loneliness. The men and women crowded beneath me were not my friends. None of them really knew me, and to me they were no more than shadows. The issue was between me and the man who came toward me, stumbling over the sprawling limbs, his dark face distorted. He snarled with furious incredulity, "What did you say, my son?"

I knew by the shrinking of my flesh that Grand'mère had crept up behind me. I felt the sickening upsurge of an old fear. I forced myself to say clearly and coolly, "You've called me bastard often enough, so, whoever else I am, I'm not your son."

"You are going—where?"

"To Paris."

"To do what?"

"To become an artist."

Someone laughed. My father grinned too, showing his broken teeth.

"That's a good joke. An artist without a sou!"

"I have enough."

"Stolen then." He beat his deformed breast with a clenched fist. "From me."

"It was not stolen."

"Who gave it to you?" Then in a flash of savage certainty, "That fornicating priest!"

He struck me in the face. Behind his blow was all the viciousness of an old hatred. It aroused in me the memory of taunts, of a dying dog, of pain and the more dreaded fear of pain. I flung myself on the hunchback, who for all his deformity had a robust adult strength. Locked in each other's arms we reeled back into the living-room, against the heavy table which with its clutter of dirty dishes and broken meats crashed over on its side. Pain seared my left arm. I had been stabbed. I heard myself cry out, and with that cry the strength of my rage drained out of me. I wasn't a man, fighting for my just freedom, but a terrified boy at the mercy of people who knew and gloated over my wretched fear of them. I fell back against the wall, covering my face with my arms, letting those two claw me and beat me with a wild lust that might have killed me. But La Baronne had lurched to her feet. Waving a shawl like a battle-flag and with a ferocious Russian oath, she flung her monstrous bulk on my assailants. She had Grand' mère by her grey hair when the now frightened Paul Bernard and a score of men charged to my rescue. They tore me loose and made a way of escape for me. I ran for my life, stumbling and gasping across the courtyard, out onto the road. The moon had gone down behind the mountains. Under the cypress trees was solid darkness. I stopped to wipe my eyes clear of blood and tears. A cold wet nose nuzzled me. I bent down, sobbing with rage and shame. "What's wrong with me, Suzon? Shall I always run away?"

She followed me uncritically, unquestioningly, as my first

Suzon had followed me. She didn't know or care what kind of a fool and coward I might be. Behind me I could hear a sullen murmur. If I turned I could see the Mas smouldering like a fire beyond the trees. But at least I would not look back.

Two days later, in a stiff, new suit, my left arm in a sling, and with the Abbé at my elbow, I stood on the Nice platform outside a third-class compartment of the Rome-Paris express. I carried an overcoat over my good arm, and a hat such as I had never worn. In the new suitcase at my feet was all the gear that the Abbé considered essential to a young man setting out in life.

The day before I had said good-bye to my friends. There were more of them than I had known. Madame la Baronne had given me something wrapped in dirty tissue paper.

"The ring belonged to my mother, Monsieur Pascal. Believe it or not, the stones are precious. One day they may be useful to you."

This time I had kissed her on both raddled cheeks. She was the first woman I had ever kissed. I knew that she was amused but pleased too.

"You learn quickly, Monsieur Pascal."

Madame Royat had collected a packet of stale *palmiers* and *cœurs sucrés* for me. Her bright eyes had twinkled with malicious and yet not unkindly speculation.

"So you are to be an artist, Monsieur Pascal, like Monsieur Renoir, no doubt. We shall be proud of you."

But between the Mas and myself was a gulf of catastrophic silence.

The engine gave its shrill feminine scream. The Abbé heaved my suitcase on to the train platform. We embraced each other shyly.

"You'll take care of Suzon for me?"

"She'll be waiting for you—she and others like her, no doubt. She is still a lusty wench. Maman will arrange the affair She is good at such arrangements."

We both laughed, not very steadily, and exchanged a last handclasp. The train jerked into movement.

"Remember . . . nothing less than the Prix de Rome," the Abbé shouted in farewell.

I knew he would wait until the train was out of sight, then he would take the bus back to Rocquedur. My heart followed him into the sacristy where he would kneel and pray for me.

The precious silver crucifix had gone. In its place was its shadow. But one day I would hang it back where it belonged.

On September 15, 1938, a young Provençal passed through the gates of the Gare de Lyon. He felt like a conqueror, with all of life before him, the world at his feet. In fact, though he could not have known it, he had just one year.

The Abbé had written to an old war comrade, René Gouges, who with his wife owned a house and café on the Left Bank. They were a homely, kindly couple, the salt of our French earth. They welcomed me as a son. I had a pleasant little room overlooking the river, and in the evening I would sit in the warm café and drink a Pernod with the other regulars and listen wide-eyed to their passionate discussions and sometimes quarrels.

"The lightning doesn't strike twice!"

A snort of contempt.

"It has struck twice already. It will strike again when and where it chooses. The Germans will be the same people to the end of time, only"—with weary bitterness—"they'll be worse."

A young man playing draughts looked up from the board to grin.

"Well, as far as I'm concerned, they can take over this filthy mess. Better to be a live German than a dead Frenchman."

His opponent threw a glass of wine in his face, and Monsieur Gouges had to come out from behind his bar to take both men by the collar and shake them apart.

"Must we quarrel among ourselves, Messieurs?"

He wiped the draughtboard dry with an indignant apron and set up the pieces like an exasperated father with obstreperous children. They went back sullenly to their game. But the explosion had torn a mere crack wide open, and on either side of the chasm the simple people who were the café's patrons looked at one another in uneasy questioning.

"We have our traitors and our idiots," Monsieur Gouges said. We sat that night together at supper in the back room, enjoying Madame Gouges' superb ragoût de mouton under a dreadful pink-shaded lamp that showed up the deep lines of care on his fat, kindly face. "Let's hope the Germans have theirs. Or it's all up with us."

I was interested, but not really concerned. (It's comical now to look back on a Pascal Guis who believed that, because he had to paint his pictures, there could not be a war.) On the strength of my work which the Abbé had sent ahead of me, I was accepted as pupil in one of the great ateliers. From sheer panic I made a late, conspicuous entry. I stood on the threshold, gazing open-mouthed and blushing to the roots of my black hair at the naked woman posed on a raised platform. My blush, my awkward clothes, my skin burnt dark by our southern sun, evoked a storm of laughter from the men and women who turned to measure me.

"Mesdames et messieurs, the Midi has sent us another genius."

There was a furious stamping of feet, a thunderous mocking welcome which did not frighten me. I laughed back at them. I could endure their mockery—I knew that I was one of them.

A pale delicate young man made a place for me.

"I am André Guerrier."

"I am Pascal Guis."

We made each other formal little bows and shook hands. He helped me set up my easel. We worked side by side. Even in that one session something good was established between us. Perhaps because he came from a desolate Brittany farm and had been lonely too, we became friends. He knew of a little restaurant in a back street whose patron, in hopes of a budding Picasso, would exchange our fantasies for a meal. We sat there late into the night, André listening with a sweet gravity as I poured out my heart to him. I think he knew how long that heart had been blocked—how necessary was its torrential overflow. He himself said very little. I thought afterwards that though he was more gifted than I, he foresaw no share in that future that seemed to be opening out for us both in a blaze of glory.

We pooled our meagre resources. One golden autumn Sunday, having fasted for a week, we took the omnibus to Chartres and stood together in the fiery reflections from the great rose windows. In a few months their glory would become fugitive for the second time in a generation. We could not have known this, yet turning to André I saw his delicate boy's face shadowed with a mature sadness, a premonition of greater sorrow.

"They must have been happier than we are," he murmured. "I think the men who created all this must have laughed and sung as they worked. They died young. They suffered cruelty and privation and oppression. But they had God. As His children they had significance even in their insignificance. At our greatest we are nobody but ourselves. Each of us is alone and meaningless."

"But if God doesn't exist," I argued, "it's useless—all this pretence at belief in Him."

"Worse than useless. It's like galvanizing a corpse. It twitches. But it stinks." He took my arm as though seeking comfort. "We are growing tired of ourselves and our cleverness. We are like the Gadarene swine, rushing to our own destruction to make an end of our intolerable boredom and futility. Well, there may be a second Revelation. It may come in time."

We were not always so serious. On the night of his birthday, armed with funds from his Breton home, he invited me to a *boîte* on the Left Bank where a Negro orchestra played stridently for the students and their girls pressed together on a tiny dance floor.

"Just wait, though!" André said wisely.

At midnight an upright piano was rolled into empty space and a girl with short red-brown hair cut to a fringe that came down to straight dark brows over lazy, smouldering eyes, sat down amid rowdy applause and sang. Her songs were French and English, sung in argot without accent. She made the most innocent of them ribald.

"A little bit of wotcher fancy does yer good."

She had a throaty, indifferent voice. She didn't seem to care whether we listened to her or not, yet each of us imagined that she was singing, secretly, to him.

"She calls herself Nina," André said. "Just Nina. Half English, half French. They say her father was an English officer in the last war, her mother a French courtesan, and that she left England on account of some scandal. But no one really knows."

> *"Du Paradis j'ai fait le tour.*
> *J'ai fait des vers, j'ai fait d'amour.*
> *Que t'importe? Ouvre ta porte.*
> *Bonjour, Suzon."*

There were no encores. She shrugged at the demands, good-humoured but adamant. She sauntered across to our table. I remember how the full skirts of her simple dark green frock seemed to dance about her slender ankles and the charming feet in their red, high-heeled shoes.

We stood up and André pulled out a chair for her.

"She's never honoured me before, Pascal," he said, grinning. "It must be your blue eyes."

"They're grey," she corrected lazily.

Then she was silent, almost as though she had forgotten us. I didn't know what to talk about. I felt like a country clod—which I was. I said stupidly, "I liked your song. At home—where I come from—I've got a dog called Suzon."

She raised her brows at this.

"Do you love her?"

"Very much."

"What other bitches do you love?"

It was a deliberate, provocative coarseness. I turned scarlet and muttered, "I don't love any," and she laughed.

"You will."

She accepted a glass of wine. She lifted it, smiling at me across the table. Her eyes, fawn-coloured, held mine so that I could not look away from her. I could not smile back. My only satisfaction was the certainty that in spite of her cool bravado she too was shaken. Her very vulgarity had been a defiance of something inexplicable and troubling.

"What is your friend's name?"

" '*Que t'importe?*' " André quoted with unusual rudeness. "I warn you—he is a virtuous young man."

"What else are you besides a virtuous young man?"

"Nothing now," I said sullenly. "I shall be a painter."

"Another painter! Give me your hand." I gave it to her. She held it palm upwards. Her hand was warm and firm. Its warmth raced to my heart.

"First you will be a soldier. You will fight in a silly battle and run away with all the other foolish little soldiers. You must be careful not to be killed. It would be too stupid. We need geniuses."

"Who told you all that nonsense?" André demanded, flushed with anger.

She glanced at him casually.

"A good friend."

"What does he know?"

"He is like me. He knows how to stay alive."

André stood up roughly and tossed money on the table in front of her and dragged me by the arm. We left her still seated at the table and counting the money as though it were all that mattered to her. But I knew . . .

It was raining, but we walked the streets together, unaware that it had soaked through our threadbare clothes to our skin.

"You rather fell for her, didn't you, Pascal? Don't. She's someone's mistress—a fellow with a title as long as your arm and a fist full of money. She's no good."

"Does she love him?"

"In the name of God—how should I know? I'd say she wasn't the type to love anyone. You heard what she said. She wants to stay alive."

I managed to laugh.

"So do I."

"So do we all—alive and free to do what we were born to do. But perhaps we want too much. If the river bursts its banks, we'll be swept away with it, God knows where." He held my arm more firmly, but he was talking to himself as out of a sort of grey despair. "Men who don't love and defend their country are corrupt and worthless. Men who turn their love to an instrument of violence and oppression are corrupt and worthless too. We little people who ask only to live and love, what are we to do?"

I think he did not quite trust me. He walked with me until he knew the *boîte* was closed. I left him at his lodgings. But I did not go home. I stood on the Pont d'Jena and watched Paris become a lovely monochrome and then a canvas of glowing colours. I knew that something tremendous had happened to me. I did not think of it as love; it was rather an opening of a door through which I passed from a dreamy, groping adolescence into fiery manhood. From now on I should see men and women with other eyes. I should paint them with an assured hand. That day Maître David, who gave rare, almost grudging encouragement, patted my shoulder.

"If God wills, I shall live to be proud of you."

God willed otherwise.

A month later André and I joined the same regiment. After a long thunderous pause, the lightning struck for the third time.

It was strange that I was not afraid. I was at first only

94

bewildered and furious at a listless regimentation that was not discipline, a preparedness that in its shabby futility was almost cynical.

"Stand firm," Monsieur Gouges pleaded with me at parting. "Don't let everything we suffered and fought for become meaningless."

The Abbé wrote me. "The foreigners have fled—all but La Baronne and Mlle Milly, who refused to desert her cats. So we are alone, wondering who we are and who our neighbour really is. They say the war will never come this far, and Lucien Sauvan maintains that in any case it is no affair of ours, that it is a trick of the rich and powerful to become richer and more powerful. Some of our people listen to him." His writing grew firmer. "I pray for you, my son, that God may protect you and give you the strength and vision to endure whatever He has ordained, for the sake of righteousness."

Even on that frightful road south I was not actually afraid. I was living in a nightmare that was so divorced from reality that I could only expect to wake from it to the peaceful morning sunlight and the orderly procession of the days. André and I had long since lost our regiment. With other refugees we stumbled along bloody, congested roads or crouched in crowded ditches hiding from the planes that almost casually sprayed us with death and wounds. Sometimes a French car like a ruthless ship would plough through our ranks, spilling us to the side, the faces of its occupants, amid piled-up possessions, set in glacial indifference to the drowning hands that pleaded with them.

A young man with a lean greyhound's face drove an American limousine. For a moment we held our ground against it, and in that moment I recognized the girl who sat beside him. Our eyes met, as they had done once before. She recognized me too, though I must have changed almost beyond recognition. I was a bloody, bearded scarecrow. She waved, and I saw her turn to her companion and speak urgently. I was sure that she appealed to him. But the appeal met with no response. The car edged forward, and the mob gave way sullenly. It closed in behind, seething and foaming. The pleading hands had become fists.

"The rats are in a hurry," André muttered. "The ship must be sinking fast."

95

That night we found a deserted barn well back from the road and a luckless old hen which we slaughtered and roasted by a fire out of sight of the fleeing crowd that would have torn us limb from limb for what we had. Two other soldiers joined us, unshaven, gaunt with hunger and exhaustion. They had thrown away their weapons. They had seen their officers desert them, flying the battlefield in staff cars with their women and all the valuables they could lay their hands on. For what should they, therefore, cling to the rags and tatters of their soldier's integrity? They were going home to their fields, their towns, their people. What happened to the world outside that orbit was no concern of theirs.

Their eyes, as they gnawed bones clutched in filthy fists, were those of hunted animals blind to everything but the vision of survival.

"I'm not going to be caught," André said. "I'm going to take to the hills. I'll come down every chance I get and kill a bastard or two, till they kill me. Who'll come along?"

I heard myself say, "I will." What motivated me, I hardly knew. It was part rage at my own frustrated and shattered life, part love of this friend who loved and trusted me. But I was still a Provençal peasant. I was not yet a Frenchman to whom the memory of a cathedral would become a battle-flag.

The two other men were coldly silent. The country was lost. But perhaps they could save themselves and the little that life had vouchsafed them.

In the months that followed I thought often of Madame la Baronne and her stories of her flight from Moscow, stealing from the destitute, killing for a crust of bread. It seemed that history was a wheel that turned in tragic repetition. Somewhere and always there were men and women fleeing from torture, enslavement and death. Some of them nursed in their tattered bosoms a spark of miraculous faith not only in themselves but in their persecutors.

André was one of them. He hated and he killed. But he loved too. By reason of that something luminous and un-troubled in his courage, he at first took the lead. But gradually as his physical strength failed, he leaned on my peasant robustness, turned to me more often for decisions. A savage cough tore at his hollow chest, and often there would be blood about his mouth. One night, hidden in a mountain cave, he cried out like someone drowning. I heard him whisper with a last flash of gaiety, "You'll have to paint my pictures for me."

All night I held the gaunt young body in my arms, trying to warm it with my warmth. But the morning light showed me that I was finally alone.

It was a loneliness more bitter than I had known even in my childhood, for now I knew what love and friendship could be to me. In it I submerged my humanity. I stole and killed like an animal, without pity but without rancour. It was only in the deadly interludes between violence that like a rift of light in the dark I remembered a woman's eyes, the warmth of her hand, the belief that for all her apparent cynical indifference she had pleaded for me. Then, deliberately, I put the memory from me.

I stumbled at length into the hands of men, hunted like myself. For two weeks they held me prisoner and subjected me to a coldly calculated interrogation. But I was forthright in my answers and savage-looking enough to inspire faith. So I entered into a new comradeship that was without mercy, even on itself. I warned them that I had a breaking point. I promised that before I reached it, I would kill myself. In any case, they did not believe me. I who had known so much fear now had a reputation for cold, ruthless courage. Also I was lucky. As disaster thinned the ranks of my cell, I rose in authority. And slowly I worked my way south, to my own country, my own people, my own village. I had the conviction that I was journeying toward some tremendous, invisible event.

At midnight the streets were empty. A bitter winter wind swept through them like a tide. An occasional overhead light intensified the shadows thrown by the tall, dead-faced houses. Here and there a shutter clattered menacingly. I felt like a ghost, haunting a world submerged in centuries. In the Place de l'Eglise a lamp burned in the presbytery window. I tapped softly. The silence became alert. I heard the scrape of a chair pushed back, the heavy, familiar tread. The door opened, and a streak of light cut the darkness like a bright sharp knife. I stepped into its path, and the door opened wide enough for me to pass. Then it closed again, quietly. A key turned in the lock.

"I was afraid that you were dead."

The Abbé led the way into his study. It was more than ever bleak and comfortless. But he scraped together some firewood and a sickly warmth fought with the dank, pervading chill. In silence, as though he knew what must come first, he produced a loaf of bread and a carafe of red wine.

"It's all I have."

"It's more than I have seen for two days."

I crouched down, cross-legged, by the fire, gnawing the bread like a starved dog. I washed down its staleness with the dregs of wine. I looked up at the big man looming over me. The florid face had been worn down to the asceticism of a Goya saint. Behind him hung that first, childlike picture.

"So you brought it in here."

"It was safer. The Germans have an eye for value. And it reminded me of you." He shook his head. "At least of a boy I knew. You've changed, Pascal. You had, in spite of everything, a look of gentleness and innocence. It's gone."

I rolled up the sleeves of my leather coat and stretched out my arms.

"Feel them. Not an ounce of spare flesh. Solid muscle. Look at my hands. A killer's hands. There was a farmer who pretended to befriend us and who planned to sell us out. Things had to be done quickly. I strangled him."

"A strange boast."

"It is not a boast. It's an explanation. I was to have painted pictures—do you remember? I was to win the Prix de Rome —for both of us."

"You still may."

"No, my time is running out."

"But you are not afraid any more. You've learned to trust and forgive yourself."

I clasped my arms about my knees. I put my face down on them, like a man falling asleep.

"I don't know—no, I don't know. They've made me *chef de résistance* in this region. I warned them: under certain pressures, I shall break."

"Do they believe you?"

"No—I have an absurd reputation, which merely means that I've had a lot of fantastic luck. So long as the luck holds . . ." I sighed to ease the aching of my body. I asked a question, fearing the answer. "My Suzon—I suppose she has gone too?"

"No, she's with my mother, nursing a last litter. Maman

98

has friends, German friends. They give her food. I ought to hate her. I persist in loving her." He smiled ruefully. "She will keep a puppy for you."

"I shall never have another dog." I felt suddenly impatient. "Go on. What has happened here? Whom can I trust?"

"That's hard to say. We have so many traitors. Or perhaps traitor isn't the right word. Can you betray something in which you have no faith and to which by consequence you owe no loyalty? Most of our people have a very simple faith. Many believe in staying alive." He asked after a moment, "Where did you learn faith in France?"

I grinned.

"I think in a cathedral—Chartres."

"A good birthplace."

I said mischievously, "I did not find God there."

"Why should you? He chooses His own time and place."

"Go on! Go on!" I had no time for a spiritual wrangle with him. I asked, "Is there no one?"

"There's my Madeleine. She has a peasant's personal constancy. They could flay her; she would scream, she wouldn't talk. There's La Baronne. She'd do what she could for you because she likes you. Not for any cause. She's through with causes. She's a good friend. To the Germans, too. They're busy massacring the people who massacred her people. You can't blame her."

"And Mlle Milly?"

"You've heard about her?"

"Something—a sort of legend, not quite believable."

"Who could believe it? An absurd elderly Englishwoman with a tribe of cats! Certainly not our Captain von Freytag. He has taken a sort of liking to her; lodges with her in her best room and occasionally enjoys a cup of tea and croissants with her and lectures her on English stupidity and decadence. She reproves him for impertinence towards his betters, a piece of temerity which convinces him that she is crazy and can be trusted. I think he would be genuinely shocked if he knew that there is a transmitting set under his own living-room floor. She's quite an expert operator. At irregular intervals she relays the Captain's tidbits to London. She seems to have a sixth sense. When the hunt becomes too hot, she closes down. Yes, you can trust her. I doubt if she would even scream." He considered for a moment. "Then there is Emile Royat. A kindly, decent fellow. Out of sheer compassion he has helped the Drouets with their escaped airmen. His two sons have been picked up as hostages. They will be shot, unless—well, Madame Royat suspects her husband. For her sons' lives she may denounce him."

I muttered drowsily, "That flint-eyed vixen with her stale *palmiers*."

"But she loves her sons. I doubt if she ever loved Emile. As to the Drouets, they're foreigners to whom she owes nothing. Poor stupid woman! From her angle she hasn't any choice."

"You're still charitable, Father."

He shrugged his massive shoulders.

"I still have an awkward faculty for seeing things as the devil sees them."

"That little spiritual trick of yours—the universal 'I'—so it still works."

"After a rather confusing fashion, I find it increasingly hard to distinguish sheep from goats. Myself, I can be a goat or a sheep at a turn of the hand! Fortunately nobody cares any more what I am. The Captain has decided that I am negligible. He thinks he has convinced me that he is a true friend to us all. What he does is in the line of duty. If he shoots the Royat boys, it will be regretfully. When he shoots me, as no doubt he will, he will give me a last hearty Teutonic handshake."

"And—and the Domaine?"

"Madame Guis lives as best she can in what the Milice left of the Mas. They were worse than the Germans. They were cruel because they felt guilty. The Germans, I gather, never feel guilty."

"And my father?"

"You know that he is dead?"

"I heard—some queer story."

"The Milice shot him because of you—his son. If he had betrayed your whereabouts . . . But of course he couldn't; he didn't know. And of course they didn't believe him. He raved and fought arrest like a madman. So they shot him in cold blood."

"That," I said, "is so damned funny that one can't laugh."

Suddenly I was utterly tired. I couldn't care any more for anyone. "Would it be possible for me to sleep a little?"

"You can have my bed."

"Too soft. I'd smother. Let me stay here."

The Abbé spread a blanket over my outstretched body and pressed a pillow under my unkempt head.

"I'll keep watch. I sleep enough."

"You're risking your life."

"It's not much to risk."

He knelt beside me and kissed my forehead. His face was close to mine. I looked straight into his eyes. A long-submerged knowledge and recognition floated to the surface of my fading consciousness.

"Father."

"My dear son."

A cold, merciless rain penetrated to my bones. I ventured to use my flashlight. What I saw briefly through the streaming lines of steel was a ruin that might have survived from some old, half-forgotten disaster. Only the walls and roof of the kitchen and an outhouse were left standing. I found a door, groaning on its hinges. I pushed it cautiously open. An animal instinct that I had acquired like a sixth sense warned me that I was not alone. Someone hid in the dark and watched me.

"Grand'mère," I whispered. "It's I—Pascal."

I heard a mouse-like scuffling. A bony, ice-cold hand fumbled at my sleeve. She whimpered childishly, "They killed him. They shot him because of you."

"I know. I'm sorry. He hated me. But still I'm sorry. Not any more sorry, though, than for other men who have been shot for less." I made her crouch down beside me. I flashed a light on her face. The eyes in their livid mask were terrible. "How do you live?"

"I have my chickens. They flew away. But they came back. Madame Royat gives me crusts in exchange for eggs. And sometimes Monsieur Robert brings me a rabbit."

"And the vineyards?"

"They left them. But they said if they did not find you they would come back and destroy them too."

"Everything has been destroyed. You must help me, Grand'mère."

She was mumbling her sunken lips as she did when she was thinking.

"There's no one to work the vineyards. They are choked with weeds. If Christophe knew, he would die twice."

"Perhaps by spring I shall weed them for you. Only you

**101**

must help me. Listen to me. I shall have to hide here till tomorrow. At mid-day someone will visit me—someone you would not suspect. It would be safer for you not to know. Take eggs to Madame Royat. If you should meet anyone on the road—forget."

She crept closer to me for warmth. She was so thin that her bones cut into mine. I held her in my arms, remembering the time, so long ago, when she had sung me lullabies. Presently I knew from her breathing that she had fallen asleep.

I hid from the rain-drenched sunlight in some overgrown bushes so that, unseen, I could watch the road. I had to smile at sight of her—a comical little woman with wispy grey-brown hair hanging about her face, huddled in an assortment of the oddest clothes, two tabby cats slinking morosely at her flat heels. But she walked with a gallant swing, as though without a fear or a care in the world. When I whistled softly, she came directly to me and shook my hand as though we were friends who had met on some pleasant social occasion. She followed me into the derelict kitchen and I made tea for her—real English tea, which she drank delicately out of a chipped cup.

"Delicious, Monsieur Pascal. Even the Captain has nothing like it."

"Thank our English air-drop. Someone must have had you in mind."

"Perhaps my nephew, Peter. Such a thoughtful boy. It was he who brought me my radio set and taught me how to use it. He landed one night just outside the Cros de Cagnes. From a submarine. Very risky, of course. But even as a child he was always trying to break his neck. Sometimes he sends me a special message. 'How are the cats, Aunty?' "

"You mustn't be here long. Did anyone see you come?"

"Two people. The Captain opened his door when I came downstairs. He has my best room, you know. And he hears everything. He told me he had some special horse meat for me. He loves cats too."

"Did he say anything else?"

"He wanted to warn me. He knows someone is sending out messages. They have their detecting machines, you know. But just when they are closing in, the messages stop and start up somewhere else. He said that if I could help, he knew I would, on account of my cats. I wouldn't want them to starve, would I? It seems that the Gestapo is very angry. That's why those poor two Royat boys have been arrested. Madame Royat is frantic. She goes about—snooping, I'm afraid you'd call it. *She* saw me."

"But she didn't follow you?"

"No. I made sure. Besides, she doesn't take me seriously." She chuckled. "No one does."

I refilled her cup for her.

"They'll catch you in the end, Mlle Milly."

Her pale blue eyes twinkled at me.

"Well, I'm getting on. There's not much you can take from old people, at most an unpleasant year or two. I shall worry about my cats, though. You see, they're my reason for living here. When I came to the village, oh, years ago, I found so many of them starving. They attached themselves to me. I don't want to fail them." She looked at me anxiously. "Do you think me crazy?"

"No one so kind is crazy. And don't worry. Your cats shall be taken care of. The Abbé will see to it somehow."

"He's a good man. The Captain thinks the world of him." She gave a light, tinkling laugh. "The Germans don't understand anyone—do they?—except themselves."

"Why do you do this?" I asked.

"Perhaps because I was a little curious. I mean I wanted to find out how I would behave under circumstances that are not usual among ordinary people like myself. And I don't like Germans. I love France. I'm proud to be English. I suppose it's old-fashioned to be proud of one's country."

"It may become fashionable again. Now please listen. On the 10th of January you should get a message from London. It will refer to an air-drop which, if things go well, will take place in the neighbourhood of St. Martin-Vesoubie. Meet me here, if you can, the next day at this time, with full instructions."

"If anything goes wrong?"

"Consult with the Drouets. They have their own contacts."

"Such nice people!" (Throughout she conducted our encounter with the well-mannered formality of a Victorian vicarage.) "They know how difficult things have become for me. I can always count on a cup of that dreadful coffee and a nice chat. So comforting."

My ears were sharp-set for the shuffle of Grand'mère's returning footsteps, or for a heavier, more dangerous tread.

I said urgently, "Please go now. Don't worry about me. I have my secret way out." I pressed a half-empty packet of tea on her. "Don't invite the Captain to share it with you. He might get ideas."

She gathered a deplorable cloak about her. The cats rose reluctantly from a patch of sunlight.

"My poor twins! They don't really like to walk. They like to prowl. Still, I think they feel they must keep an eye on me." She smiled at me rather charmingly. "You were such a lovely boy, Monsieur Pascal. Now you're a very handsome young man—at least you would be if you shaved and cut your hair properly. Hasn't anyone else fallen in love with you?"

"No one." I crushed down a resurgent memory and laughed and kissed her cheek. "I don't stay around long enough."

I stood, submerged in shadow, and watched her plod back up the road, her two companions at her heels. I wondered if I should ever see her again. It was possible, of course, that we might die together.

Things did not go well. What had gone wrong, I didn't know, only that I had played my luck for the last time. The air-drop was a disaster. We were ambushed, and half my men killed or captured. I escaped to the Domaine but was caught the following night. They found me in the cave on the face of the cliff. It was as though they knew exactly where to find me. I was asleep. I had no time to keep my promise.

They took me to the Gestapo headquarters at Nice. The last I was to see of my world was contained in that bleak room: the oversized portrait of a fanatical clown's face, a man in civilian clothes seated at a desk so rigidly that only his mouth seemed alive, sinister black S.S. guards, rigid too, and, seated aloofly against the wall, like the spectator at some rather intriguing show, an officer of the Wehrmacht. I did not know why, for a moment, I forgot everything else—even my own immediate deadly crisis. The man was older than myself, strangely arresting, almost attractive, well-built, immaculately uniformed. His eye-glass, catching the light from an opposite window, flashed at me like a warning beacon. He had a long, closely folded mouth that seemed on the verge of a friendly, reassuring smile. But in the dark afterwards it was the heavy-lidded eyes that I was to remember.

They held mine. I knew confusedly that mine held his. It was as though this stranger and I had travelled a long way to this encounter and that now we were locked together in a final conflict on some other level of experience, that neither now nor until that conflict was resolved could we free ourselves. The German put a white, manicured hand to his military collar as though suddenly it had become too tight for him.

"Your name?"

I did not answer.

"You are Pascal Guis, so-called *chef de résistance* in this region?"

Silence. (But for how long could I maintain it?)

The mouth moved on. "If you tell us everything you know, you will escape with your life. Otherwise we have infallible means to make you."

So it had come. I was alone with myself, a self I had never trusted. They had taken my means of escape from me. They were strong. But also they were slow. With the swiftness of light I had wrenched the revolver from the holster of the man next to me. I shot myself into darkness, as I thought, to safety.

I believed at first that I was dead and in the hell reserved for painters, a lightless, featureless hell. But then someone whose voice was soft, almost caressing, spoke to me in French.

"I'm afraid you've made rather a mess of yourself, my poor friend. You precisely hit the optic nerve. When you are well enough I shall have to produce you for further interrogation. An ugly business. I beg of you, spare yourself and us." The voice became strangely urgent. It said incredibly, "I ask it as a personal favour. We are both soldiers. I should like to save you, if you would make it possible."

I knew instinctively that he was pleading with me, not to save me, but in some obscure way to save himself. He needed me to fail.

I managed to whisper, "I shall try not to oblige you."

Two weeks later they turned me loose, for their own inscrutable reasons or because a blind man on whom they had inflicted their most ingenious worst and who had remained implacably silent was of no further use to them. Throughout the proceedings I had felt that man's presence. I had known that he watched and waited breathlessly. I had felt his tension mount with my agony. But I never heard his voice again.

An officer of the Gestapo drove me through the Var valley and across the river. At the bottom of the rough cart track which twists up to the mountain to the Domaine Guis, he kicked open the car door.

"Find your own way home, stubborn French pig!"

# III

## OF MLLE MILLY

THEY say that we English have two countries, our own and Italy.

My second love is France.

I love her wide, pellucid skies, her benign sunlight, the gently drifting clouds, the small, perfect husbandry of her fields and vineyards, the wild *Causses*, the friendly mountains and great and little rivers—the noble Loire, the smiling Dordogne. I love her cities whose people know how to enjoy the life they work for. When I am dying I shall try to remember all the things I have loved so much, the places where I have been at home and happy.

My good friend La Baronne tells me I see France with the eyes of a foreigner, that the French themselves have ceased to love her as the source of their virtue. They won't die for her any more. They won't even live for her—only for themselves. Perhaps that's true. But I'm glad I see France with my English eyes.

I love the people. La Baronne grumbles that they have intelligence and passion but neither heart nor wisdom. That may be true too. But they have something so rare and wonderful that it is perhaps right that we others should have to die for it in their stead—*le douceur de vivre*.

I love these Rocquedur peasants. They don't love me. Indeed love, as we English understand it—part kindness, part loyalty, part compassion—is a stranger to them. They tolerate me. They don't want to understand me. I don't blame them. I'm just one of those wispy English spinsters with enough money to barge about the world and sometimes make a nuisance of themselves. I suppose the people here think my cats are a nuisance—or at least a proof that I'm a little crazy.

They would shake their heads or lift their eyebrows if I tried to explain how I feel, that we owe animals a tragic debt. What awful things we humans do to each other is our affair. But animals have no redress. We have taken their world from them. We use them for our sustenance and pleasure. They are at our mercy. And we are not merciful. No one can make me believe that they are not God's children too. They are my brothers and sisters. I have tried, in my small, no doubt foolish way to pay my debt to them.

Pascal Guis would understand. Madame Royat, whose sons are like sleek, bright-eyed young foxes, used to call him *farouche*. But his funny little dog knew that his sullen fierceness hid a loving, desolate heart. I was so thankful when the good Abbé helped him to escape those two dreadful people. When the war broke out I prayed for him too.

So of course I was willing to do all I could.

It was too bad, of course, about that poor German captain. He trusted me. And he was such a lonely fellow. But after all, as he said, war is war. Or, as the French say, *à la guerre comme à la guerre*. He would have had to shoot me if he had found me out, but I think he would have been sorry. And I should have been sorry for him too.

Anyhow, something went wrong. No message came through. My nephew Peter calls me a grand old trout. But after all I am an amateur trout. I may have failed somehow.

I was on my way to the Mas when an open car filled with armed men drove past me at top speed. But I caught a glimpse of him. Pascal's face was grey and set and expressionless. But I knew he had tried to signal to me, "Warn everyone."

I went on as though nothing had happened, hoping against hope that he had had time to leave a message for me. I found his grandmother in the kitchen, standing by the table. She looked demented.

"Who betrayed him?" I asked.

Her sunken mouth was like a trap that had snapped to, that nothing could pry open.

All the same, I knew.

# IV

## OF ULRICH VON FREYTAG

A MAN springs from his roots. He can't change his roots, so he can't change himself. He is what he is born to be.

As a German I suppose I should say that my roots are planted in our good German earth. But in fact I trace them to our one-time ancestral gallery in Schloss Freytag, which is perched above Baden-Baden on the fringes of the Black Forest. It is really more a French chateau than a German castle; outside a jumble of coy little towers and turrets, and inside a jumble of French Rococo and German Biedermeier —all very stiff and comfortless. When I was quite small I thought it all splendid, until my English nurse laughed at it and told me it was awful. I hated her. (She was shortly thereafter sent back to her native fogs.) But I am not stupid. I had learned my lesson.

One day, when I was five years old, having escaped my French *bonne* I set out on a hazardous exploration of our vast and gloomy corridors and finally stumbled, by accident, upon my past. It terrified me. The men and women lined up side by side in their gilt portraits were life-size, but they grew monstrous as I stared up at them. They loomed over me. When I tried to turn away, their cold blue eyes held me. My small legs turned to water. Some, as I learned later, were actual portraits of soldiers in every kind of uniform, from that of an officer in Frederick the Great's Grenadiers to that of General Eric von Freytag, my father, in the pale blue, tight-waisted frock coat and high yellow collar of the Durlacher Dragoons, as they had been before 1914. The legendary portraits were of Teutonic knights and even Vikings, with flowing red beards and winged helmets. The women, with one exception, were ugly. Even court dress and piled-on jewels could not redeem their fat, expressionless faces. The exception was my mother, who had an unsubstantial moonbeam beauty and look of childlike wistfulness.

It was she who found me, howling in hysterics. She tried to comfort me.

"You mustn't be afraid of them. They are your own people. You must try to be worthy of them."

When my father came home on leave, she must have told him. He was like God to her. She had to confess everything.

I was dressed in my best sailor's suit, and she went with me to the door of my father's library. She knocked and turned the door handle for me and gave me a gentle push. Then I was alone.

"Come here, Ulrich."

I came at once, not very steadily, and stood as I had been taught, stiff and straight, heels together, my hands pressed to the seams of my short trousers. My father, wearing a dark blue Letewka and strapped trousers which outlined the slender-hard-muscled horseman's legs, stood in front of his desk, his white hands clasped in front of him as though on the hilt of an invisible sword. He was young to be a general. But his thick, close-cropped hair was steel-grey. His lean face was cut with deep lines. His mouth under the clipped moustache was the deepest, straightest line of all. I had never dared to look into his eyes long enough to be sure whether they were grey or blue.

"So you cried, Ulrich?"

"Yes, Papa."

"Why?"

"I was frightened."

"Of what?"

"Of—of all those people."

"Those people, as you call them, are you. You are what they made out of their German flesh and blood. It is futile cowardice to run from them." He made a faint gesture of distaste. "There's loose talk of environment as an explanation for what we are. Effete nonsense. A man springs from the loins of his past. Do you understand?"

"Not—not quite, Papa."

"You will. Meantime remember this: that a Freytag cannot be afraid, least of all of himself."

He leaned forward and slapped me on both cheeks with the back of his hand. The big crested ring drew blood. My eyes filled with tears. I swayed a little. Then by a desperate effort I stood stiff. The tears did not reach my cheeks.

"That's better. At ease." He relaxed too. He took a cigarette from his gold case, so thin that it did not break the perfect lines of his Letewka, and I hurried forward, as I had been taught, to strike a match for him. I felt his hooded eyes considering me over the steady flame.

"One day soon Germany will be fighting a great war. We believe that we shall be victorious. But in the worst event

victory will be only postponed. It is for you and your generation to make it inevitable and final."

"Yes, Papa."

"So you won't cry again?"

"No, Papa."

He put his fine white hand on my shoulder and paced with
me down the long corridor to the gallery. He stopped for a
moment before each portrait. I understood dimly that he was
introducing the future to the past, the not really dead to the
living who would never really die, and that I, a link in that
unbroken chain, must not break it. I wasn't frightened any
more. I was proud.

"This is your great-grandfather who fell at the head of his
regiment at Waterloo. This is your grandfather who killed
ten men with his own sword before he died gloriously at
Sedan. This"—I could feel him stiffen—"is your father, who
by God's grace will be no less fortunate."

So I understood that death was not terrible, but wonderful.
To inflict it and to die was a man's whole purpose.

My father passed over the women of our race without comment. Even my mother didn't really count. From that time
on I secretly despised and disregarded her.

On Sundays my father, if he was on leave, my mother and I
would drive to the little Lutheran church in our village. The
three of us would sit stiffly apart in the front pew, and to
prove that I was wide awake I would sing loudly out of the
black hymn-book.

*"Ein feste Burg ist unser Gott—"*

The black-clad pastor with his starched white neck-band
thundered and thumped the velvet edge of his pulpit so that
the dust flew. He shouted that God loved us Germans and
had a great destiny in store for us. (I could almost see Him,
a huge fellow with a flowing yellow beard and cold blue eyes
and a winged helmet.) Sometimes the pastor and his fat,
terrified wife would be invited to the Schloss for Sunday
dinner. He didn't thunder any more. He mumbled over his
heaped-up plate and bobbed his head in anxious agreement
with everything my father said.

*"Aber gewiss, Herr General, gewiss."*

When I was fourteen I was to be sent to the Kadettenschule

in Karlsruhe. Meantime my foreign nurses gave place to a Captain Schulz, A.D., who came to live in the Schloss and taught me strategy and tactics, the history of Germany in relation to Europe, and of her great soldiers. I despised him. I knew he was a commoner and a mere captain of the reserve in a line regiment. He had a sick wife in the village. I caught him stealing our food to take to her. He begged me not to betray him. He almost wept. It gave me a delicious, giddy sensation to make a grown man afraid of me.

Those were splendid days. Officers in brilliant uniforms came to the Schloss and kissed my mother's hand to the musical jingle of their spurs. Then they ignored her. They withdrew to my father's library. From my overhead bedroom I could hear their strong voices rising to me as from the depths of the sea. I knew they were weaving a pattern of Germany's future, and that I would be woven into it.

On my seventh birthday my father gave me a brown Shetland pony whom I called, for no reason that I can remember, Mitzi. The head groom, Karl, taught me to saddle and bridle her and walked beside me until I learned to grip her fat, shaggy sides with my short legs. I learned quickly. In a few days we were trotting and galloping along the grassy allées of Schlosspark. When I fell off—as I did sometimes—Mitzi would stop and nuzzle me with apologetic sympathy.

I was allowed to ride her every day for an hour, unless I had failed to learn my lessons. I was very rarely punished. Captain Schulz, blinking humble appealing eyes at me, would report excellent progress.

"You will be proud of him, Herr General."

The day for which we all waited came at last. War. A huge map of Europe dotted with our flags was hung up in my schoolroom, and every day Captain Schulz moved the flags triumphantly forward. It was a matter of course that they should move forward. Then one day they stood still. They fell back. "*Il faut reculer pour mieux sauter*," Captain Schulz said in excellent French. But the flags drooped and faded.

The officers who came to Schloss-Freytag wore strange drab uniforms. Many of them came to say good-bye to my father, who had been slightly wounded. Only much later a few of them came back. The great staff of servants melted like wax in a fire. The ceremonial rooms were closed. Food was scarce. Everything became something else that was called *Ersatz*. At last Captain Schulz disappeared. It seemed he was needed on garrison duty. There was no *Ersatz* for him. I ran wild. Mitzi and I spent whole days together.

One night my father, home on leave, called me to his study.

"The time for superfluities is past. We have to strip ourselves to the bone, all of us. You too, Ulrich. And there must be no flinching. Besides," he added casually, "you are too big to ride a pony."

The next morning he took me to the stable yard where old Karl and Mitzi waited for us. She wasn't fat any more. She looked at me with puzzled yet trusting eyes. She might have been saying, "Where is my carrot? What's wrong? Why don't we go for a ride together?"

Karl looked at me too, sadly.

My father put a revolver in my hand. It was a pretty little thing—it might have been made for me.

"In the ear," he said. "If your hand is steady, it will be instantaneous."

So my hand had to be steady.

The explosion that answered my pressure on the hair trigger shook the earth. It seemed to take place inside myself, tearing me apart, so that I was astonished to see Mitzi break at the knees and crumble at my feet like an empty sack. For a moment I wanted to fling myself on that poor, still twitching body and die too, but instead something strange happened to me. Some blood from that shattered brain had splashed onto my lips. I licked it. It tasted warm and sweet and good. I felt as I had done on the Kaiser's birthday when my father had made me drink a champagne toast to the dregs. I was intoxicated, reeling a little, only now with the wine of power and death. I had killed something I loved, without flinching. It was the first great act of my life. I would never love or flinch again.

Our old groom turned his face from me.

My father laid a firm satisfied hand on my shoulder.

"*Also—doch ein ganze Kerl!*"

A fine fellow. One of those other fine fellows who through the ages had begotten me. One day I would fill the space that they kept waiting for me.

My mother faded. Then they told me that she was dead.

But the death of a woman was of no great account. She had played her part and gone. In any case, death had by now become familiar to me. To die of sickness or old age was a woman's fate. Men died on the battlefield.

The little flags continued to fall back. I learned to my astonishment that Germany could lie in the dust, with base, cowardly peoples trampling her underfoot, and a German general could still stay alive. My father came home. He never left the Schloss grounds. He wore shabby shooting clothes; except that he still carried his shoulders haughtily straight, he might have been his own gamekeeper.

The Kadettenschule in Karlsruhe had closed down. Except in the minds of the grey-faced, stiff-necked men who sat with my father behind the closed doors of his library, there was no Wehrmacht. On my twenty-first birthday I sat in with them. I learned that, not for the first time in history, Germany was fooling the men who thought they had conquered her. A hundred thousand men! A hundred thousand trained, dedicated officers! The ghosts of von Stein's secret army were rising out of their graves.

"Give the vulgar guttersnipe his head," my father said. "We can use him. When he has served our purpose . . ." He snapped his fingers, as though breaking the back of some repulsive insect.

I joined the S.S.—not the Allgemeine S.S. which did dirty police work, but the Waffen S.S. which was held in readiness for the great battles.

The young men of my Abteilung were tall and handsome. I had the strong, clean-cut features of my race and an elegant body of whip-cord strength that gained their respect. We did not love one another with the love that devoured the S.A. like a foul cancer. We did not even indulge in friendship. We were bound to one another with the cold loyalty of priests whose merciless ritual tested them to the limit of endurance —sometimes beyond. Those who broke under it were ruthlessly discarded. If they were wise, they shot themselves.

I did not break.

I became Standartenführer. On the night of June 29, 1934, I killed men for the first time. They were lined up on the parade ground of the Lichterfelde-Kadettenschule, waiting for the firing squads. I preferred to shoot my section with my

113

own hand. I shot them through the ear, as I had shot Mitzi, and kicked them as they fell, like rabbits. The parade ground was laid out neatly with their brown-shirted bodies, for once bloody with their own blood. I had never loved a woman, but I had made love often enough. It was like that—a brief ecstasy.

I was given leave. I went home in a fine new black uniform and black boots. I greeted my father with a raised arm and a challenging "Heil Hitler!" He shrugged his shoulders. He had never loved me, or perhaps anyone. Now I thought he looked at me with sour distaste.

The war came for which we had prepared.

I saw hard, victorious fighting. Some of my best men were killed alongside me. I avenged them. Vengeance only slaked the thirst of what had become a low but chronic fever. There was that episode at Paradis. The English prisoners who greeted us almost as comrades, who seemed to imagine that wars were still fought with courtesies, were almost comical in their aghast disbelief. Even in death they looked childishly astonished.

My battalion was ordered to join our occupation forces in the South of France.

Gauleiter Bach sent for me at his Nice headquarters on the Promenade des Anglais. Bach loathed me as a ci-devant aristocrat who, in turn, despised him as an upstart from the gutter. It amused him to keep me standing at attention whilst he riffled through his official papers. Finally he looked up, his eyes sharp and hard as a ferret's behind their glasses.

"Sit down!"

Though I was aware of catastrophe behind his rudeness, I remained insolently standing.

"I have to inform you that your father, General von Freytag, committed suicide two days ago. The motive for his cowardly act is unknown. He may have been insane. Otherwise he deserted in the face of the enemy." He made a brutal gesture. "Sit down!"

This time I obeyed him.

"You are changing uniforms, Freytag. You are to join what was, I believe, your family regiment. Your personal record in the S.S. is satisfactory enough, but it detracts from your remaining usefulness. The Paradis affair has, for instance, put you on the enemy's blacklist. So we have erased you. From now on there never was a Freytag in the S.S.—only a Wehrmacht captain of that name and who was, at that time, fighting on another front." He referred to his papers. "I understand that you speak good French."

"The French have told me so."

"Also that you have good manners—when you choose. They too will be an asset. You are to proceed with your company to the village of Rocquedur and take up quarters there. As far as the inhabitants are concerned, you are merely an amiable officer who does his strict duty with regret. It need not be too strict. Handle the bastards with kid gloves whenever possible. There is some aristocratic family in residence which claims to be collaborationist. You do not need to bother too much with them. We have their measure. Watch out for the small fry. The Gestapo is very annoyed. They maintain that someone is helping allied airmen to escape from the Fort de la Revère. Someone is sending out information. Keep a sharp eye on a farm called the Domaine Guis. The Gestapo wants its owner brought in dead or alive—preferably alive."

I polished my eye-glass with a steady hand. I could not imagine what had prompted my father's act. (When I learned later of the Valkyrie plot against the Fuehrer I understood that his soldier's oath had been too strong for him.) I did know there would be no forgiveness for his son. I was being deliberately degraded and humiliated.

"A spy," I murmured.

Bach grinned maliciously.

"Let's hope, my dear fellow, a successful one."

I led my men up the dusty, winding road to Rocquedur. They were the dregs of the pail—a sloppy lot of uniformed civilians who wanted sheepishly to be friends with everyone and to get home to their families. No amount of discipline would make them soldiers. They were just cowed enough to shoot their own mothers if given the command. I despised them as I despised the mayor waddling across the Grand' Place to greet me, his sash of office draped about a once solid, now sagging stomach.

We shook hands like long-lost brothers. I think if I'd given him the chance he would have kissed me. We understood each other perfectly: live and let live.

115

I called promptly on the Fouqué-Basdurs in their walled and gloomy residence. The two elderly people and their son Victor, as the Count explained, had fled Paris under a stupid misapprehension.

"We were afraid that, in the first flush of victory, you would not appreciate our real position." The white-faced elderly man filled my glass with a delicious sherry. "We need discipline, we poor French. With your discipline and our genius we shall master Europe—perhaps the world."

I smiled politely. The poor fool. Young Victor, a decadent rat with the elegance and charm that sometimes accompanies decadence, had other illusions. He was smirking at one of them, a slender girl standing aloofly at a window that over-looked the valley. The Count introduced her. "Mlle Nina Gifford, my wife's companion. A loyal Frenchwoman, and," he added suavely, "a charming singer."

I made her a correct bow.

"I shall hope to hear her."

She stared at me, unsmiling. A casual nod responded to my courtesy. Though she was lovely after a fashion, it was not my fashion. And I did not believe that she was French or Madame la Comtesse's companion. All the same, she might be useful. Anybody sailing under false colours is vulnerable and amenable.

The Count accompanied me through the paved garden to its high protecting wall. He mumbled apologetically, "My son's mistress, of course. He would not leave her behind."

"I don't blame him," I said, laughing.

I refused the invitation to take up my quarters in the gloomy chateau. I did not want to be identified in the village mind with so-called "collabos" who were, in any case, of no account. Instead I came to friendly terms with a crazy English-woman who had a house on the Place de l'Eglise. As I pointed out to her, I could have shipped her to Buchenwald. On the other hand, I had a certain feeling for the English, for all that they were a stubborn, stupid people. I even in-vited her to tea with me in her living room, which, in spite of my batman's best efforts, remained a clutter of ancient souvenirs and photographs in silver frames of a dreary-look-ing country house and appallingly dull women in awful clothes and comic hats.

"My father's vicarage, Captain." She spoke French so badly that it was easier for us to converse in English, which I spoke fluently. "Such a dear place. I expect it's gone now. Such dreadful, foolish destruction. I'm sure no one wants it really. As I wrote my sister—my last letter, and I daresay she never got it—I'm sure we all mean well. If only sensible people could talk things over quietly, just as you and I are doing."

As though I had been her guest, she made tea for me. She lit my own fire. She treated me as she might have treated her favourite nephew, who was something or other in the navy—if he were still alive, of course. "Those poor, dear young men. Yours too, Captain. There are fine young men everywhere."

She amused me. She was harmless. I could relax with her, undo my heavy tunic and stretch my booted legs.

"So kind of you to let me stay on, Captain. Of course I should have gone home. The Consul at Nice was most annoyed with me. But after all I should have been of no use, and my cats do need me. I couldn't desert them, could I?"

I agreed politely. I even brought her horse meat for her wretched waifs. There were ten of them, and more to come. It was impossible to enter the ill-lit, crumbling house without stumbling over them. It was like stumbling over ignited squibs that went hissing and sputtering in all directions.

"Cats are such queer creatures," she apologized. "They really ought to love you; you're almost our only friend. It's such a comfort to have you chat with me and let me know how things are going. One feels so shut off. Is it true that there is going to be an invasion? I'm sure you Germans won't permit it. You are so strong and clever. Real professionals. We poor English are such amateurs, we do so like to muddle."

I expected nothing of her. It was unlikely that she knew anything of importance. The villagers, who had hitherto tolerated her oddity, began to be resentful. To feed animals when they were hungry was an outrage. She had, in addition, an attic lodger whom she called mysteriously her "P. G."—a mad Russian woman who had welcomed my batman by emptying her pot-de-chambre over his head. The pot-de-chambre, which was of iron, followed, and the luckless fellow was laid out unconscious. However, his aggressor was drunk at the time. It also appeared amidst apologies and explanations that her father during a visit to Berlin had met my father. National antagonisms had been submerged by aristocratic and soldierly affinities. They had become friends. Now my people were helping to wipe out a common enemy. So the pot-de-chambre had been an error, an impulsive if not misguided missile.

She and I drank to each other. At the bottom of a bottle of excellent brandy she discovered that she loved Germans. She loved me. I could count on her. She kissed me lustily on both cheeks.

The Abbé was, as the French say, another pair of shoes. He had to be handled firmly. He was a big, powerful fellow who had distinguished himself as a soldier in the First War. But as men grow older they lose fire; they cling to their little comforts and securities. After those two first sermons I spoke to him as man to man. I hinted at the fact that I had his Curé and Bishop behind me. After that I had no trouble with him. He preached with the utmost correctness: "Render unto Caesar", etc., etc. He even consented willingly to posting my proclamation on his church door, especially as it was worded with conciliatory moderation. If any of Rocquedur's citizens had a problem or information that would further peace and good order, I could be reached at my quarters.

It had results. The village gendarme came after dark like a man afraid of his own shadow. A nice-looking young fellow with crisp black hair and soft round brown eyes. He sat opposite my desk, crushing his shabby kepi between shaking hands.

"I have a problem, my Captain."

"Perhaps I could help you."

"My name is Paul Bernard. I am an officer of the Law, my Captain. My business is to take orders from my superiors and obey them. When the Marshal was at our head, I obeyed him. Now no one seems to know what has become of the poor old fellow."

"He has delegated his authority to us. In Rocquedur I represent him. You owe obedience to me."

"Yes, Captain. That's what I thought."

"Go on, go on."

"It's Pierre, my Captain. Pierre Estable." There was a band of sweat along the edges of his hair. "I know for certain he helped an English airman to escape. I met them on the road to Basdur, and he begged me to hold my tongue. He went all the way with the Englishman to Perpignan."

"Who else was in on this?"

"I don't know."

"How long ago?"

"Two weeks."

"Why didn't you come to me before? I could have you shot!"

The brown eyes dropped.

"It was difficult, my Captain. Pierre is my friend." His voice became almost inaudible. "Before their marriage, his wife and I were sweethearts."

To my disgust the fellow broke into a storm of weeping. I laughed and came over and patted him on the shoulder.

"You may be again."

The next morning I took two men and a sergeant and went down to Pierre Estable's little farm outside the walls. It was a Sunday, and the man was busy weeding his carnations. But he looked up and like a panic-stricken fool leapt the stone wall and went headlong down the road, like a scarecrow, all waving legs and arms. It was a long time since I had killed anyone. The need, like a torrential flood suddenly released, poured over my calculated purpose. I put up my men's guns. I am an excellent shot. The fugitive fell flat on his face, his arms and legs still ludicrously outspread. When we picked him up he was dead. His criminal knowledge had died with him. (Gauleiter Bach, I thought, would be cynically amused and pleased to learn that the damned, high-nosed aristocrat had made a mess of his assignment.)

Pierre Estable's young and pretty wife raced out of the house. There was no need to tell her. She flung herself on me, screaming curses and clawing at my face like a mad vixen. Beside myself with rage at my own blunder, I struck her down with the butt end of my revolver. She crumpled to my feet, and the blood, dripping along the strands of her black disordered hair, made dark little patches in the dust. I stood over her, breathing hard. I ran my tongue over my lips. I must have bitten them. I tasted my own blood. Gradually, under the furtive eyes of my men, I regained calm. I lifted her to her feet.

"I regret, Madame. But you and your husband have been unwise."

The two soldiers carried her off between them. She was like a half-emptied sawdust doll, its feet dragging.

A week after Madame Estable went on her way to an un-

119

specified German destination, the gendarme Paul Bernard disappeared. His uniform was found on the banks of the Var, then in full spate. Either he was the victim of *Résistance* vengeance, or he had committed suicide. There was another cautious rumour that he himself had gone underground. This rumour I discounted. In my experiences, a petty official remains petty to the end.

There were other incidents of a like nature. I played on the fears, hatreds, self-interest and cupidity of the villagers like a virtuoso, and most of them responded. I took note of those who did not. It was only a question of time before the Drouets fell into my hands.

There was a fellow who called himself Freddi Waldkirch who drove up from Nice in an elegant sports car to call on me. He was a lively self-assured mongrel without any of that sense of guilt which made so many collaborationists tiresome. It must be a tedious business, he suggested, for a man of the world like the Herr Hauptmann—he spoke German perfectly—to be stuck fast in a dreary nest like Rocquedur. Also, owing to the threat of invasion, there was a certain uneasiness everywhere—what the French would call a touch of *cafard*, not serious of course, but a mild ailment that, if neglected, might become serious. What we needed was diversion, a break in the monotony. Suppose, for instance, the deplorable *bistro* in the Grand' Place was turned into a night club, with music, a dance floor, and a first-class chef? Officers from Nice and Cannes could escape the oppressive heat and even more oppressive boredom. The Herr Hauptmann, of course, would have to give the proposed Café des Artistes his official blessing. I shrugged and gave it. I rather liked the scoundrel, and his notion appealed to me.

One pleasant spring evening I strode down the cypress avenue to the Mas Guis. I had to marvel at the savagery of Frenchmen's hatred of one another. The Milice had performed an act of ruthless destruction that would have put our men to shame. The old woman, lurking in the ruin's shadow and watching me like a hunted animal, was so obviously half-witted that I ignored her. (All the same she might serve as a bait in the trap.) But I took note of the goat track up the mountainside, a very obvious line of escape for a desperate man. It had been kept significantly clear of weeds and stones. I was able to climb past a cave to the summit. The cave had certainly been occupied, and not so long ago.

I stood for a moment on the ledge outside its mouth, with an uneasy sensation that I was not alone, that its late occupant watched me, not threateningly, but with good-humour. I knew then I would have to deal with him.

Shortly afterwards he was captured.

I suspected that Gauleiter Bach was delighted that capture took place at a time when I was on leave in Nice. I was to have no credit for it. There had been an English air-drop outside St. Martin-Vesoubie which had ludicrously misfired. Most of the *Résistance* were either killed or captured. The dropped arms and supplies fell into the hands of the Communist band of P.F.T.F. who had watched the brief and bloody encounter from the sidelines—an oddity of patriotism that suited us well enough. The more bitter Frenchmen became against one another, the easier they would be to handle, both then and later.

Pascal Guis himself escaped for the moment. But on information of a secret nature he was picked up almost at once on his own territory, in the very cave where I had become for the first time aware of him. As a gesture of insolent disparagement of my part in the affair, Gauleiter Bach invited me to sit in on the subsequent interrogation.

I have difficulty in understanding, in explaining to myself, this curious episode in my life. It persists in my consciousness like an ulcer that never heals. Somehow I must cut it out to be free of it.

Bach conducted the affair himself. I hated him, but I had to admire his passionless technique. Also I was vitally concerned in his success. The prisoner standing between the two S.S. guards had to be broken. I had to hear him scream and see him grovel to us. It was a necessity. I did not believe it would be too difficult. I had learned to estimate men with a machine-like accuracy. This Pascal Guis had courage but not much endurance, what the doctors call, I believe, a low threshold of pain, so that he would offer only a brief resistance. I suspected that he knew this and was, under his steadfast exterior, panic-stricken. Yet ragged, blood-stained, and vulnerable, he had an arresting, almost luminous quality, so that all the light in that drab room seemed to emanate from him. His eyes, seeking perhaps some help or reassurance, met mine. They were of great, almost feminine beauty, a clear, translucent grey shadowed by long black lashes. Their expression, at first one of profound distress, became one of surprise, of baffled recognition, as though he had met me before somewhere but could not remember when or where. I too felt myself involved with him. In some inexplicable way he challenged me. We could not both survive. I felt stifled. I had to fight down an impulse to escape into fresh air, out of this stench of unclean uniforms and sweat and fear.

Discipline can be too rigid. Strength can be muscle-bound. I knew afterwards that I had been aware of the prisoner's purpose. Yet I made no effort to frustrate it. Why? Was it a desire to witness Bach's discomfiture, the old thirst for death, or was it something else—the realization that death would resolve a conflict I wasn't sure of winning? With Pascal Guis dead I could always believe that I could have defeated him, that he would have screamed and grovelled to us.

The interrogation had to be postponed.

I resumed it at the prisoner's bedside. I had had to humiliate myself to Bach to obtain the privilege, to convince him that I had an infallible technique of my own. Actually I had no such confidence. I was beset with an insatiable need to understand what this man meant to me.

I sat beside him. The powerful body lay peacefully outstretched, the beautiful mouth was composed, the hands folded on his breast as if already they had accepted death. The heavily bandaged head turned slightly as though the lightless eyes were still seeking mine.

"You're wasting your time, Captain."

I had foreseen that I would be wasting it. I had come for that other undefined, unrecognizable purpose.

When he was well enough to stand, Bach resumed the interrogation.

"You're a painter, Monsieur Guis?"

"I was."

"Of what use is a blind painter?"

"Of no use."

"Well, perhaps he can learn to sing instead—for his life."

They did their utmost. They laid his hands on Bach's table and the young Standartenführer broke the bones with his revolver butt. They burned his breast with their lighted cigarettes. They stopped short of emasculating him—I believe by that time they too were afraid of him. Something had happened to the man. He had found, it seemed, in his perpetual darkness some force, some vital knowledge, that defied us. He breathed heavily like a man labouring under a great burden, but otherwise he gave no sound. The sweat ran down his livid-grey, bloodied face. But I swear he half turned it toward me with a sort of terrible good-humour, almost with compassion.

When he fainted I felt a profound relief, as though I too had temporarily escaped from an intolerable pressure.

Bach may have suspected an insubordinate satisfaction in his defeat. He motioned me to stay on after the unconscious man had been carried out.

"One can do nothing with these so-called saints," he said. "They become martyrs at our expense. As soon as he is presentable we shall let him go, under condition that he goes home and stays there. Sooner or later his men will try to get in touch with him. Then we shall bag the lot—that is, of course"—his grin was venomous—"if this time you manage to do better, my dear Captain."

Nice, in those days, was like a gay, brilliant demimondaine who had become a drab and listless prostitute.

The unclouded mid-day sunlight pouring down onto the Promenades des Anglais blinded me. I felt physically sick. I had to have someone, a woman, not one of Madame Rose-Thérèse's girls, who beneath their apparent submissiveness were volatile and illusive, but a woman such as my mother had been to my father, aware of me in my absence, cringing under my ill-temper, responsive to my good-humour—a humble, devoted extension of myself. Anyway I could take my pick. Any one of these hurrying, furtive women could be mine at my own price.

I chose her because, in spite of months of Occupation, she carried herself well. She was neatly dressed and had a round, pretty little face, rounded hazel eyes, a sweet, greedy little mouth. Her high-heeled shoes clicked gaily. I let her pass, and then I overtook her and saluted. I was feeling better already. The pressure in my breast had eased.

"Mademoiselle . . ."

"Madame, if you please. And I do not talk to German officers."

"Not even German officers with champagne and caviare and pâté de foie gras?" (For I knew already that she was hungry.) "What is your name?"

"I shan't tell you."

"But you must. It is your duty to reply to an official question. Otherwise there might be trouble. You don't like trouble, do you?"

She gave a gasp. Somehow she reminded me of little Captain Schulz. I was myself again.

"Madame Marcel Passano."

"Where is your husband?"

"I don't know." She sounded on the verge of angry, frightened tears. "He's a prisoner somewhere."

"Perhaps, if you're as nice as you look, I could find out where. What is your own name?"

She whispered, "Francine."

"I shall call you Mitzi. You remind me of a pony I had once. No—you are more like a brown partridge."

I heard a little irresponsible gurgle of laughter.

"That's what Marcel—my husband—calls me."

"You see—he and I are going to have a lot in common."

"Please, Monsieur, I am not interested."

"Where do you live?"

She gave me a sidelong glance, half piteous, half speculative.

"Boulevard du Cimiez, No. 5, bis."

"If I rang the bell tonight, couldn't we have a little celebration party?"

"If my neighbours were to see a German officer . . ."

"Not a German officer, Mitzi—a mere civilian, an old friend, perhaps from Paris, come to call."

So it started. The brown partridge became plump again. She ate out of my hand. She adored me. She would have adored anyone who fed her. At night I rang her bell, pleasantly expectant. I left her angrily frustrated. I was aware that in that still unresolved conflict, I was alone.

The Café des Artistes had its première on a stifling June night. I had invited Mitzi, La Baronne, Mlle Milly, the Comte and Comtesse de Fouqué-Basdur, Victor and his girl Nina (it was, I think, the first time that the Fouqué-Basdur menage had ventured its collaborationist nose outside the ancestral walls; they had hated and despised our Italian predecessors); also some officers of my regiment. The party started brilliantly and gaily. It degenerated into a sort of grey, irritable uneasiness, which may have had its source in the black, faceless circle of villagers surrounding us. The girl, Nina, wearing pseudo-Provençal dress, perched herself on a table amid a clutter of plates and spilled wine and sang, unaccompanied, innocent little songs that she managed to make insolently provocative.

> *Auprès de ma blonde,*
> *Qu'il fait bon dormir . . .*

Afterwards I danced with her to a French notion of a rumba. She was by then a little drunk. Even so, she was a beautiful dancer. I smiled down at her.

"May I ask you a question, Mademoiselle?"

"You may ask."

"Are you very much in love?"

"Do you think I am?"

"No."

"How did you guess?"

"I didn't guess. *Ça se voit.*"

She said with apparent inconsequence, "Victor doesn't believe much in that thousand-year Reich of yours—though I am sure he's too polite to say so. He's planning a trip to the Argentine. I expect he'll manage it. He has plenty of money over there. He says he'll send for me."

"Do you think he will?"

"No."

"What will you do?"

"I haven't the faintest idea. I'm what in English is called a 'bad hat'. What happens to bad hats?"

I said in her own tongue, "So you are English!"

"Partly." She looked up at me quizzically. "You're a good linguist and a good guesser."

"A good observer. Only Englishwomen have those long straight legs. Well, why didn't you go back to England?"

She gave a husky little laugh.

"They'd have slapped me into jail. I daresay I'll end up in jail somewhere anyhow."

"Perhaps I could keep you out."

"That would be nice. What do I do?"

"I don't know yet. I just want to know what you would do."

"Anything. Why not?"

Freddi Waldkirch, in impeccable white, moved from guest to guest, refilling empty glasses, murmuring into half-attentive ears with an intimacy that was neither subservient nor impertinent. The perfect collaborator. He would collaborate perfectly with the so-called Allies when and if they landed. They would appreciate him too. The orchestra drifted into silence, which he filled promptly. He may have felt that silence, under the circumstances, was dangerous.

Nina and I, still linked together, stood on the dance floor to listen to Freddi. (I knew that Mitzi, from her place between two of my younger officers, watched us with round, distressed eyes. Was the source of caviar and champagne threatening to run dry?)

"I was just telling Monsieur le Comte of a curious little encounter. Perhaps, Mesdames et Messieurs, it would interest you too. I was on my way back from Nice when I came upon a man standing where the dirt road leads up to the Domaine Guis. He seemed in some distress and confusion, and I stopped to ask if I could be of assistance. I discovered that he was blind. He asked me if I would be kind enough to bring him home. He said his name was Pascal Guis."

I must have stiffened or made some involuntary movement. The girl Nina looked up at me. So Bach had baited his trap. It was now up to me, with my career and possibly my life at stake, to see that I closed in on our quarry. Freddi went on talking. But the orchestra began to play again, a languid fox-trot. I drew Nina back into my arms. She was almost my height. I could rest my cheek against hers, American fashion. I could feel the vitality and warmth of her lithe body pressed against mine—and also her total indifference to me.

I realized that I was dancing rather badly.

"Anything?" I asked again.

"Anything," she repeated.

"Would you take me on—in Victor's place?"

She pulled back to laugh at me.

"Enchanted, my dear Captain—except that I too don't believe in those thousand years. You're not permanent enough. I'd like to be permanent—well, for a time anyway."

It was then the idea came to me.

# OF FREDDI WALDKIRCH

I was born without a country, a name, or faith in anyone but myself. Or at least I have changed countries and names so often, forged so many impeccable passports, that, frankly, I have forgotten them. My faith, I'm glad to say, remains unchanged. I am like a sparrow. There are sparrows everywhere. I pick up what I can. I steal and cheat when I must. I don't owe anyone so much as a kindness, so I am free of gratitude. No one asked me if I wanted to be born, but having been born I intend to stay alive. I am the perfect product of a world in dissolution. I am the ultimate survivor.

As a matter of strict fact, I was born in some forgotten, rat-infested village on the Volga. Wars and revolutions swept my family from its moorings. Until I was ten we fled from one form of persecution to another. I remember dimly that I was fond of my father and mother but not so fond as I was of my own life, so that when they were murdered by a band of young Bolsheviki I was conscious of relief. They had become something of an encumbrance, for they belonged to a generation that had had roots and craved them. They had simple ingrained rectitudes which were incompatible with the business of survival. Having buried them decently, I travelled on my way alone. I travelled light. There were none of my parents' old-fashioned moralities in the dirty knapsack which contained my few belongings. I was, outwardly, a mere child, a hapless orphan. Occasionally I excited pity. More often I stole from Peter to bribe Paul. I made profits. I learned to forge passports at a price. I picked up languages. I became a citizen of whatever country happened to harbour me. I was a Parisian when war was declared. When I saw which way the cat was going to jump, I sold my car to the Fouqué-Basdurs, who were in a state of panic and paid through the nose with some of the famous Fouqué-Basdur jewels, at the moment not negotiable. (But I foresaw that they would be.) I was able to purchase a serviceable two-seater for myself and, being in funds, could afford to travel leisurely off the main roads and pick up supplies from an astute peasantry long practised in the art of hoodwinking the rationing authorities. On my way I made acquaintance of chiefs of police whose wives demanded butter and flour at all costs, of refugees from the north who had brought fortunes hidden in buxom feminine bosoms and who saw no reason for altering their way of life. Let the canaille queue up for their rotten potatoes; it was the canaille who deserved to suffer. They deserved chastisement. Good Frenchmen owed the Germans a debt of gratitude.

But that was as might be. I had no opinions in the matter. By the time I reached Nice I was a stout supporter of the dear old Marshal. With full German occupation I became a German business man with useful connections *outre mer*. No one suggested, of course, that Germany was fighting in the last ditch, but it was a good idea for the Big Brass to lay away nest-eggs out of reach of allied rapaciousness. The Argentine became popular. I learned to juggle currency as a conjuror juggles with his hoops and coloured balls.

I made friends of Gauleiter Bach and the charming Captain von Freytag. With the latter's blessing, I turned Rocquedur's deplorable *bistro* into the Café des Artistes. Its opening was quite a gala occasion for the Wehrmacht, the S.S., and their whores and good French friends.

One of my patrons, though rarely a paying one, was Madame la Baronne. I had a slinking affection for the obese horror. She came from my part of the world. If it can be said that I had a countrywoman, she was one. She had, like myself, survived, and she was always able, at someone else's expense, to drink herself blind and hilarious. Her rendering of the Russian national anthem was one of the café's high-spots of entertainment. At the end of a good evening her pal, the crazy little Englishwoman, tottering under her reeling enormity, would bring her home to the filthy attic that she called her "atelier". On extreme occasions she slept herself sober in the local jail. In the morning Monsieur l'Abbé would persuade the authorities that she had merely suffered a bout of artistic temperament. I liked and respected the Abbé. He was not at all my notion of a Christian.

When it was obvious that the Thousand Years' Reich was counting its days, I prepared to welcome the Allies with enthusiasm. Certainly I had been a collaborationist, but I was a universal collaborationist, one of those necessary people who at all times make the best of everything for everybody— including, of course, myself. Why not? The labourer is worthy of his perquisites. At least I was sure the Americans would appreciate me. They are not decadent, but their famous American way of life lays them wide open to corruption. (If you can't get what you want one way, get it another, and the devil take anyone less smart than you are.) The English, on the other hand, are a different people, deep-rooted in prejudices that make them difficult to handle. And there are still quite a few of them.

Meantime I had bought up, at practically no cost, valuables which when currencies fell apart, as I foresaw, would be still valuable. Their safe-keeping, however, bothered me. Banks, of course, were out of the question. I had been careful to have no dealings with them. Then my good-nature in the *"affaire Pascal Guis"* solved my problem. It just proves that when self-interest becomes a dominant principle in a man's career his most disinterested actions turn automatically to his advantage.

I helped the poor devil out of my car and led him carefully. I gathered that his blindness was recent. He had none of a blind man's acquired adroitness. We stood together on a ruined patio under a giant vine that grew overhead in wild, unpruned profusion. The French Milice had dynamited the Mas itself so that there was nothing left of it but one section: four walls, a roof, a door hanging on its hinges. An absolute silence lay behind it, yet I felt in my well-trained nerves that it was a watchful silence. I smelt life somewhere. I took a look at my pick-up. To this day I can't explain his effect on me. I have always considered myself a man completely adjusted to his times, so amoral as to be moral after my fashion, that is to say, predictable. I have always been able to count on myself and my own reactions. I have never been deflected from my course by emotion or seriously disconcerted by anybody. This man disconcerted me. There he was—a battered, blind, unshaven, helpless remnant. The neck of his blue shirt was open, and on his naked chest I recognized those small red scars; I dared not look at his hands. His eyes just missed mine. They were very grey and very dead. My German friends had done their worst. Yet they had left him unbroken, with a young, untroubled beauty. There was no reason for my recoil from him. He was friendly, grateful and even smiling. But in some way I was afraid of him. He shook my security.

I heard myself ask, almost sullenly, "What more can I do for you?"

"Why, if there is a barber left in Rocquedur, and a doctor, persuade them to come and shave me and try to get my hands into some sort of shape. And then, if you would, tell the Abbé that I have come home. I don't think I should be involving him in my difficulties. He would be only doing his duty as a priest. Tell him I wish to confess and that I am still too weak to walk that far."

I went on like a man under a spell. "I could do more for you, Monsieur. I have a few villagers who work for me. In their spare time they could make this place habitable. Some of your vineyards too might be saved for next year's harvesting."

I saw the nostrils of his short straight nose flare. He said, "They have left the lavender."

"Even they overlook something sometimes," I muttered.

"What is your price?"

I was irrationally angry. "Does one have to have a price?"

He made a gesture of courteous apology.

"No—of course not. You have been most kind. Forgive me."

Then it happened. He must have heard some sound beyond my hearing. He called gently but imperatively, "Grand'mère! Grand'mère!" There was a moment of hesitation, of some secret conflict. Then from behind the broken door an old woman crept out into the sunlight. She seemed so old that her youth was unimaginable. But probably, like most peasants, she was bowed and crippled before her time. She came toward this Pascal Guis like a lost cur that expects nothing of men but cruelty. She came to him because she had no choice.

In a way it was quite horrible.

Afterwards I described the scene to my café patrons. It helped me to get it out of my mind. By that time they had drunk themselves free of their inhibitions. The black-uniformed men had loosened their tunics; their gross faces were flushed and insolent and contemptuous. Captain von Freytag was dancing with Victor's girl. They too stopped for a moment to listen.

"She knelt in front of him," I said. "She might have been pleading forgiveness from a resurrected Christ." (One of the officers guffawed, and I had a crazy impulse to put my fist in his goddamn grinning face.) "He bent down and lifted her to her feet and held her in his arms. She wept, though I didn't think she had a tear to shed. I thought she'd sob herself to pieces. He kept on saying, 'Don't Grand'mère. It's all right now. I'm safe home'."

Then I laughed too—at myself. It was idiotic to be so angry with these fools.

Later on I managed to get Captain von Freytag alone. By that time the party had drunk itself into a sulky apathy. We stood together at the ramparts. The dawn was breaking.

"You know I am a friend, Captain," I said. "You can trust me—at any rate to know on which side my bread is buttered. Is it true that we shall be invaded?"

His monocle shone in the brightening light. I didn't wonder that some of the peasants called it the evil eye.

"We are invaded."

"I mean—here."

"Probably."

"Then surely, Captain, intelligent men like ourselves should take precautions. After all, one of these days the war will be over. We shall be—as we were. Everything will be normal again." I took the plunge. "I have certain possessions. I should be glad to share them with you."

"In return for what?"

"Your co-operation."

I went on to describe the Mas and certain details that he might have overlooked. I had underestimated him. He was not apt to overlook anything. He too had noted that goat track. He had even explored it to the cave which was a perfect cache for loot and beyond that to the summit of the Baue. It was a tricky path, but perfectly negotiable by agile men. In time it would be overgrown with weeds. In the meantime Pascal Guis was blind. As to the old woman. . . .

The Captain smiled.

"She will do whatever she is told," he said. "She has her reasons. When I require it of her, she will be blind too."

## OF MADAME ROSE-THÉRÈSE

IT touches me and pleases me very much that my son Thomas visits me so often in my charming little Niçois apartment. I know that it is not a mere matter of filial duty. He likes to come, and he loves me against the better judgment of his superiors. Indeed I am not a suitable mother for a man of God. I think it is his capacity to see life through the eyes of all God's children, however much he happens to dislike them or disapprove of them, that helps him to see me as I am—a simple, but very practical woman who has estimated the assets provided her by whoever does the providing and made the most of them. Also that I am honest and that unlike a number of worthy souls I have never consciously hurt any of my fellow creatures. Also that I have had a hell of a good time. That too, I fancy, Thomas regards as a certain virtue in me.

Now that I am elderly and rather fat and lazy and almost respectable, I expect he finds it easier to accept me. But even in my liveliest days he never failed me. They never bullied him into disowning me.

Usually he comes on Thursdays. I always have a delicious déjeuner for him. I slip money into his soutane pocket. God knows what he does with it—no good to himself, I'm sure.

I learned of my grandson's existence by a simple process of addition. Two and two makes four. It was one of my girls howling that the crooked-backed gentleman had gone mad and tried to strangle her that started my calculations. Of course we often had to do with gentlemen like that—to convince them as tactfully as possible that they were wasting our girls' time and their money. They *are* often difficult, maintaining that it's everybody's fault but their own. Anyhow, when we heard that Monsieur Christophe Guis had had a son we all had a hearty laugh. And then there was Thomas's air of abashed pride. He was young in those days and quite incapable of keeping a nice little light like that under a bushel. Of course I was delighted. I felt that the poor fellow, after all, had managed to get a little fun out of life.

I caught unobtrusive glimpses of my grandson. I would take the bus up to Rocquedur, and La Baronne and I would *faire la noce* together. We were good friends, and of course had a lot in common. The main difference between us was that whereas I am a careful French bourgeoise who counts the sous, she was a crazy Russian who wouldn't even buy an umbrella against a rainy day. It was she who pointed Pascal out to me. He was sitting on the steps of the church opposite our *bistro*, his dark head—so like Thomas's—bent earnestly over what looked like a copy-book. There was a comical little dog asleep beside him.

"He's probably drawing an outrageous caricature of us both." La Baronne hiccoughed. "An artist—perhaps a genius. But a wild, unhappy, lonely little boy."

I didn't mind his being wild—I had been wild myself—or even lonely and unhappy. One outgrows childish unhappinesses, and if one has any sense one accepts the fact that one is born alone, one lives alone and dies alone. One makes the best of one's own company. But it would be nice to have a genius in the family. It would prove to Thomas, if he needed proof, that some of the fool things we do turn out extremely well. Anyhow I was delighted when Pascal went to Paris, even though Thomas was likely to starve to death to keep him there. When he disappeared in the flood of another silly war, I grieved. Poor Thomas couldn't hide that he was half-demented with anxiety.

One day he came to me and knelt beside me and cried into my lap like a broken-hearted child. It is painful to see a big, fine fellow like Thomas crying. Oddly enough, in his distress he reminded me of his father, who was so young and ardent and who wept too when he had to leave me. He was a sailor. Perhaps he was drowned somewhere. More likely he found another girl in another port. I never heard from him again. (Why I picked on Alois Clerissy to make Thomas legitimate, or why I even wanted him to be legitimate, I don't know to this day. We all have our frailties.)

I was patient, stroking his dark head until presently he sat up and blew his nose. (His handkerchiefs, in spite of all my efforts, suggest that he dusts his presbytery with them.)

"He's come home," he said. "They tortured him. He shot himself—clean through the optic nerve. He's blind. And after all it was a terrible mistake. They did their worst, and they never got a word out of him." (I could see his big chest swell with pride.) "They let him go, and he sent for me to the Mas. Frankly I was afraid. I didn't dare imagine his state of mind. But he took me in his arms and kissed me and patted me on the back as though it were I who needed comforting. He had been terrified of pain. Something extraordinary had happened to him."

"I suppose you think it's one of your miracles," I said, rather tartly. "You might remember that he inherits guts from his father, his grandmother, and his grandfather, who was a brave man too."

"You don't even remember his name," Thomas grumbled.

Which was true. But after all, it was a long time ago. A lot of water, not to mention gentlemen, has flowed under the bridge since then. And as I get older my memory fails me a little.

Thomas settled himself with more composure on my one chair that is capable of containing him. He went on to tell me how the boy had tried to spare him the sight of his pitiful hands and had made light of his future life in the ruined Mas with no one but that crazy old woman to look after him. His one concern was that the men who had survived the Vesoubie disaster might try to get in touch with him. He was sure that he would be watched. Ugly things were happening. There was a rumour that Jean Barberis, the baker's son, had been picked up in Nice. Poor kindly Emile Royat had been arrested, and if he cracked, as no doubt he would, the Drouets would be the next. The Royat boys, on the other hand, had been released. Thomas shrugged his big shoulders. "I can guess the price."

"Wars are ugly," I said, "and civil wars are the worst. You men must enjoy them or you wouldn't keep them up."

On the other hand, Thomas said, there was a side to men that would make the Day of Judgment—if God could be supposed to indulge in such trivial bookkeeping—a very tricky business. Some of the villagers, perhaps in their sullen way remorse-stricken or moved by the blind man's good-humoured acceptance of his fate, were helping to rebuild the Mas. Madame Royat had sent a ham from her mysteriously well-stocked larder, and a school-child delivered daily bread from the Barberis bakery. But Pascal didn't want to live on ill-gotten charity. Thomas took a little packet from his soutane pocket and unwrapped it. To my astonishment I recognized La Baronne's ring, a heavy gold affair with a roughly cut but magnificent emerald.

"She gave it to him when he went to Paris," Thomas explained. "We wondered if perhaps"—he coughed—"one of your rich friends ..."

"I know plenty of them," I said, "who will pay a lot of rotten French francs for a good stone, if you trust me."

"You know I always do, Maman."

But after all, as even I realized, money could not relieve a tragic loneliness and helplessness. I had another idea. I went into the kitchen and came back with a small shadow dancing at my heels.

"Behold Suzon III or IV—I have lost count. Give her to him. She is the apple of my eye. She may become the light of his."

Thomas held my pet in his arms. By contrast her coal-black coat made his soutane look positively green. He had begun to sniff again.

"Maman—if things get bad, could I hide him here?"

I have always been a sensible woman. I responded like a fool. Though, for that matter, Pascal would be fairly safe with me. I had powerful friends. Not even that filthy, snooping Gestapo would dare knock at my door.

"This is your home, Thomas. My grandson will be welcome."

He grinned at me shyly.

"Thanks, Maman."

I waited. I believe I actually hoped that Pascal would come. He never did.

# VII

## OF NINA GUIS

My first picture of myself is of a scrubby little girl hiding under my grandmother's dining-room table in a vast Victorian room in a vast Victorian house in a mouldy Victorian London square. It was my favourite hiding place. (I expect modern psychoanalysis would diagnose a symbolic womb.) Anyhow it was there that I told myself my best stories, and they were always of my mother. She was an angel come to my rescue. I would be lost, in a crowded street in a strange city, and suddenly she would be there too, coming toward me, gravely smiling, incredibly beautiful, and clasp me to a warm, delicious-smelling bosom. My heart would almost burst with happiness.

I understand that orphans and even children who are not orphans are given to such fancies. Their real parents aren't good enough. They imagine beings who never existed or could have existed but who fill their hunger for perfection. Oddly enough my imagination never conjured up my father, who, in the last month of the First War, had been reported missing and had never been found. (Grandmother was firmly convinced that he was the Unknown Soldier buried in the Abbey.) His uniformed photograph stood on a Paisley-shawl-draped Steinway in the drawing room and was an object of her constant adoration. He never rescued me. I did not want him to. Though he was undeniably handsome, I did not like the look of him. I was in love with my mother, whom I couldn't remember either. I had never seen so much as a snapshot of her. But I knew that she was somewhere, waiting for me to find her, and that she loved me too.

No one else did. I was just endured. One day I fell asleep in my hide-out and woke to a lunch party and learned the reason why. Grandmother's lunch parties, in spite of the restrictions, were still quite lavish. I think it was the smell of roast duck and the rustle of the hired waitresses' skirts that woke me to the dry crackle of Grandmother's voice.

"No, I'm afraid not. A plain child, like her deplorable mother. What my poor Rodney saw in her I shall never understand. She was a refugee. He may have been sorry for her. Nina has her temperament—irresponsible and untrust-worthy. French, you know. It's a great grief to me."

I had a brief impulse to give the white damask tablecloth a jerk that would have spread gravy and devastation over their smugness. But even then I had a strong sense of self-preservation. I could bide my time. One day Mother and I would be happy and irresponsible and untrustworthy and French together. If we were refugees too, it wouldn't matter.

In the meantime I set out to be deplorable all on my own. I tormented in turn nannies and governesses. I stole pennies out of Grandmother's purse and bought sticky chocolate mice that brought me out in spots. I lied fluently.

We Giffords are all Catholics. I took my first Communion as I took medicine: because I had to, but without conviction. At fourteen I was sent to a French convent where I learned perfect French and to sing "Sur le pont d'Avignon" and other innocent French chansons. I sang them in my dormitory after "lights out" with implications of my own that filled my schoolmates with alarm and awful glee. Finally the good Mother Superior, for the peace of her Order, requested that I be called home. Only it had never been my home, and I could no longer hide under the dining-room table.

By this time Grandmother had washed her hands of me. She engaged, in her stead, a youngish woman called Miss Keith. I called her Vera. She was to act as my chaperone. She had her own ideas, masked by a prim exterior, of chaperonage. Evening lectures turned into night clubs. Before she left, under a black cloud, her friends had become my friends. The young men took me riding in their rakish sports cars, assured me that I was beautiful, and had what it takes—whatever that meant. They introduced me to their subterranean haunts where, invited or uninvited, I sang my French and English ditties. The young men were, with one exception, not the right young men. They could not be counted on to make me a respectable wife and mother. They never came, with that exception, to call on Grandmother. If they had, they would not have called again.

"We have lost all control of her," Grandmother lamented. "I dare not think what the end will be."

The exception gave her a moment's hope. Tony Walters was of good family. He was a Flight Lieutenant in the R.A.F. He had money. He was handsome. I thought he was a god. He became my mother's rival. I began to dream of him.

The end, so far as Tony and my life with Grandmother were concerned, came one night in September, 1937. Tony had a wonderful sports car which at a touch of the accelerator leapt to ninety. It finally leapt into a ditch. Tony's closest friend and brother officer, who was with us, was killed instantly. When I recovered consciousness I found myself in the driver's seat. I could have sworn that I hadn't started out there. But the evidence was all against me. Tony seemed to be frightfully decent. He explained that, as an officer and a gentleman, he couldn't lie about it—he'd be cashiered. But he went bail for me, and even with all that money at stake he advised me to skip it. I skipped it. After all, when the heat died down I could probably skip back. I didn't care if I never did. Fortunately I had an up-to-date passport, and with the remains of a month's allowance, Tony's lavish help, and a few bits and pieces of jewellery, I found myself in Paris.

I was not without hope or purpose. Vera, who had been an expert snooper, had discovered that Grandmother's lawyers paid a regular sum into a Madame Rodney Gifford's bank in Paris. The bank refused information, but I beguiled a clerk into accompanying me to a shabby apartment house in a down-at-heels *banlieu*. (For some time thereafter the misguided young man haunted the place until I convinced him that kindness is its own reward and that I had no further use for him.)

Well, Grandmother had been right. I was my mother's daughter. At least I could see what I might become—an ornate slattern living amid the débris of a hilarious if misspent life.

"*Ma chère petite,*" the fat billowy woman exclaimed, clasping me to an ample, perfumed, but not stainless bosom, "*d'ou viens tu?*"

I explained. It was a bleak reunion. We sat together over a tough omelette and a cheap bottle of wine and discussed my future.

"My child, what can I do for you? From that insufferable father of yours I inherit a doled-out pittance. It is not, as you see, sufficient to keep me in decent comfort. The two of us would starve. Had you not better return and explain the circumstances to the *Juge d'Instruction,* or whatever he is called in that sodden, depressing country? You are charming. You will be certainly exonerated."

Being half English, I had no such illusions as to the gallantry of English justice.

I slept that first night on my mother's Récamier sofa whose springs had long since broken under various burdens. I had pretended a cool sophistication, but I was desolate as I had never known desolation. I had dreamed, I believed, my last dream. I was finally and utterly alone, with no one but myself to turn to. And I did not like or trust myself.

My mother tried to be kind. She kept me whilst I hunted for a living. In the process I encountered more undesirable young men. But by now I was as smart, as tough, as coldly intent on my own survival, as they were. (No one would catch me for a second time in the driver's seat.) One of them introduced me to a Left Bank *boîte* where I sang my innocent chansons with deepening *double-entendres* to the increasingly enthusiastic patrons. Finally the management gave me a sort of contract—not a good one, but good enough to provide me with a room of my own and the chance to swim and an even better chance to sink.

"I too had talent," my mother told me as she stood around gratefully watching me pack my suitcase. "I would have been another Yvette Guilbert. But I fell in love with and married your father. Never marry an Englishman, *chèrie*. Indeed it is better not to marry anyone. Pick your man. Keep him on tenterhooks, put money in the bank, and retire in comfort."

My worst problem was an expiring *permis de séjour* and the fact that the authorities kept a sharp eye on foreigners whose talents took the food out of French mouths. To those *fonctionnaires,* the English, especially, were at the bottom of all French troubles. They were worse than the Germans, who at least were a success, who knew where they were going and how to get there. It might be better, some of my friends said, to string along with them.

Tony flew over to see me. We spent a rather awkward evening together. He said he didn't think the police would apply for extradition. They'd just wait for the mouse to try to slip back to its hole. The thing to do was to wait and see. He'd keep in touch with me. He struck me as oddly shoddy and furtive. I couldn't imagine why I'd ever dreamed about him.

I never heard from him again.

The time came when I was scared stiff. My contract was running out. Without the unlikely permission of the Préfecture, it would not be renewed. I knew better than to go back to my mother. The radiant figure who had rescued her little girl in a big wicked city was a memory that made me laugh.

Opposite my piano hung a mirror. I could see the faces of my audience floating like coloured balloons in a grey haze. I could see myself. I supposed I was rather beautiful in an end-of-everything sort of way. I wasn't eating much, and there were hollows under my high cheekbones. My long jaw bone, which is my best asset, was razor-sharp. My mouth looked very red and my eyes very dark and probably provocatively unfathomable. The spotlight polished my red-brown hair to bronze and my white shoulders, rising out of a simple green silk dress, to marble. I looked as slyly innocent as I sounded, with my husky casual voice bawdy. I sang one of Gounod's little songs. I could make even the genteel Gounod scabrous.

> *Quand tu dors*
> *Bercée le soir*
> *Entre mes bras . . .*

All the time I was thinking, "Where the hell do I go from here? Into the Seine probably."

He might have been an answer to despair. He stood at my elbow, very tall and thin and, unlike most of the *boîte's* patrons, elegant—in fact, a gentleman. He had a long white face and eyes that seemed to dissociate themselves firmly from his rather pleasant smile. They never smiled. They never did anything.

"I want to thank you, Mademoiselle. It's a long time since I've been so charmingly amused. Won't you take a late supper with me?"

I hadn't had an early supper. I would have supped with anyone who could pay for it. He could. I wasn't used to such rich food and drink, and I got a foggy notion that Rodney Gifford, at last concerned with his duty as a posthumous father, had inspired this man to come to my rescue. They had, I sensed, a lot in common. Victor Fouqué-Basdur, as an adjunct to his good manners, had a polite capacity to listen. By daybreak I had told him the story of my life.

"It's all very simple," he told me, "if you have the right friend."

He was the right friend.

We were walking along the Pont d'Austerlitz to my room on the Left Bank. We stopped to look down on the Seine flowing in a tide of silver under the brightening light. I remember how tired I felt. I was afraid I might faint, as I do sometimes when things are too much for me. Victor kept on talking. I was half-French, wasn't I? Actually born in France. Forget that tiresome Englishman. If you knew the right people, he could be transformed into an honest French poilu—one of the unknown kind. Everything could be arranged.

He knew the right people.

I was going to have everything I wanted. I was going to be safe. But in fact I had lost my last foothold. I was being swept out of my depth—I didn't know or care where.

Mother came to visit me in my discreet, charming little apartment. She approved of it. She approved of Victor, though she took care never to meet him. She had the good sense to realize that with our unfortunate resemblance to each other, he might be discouraged.

"*La haute noblesse*," she commented contentedly, "in steel. You couldn't have a better combination."

So everything was arranged. I continued to sing at the Café du Chat Gris. I liked the excitement and—secretly—the assurance that I had still a shot in my locker. Victor would drift into my midnight show and sit at his special table, haughtily remote, convinced that though the scrubby patrons might call me "*notre Nina*", he possessed me. Sometimes he brought officers from his regiment—in mufti, *bien entendu*—and I would sit with them and listen indifferently to their talk. It was often about an inevitable war that would not be fought.

"We have to choose," Victor would say in his thin, well-bred voice, "between the Germans and our own canaille. I prefer the Germans."

One night two students sat at a near-by table, so that when I turned my head a little I looked directly at them. At least I looked at one of them. He was a black-haired, olive-skinned youngster whose eyes, almost too beautiful for a man—a sort of sunlit grey—wouldn't let mine go. You read of things like that in silly, romantic novels. You laugh at them. And then it happens to you, and you can't laugh. I broke off singing, in spite of the applause, and strolled over casually to their table—Victor hadn't arrived yet—and sat down and let them fill my glass. I knew André Guerrier. He did not introduce his companion. I was so deeply troubled that I must have talked like a flippant fool. André was so angry with me—or perhaps already afraid of me—that he yanked his friend to his feet and threw money on the table. I was left counting it, as though it mattered to me. But nothing mattered to me but a strange confusion which left me dry-throated. I was moved deeply by someone for the first time. Tony had never made me feel what I felt at this moment. It was real. It was disturbing. It was inexplicable. It took possession of me. It was

141

everything. And already it was nothing. It was too instantaneous to last. It had flashed and was gone—finished.

But it wasn't. Perhaps it couldn't be. I was to see him again, on that frightful road south.

Hitherto the war had passed me by. I still sang, but to an audience of sullen, uniformed men. Victor said, "There'll be a few token battles. We'll make a few correct gestures before we come to terms." But then he became angry. Those damned English. Always ready to fight to the last Frenchman. Sometimes, remembering Rodney Gifford, perhaps mouldering as the Unknown Soldier in the Abbey, I grew hot with an obscure resentment. But you don't stay resentful with security, comfort and good food that for most people was becoming painfully scarce. Sometimes, in Victor's absence, I'd invite Mother to lunch. The poor woman was actually emaciated. She forgot to dye her hair, which was a dirty grey at the roots. All the same I felt a kinship with her that I had never felt before—almost a respect.

"There's one thing to be said for those English stuffed-shirts," she snorted. "They don't run. Your father didn't. And, name of God, I shan't."

Perhaps she didn't. I never knew. She vanished into the chaos that threatened to engulf us all. The *boîte* closed overnight. Victor had vanished. I used to sit at my apartment window and watch the terrifying spectacle of a people in full flight. One day a big limousine stopped at my door. A fat man and woman, pale as ghosts, sat on the back seat amidst piled-up luggage. Victor drove. He clambered out and ran up my steps.

"We're going south to our property in Provence. I have connections along the road to help us. You are to travel as my mother's companion. Take a suitcase with your immediate needs. We haven't room for more."

The Comte de Fouqué-Basdur raised his black Homburg to me—slightly. Madame la Comtesse nodded, her mouth pursed. Evidently she accepted a mistress as an inevitable piece of gentleman's baggage.

The big, powerful car pushed through that poor dreadful mob like a ship ploughing through a rough sea of misery. Faces were lifted to us, sometimes in wonder, sometimes in abject appeal, sometimes in menace. From time to time after-

142

wards I would remember, as in a recurrent nightmare, a thin claw that lay hold of the open window at my side. It was a drowning hand. Victor leaned across me and struck at it viciously, petulantly, as though at some unwarranted and disgusting intrusion. The hand relaxed instantly. Whoever owned it vanished under the tide. I had never really hated Victor until then. But what right had I to hate him? I too—perhaps—had killed and run for my life.

Victor drove steadily. He was ruthless. When a black plane skimmed overhead, spraying the crowded ditches with wounds and death and terror, he coolly took the opportunity of a clear road to drive faster. It was then I saw *him* again. He wasn't cowering in a ditch. He stood furiously upright, bearded, clad in the rags of a uniform, his black hair hanging to his eyes. For a crazy moment I imagined that he was not just a man, but France, a real France that I had never known till then—splendid and ruined and indestructible. We recognized each other. It was for no more than an instant that our eyes met again. But it was an encounter which endured with me like a mortal anguish. I laid my hand on Victor's arm. I heard myself appeal to him. He shook me off coldly.

"We are already overloaded."

At a crossroad he turned off. It seemed that he had connections scattered over the countryside. They supplied us with food and petrol. We slept every night under a different roof. I was exhausted. But I slept badly. I hated myself too. I deserved to be what I was—utterly and forever lost.


The torrent slackened. By the time we reached the Mediterranean it had thinned to a trickle of luxury cars on their way to safety. I found myself in a neglected garden behind high walls and then in a big musty bedroom whose windows overlooked a deep, narrow valley and mountains that mysteriously changed colour and shape and distance with every movement of the sun. I would sit for hours at that window and watch them. In my fear and desolation they were a reassurance of something indestructible and lovely that transcended my own devastated, unlovely life.

The chateau was very old. At night the dust of centuries seeped out of its walls and laid itself like a fine grey mist over the stiff, comfortless furniture. At a touch the brocaded curtains might have shredded to nothing. The place was both a sanctuary and a prison, from which no one except old

**143**

Julie, the housekeeper whose people had served the Fouqué-Basdurs for centuries, ever ventured. For it was understood that the inhabitants of our strange, high-perched village hated the Fouqué-Basdurs with an ancient, deep-rooted and even dangerous hatred. I did not hate them any more—not even Victor. They were like wax effigies animated with emotions that against that sombre background seemed inhuman. They tolerated me.

Once a week the Curé drove up from Basdur to hear confession and celebrate Mass in the chateau's chapel. I made all the correct gestures, like a performer in a ritualistic dance. I confessed to perfunctory sins for which the pink-cheeked, anxious-eyed priest prescribed perfunctory penances. Afterwards he dined with us. He was our one contact with events that were sweeping down on us, encircling us, pressing us closer and closer to one another in a suffocating proximity.

It became intolerable. At daybreak I unlocked the iron-studded garden door and stole out into a narrow, still-empty street that led to an open square over which a tall, ugly church threw its deep shadow. As I stood there, lost and uncertain, a priest came down the church steps. Though I had never seen him before, I recognized him as the Abbé Clerissy, who was, the old Count said, a traitor to the true France—the France of the Fouqué-Basdurs. He was the type of man who should have been robust and ruddy. He was gaunt. His soutane flapped about him like the rags of a scarecrow. From his grey, exhausted face I guessed that he had spent the night in supplication before some tawdry village altar. How fantastic that a grown man should still have faith!

The Abbé, lost in his thoughts, passed me without seeing me.

I walked on down another street which led me outside the village walls to a cypress-shaded avenue. At the end of it was a ruined house and vine terraces choked with weeds and old walls over which roses poured in an unchannelled flood of colour. I didn't see anyone. Yet I felt that I was being watched. I wasn't frightened, only deeply troubled, as though I had stumbled on a tragedy that was in some mysterious way related to my own rootless despair. I turned and fled from it. By this time the village was awake. Strangers glanced at me with astonished and lowering dislike. I was breathless and panic-stricken when I reached the garden door and hammered at it. Victor, it seemed, had been waiting for me.

144

He was white with anger. He said, "You took a stupid risk. Why? Where have you been?"

I pushed past him. I managed to say, laughing, "You forget —I'm half English. I have to walk."

I became less and less Victor's mistress, more and more Madame la Comtesse's nurse—not quite her friend. The old woman was dying, almost literally for Paris, a lost life. Of the three of them she was the most nearly human. I could at least see her as a sort of victim, a tragic leftover from another century. What she was—bigoted, contemptuous, and terrified of change—wasn't all her fault. It was built into her by countless generations. I grew to pity her. And in a stiff, reluctant way, she clung to me.

Victor was deep in some plot or other. A lively, well-dressed fellow called Freddi Waldkirch would drive up from Nice in the kind of sports car Tony would have envied, and the two men would talk together behind closed doors.

At last the Germans came. It was like the bursting of an infected abscess. At least no Frenchman could boast any longer that he was master in his house. But the Fouqué-Basdurs sighed relief. For them the long siege had been raised.

The first day of the Occupation someone knocked at the garden door. Julie went to open it. She ran back, tottering and trembling all over her meagre body. Close behind her came a man in field-grey, with a high-crowned cap and a swastika dangling from an eagle's claw on his breast. He wasn't tall, but so beautifully built and uniformed that he seemed tall. He had a bold-featured face that, except for the long, half-smiling mouth, might have been carved out of some pale wood. He stood on the threshold of the salon, saluting, clicking his heels. A late afternoon sunlight, pouring through the window in whose embrasure I stood, caught his monocle. It flashed at me like a miniature searchlight.

"Forgive this intrusion, Monsieur le Comte. I was hoping you would remember me."

Victor advanced with outstretched hand.

"Why, my dear Ulrich!"

So they were friends. They had met, it seemed, first in Berlin and then in a salon of the Faubourg St. Germain. That night we dined together in the gloomy, oak-panelled dining

145

room. Captain von Freytag brought champagne and a famous pâté as a contribution to the celebration. He sat beside me and talked in almost too perfect English. It was his way of telling me, "I know who and what you are."

Much later Victor came to my room, but not to revive a half-forgotten relationship. He stood at my window, his arms folded, looking out over the moonlit valley—perhaps in order not to look at me.

"It won't last," he said. "I know, and they know. It is only a question of time before we are overrun by those pious Allied pigs and subjected to their so-called justice. The villagers won't wait for it. They'll try to whitewash themselves with a wholesale patriotic massacre." He unfolded his arms and began to pace the room, still avoiding me. "I have friends and money in the Argentine. With von Freytag's help I shall make my way there."

"Your way—alone?" I asked.

I didn't try to keep contempt out of my voice. Either he didn't hear it, or he didn't care. We had taken what we wanted from each other. Now we were both finished.

"My mother is too sick to travel. My father won't leave her. In any case, he would refuse to be driven out. I can't take you with me. But as soon as possible I shall send for you."

He knew that I knew that he was lying. He was making the conventional gestures of his code.

"And in the meantime?"

"Von Freytag has promised to take care of you. He has some plan. He will tell you himself."

I guessed at the plan. I was to be handed from one man to the other until I reached the bottom of the heap. Then I could fend for myself in the gutter.

I guessed wrong.

The night of the gala opening of Waldkirch's Café des Artistes, Captain von Freytag and I danced together. I had drunk too much to care what awaited me tomorrow. He danced beautifully. He made me feel young and passionately alive. (Tony had done that to me too.) At first I hardly understood what he was talking about.

He said, "The fellow is blind, and his grandmother half crazy. He is in desperate need of someone to give him a helping hand. You are a refugee. You are in desperate need too—and are prepared to work for a living. He will be thankful. All I ask is that you keep your eyes and ears open. Whenever strangers come—and they will come—you are to let me know at once."

"You mean, don't you, I'm to spy on him?"

We were dancing cheek to cheek, like lovers. I felt his jaw tighten as though I'd touched a raw nerve.

"We don't call people who work for us spies. They are secret agents—a dangerous but honourable status."

"What is there in it for me?"

"Safety, as much as there is for anyone these days. If we come out on top—and we still may—you will be under my protection."

I was sober enough now.

"If you don't?"

"This Pascal Guis is a *chef de résistance*. As a member of his household, you will be respected."

"And if I won't?"

He withdrew a little so that his curious stone-grey eyes looked straight into mine. The corners of his long mouth lifted in an almost playful smile.

"Then you *will* be a spy—an English spy. And we have no time these days to put on kid gloves, even to handle a pretty girl."

Two days later the Comtesse de Fouqué-Basdur died in my arms. Before the end, she rolled up her pale, emptying eyes at me and said, "Thank you, Mademoiselle," coldly and formally. To the last she couldn't forget who she was and who I was.

A knock-kneed skeleton horse was harnessed to the shabby black and silver hearse that they dragged out of the church vault. Julie and I followed at a respectful distance behind Victor and his father and Captain von Freytag. (No villagers were to be seen. Everything in the village was wrapped in sullen silence except for the tolling of the cracked church bell.) The old Comte de Fouqué-Basdur was a half-tragic, half-comic figure in his old-fashioned black suit, his bowler hat, and high buttoned boots. It was a long walk to the cemetery outside the walls. He teetered on his small, unaccustomed feet, and every once in a while Victor would take his arm to steady him.

We stood bunched together outside the huge granite family vault. I thought of all the bold, tempestuous men and women who had preceded this foolish, bewildered old woman and whom this stout, foolish, white-faced man would follow. Everything peters out—nations and peoples. No one seems to know why.

The mistral blew dust into our faces and rattled the old tin wreaths as though the dead were shaking them, trying to make us remember that once they too had been alive. The Curé at Basdur was ill. I remember his Vicaire, the Abbé Clerissy's powerful voice.

*Dominus vobiscum*
*et cum spiritus tuo.*

I went back and packed a battered suitcase with my few possessions. I didn't say good-bye to anyone. I knew Victor would be thankful to be rid of me and the necessity of making gentlemanly gestures. On the road under the cypresses I had time to look ahead—as far ahead as I ever looked, which wasn't far. Tony had said once, "My child, it's only important to be one thing—to be alive." At all costs. Up to now I had paid for life with myself. Now a blind and helpless man would have to pay the price. But I had no hesitation and no particular reluctance. I had jettisoned scruples—if I had ever had any—so long since that I couldn't remember what they felt like. I was a hand-to-mouth tramp with nothing in my kit but good looks and a stubborn will to survive. Why I wanted to survive I wasn't sure. I meant nothing to anybody, not even much to myself. I suppose, mainly, I was afraid of pain and death.

I passed the press house in the mountainside which gave out a musty smell of old fermentation, across the courtyard, still cluttered with a sad neglect, to the patio, shaded by a giant vine. A man was seated at the empty table, his face buried in his arms. He might have been asleep or overcome by some bitter grief. I stood there, rigid, looking at his dark head with sick foreboding. He must have felt my presence, for he straightened up, his strong brown arms with their distorted hands stretched out in front of him. His eyes just missed mine. They were still grey. But the light in them had burned out.

In that moment I felt no pity, but a sort of rage—against everything, everybody, even against him. It was as though everything I touched had to turn to ugliness. The man whose virile beauty I had carried in my memory like a talisman

148

against utter disgust of myself and life had become this broken, unkempt wreck. I actually hated him for what he had done to me, for the destruction of a last silly schoolgirl's illusion.

He must have felt my recoil too. Like a child caught in some transgression against good manners, he put his hands under the table and bowed his head so that his eyes were hidden, not from humiliation, I guessed, but to spare whoever I was from an unsightliness.

He asked quietly (his voice had not changed; it had a well-remembered resonance and warmth), "Who are you?"

I heard myself answer. I might have been repeating a well-rehearsed lesson. "My name's Gifford—Nina Gifford. I'm half English. The war caught me in Paris. I came south with other refugees. Someone told me you needed help. I'm strong and willing. Perhaps you would let me work for you."

"I know your voice."

"I daresay you do." I sounded brash and defiant. "I used to sing at the Café du Chat Gris. I was just Nina. I remember you too. I knew your friend André."

He said nothing for a moment. I guessed that I had touched an old but aching hurt. Then he asked, "Do you still sing?"

"I can."

"Please sing to me. I want to be sure." He made an apologetic gesture. He had forgotten about his hands and eyes. Strangely they seemed less terrible. "You see, I'm rather at a disadvantage."

It was ridiculous. But as I was to learn afterwards, he had an odd capacity for getting what he wanted out of people, not by way of pity or authority, but of a confident friendliness. Anyway there I stood, with my hands behind my back, and sang "Sur le pont d'Avignon", just as children sing it. An old woman peered out at me from a half-open doorway and vanished instantly. She might have been a daytime ghost. Pascal Guis nodded.

"Of course it's you. It's the same, only much better. It's the way you would have sung if it hadn't been for us ribald scamps." He held out a brown hand. "Do you mind? I can only see you if I touch you."

I didn't want to touch him. The very sight of that hand sickened me. Yet I seemed to have no choice. His clasp was stiff, like the claw of a bird, yet it was warm and somehow compelling. I had to blurt out a half-truth.

149

"I ought to tell you—I'm not an honest refugee. I was Victor de Fouqué-Basdur's mistress, up to this morning. He brought me south with him—in the greatest comfort."

"Yes—of course. I saw you."

"I tried to make him stop for you. Please believe that I tried."

"But I do. I knew then. It helped enormously.'

"He wouldn't."

"He couldn't. I was the enemy. I waved, but you didn't see me."

"I didn't dare look back."

A faint colour had flowed into his grey, sunken cheeks. It made him look almost young again.

"May I ask impertinent questions?"

"All employers ask impertinent questions," I said flippantly, "even Victor."

"Why are you leaving him?"

"He's leaving me. He's going to the Argentine. I should be excess baggage."

"Do you love him?"

"No. I never did. He was a means to what I wanted—life."

"But you're half English. Couldn't you, when you had the chance, have escaped home?"

"I didn't have a home. Besides—I was in trouble—bad trouble. At least, I thought I was. Anyhow I was frightened. I ran away." I added with an attempt at flippancy, "I'm still running."

He smiled rather grimly.

"Running away is no good. I've tried it. In the end you have to stop and turn and face things out."

He still held my hand. He made me sit down beside him. "Now it's my turn to show my cards. I've almost nothing to offer. No money. Not always enough to eat. A bare roof over your head. Even that leaks. And I'm a dangerous fellow. The Germans are just waiting to pick me up again. They might pick you up too."

(But they wouldn't. I had Captain von Freytag's word for it.)

There was such quiet between us that I seemed to hear the sunlight moving among the vine leaves overhead. I began to cry, out of a sort of weariness and disgust with everything. I hadn't cried like that since I was a little girl under a mahogany table and had learned for the first time that I was no good to anybody. It was a silent crying. I just let the silly tears run down my cheeks. But the man beside me seemed to know. He put his arm over my shoulder.

"Don't. We'll do the best we can for each other."

My best! I nearly laughed—the kind of laugh that rises in one's throat when it's no good crying any more. One day, perhaps quite soon, I'd lay my last card on the table, the ace I was hiding up my sleeve like a common sharper.

Ours was a strange life together, a sort of intermission between two acts of a violent play, a breathing spell. If ever Pascal had felt anything for me in those two brief encounters, it was buried under the rubble of his world. I felt that he had put himself aside, as of no account. He would never paint his pictures. He would never be happy as most men understand happiness. But he had what was for me an inexplicable, almost gay serenity. As for me, I was alive. And that, as Tony had said, was all that mattered.

Almost every day timid little Dr. Chinot sneaked down from the village and taught me to massage Pascal's hands to some degree of flexibility. I hated the job. It wasn't that his deformity revolted me any more. It was just that I was afraid to touch him.

When their own work was finished, men would drift down surreptitiously to weed the vineyards and rebuild the crumbling walls of the terraces. Afterwards in the dusk they would huddle on the patio steps and wash down their stale crusts with Pascal's wine. They risked their freedom—perhaps their lives. And they were not, I was sure, brave. They had some imperative need of this blind and broken man. I could see how they watched him from under lowering, troubled brows as though he had an answer to their bewilderment.

I worked hard beside them. They ignored me as beneath even their contempt. Though Grand'mère Guis never spoke to me, she was intensely aware of me. She watched me, and sometimes I caught in her sunken eyes a gleam of detestable understanding, almost of complicity. She cooked our poor meals. But she ate alone.

The Abbé came every spare moment. I knew why the Fouqué-Basdurs hated him. He was afraid of no one. And he hated them with an un-Christian heartiness. He should have hated me. He didn't. I guessed that anybody who helped

Pascal was a friend of his. He would just nod to me and roll up the sleeves of his deplorable soutane.

*"Allons, ma fille!"*

He was a vigorous if not expert mason. Gradually the Mas took shape again.

Leading Pascal along the terraces, I learned the names of the vines and how to prune and graft. I taught Pascal to shave himself. Until Suzon, the black woolly dog that the Abbé brought from Nice, took over, I led him to the outside privy. The first time I was embarrassed, and he turned to me, teasingly demure.

"The English half is just a little shocked, isn't it?"

"Shocked stiff," I said. "But the French half thinks it awfully silly."

We both laughed. It was our first laughter. And for a moment we were both young and everything was possible.

One day, going to the village to sell our eggs, I met Captain von Freytag coming out of Mlle Milly's house on the Place de l'Eglise. He saluted courteously.

"Have you any news for me, Mlle Nina?"

"None," I said. "Nothing has happened. No one has come."

"They'll come, sooner or later." He hesitated, rocking on his heels with what seemed to me an assumed negligence. "How is he?"

"Better. He is out of pain."

"Our friends, the S.S., were rather rough with him. He was rougher with himself. A strange, interesting fellow. I have been tempted to look him over." He laughed. But the laugh sounded to me forced. "Well, he would hardly appreciate my interest." He saluted again. "You won't forget, I'm sure."

His smile left me no illusion. A hint that I was running out on my bargain and he would have me arrested—Pascal too, perhaps. I knew what happened to people who Captain von Freytag had arrested. And yet it was strangely possible for me to forget for long stretches of quiet such as I had never known. It was as though everything in me had stopped—thought, even the capacity to feel afraid. Only sometimes I would wake at night in my attic and a tide of horror would break over me. I wanted so passionately to live, on any terms. But I wished too that I could fall asleep and never wake.

I lived from day to day, as I had always done. And then,

suddenly, the intermission was over. The bell rang for the curtain to go up.

Just beyond the walls of my French convent had been a wood. Nightingales sang there. I used to listen to them from my hard dormitory bed. The nuns explained that nightingales only sang in springtime. (They did not explain love to us.) But the nightingales of the Domaine must have been of another breed, for they sang deep into the summer—a different song, broken and dreaming, as though love were satisfied and falling tranquilly asleep.

It was a night in August, 1944.

Pascal and I sat over the remnants of our poor supper, ourselves silent, listening to the lovely, drowsy sounds of a Provençal night. We never talked much. We were both tired after the day's work and content to sink into the peace of a besieged island. The enemy was all around us, perhaps at that very moment closing in on us. But where we sat together was a fragile, tender peace.

That night Pascal seemed to know that its time was running out. Or he had been made restless by the feverish heat that would not be relieved until, just before dawn, a wind like a cool stream would pour down from the mountains over our exhaustion.

"We need rain," he said. "The grapes are withering to sugar. And it might have been our great year." He waited. I guessed that he had reached a familiar barrier and that this time he had determined to surmount it. He meant to reach me—to lay hold of me. "The vineyards were all poor Christophe loved. He hated everyone—his mother because of his deformity, me because I was not his son and not deformed. So it was bitter-hard for him to have to die because of me. But if he saw me as I am now, if I grow his great wine for him, he might be reconciled." He sighed and then went an ruefully, "I promised André, when he was dying, that I would paint his pictures for him. I took a lot on myself—so much I can't fulfil."

I blurted out almost angrily, "You didn't have to fight. You were an artist, not a soldier. The war was over."

"Not for André. And he was the only friend of my own age that I had ever had. I had to go along with him .Afterwards I fought out of fury at his death, at my own frustration, then against cruelty, then I suppose for compassion and justice—a man's right to be himself. Then"—he bent down and gathered up a handful of crumbling soil—"for this."

I kept silent. I even withdrew a little, physically, as though to evade his blind pursuit. I did not dare allow myself to be drawn into this closeness to him.

"When they caught me," he went on, "I shot myself to escape. I didn't trust myself. I was so frightfully alone and so afraid of pain and of breaking under it. And then, in the dark, I wasn't alone or afraid any more." He bent toward me, urgent, almost pleading. "You must believe this, Nina, and not laugh at me and think I'm imagining or boasting of some unique experience. I know it wasn't unique. With me, in the dark, were unknown men and women, simple people like myself, who down the ages have suffered for their faith, even if afterwards it came to seem a foolish, mistaken faith. And behind them was whatever power had comforted and upheld them." He smiled rather shyly. "The Abbé insists that it was God."

I saw his outstretched groping hand tighten to a fist. He had heard, before I did, the hurried scuffling on the mountain path behind the Mas, the hard breathing of exhausted men. He stood up. He must have been expecting and dreading the five shadows that lurched into the lamplight. They were strangers to me, armed, ragged, brigand-like men. One of them had a bloodstained shirt. He must have been badly wounded and reached us only by a supreme effort. He pitched forward on his face like a marionette whose strings have broken.

Pascal drove his fist down on the table.

"I tried to get a message to you. This is a baited trap. You've fallen into it." He told them something that he had kept from me. (But I remembered that Mlle Milly had paid us one of her seemingly inconsequential visits.) "Yesterday they shot ten of our villagers—as a warning."

The foremost of the five men shrugged.

"We had to come. We're at the end of our tether. Ever since St. Martin the cell has been shot to pieces. We've been on the run. We had to get in touch with you. By bad luck we ran into a patrol—they got Sebastien in the chest."

Pascal knelt and groped for the wounded man, and took him in his arms. I heard a tortured whisper.

"The pain—I can't stand it. For God's sake shoot me, Pascal."

"I won't," Pascal said. "You're too good a man." His eyes groped for me. I could have sworn there was fire in them. "Help us, Nina. Find Chinot. We shall have to trust him. Be careful. Don't let them catch you. I've got to risk you too."

He was more than risking me. He did not know, of course, that he was challenging me to make my choice.

But, as it happened, I had no choice.

I found myself on the black road under the cypresses. I was like an automaton, obeying some other will than my own. I didn't know what I was going to do. Was I going to save myself? Was I on an errand of mercy or betrayal? Was I innocent or guilty? The awful thing is that to the end of my days I shall never know the answer. Because just inside the village gateway I was flooded by a red glare that poured over the roofs of the houses from the Grand' Place. I heard frenzied shoutings and one shrill scream of pain and terror. A woman stumbled against me. I recognized the wife of Monsieur Millo, the tax-collector. She stared at me like a spiteful, demented witch.

"They've killed him. They've hung him. They're killing one another. They'll kill you, you foreign bitch. Your German friends won't save you now."

It was like one of those nightmares in which you try to escape some terrible, invisible pursuit but your feet are rooted to the ground. The woman fled into the dark. But they were after her—a wild-roaring tide of shadows that poured down the narrow street, lapping its high walls. Someone must have recognized me, standing there, spellbound. I heard a yelp of bloody delight and lust.

"There's one of them! Get her!"

The spell broke. I turned and fled. I was possessed of such terror that even on that black, treacherous road I kept my footing and outdistanced the pursuit. It lost sight of me. But it knew where I was going—where I had to go. I didn't reason. But I knew that the time for cheating and bargaining for life was over. I had only one hope. I was like a frantic homing pigeon with nothing but an instinct left in me.

He stood alone under the naked lamplight. The wounded man and his companions had vanished. But I guessed they were hidden somewhere in the dark, guns in hand. In that confused, desperate moment I regained what I had thought lost—the radiant, splendid boy whose eyes had met mine through the fog of that depraved *boîte* and had held them— the bloody, ragged soldier who out of defeat had waved to me in recognition and reassurance. I remembered what he had said: "In the end you have to stop and turn and face things out." I did stop, I did turn, to face men and women who only yesterday had been my neighbours. I believe, I hope, that I intended to throw myself in the teeth of their unbridled hatred of me—perhaps of themselves too. But Pascal must have known. He reached out and caught hold of me and drew me into the hard circle of his arm. My frantic heart felt the strong steady beat of his.

"Have you all gone crazy?" he asked, cool and good-humoured. "What the hell do you think you want?"

Lucien Sauvan stood out. For months no one had seen or heard of him. Now he had emerged from wherever he had been waiting to assume leadership of this frenzy. His lean handsome face was a mask of proper patriotic passion. It slipped for a moment as he glanced at me. Behind it was a cold cynical calculation.

"It's all over, Guis," he said. "The Allies have landed at St. Raphael. But before the so-called Liberation we propose to liberate ourselves. We're cleaning house. We want this woman. She's a collaborationist. She ate cake whilst the people starved. She was Victor Basdur's whore."

"Well," Pascal interrupted, "now, if she will, she is going to be my wife. What do you propose to do to my wife?"

They were surging back and forth like a flood that has broken against a barrier. "Do you want to shoot out my last pair of eyes?" he asked of them. He held out a mutilated hand. But he was really teasing them, laughing at them like an affectionate brother. "What more do you want to do to me?"

He was, I thought, their sick and ashamed conscience. They loved him, but for a moment they came near to destroying him because so long as he lived he would remind them of their own guilt. But there was his serenity, his almost lighthearted assurance that there were meannesses to which they could not and would not sink. They wavered. Sauvan must have known that the explosion point had passed.

"All we want," he said, "is to shave this pretty head, as a reminder and a warning."

"But it's my head, too," Pascal said. "I have a proprietary interest in it." He ruffled my hair with his crooked fingers. "And I like it as it is."

Someone laughed. The foremost men and women nudged each other. They had been eager to tear me apart. Now they exchanged knowing glances with me. It was, after all, a good idea that their Pascal should have a woman.

"You were always a romantic fool, Guis," Sauvan said. His dark, brilliant eyes looked me over in a cynical appraisal. He was like an executioner, aiming to kill. "She's a rotten tramp. She's an English spy who would sell out you or anyone to save her skin. You'll find out for yourself."

It was a clever aim. It hit the intolerable truth. I took my coward's way. I crumbled out of Pascal's arms to his feet, into a protective dark.

With reluctantly returning consciousness, I heard a nightingale's sleepy singing, the cheerful chirp of the cicadas, the ugly yet friendly chatter of the frogs. The earth quivered under me like a drum under the fist of a victorious giant. But immediately around me was peace. I lay where I had fallen, my head on Pascal's shoulder. The Abbé, dishevelled and dust-stained, mopping a red, dirty face with an even dirtier handkerchief, loomed over us.

"I ran," he said. "But my wind isn't what it was. I was afraid I'd be too late."

"You've come in the nick of time, Father," Pascal said, "to save me from what, I believe, is venial sin. Please marry us." He bent over me and found my mouth with his. "Will you, Nina? I've loved you very much for a long time."

# VIII

## OF GRAND'MÈRE GUIS

I AM old. On account of my club foot I was never young. I couldn't play with the other children. When I tried, they laughed at me. They pretended to be lame too, and hopped about me like maimed sparrows. Marie Ribout—she is Madame Royat now—used to wrinkle her button-nose at me as though I were a bad smell.

At daybreak Mother would drag me from my bed, and the three of us would trudge down to our carnation gardens and pick carnations and pile them into a handcart, which we dragged uphill to our stable. There in the half-dark we would clean the flowers for market. We never went anywhere except to the gardens and to the market at Basdur where the flower merchants held their auctions. I used to wonder where our flowers went. Someone said to Grasse, and to the shops in Paris. I knew I would never see such places, so I stopped thinking about them.

Once a year, at the fête of St. Roche, a fair was set up in the Grand' Place. I would stand outside the bright lights and listen to the music and watch the young people dancing. I never had any money, so it was of no use wandering among the booths, looking at the coloured candies and toys and pretty clothes.

My father and mother scarcely ever spoke to each other or to me. They were too busy thinking about their money. No one knew where they hid it—except me. One day I caught my father on a ladder climbing to a hiding place in the ceiling of my attic. He beat me. He said if I ever told anyone he would kill me. As I knew afterwards, he was afraid of our tax-assessor whom everybody hated and who later hung from the oak-beam on the rue des Princes.

When I was eighteen I married Guillaume Guis.

He was old and short and dark and ugly. But he owned the Domaine Guis. He would sit at the *bistro* on the Grand' Place and boast that one day his vineyards would produce a great wine. People said he was crazy about his vineyards, just as my father and mother were crazy about their carnations and their money. At any rate, they and Guillaume got together. He wanted to build new terraces, and they wanted to be rid of me. Besides, the village doctor had told them that Guillaume had something the matter with his lungs. When he died his widow and children would inherit everything.

It was quite a grand wedding. I was dressed in a long white dress that hid my foot. When I stood still I wasn't so ugly. But I had to limp up the aisle, and though I could not hear them I knew that the young people were sniggering to themselves. I came down the aisle on Guillaume's arm. He wore a stiff new black suit. But he was still ugly.

Soon afterwards my old home burnt down. And Father

and Mother were burnt too, trying to save the money.

At first I thought life would be different. Now I was Madame Guis, the wife of an important man. But it wasn't really different. I worked in the vineyards, had to cook and to clean the dark old Mas. Guillaume never spoke to me except to complain or give orders. When he slept with me he was cruel. When he knew I was going to have a child, he was more careful of me. I was like a valuable cow in his stable. He used to stare at me as though he could see his child growing in my womb.

I was terrified. If I did not bear him a son, I felt sure Guillaume would beat me, perhaps to death. He knew he didn't have long to live. The doctor said he was coughing out his lungs. He had to have a son to gather the harvests. The night the labour pains started, he sent for Madame Vivando, the *sage-femme* and they sat on either side of me so that I could pull on their hands. It was a terrible pain. It came in gusts and seemed to tear me wide open. I felt that the child who was coming hated me too.

Out of a sort of fog I heard Madame Vivando trying to make the best of things. "He may grow straight," she said. But he never did. My Christophe was born with a crooked back and a lame leg.

I held him close to my breast. He was mine. Just because he had inherited my bad blood, he belonged to me. But I don't know what Guillaume would have done to us if he hadn't died one night of a hemorrhage that poured all over our bed. The doctor blamed me for not sending for him. I think he guessed that I wanted Guillaume to die so that Christophe and I could live in peace together.

I gave Guillaume a grand funeral. The important men of the village carried his coffin to the crowded cemetery on the mountainside. It is so steep that one day, they say, the dead will go sliding together into the valley. There are so many of them that it would be something to see.

Christophe had his father's love of the vineyards. I used to fancy that Guillaume returned at night from his grave and would talk to my son about them and make him hate me too. The schoolchildren made fun of him, just as they had made fun of me. He would come home and refuse to eat the good things I had made for him and glower at me from under his black brows.

But when the war broke out, he should have been grateful to me. Young men were taken from the village. Few of them came back. He stayed at home and alive. He even found a woman. None of the village girls would look at him. Though their parents wanted a rich husband for them, they never came to bargain with me. They believed that Christophe and I were under God's curse.

Christophe found the girl in Nice—a white-faced little thing who had no people and who had lost her job. I think at first she was grateful for a home. And then she became frightened.

I didn't understand. Something queer went on between those two. I came upon them once—I had heard screams like those of a trapped rabbit. They were lying together on one of the terraces, struggling and fighting between the vines. It would have been called rape no doubt, if he hadn't been her husband. I hurried away, but not before I had heard him slap her across the face twice, like pistol shots, and her smothered sobbing.

Then one day she had to tell us that she was with child. I would have been glad if I hadn't seen Christophe's face. It was black as murder. He went about the village, drinking and boasting, but he never spoke to her or touched her again —until the end.

The child was born late one night. I heard her screaming in labour. But Christophe wouldn't send for the doctor or even the *sage-femme*. He locked the door against me. In the morning she was dead. Dr. Chinot signed the death certificate. He looked at Christophe strangely. But he was very young and a newcomer and afraid of us.

The child lived. Most babies are ugly things, but even in those days you could see that Christophe's son was beautiful.

Only he wasn't Christophe's son. He couldn't have been. That was what Christophe told me in his rage and shame. I was responsible. If he had laid a pillow over his wife's mouth and held it there with his great strength, it was because I had handed down to him my ugliness. I had made him what he was.

I couldn't help loving little Pascal. I didn't know whose son he was. I kept him alive, so he belonged to me. I helped him to grow strong and straight. I had to hide my love because Christophe hated him. Christophe was my son, and I had wronged him. When Pascal was a baby I sang him to sleep. When he was ill I sat beside him and told him stories. I didn't know many. But he liked the one about Christ's entry into Jerusalem. I remembered that when I saw the picture he had painted hanging in Monsieur l'Abbé's sacristy. It was then I began to suspect. After all Monsieur l'Abbé had not always been a priest. He had been a lusty young soldier. He came of bad stock too.

Pride must have made Christophe acknowledge Pascal. Besides the boy would carry on the Domaine. One day he would press the grapes that would make the vineyards famous. When Christophe knew that he wanted to be an artist he was like a madman. When Pascal ran away to Paris he never spoke of him again. He closed the door on both of us and locked us out.

There was another war. At first it didn't seem to touch us. We had a fine wine year. The grapes had never been so swollen with goodness. Christophe was so sure that his great year had come that he invited all the village to the *vendange*. We had never had such a feast. In the middle of the singing and dancing, the Milice came.

"Your son is *chef de résistance*," the officer said. "Tell me where we can find him."

Christophe would have told him gladly. But of course he couldn't. He didn't know. He raved and fought arrest, so they shot him—right there, under my eyes.

My son my poor hunchback son.

Pascal came home. In the dead of night. He was different. He had grown hard as steel. When I told him what had happened, he said simply, "Well, Grand'mère, at least we have a hate in common."

He thought I hated the men who had killed Christophe. But it was Pascal I hated. He was the cause of all our trouble. When the German officer with the glass in his eye came and talked to me I listened carefully. He said, "When Pascal Guis returns, you are to let me know. Otherwise my men will tear up your vines."

The vines that had been my son's life.

So when the time came, I went up to the village. The officer was away on leave. But I told a German *sous-officier* that Pascal was hiding in the cave on the goat track. He was asleep when they caught him. They took him away. I didn't know what they did to him until the day Monsieur Waldkirch drove into our courtyard. A man climbed out of the car. At first I didn't recognize him. He was like a dreadful scarecrow. His eyes that were not Christophe's or mine were empty.

I don't know what got into me. I seemed to be back in the time when he'd been a little boy and all I had, the only living thing that had ever loved me or clung to me.

I went down on my knees to him. He was so kind. His poor hands groped on my shoulders. He lifted me and held me in his arms.

"It's all right, Grand'mère. Don't cry. I've come home."

That's a long time ago. I don't know how many years. I don't count them any more. Time just seems to go on and pass me by. I don't seem to grow older. I can't die.

Pascal's strange young wife is kind to me too. But I know she thinks I'm crazy. I wish I were.

## IX

### OF LA BARONNE

THE title is absurd. But it's good enough. I've been a lot of people in my time—Grand Duchess, a half-witted peasant, a fabulously kept woman, a prostitute. Now I'm a dirty old piece of flotsam swept along by a river in full spate and caught in a backwater. There I'll rot until the day when the good Abbé will knock at my door and I shan't answer. I'm sorry for him. I shall make a more than usually disgusting corpse, and it will take all his charity to be hopeful about the rest of me.

As it is, I'm disgustingly alive. I get drunk. I paint awful little water-colours. When the tourists buy them, I celebrate. All the foreigners crowd into my "atelier" and bring sandwiches and bottles. Mlle Milly bakes what she calls scones. I don't know what happens to my guests. When I wake up, it is quite often in the village lockup, where I wait for the Abbé to explain the aristocratic-artistic temperament to our gendarme. He is sympathetic. I must say this for the French; they have an amiable understanding for large-scale lunacy. Indeed I've an idea the inhabitants of this rat hole are grate-

162

ful to me for raising occasional hell, for reminding them that though we have lost our souls we can still empty a pot-de-chambre over the heads of authority.

The Revolution overtook my family on our country estate near Rostov. We all knew that it was coming, but of course we did nothing about it. The peasants, who loved us as nice children love their kind parents, became animals infected with rabies. They may have been right to bludgeon my young husband to death and to leave me for dead. But it was idiotic to burn our crops and our house. I must have had a tough peasant or two among my forebears. I bound up my wounds with filthy rags, and they healed. I crawled south from one village to another, whining, begging and stealing. It took me three years to reach Constantinople, where other Russians of my kind had taken refuge. I'd managed to conceal some jewels in my rags, and I had a year or two of high living. I became beautiful again. Which was fortunate. I needed to be beautiful.

I was the mistress of a succession of high-ranking Turks. They became less high-ranking. Finally I joined forces with a Russian princess who had been a friend of our family and in whose brothel I was treated with respect. When she died I came here—to this perch of the Alpes-Maritimes. I can't remember now why or how.

The people here have been kind—after their fashion. I have some good friends: Mlle Milly, who is so understanding about the rent, the Abbé, who though I'm Orthodox remembers me in his prayers, Madame Rose-Thérèse, his shrewd, delightful mother, with whom I can exchange many a good joke, and the poor old Comte de Fouqué-Basdur, who had guts too. (At any rate when the villagers tried to burn the chateau about his ears he stood in the doorway with a revolver in either hand. So they hanged the tax-assessor, Monsieur Millo, instead.) Even the Communist fellow, Lucien Sauvan, has a weakness for me. Neither of us believes in all this democratic nonsense. The canaille are just canaille. They'll always be booted in their behinds by someone. Sauvan happens to think it's his turn to do the booting. He plans to be mayor of this rat's nest and one day Commissar, no doubt. He holds meetings on the Grand' Place, and the young people gape at him open-mouthed, like silly, hungry fish. He tells them that they have been cheated of the products of their labour and suggests that they cut the throats of the fat bourgeoisie who ride along the Promenade des Anglais in their big American cars and spend money at one sitting at the Bonne Auberge that would keep the village in comfort for a month. He does not tell them that cutting throats won't help them. They'll still be canaille. They'll still eat the scraps tossed to them and live in hovels, working for a millennium that will never come.

Lucien Sauvan and the Comte de Fouqué-Basdur have a lot in common. They ought to get together. Perhaps they will.

At first Sauvan took no part in the war except to rail against it as another capitalistic trick. But when my ci-devant compatriots were kicked into it, he changed his tune. He became a chef of the P.F.T.F. in our region and went underground. What he did there, no one quite knows. Captain von Freytag observed that it was a good thing the French hadn't fought Germans the way they fought one another. He and I had a good laugh about it.

A charming fellow. I was more than usually drunk the day he and his men occupied the village and ready to throw anything at anybody. At first he was annoyed. He had me arrested. But when he found out that I was an aristocrat too, he behaved with the utmost courtesy. One of his men returned my pot-de-chambre which fortunately was of metal. Since there is no toilet attached to my so-called "atelier" I would have missed it.

The Captain gave wonderful parties at Freddi Waldkirch's dressed-up bistro on the Grand' Place. He invited me and Mlle Milly, who could be counted on to get me home, the Fouqué-Basdurs and the English girl who was Victor's mistress. (Freytag brought his own, a plump, pretty little nobody who looked as though she would die of fright.) The English girl was a beauty. She sang songs as I remember Yvette Guilbert singing them, in the same husky voice, but she put suggestions into them that Yvette never dreamed of. Victor, of course, deserted her when he took off for the Argentine. She went to work for Pascal Guis and eventually married him. She has made him happy, and I'm glad. Ever since he was a little forlorn boy, I've loved the fellow. I'm glad for her too. Because when the Allies landed, the villagers got out their knives. They reminded me of our peasants, looking for someone to kill, for things to destroy, for vengeance on everybody—including themselves—for everything. But they couldn't touch Pascal Guis and what belonged to him.

Why they didn't cut my throat, I'll never know. I was drunk at the time. As they were drunk, too, they may have had a fellow-feeling.

The Drouets are good people, the salt of French earth, what remains of it. When all else fails, I can always count on them to help me *faire la bombe* in a big way. But the villagers squint sidewise at them. During the war they got into bad trouble. I don't know who betrayed them. I saw them marched across the Place de l'Eglise with a squad of soldiers, as though someone might try to rescue them. No one did, of course. The villagers were thankful to be rid of them. Captain von Freytag took their Auberge literally apart. He hated to do it, he said. It was too bad some French people were so foolish.

They came back from the concentration camp a year after the war. We didn't at first recognize them. Brick by brick they rebuilt the Auberge. They became people we had known. There were no scars on their faces, but you knew the scars were there. English and American airmen for a time made the Auberge a place of pilgrimage. A lot of high allied mucky-mucks presented them with citations, extolling their patriotism. But some of the villagers look at them with sullen dislike. They even mutter that the Drouets had been really English and American agents. It is an accusation that camouflages their own disloyalties. The Drouets rub salt in old wounds. They too are bitter against those who played it safe.

But they don't blame me. They understand that I couldn't take sides. I didn't have any side to take. I'm just a lost old tramp who wants to go on getting drunk and living—God knows why.

## X

### OF RAYMONDE DROUET

BECAUSE of my health we left our grey bleak town on the Normandy coast and came south. But Normandy is still our *pays*—our own corner of France. To us the sunlit, sometimes burning village seems at heart cold and sombre. We don't belong to it. To the end we shall be foreigners. The villagers say we made trouble for them. But we had no choice. When the allied airmen, disguised as workmen, tapped a signal at our door, we hid them. We forged papers for them. We sent them from one post to the other till they reached the Spanish frontier. One of them, a young Englishman, was shot on his way down from the Fort de la Revère. By the time he reached us he was dying.

All we could think of then was that in a few minutes he might be dead. And a dead man on our hands was more dangerous than a living man. Richard had gone to fetch Dr. Chinot. To trust him was taking another desperate chance. But we had no choice.

It was then I heard the faint tapping at our door. It wasn't our usual signal. The Germans, when they came, banged with their rifle butts. I had to answer. I saw Madame Royat huddled on our doorstep. I had never liked the woman. Now with the light falling in her eyes she looked vixenish. She whispered, "Emile sent me. He says the Germans are planning mass-arrests. He asks you to give me the list of our people in Nice so that I can warn them."

She had said "our people", Emile was a good man. I had to trust her. I can see her now, tucking the paper into her bosom, almost greedily.

Dr. Chinot did not come. That night we dug a grave in our cellar for a still warm body. When the Germans tore our Auberge to pieces they did not find it. It is still there. The Auberge has become the monument to our Unknown Soldier. For we forgot his name. The next day we were arrested.

To this day we are not sure who betrayed us. We have no proof. All we know is that Madame Royat spread spiteful tales about us, and that when the Allies marched up to Grasse her two young sons welcomed them, wearing the brassards of the *Résistance*.

The Germans didn't allow Richard and me to say good-bye to each other. And we had loved each other since we were children. We could only exchange signals of farewell. They sent Richard to Buchenwald. I went first to a prison in Nice, then to Dachau. I didn't know whether Richard was alive or dead until years later when I saw him waiting for me on the platform of the Nice station. We just stared at each other. We couldn't even weep. What had happened to us had dried up our tears forever. It had exhausted our capacity to love or hope or hate. We were like two small islands separated by such black seas of memories that we could not, dared not share. We are no longer sure even of ourselves. If it were all to happen again, would we betray one another? Would we betray France? There's no real blood in our veins, only a thin bitterness. We have been drained dry of faith.

The walls of our new Auberge are festooned with engraved thanks from de Gaulle, from Eisenhower and Churchill. We don't look at them any more. They would only remind us how completely we have been forgotten. German tourists look at them and turn to grin at us with their brutish friendliness. After all, they won, didn't they? We are the defeated.

Only when Pascal comes to visit us, holding his wife's hand, his mouth at peace, his dead eyes to the sun, something stirs in us—not pity, for we have left pity far behind us. The two of them sit at one of our little tables under the plane tree and drink a Pernod with us. And for just a little while we have the illusion that it was not all in vain. There is still love and goodness in the world. All is not lost.

# XI

## OF DR. GABRIEL CHINOT

WHEN my mother had one of her terrible headaches, I used to stroke her head. She said I had good hands and that I must be a doctor. I wanted to be a doctor more than anything in life. The idea of bringing comfort to the suffering filled me with happiness. My people were poor. It took all their savings to put me through my medical training. Soon after I took my degree they died in a flu epidemic.

In a way I'm glad. They died believing in me and that I justified their sacrifice. But a doctor needs more than good hands and even good brains and diplomas.

I didn't really know myself. Outwardly I'm small and rather colourless. But in my secret life I was someone quite different—a brave, splendid fellow who sacrificed himself for others and performed miracles of healing. I never told even Louise of this secret life of mine. Perhaps she has one too. I don't know. We are all alone.

I married Louise in 1914. She had a few thousand francs of *dot* so that I could set up practice in this village. In a quiet way we love each other. But she is delicate. She needs things that I can't give her.

Ours is a hard life. The villagers would rather pay me with their souls than with money. They give me eggs and sometimes an old hen too tough even for their pots, and Madame Royat sends me stale pâtisserie that she can't sell. But the fact remains that I have to have money to pay the rent. Monsieur l'Abbé understands. I don't believe in God, but if he existed Monsieur l'Abbé would be His man. He bullies Monsieur le Comte into contributing to my support. The Comte detests him and despises me. When his wife was dying he sent for a big Niçois doctor who, in spite of the war, drove up in a high-powered limousine. Madame la Comtesse died just the same.

I come of small-town stock. Sometimes these peasants frighten me. I remember the time that Christophe Guis sent for me. His wife had given birth. She was dead by the time I reached the Mas. Heart failure. At least that is what I put on the certificate. I explained to myself that I had no proof. But I was a newcomer. I was frightened at the way Christophe and his mother looked at me. It took me a long time to recover my secret life. I tried not to think about myself. After all, I did my best.

I wasn't good enough for the Army. "Thank God, they've left you in peace," Louise said.

Peace is a strange word. What does it mean?

I had a few friends. The Drouets, who were "foreigners" too, were kind to me. They are people of education and intelligence. My happiest hours—but who is really happy? —were spent outside the Auberge under the plane tree. A pretty shaded lamp would spread a warm pool of light about us. Madame Drouet would cook a famous omelette aux champignons, and Monsieur open a good bottle of Burgundy. Sometimes Monsieur l'Abbé would join us, and we would discuss life, death and eternity and imagine that our ideas were important and our lives worth living.

Even when the Germans came, we still met. There were no more golden-brown omelettes. But it was wonderful what Madame Drouet could do with a handful of crusts and potatoes and a sauce made of God knows what. They tasted good, and the gnawing of our stomachs eased. But we didn't talk much. When we did, we kept looking over our shoulders, as though there were someone invisible behind us, listening. When we heard the heavy mechanical tread of soldiers patrolling the streets, we dropped into silence.

The soldiers tried to be friends. Either they were obeying orders or they were lonely and frightened too. Their Captain was most correct. I had to admire him. He was so sure of himself and what he stood for. I felt that he had a god of sorts and that perhaps any god is better than none. He was his god's high priest and owed himself respect. His uniforms were beautifully cut, and his knee-boots polished so that they shone like ebony. His face was immaculate too—such hard, clean lines. He had a long mouth, lifted a little at the corners so that you felt that at heart he was a good fellow, just on the point of breaking into a friendly smile. On account of the monocle perhaps, his eyes made you less sure.

One day he strolled down to our house, which is outside the village walls. He brought me a package of American cigarettes which, as he said, laughing, were one of the spoils of war. He knew how I hungered for cigarettes. We sat and smoked together like comrades. He blew rings of smoke, which is something I have never been able to do. He tried to teach me. Even Louise was gay.

"You see how easy it is for us to be friends," Captain von Freytag said. "You are a sensible man, Doctor. But some of your compatriots are not. They force us to do things which we regret. There are misguided people in your village, for instance, who are in touch with our common enemy. Sooner or later we shall track them down. We shall have no mercy." His mouth was now straight and thin. His eyes were the colour of grey stones. "Don't be misled yourself, Doctor. You have a duty to your patients and your wife. And you have my assurance that whatever you do to help us will be known only to us two."

He kissed Louise's hand and clicked his heels and touched his high-crowned cap in an old-fashioned military salute. None of that outstretched arm, "Heil Hitler" nonsense. He wanted us to know that he wasn't one of those S.S. swine.

He was an officer and a gentleman. He would keep his word. He wanted to be friends. Yet he would destroy us without flinching.

Some memories are like red-hot irons. They scar the mind. They wake me out of deep sleep with their agony.

One night I heard a surreptitious knocking at our door. There was a mistral blowing, and I pretended to myself that it was just a broken branch of our apple tree. But in my heart I knew. I lay dead still. Louise whispered to me, "Let me go. It is safer for a woman."

She pulled on a wrapper and scurried downstairs. I heard the unlocking of a door. The wind rushed up the stairs and flowed about me so that I shivered. They say that drowning men relive their lives in their last moments. It seemed to me that everything I had experienced and hoped and worked for crowded down on me—my father and mother, their sacrifices, my own starved life, Louise who was so frail, my patients who depended on me. It was as though everything urged me: "You have a right to survive. It is all that matters."

I heard whispering, a long silence, and then the closing and locking of the door again. Footsteps like those of a fugitive faded in the distance. Louise stood in the doorway. She was white as death.

"It was Richard Drouet. They have an English aviator hidden. He's wounded. They wanted you to come at once."

"What did you say?"

"That you were not at home. You had a call to someone in the valley. Richard saw your bicycle in the hall. I said it had broken down. You had had to go on foot. I did not know when you would be back."

"Did he believe you?"

"I don't know—I don't care." She came and fell on her knees beside me, clinging to me, shuddering like a little tree caught in the teeth of a cruel wind. "Oh, Gabriel, I'm frightened. We have so little. If they take it from us . . ."

I held her close.

"They shan't," I said.

I never knew what became of that Englishman. Perhaps he escaped. Perhaps he died and was buried secretly. The next day the Drouets were arrested. It was terrible that I should take a deep sigh of relief. They were our friends.

Now, so they say, we are at peace. The Germans are gone. Captain von Freytag has been condemned to life imprisonment. He won't trouble us again. The Drouets have rebuilt their Auberge. They invite us once in a while to share an omelette, but it is not the same. Its goodness sticks in our throats. And somehow we seem to have nothing to talk about, even to each other.

I am not a good doctor. That one failure seems to have pulled out the keystone of my integrity. Since I am that kind of man—what does it matter? Sometimes when I'm called at night I refuse angrily, or I make some excuse. But I have worked hard on Pascal Guis's hands so that they have become quite flexible. It is odd that they do not reproach me. But then he wouldn't. If I told him what I had done, he would just say that we little fellows weren't built to stand up to such pressures. He would take off the dark glasses which hide the tragedy of his eyes. "I know. I ran away too." So he would try to comfort and reassure me.

Louise says it's all in the past and that we should forget. I do try. I think I'm succeeding. At least I wake up less and less often to remember.

# XII

## OF LUCIEN SAUVAN

MY father owns the hardware store on the rue des Princes, close to the oak-beam on which we strung up Félix Millo that night in August. (I had nothing against the fellow myself. But the cat has to have its mouse. And you never know which way a cat will jump.) My father is a poor man. I am his only son. He used to be ambitious for me. I was sent to the Lycée at Nice. Eventually I was to become a lawyer. (It is ridiculous how the little bourgeoisie regard lawyers as a sort of end-all of success and respectability. They have a natural tendency to admire parasites.) I am ambitious myself. Even in the Lycée I was noted for my eloquence, or, as rivals put it, my capacity to talk black into white. I was tall and dark and good-looking then in a lean wolfish way, due to the fact that in order to become a lawyer I didn't eat enough. I was a brilliant student. But I never passed my exams. Instead I went into the Army—or rather I was dragged into it. I despised it and the men who led us. Little Georges Robert, our postman, knows what I know. We served in the same regiment. Anyhow, as our Comrade Léon Fouget said, it wasn't our war. Our war began when France collapsed. We fought not for France but for a new world, and not always against the Germans, who according to our dialectic were part of the historical process of the inevitable means to an inevitable end. They served our purpose. They were like housebreakers who tore down an old, rotted civilization so that we could rebuild. The real enemy were men like Pascal Guis, who was *chef de résistance* in our region. We were supposed to fight together. When our mother country came into the war we fought for her and sometimes against him. We needed arms and supplies. When the English made that air-drop at St. Martin, we got them. This episode, fortunately, is known only to the Germans, most of whom are dead or safe in prison, and to our inner circle. It is not yet the time to boast about it.

I did not go back to the Lycée. It was too late. Besides, by then I had other fish to fry. Comrade Léon sees to it that I have enough money to live well and get around. Sooner or later I shall be mayor of this rat's nest and run things our way. No one knows where I shall go from there. Léon says that in our new world men like ourselves will rise to the top like powerful submarines that after they have torpedoed stupid, obsolete battleships rise to the surface. A lot of torpedoes will be necessary. You can't make omelettes without breaking eggs. Most of the eggs are rotten anyway.

My father and mother don't understand. They are bewildered and unhappy, and their unhappiness exasperates me. They think I'm a loafer and a ne'er-do-well. They don't know how hard I work. I don't spare myself. I even work on small fry like the postman, Georges Robert. He is disgruntled. He hasn't enough money to keep himself and his family. He sees people swaggering round in big cars, not even paying the taxes that bear down on him so heavily. He knows something is wrong, and I tell him how it is going to be put right. He is a stupid little fellow, but the stupid little fellows are the torpedoes. They blow up the big battleships. That they blow up with them is just too bad.

I made no friends. I was a lonely youngster. I am not alone now. I march in a huge and growing army. There are men all over the world who are my comrades. I have a faith. It is not like the opiate which Monsieur Thomas Clerissy feeds to superstitious old women and helpless children. But when the glamour of their first communion has faded, we'll get the children. We shall plant our teachers among them. Gradually the churches will wither away, dead at the roots.

The Fouqué-Basdurs and their like play into our hands. Nothing teaches them. It is men like Pascal Guis whom we must wipe out. They have a quality which makes them dangerous. Fortunately there are too few of them to matter. We have a list of them.

I have never loved anyone. I have had women. If they mistake a passing passion for love, it is a mistake for which I am not responsible. I have never allowed any of them seriously to concern me for a moment. I am a dedicated man—a revolutionary conditioned to shoot down his mother and father without flinching. It may be that I *shall* shoot my father and mother. For they are obsolete. They are like small, stubborn rocks in the great torrent of the future.

But before they die they must realize that I am not a failure —that I am a great man. They must be, in spite of themselves, proud of me.

On summer's evenings when the scum of Nice and Cannes crowd into Freddi's café, I gather the young villagers round me and talk to them. It is easy. They are exploited and sick of exploitation. We stand together outside the circle of gaudy lights and watch the besotted fools dance on the mine which we are digging under their feet and which soon will blow them to dust.

## XIII

### OF THE LITTLE PEOPLE

I AM Marie Royat, Emile Royat's wife. My people have owned the little general store on the rue des Princes for generations. Our recipe for *cœur sucrés* is a secret handed down from mother to daughter. If you walk through our shop and the back parlour, you come to Emile's fruitstand in the Place de l'Eglise. It makes a gay spot of colour.

We have always been good citizens. We deal honestly with our patrons. We save money. All we ask is to be allowed to carry on our business in peace. We don't like hotheads. We distrust foreigners. They have always brought trouble. Why don't they stay in their own countries? If we charge them double it is only reasonable. We didn't invite them to come, did we?

We don't like the big cities and their goings-on. We don't even like Basdur. It's no concern of ours. I have my family to worry about. That's quite enough for any woman.

Emile is different. He has a hot head with no sense in it. He got himself mixed up with the brigands who made such trouble for us during the war. I didn't blame Captain von Freytag when he took Louis and Claude as hostages. He explained how much he regretted the necessity. They were seventeen and eighteen—just terrified children who had done no harm to anyone. The Captain said if only I would help him a little . . . After all, a mother's first duty is to her children.

I was half mad with fear. They were innocent. Emile was a man. He had chosen his road; if it led to a concentration camp he had no one to thank but himself.

Well, that's all in the past. Louis is a croupier at the Cannes Casino. Claude has married a girl in Lyons—not pretty, but with a *dot* which has set him up in a good business. Emile is back at his fruit stall. He is short of breath and stoop-shouldered like an old man. He has become very silent. But between the two of us we do quite well.

So I have nothing to regret. I make my confession twice a year and go to Communion. I confess what is God's concern. There are matters which don't concern God and which I have a right to keep to myself. Even a good Christian must be reasonable.


I am Antoine Barberis. I bake the long golden loaves which Jean carries in his *pannier* and delivers to our patrons. I am very proud of them.

In the daytime I sleep. At night I put on my white coat and build up the furnace with the brushwood which Jean has gathered from the hillside. I plunge my hands in the beautiful white mounds of dough. The furnace throws a red glare on the faces of the children who crowd on the steps of my bakery like hungry sparrows.

Jean is a grown man now, but in his mind something has stopped growing. He is not quite an idiot. He remembers names and places, he never fails to make the right deliveries, and he works in his spare time at the Domaine Guis, which I do not like. (Pascal Guis was and is a trouble-maker.) But a little extra money is always welcome. If Guis likes to throw it away on a half-wit, that's his affair.

Whatever happened to Jean in the concentration camp is not my fault. I warned him. I said, "You will bring misfortune on yourself and me too." After all, if I was to do my duty and bake bread for the people, I had to have flour, didn't I? The German Captain said to me, "You shall have your flour." He was reasonable. He even quoted the Bible to prove his point. "If your right eye offend you, you should pluck it out. You must have courage, Monsieur Barberis. To side with the enemies of France is to be a traitor."

The people were clamouring for bread. I was confused. How was a simple man like myself to know what he ought to do? It isn't as though I didn't warn Jean. I told him. "You will destroy yourself. We have only one life—why not live it sensibly, in peace?" But he wouldn't listen.

I swear I hadn't any choice. It was him against the rest of us. Well, it's all water under the bridge, as the saying goes. Jean doesn't talk. I don't think he remembers. And the German Captain is safe in prison. I am beginning to forget.


I am Georges Robert, the village postman. Every day I ride down on my bicycle to the main post-office at Basdur. My bicycle is very old, and I'm afraid that one day the brakes will fail. I ride back too. I'm very strong. It's only on hot summer days that I have to dismount and walk. It's surprising how many people write letters. Sometimes my old leather satchel is almost too heavy for me.

Grisette and I and our baby live in one room in Madame Royat's house. There are no conveniences. Grisette has to cook when Madame Royat permits in her kitchen. Grisette isn't strong. She has a nasty cough. Madame Royat says it's infectious and that we shall have to move. I don't know where.

I was called up at the beginning of the war. I was in the young Victor de Fouqué-Basdur's regiment. When the

Germans attacked at Amiens, a front-line lieutenant sent me back to Captain de Fouqué-Basdur for reinforcements. But the Captain had gone. A sergeant who had had his bowels shot out of him and was dying fast said he had seen the Captain drive off towards Paris in a staff car. So Lucien Sauvan, Léon Fouget and I took off too. Follow my leader. But if I'd caught the Captain I would have shot him with a lot more pleasure than I'd shoot some poor devil of a German. Afterwards, when I met him on the street in Rocquedur I touched my kepi to him. *"Bonjour, Monsieur le Vicomte."* It's hard to believe. But I did.

I don't know whether he remembered that I had been in his regiment. Probably not. What's the use of remembering? We're told we ought to live and let live. But I'm not sure about that either.

When I'm not too tired I go up to the Grand' Place and play *boule* with the other fellows. We play in silence. My *boule* is the only thing I really possess. I am paid 900 francs a day. When my legs give out, I shall get a pension that wouldn't keep a dog alive. I can't give Grisette and our baby what they need. If I don't, Dr. Chinot says they'll die. Then I'll be quite alone.

I don't go to church any more. I don't believe in God. If He exists He doesn't concern Himself with me. Sauvan says religion is just dope to keep us quiet. But I used to like the lights and the music and even the words I didn't understand. I like Monsieur l'Abbé, who is a good fellow. He stops me sometimes and asks, "Won't you ever come to confession, Georges? Haven't you any sins?"

We both laugh.

The old Comte goes to confession at Basdur. He doesn't like Monsieur l'Abbé. I wonder if young Victor, before he took off for the Argentine, ever confessed to that little affair outside Amiens. But perhaps that wasn't a sin. Perhaps Monsieur Victor was just living for his country, instead of dying, like so many of us.

Besides my game of *boule*, my chief pleasure of an evening, before the rich mob swarms up into the café from Nice, is to perch on the ramparts and listen to Sauvan. Now there is a real patriot. He fought with the P.F.T.F. He has a right to talk to us and tell us what fools we've been. He says that when he is mayor everything will be different. I shall have my own house, and Grisette and the baby will grow well and strong.

It's queer about Sauvan and Pascal Guis. After all, they were both in the *Résistance*. But they are not friends. When Pascal and his wife, hand in hand like children, cross the Place on their way to the Drouets', they stop for a moment to listen. Then Sauvan falls into a black silence. But why should a blind man trouble him?

We all know that our Pascal Guis tried to kill himself for fear he might betray his friends. All he did was to shoot himself blind, and he didn't talk anyway. So it was all to no purpose. Sauvan says he's a fool for that and for marrying Victor de Fouqué-Basdur's cast-off whore. But that's all of eight years ago. And she's a hard worker. You can see that he's happy. What more does a man want than to be happy?

There's something peaceful and strong and kind about the fellow. I feel he'd listen to me and that my trouble about Grisette and the baby would really matter to him. Sauvan says that individual troubles aren't important. Only the proletariat is important. Who is the proletariat? Who am I? Where am I going? What does it all amount to?

Perhaps Pascal Guis knows. But if I talked to him, Sauvan would have me kicked out of the Party. The Party means a lot to me. When a man raises a clenched fist to me I know he's my comrade. It's not perhaps a friendly gesture, but it means that we're all working and fighting for the same thing—I mean for things to be different.

Grisette says I'm confused. I know I'm a stupid fellow. But even a stupid fellow has to make some sense. He has a right to know why he was born and why he's hungry and frightened and alone.

I am Paul Bernard. A long time ago—it seems like another life—I was one of the two young gendarmes who kept order at Rocquedur and Basdur. Not that there was much disorder. La Baronne was our worst headache. Getting her to the Rocquedur jail—it's really only a cellar in the Mairie—on one of her big nights was quite an affair. In the morning she would apologize handsomely, and we would shake hands all round.

Now, on sunny days, I sit in front of our little house. My wife covers my stumps with a blanket and sits beside me and sews the little cambric bags for the Guis lavender. With her tiny pension as Pierre Estable's widow, we live well enough.

My wife loves me. She'd spit in my face if she knew.

Pierre was my best friend and her husband. We used to sit together of an evening and smoke and gossip. We'd joke about the time when I'd courted Jeanne myself, and Jeanne would blush angrily. "Well, anyhow, I chose the better man!" she'd flash at me.

I tell myself that I only did my duty. I was an officer of the Law. I was under oath. It isn't as though I didn't warn Pierre. He just twinkled his nice brown eyes at me and told me I had bees in my bonnet. But I knew what he was up to. It seemed to me that I had no choice.

Captain von Freytag shot Pierre with his own hand. They arrested Jeanne and sent her away. (I didn't see her again for two years.) I knew then that I had always loved her, and I went half crazy. I couldn't be sure any more that I had only done my duty. I didn't know what was at the bottom of what I'd done. I tore off my uniform. I went underground with Pascal Guis. I was almost glad when my legs were shot to pieces. I wanted to die and be quit of myself. When I came home, Jeanne took care of me. I was a hero. She asked me to marry her. She said she knew it was what Pierre would have wanted.

I tell myself that it's stupid to brood over what's past and can't be helped. No one knows what I did except that Captain who won't come back. Besides, even he doesn't know the real truth. I don't know it myself.

It's a frightful thing to sit here wondering—never to be sure.


# XIV

## OF MITZI

MITZI is an absurd name. He gave it to me. He said I reminded him of a pony he'd ridden as a little boy. I didn't feel like a pony. But I didn't argue with him. I'd learned not to argue.

My real name is Francine Passano. I'm Marcel Passano's wife. Marcel's people were Italians when Menton belonged to Italy. Now they're French. Marcel has a good position in the *Bureau de Poste et Télégraphe*. His brother is a captain in the Nice gendarmerie. On both sides we come of good, solid stock.

Marcel calls me his little brown partridge. I suppose I am brown—a golden brown, my hair, my eyes, and even my skin. I have to fight all the time against becoming too plump. Marcel says, laughing, the more of me the better.

I must have been born hungry. I love cakes with cream and love and fun. I just can't help myself. If I hadn't been so hungry I should have been good. I wouldn't be so dreadfully frightened.

Marcel and I are so happy. We have such a cosy little life together. With his salary and the money I make with my shop, we can afford a nice apartment on the Boulevard du Cimiez and to give little parties to our friends. We have wine and lots of good things to eat.

It was that stupid war. I never understood why Marcel had to volunteer. He was a government official; he didn't have to go. I loved him to desperation, but I was so angry and bewildered that I wouldn't speak to him on the way to the station. Only at the last moment I flung myself into his arms, sobbing. He whispered to me, "Dear little partridge, wait for me."

Well, I did wait, for months and months. I went to work at a café to keep his home for him. At first he wrote regularly. Then his letters stopped. They said he might have been taken prisoner. Or he might be dead.

That awful, stupid war!

The Germans came. I never understood why. After all, we were supposed to have made peace with them. I must say the officers were very *chic*, so well uniformed, not like our poor men, who looked like scarecrows. Of course decent French-women wouldn't speak to them. When that officer overtook me on the rue Meyerbeer and touched his cap, I told him at once that he was making a mistake. He just laughed and kept on walking beside me and talking, about food and being reasonable. I was so cruelly hungry. And then it occurred to me that if I was polite to him he might find out about Marcel. So I gave him my address.

That's how it began. He was so discreet and correct. (Only sometimes he was so cruel that I wondered if he were sane.) He came late at night in civilian clothes and brought champagne and caviar and the little pâtisseries we couldn't buy any more. He said he had written to Germany to find out about Marcel. Perhaps he did. I don't know. Anyhow it was too late even to try to think.

When the Allies landed at San Raphael, he came to say good-bye. He said that if he was caught he would be shot. But he wasn't frightened. He hoped Marcel would show up. And one day he would come back too.

Of course I didn't believe him.

Marcel was lucky. He was released almost at once. I'll never forget the day I met him at the station, almost on the spot where we had said good-bye. He was so frail and thin! We both burst into tears. I took him home. He looked about him. He said, his voice trembling, "You've kept everything —just as it was."

I could never, never tell him.

We are so happy. We are saving to buy ourselves a car, one of those little Volkswagens. Freddi Waldkirch says he can get us one second-hand almost for nothing.

Today I saw one, drawn up outside Queenie's on the Promenade des Anglais. I stopped to look at it. It was then I heard him. He said, "What a happy chance, Mitzi!"

180

PART THREE

ROCQUEDUR, SUMMER 1953

# I

THE orchestra at the adjoining Casino was playing excerpts from *Carmen*. Francine Passano came out of a fog of semi-consciousness to hear a violin sing a sultry solo, *"Si tu m'aimes, je ne t'aime pas"*. She also heard a deadly, pleasant voice say in perfect French, "Madame, it seems, is not hungry. But bring coffee and a couple of *mille feuilles*. She may change her mind."

She swallowed down nausea. She managed to lift her eyes to his. They had changed. They had faded and become more secretive. Without the monocle, the left eye had a naked look. The lower lid was drawn down and a little inflamed. There was still a ridge of flesh on which the monocle had rested. His skin, drawn tight over the flat cheekbones, had an opaque pallor. Even in her sick terror of him she noted shrewdly that though his clothes were new they did not fit him very well.

She tried to say something—she did not know what. He spoke for her, between mouthfuls of *mille feuilles,* which he seemed to be enjoying zestfully.

"You don't have to behave as though I were a ghost. I'm not. And as I remember, Mitzi, we parted friends."

At that moment something stirred under the table. She suppressed a little scream. But it was only a small shaggy dog with hair hanging over its amber friendly eyes. Ulrich von Freytag smiled. She noted that one of his fine white teeth was missing.

"Permit me to introduce one Mitzi to another. I have a knack, it seems, for picking up hungry strays. She was looking for someone to whom she could belong and who would feed her. She's a nice little bitch. I called her Mitzi inevitably—out of a delightful memory and because she has your eyes and colouring. I hope you're not offended."

Francine laid her hand on the dog's rough head. It was an instinctive gesture. She might have been seeking reassurance from someone as lost and helpless as herself.

"Why don't you eat, Mitzi? These pâtisseries are as light as ever."

"I—I'm not hungry."

"That's something new, isn't it? Have you been living too well? You have put on weight. It becomes you—gives you a comfortable, maternal look. But you are not a mother?

"No," she whispered between dry lips.

"Didn't Marcel come home? He should have. I knew he was alive."

She stared at him with incredulous horror.

"You never told me!"

"Of course not. We were happy together. You made my visits to Nice delightful. I had a feeling that if you knew Marcel was alive, for certain, he might have come between us. You might have had tiresome pangs of conscience." He narrowed his eyes quizzically. "Do you have them?"

She said faintly, "I always knew that you were wicked."

He shrugged and beckoned a white-coated waiter.

"Another *mille feuilles*, please. They are delicious. No—I am not wicked. But I don't lay claim to certain effete virtues, as no doubt you do." He attacked his third *mille feuilles* with a sort of viciousness. "You know, I often tried to imagine Marcel's homecoming to my *nid d'amour*. I'm sure you went over it with a fine tooth comb. It would have been disastrous if Marcel had found one of my razor blades. What would he have done? Killed you in the best French tradition?"

She said hoarsely, "He would have killed himself. He had suffered too much. He could not have endured more."

He sat back with a sign of repletion, his white, beautiful hands spread out on either side of his plate. She remembered the signet ring on his little finger and the night he had talked to her about Schloss Freytag and his people. That was the night that she had submitted to him for the first time. She had had no choice, of course. But also she had been weakened by an inexplicable pity for him.

He saw her glance.

"All that is left," he said. "They have turned Schloss Freytag into an asylum for the shell-shocked. There is perhaps an ironical appropriateness in our ancestral gallery being populated by demented soldiers."

"Where have you come from?"

"Prison," he said equably. "Spandau Prison, to be exact. I was given, if you remember, a life sentence. But a subsequent Military Tribunal, after much erudite discussion, decided that a grievous mistake had been made. I was not present at that Paradis affair. I was not responsible for the shooting of those hostages. Anyhow Germans had become *gemütlich* and lovable again. I was amnestied. So here I am—on my old hunting ground, with an old friend."

"They gave you a passport?" she asked incredulously.

"My dear Mitzi—you were always charmingly naïve. A Freytag is still a Freytag. Americans are peculiarly susceptible to a resounding title—and even more susceptible to, shall I say, a quid pro quo, in this case a van Dyck portrait which a faithful retainer had rescued from the deluge."

"Why have you come back?"

"Can't you guess?"

His smile teased her. The passers-by in their gay, awful clothes made up a whirling, sickening kaleidoscope. He laid his hand on hers. "Don't faint. A scene would be deplorable. If I had to drive you home, Marcel might be frightened—perhaps puzzled."

"Leave me alone, Ulrich. For God's sake, leave me alone."

"I'm afraid I can't do that. I am in need of help. We poor Germans! I spent almost my last penny on that little car you were admiring."

"You need—money?"

"I do. Very much."

"I—we are not rich people."

"But you have a little nest-egg. All good Frenchwomen have nest-eggs. I shall not be unreasonable. You might introduce me to Marcel as a kindly German officer who had helped keep him alive."

"My God!" she whispered.

"He and I might become friends too. It is the fashion for Frenchmen and Germans to be friends. I could take you both on little drives along the Corniches. Marcel would enjoy them. We might drive up one evening to Rocquedur. Do you remember our gay parties? I have often thought of them, and my friends. I haven't forgotten one of them. I hope they haven't forgotten me. How many can I count on?" His eyes had sharpened. "Freddi, I hope?"

She nodded speechlessly. To have called him "blackmailer" would have been futile and too simple. He was much more than that, and the "more" terrified her as indecipherable forest shadows terrify a lost child.

He asked, "And the Café des Artistes still flourishes?"

"Yes."

"Good. I was sure of it. Freddi has the Midas touch and

like myself an infinite capacity for survival. And Madame Rose-Thérèse, the good Abbé's remarkable mother?"

A little irrepressible laugh gathered in her throat. She laughed so easily—too easily. Her need to laugh, to be happy and well-fed had been disastrous.

"She has retired. She has become respectable."

"That I must see with my own eyes. And that admirable patriot, the Comte de Fouqué-Basdur?"

"He lives alone in the chateau. They say Victor is coming home from the Argentine."

"Bringing a charming English wife? For I hope he kept his gentleman's word and made an honest woman of our Nina."

"No. She married Pascal Guis." She added with a flash of defiance, "They are very happy."

She had a curious feeling that something she had said had checked his assurance, that for a moment he was disconcerted. He said, "Then inadvertently I did them a good turn." But the irony sounded forced. He went on, "Well, one good turn deserves another. I owe Monsieur Guis valuable support. Years in prison are apt to wear down one's mental and physical self-respect. Monsieur Guis set me a standard against which I measured myself, day by day. I proved that it is not necessary to be what the late unlamented Gauleiter Bach called a saint in order to be a man—how shall I express it?—of impeccable endurance."

She looked blank. She did not know what he was talking about. But she did know confusedly that he had let down a barrier and immediately and angrily resented it. He managed to regain tolerant amusement. "As to that, don't worry your pretty head. That's between Monsieur Guis and me.— Go on. Is the old grandmother still alive?"

"They say she's crazy."

"How fortunate for her! Craziness is a refuge from the facts of life—one's own life anyhow. Must you go?" For she had stood up waveringly. "Where shall I find you?"

"I—I have a little shop on the rue Meyerbeer, 'Mille Choses'. I'm there almost all day."

"How clever you are, Mitzi! A good wife and a successful business woman! Marcel is a lucky man. I shall tell him so one of these days." He drew out a rather shabby wallet and tossed a 1000-franc note on the table. "This time the party is on me."

He pushed past her with a rudeness that was unlike his remembered polished cruelty. But she was too desperate to assess the change in him. Through a haze of physical sickness, she saw him climb into the green Volkswagen and his little mongrel jump in confidingly beside him. She heard the car's soft, venomous purr as he steered it into the stream of traffic. Then he was gone. He might have been a hallucination—a waking nightmare.

Her legs shook under her. She had to hold on to the littered table to avert a total disastrous collapse. A waiter, looking at her curiously, picked up the saucer with the 1000-franc note as though he didn't trust it.

"Monsieur is coming back?"

"No—no." Then she gave a little gasping sound—a sob on the verge of hysterical laughter. "Yes, of course. He will be coming back."

## II

THE kneeling man held a bunch of darkening grapes with delicate question between his brown hands. He asked, "Are they as splendid as they feel, Nina?"

"I think," she said judiciously, "that our great year has come."

"The rain must come first," he said.

He stood up effortlessly and took her arm. They strolled together along the path between the carefully tended trellises of vines. A shaggy old dog, trailing a lead, kept her distance with an air of saying, "Since she is with him, I can amuse myself." A July sun was sliding down in splendour behind the mountains, and the narrow valley filled with shadow like a chalice filling with dark wine. The frogs had begun their evening gossip. Their comical chatter was part of the summer pattern, like the broken singing of the nightingales, who seemed reluctant to believe that the time for love and singing was over.

At the end of the terrace the man and woman climbed the steep stone steps to the courtyard. The man had grown stockier with the years. There was grey flecked in the dense black hair. He wore dark glasses to cover the emptiness of his eyes. But his face had regained something of its youth. Like the woman, he wore a workman's faded denim slacks and a loose shirt open at the neck. He looked a handsome Provençal peasant.

He stopped abruptly and turned. He ran his hands over her tranquil, attentive features, much as he had felt out the quality of the grapes.

"I want to be sure that you're as lovely as you were."

"I shall never change—not for you." She quoted in English. " 'Do not grieve; she cannot fade . . .'"

"What does that mean?"

"It means that when I'm an old hag you won't know it."

"That's nice. What about me?"

"You'll be forever young."

"That's nice too." His hands paused. "Why do you keep your eyes shut?"

He felt her smile.

"So that you won't poke them out, by accident. You still need them."

"No. You are pretending to be in the dark too."

"Perhaps. I try sometimes to see things as you see them."

He put his arm through hers again, and they crossed the courtyard to where the cypresses made a black tunnel of the upward winding road. She was thankful that he had never seen it as she had seen it on that mad, dreadful night and as, for a moment, she saw it now. (Yesterday the mere mention of a man's name had resurrected phantoms. It had shaken the ground under her feet—the whole strong edifice of her life —built with the love, patience and faithfulness of years. It was absurd to be so easily shaken—to allow a shabby ghost to blight the tranquil evening sunlight. Ulrich von Freytag might be free. But he was gone out of their lives. He would not trouble them again.)

"I do see them," Pascal was saying, "against the back of my eyelids. At first there was nothing but black whirling chaos— the sort of chaos God must have tackled that first day. Then, gradually, came the wind and the rain and the sun and the good earth." He added half to himself, "And you and your voice."

In those nine years together he had spoken rarely of that transition, and she had never tried to break his reticence. She only knew that whatever had happened to him gave him a lighthearted faith, peace, and a certain power over others so that the villagers who, in their spare time, worked for him

188

did so with a good-humoured willingness that was not native to their sombre temper. She thought sometimes, "When I am dead, I shall perhaps find what he has found." For she had not found it. Perhaps it was her unresolved guilt that hindered her. She wondered, when at night she lay awake beside him, why he was not aware of it. He believed in her. He believed in God. Both beliefs at times exasperated her by their simplicity. At other times she felt that, in the end, they might break her heart.

She had done what she could. She had crept back humbly to the church of her childhood. She confessed to little daily sins. She took Communion, kneeling at the altar rail at Pascal's side. She had never lost the feeling that she was an intruder in the house of a stranger who was never at home for her.

"You make it very difficult for God," the Abbé had said once. (He had seen her, kneeling perfunctorily in the depths of the church and had come billowing down on her, his biretta a crown, somewhat askew, against the glitter of the tawdry altar, and had plumped himself down beside her.) "Relax. Be quiet. Keep the doors open for a miracle."

She had said drily, "Pascal believes in miracles."

"He has good reason."

"Do you?"

"Don't be a fool, Nina," he'd said crossly. "I'm not one. Or rather, I'm lucky. I believe in miracles, as I believe in God." He had folded his arms across his powerful chest and became, as he did when angry, sententious. "Our human dilemma is quite simple, my daughter. For us it's God or that final bomb. If there is no God—and I mean a God who is concerned with the fall of sparrows and who fights with us against our devil, not always successfully, of course, or the fight would be a farce—then we human beings are such bad jokes that we can only weep over them. Our idiot civilization becomes more idiotic, without present significance and without a future. In our hearts we know it. We kowtow to science, we throw ourselves in the arms of new material faiths, we nail our so-called happiness to new material gadgets. But nothing fills our emptiness or relieves our boredom, our appalling loneliness. Observe"—he had shaken his finger as though at an invisible audience—"that in direct ratio to our loss of faith in God is the development of our death-urge, the increasing lust for self-destruction. We rush up to the verge of the abyss. We pull back. But one day, short of a miracle, a second revelation, we shall pitch ourselves over." He added glumly, "And serve us right." Then he had cheered up. "That's quite a speech," he'd said. "I must remember it for my next sermon. Even my confounded old ladies may wake up."

She had hardly listened. She was tired of her burden. This was one of the days when it seemed unbearable. She had an almost overwhelming need to shift it to his shoulders. He had asked abruptly, "Are you happy, Nina?"

"You are so good at definitions. What is happiness?"

"That's easy. Peace with oneself."

"Then I'm not happy."

"But you love Pascal."

She had murmured, with subdued passion, "So much."

He had stood up, looming over her.

"At some time or other," he said, "we all make a mess of things. We fail each other and, worst of all, ourselves. Atonement sometimes lies in keeping our mouths shut about it." He had laid his big hand on her shoulder. "Whatever burden you carry—have the guts to carry it alone."

As though he'd known and had challenged her.

She lifted Pascal's hand and kissed it, and he laughed at her.

"I can do better than that."

From where they stood she could see the lights of the cars, swinging up from the valley, clawing the mountain flanks with long gold fingers. They could hear music that, coming to them from a kindly distance, had a mysterious sweetness.

"St. Roche invites us to dance in his honour," Pascal said. "Thanks to him, no doubt, I have a charming wife and a sound pair of legs." He made her a formal little bow. "Will Madame do me the honour?"

They wore their best—Pascal fawn-coloured slacks and a white shirt and new espadrilles, Nina a gay Provençal skirt and blouse and red, high-heeled shoes. Because of the shoes Pascal perched her on Annette, their donkey, and walked beside her. She rested her hand on his shoulder, guiding him, protected by him. The soft clop-clop of small hoofs in the dust, the fairy music, the dark, the man's warmth under her hand, enclosed her in a magic separateness from reality.

Afterwards she was to remember that quiet journey as an oasis in which she had rested her heart and mind for the last time.

Freddi Waldkirch, plump but still elegant in white shark-skin, welcomed them, shaking them warmly by the hand. He gave them a table near the ramparts and commandeered a scurrying waitress.

"These are my very special guests. We don't see them often enough." He opened a bottle and filled their glasses. "A little wine from Cassis—excellent, I think, for a hot night."

His affectionate respect for Pascal Guis was not feigned. If he had not had his own infinite capacity for dodging trouble, he would like to have had the blind man's capacity for meeting it. But he preferred to be himself. "Let me recommend our boula-boula, a delicious sole meunière to follow . . ."

His own tribute to St. Roche was lavish. Paper lanterns strung across the Place flooded it with a gently undulating sea of colour. The up-flung waters of the fountain danced in rainbows. An orchestra of swarthy young men, red sashes round their narrow waists, had driven up from Nice. The temporary wooden floor swayed under pounding feet about which the dust swirled in low clouds. Expensive strangers who had escaped the fever-heat of the coast and villagers danced together—young men with young women, girls with girls, children awkwardly with children. Dogs ran in and out among them like small unheeded ghosts. Extra tables had been set up and drinks, within reason, were on the house, so that even Georges Robert and his pale-faced wife, nursing a baby at her thin breast, could drink their Pernods and tell themselves that, after all, life wasn't so bad. Madame Royat had ordered a special table in celebration of the visit of her two sons and their wives. She had no illusions about the wives. They were plain, dull young women. But she had reason to be proud of Louis and Claude—Louis in his chic white gabardines, Claude, as became a Lyonnais merchant, in a conservative dark blue suit. Tall, sleek, prosperous young men. But if she hadn't been so sensible they might be lying in that half-forgotten burying-ground, side by side with those luckless ten. As it was, thanks to her good sense there they all were, even Emile, though it was true that he didn't seem to enter into things, but sat apart, stoop-shouldered and, as she thought impatiently, almost senile.

She drummed out the rhythm of a fox-trot with her blunt fingers.

"Tum-tum-ta-ta—"

The old women sat on the sidelines like unblinking, not ill-natured vultures. Lucien Sauvan stood with his back to the ramparts, his arms folded. He said to the sharp-featured stranger next to him, "I wonder what those fools have got to dance about?"

His companion tapped his shoulder good-humouredly.

"Tomorrow, comrade, when they wake up with sore feet and sore heads they will wonder too."

Both men watched Pascal and his wife as they danced past. She led him without seeming to, her smiling face lifted to his dark-shaded eyes. They seemed to be talking to each other without speaking—two bodies that had a language of their own. Even strangers who did not know them or realize the man's blindness made way for them. They were two charming people who danced beautifully.

Cars continued to drive up and park themselves under official direction, in the Petite Place. They honked and ground their gears at each other, and when a dark green Volkswagen edged into the last space, ahead of a stately and solemnly manoeuvring limousine, there were indignant protests. The driver, a little dog under his arm, merely shrugged. He reached the Café des Artistes just as the orchestra petered into silence and the dancers, applauding perfunctorily, began to drift back to their tables.

Freddi never missed a newcomer. He recognized instantly the inconspicuous, somehow conspicuously isolated man. He said something under his breath in a language that he had thought forgotten and started forward in involuntary concern. For Pascal Guis, blindly groping, stood alone in the widening circle, an unconscious woman at his feet.

On second thought, or rather obeying an instinct that had never failed him, Freddi stayed planted where he was. A stone had been tossed into a placid pool. It had stirred to life ugly things that might come to the surface and prove dangerous. And he had done with danger. Someone called to him, and with a little forward bend of the body, ingratiating but not obsequious, he crossed over to the table where La

192

Baronne with Mlle Milly, like a watchful, anxious terrier, was starting out on one of her big nights at his expense. She asked through rings of cigarette smoke, "Why has that fellow come back?"

"The Germans," Freddi said smoothly, "like to travel. They adore France. And no doubt he has old friends here."

The Abbé had marched out from the sidelines. He took Pascal's arm in affectionate reassurance, and the younger man half-turned to him, bewildered and questioning.

"What happened to her?"

"It's nothing. Perhaps the heat. Perhaps you were too vigorous. She's fainted."

"She fainted once before—when she was frightened."

The Abbé had lifted Nina in his powerful arms. He pushed his way through the crowd that peered at the white face against his shoulder with the naked avidity of the simple for a misfortune not their own. Pascal held to the Abbé's sleeve like a lost and anxious boy. "We'll take her to the Auberge," the Abbé told him. "It will be cool there. The Drouets can telephone for Chinot. Don't worry. Women still faint, you know. In my mother's time it was their privilege."

They passed close to the newcomer's table. He rose and bowed. He said politely, "Good evening, Monsieur l'Abbé."

The Abbé seemed not to have heard him.

By the time they had reached the deep shadow of the Auberge plane tree, Nina had begun to stir against the Abbé's shoulder. He murmured to her, "It's all right. It was just a bad dream. You're awake now."

He set her down gently at one of the iron tables, and she leaned forward, her face between her hands. Pascal groped for one of them and held it against his cheek as though his very urgency could make him see her. They might have been alone together.

"What is it? What did I do? I said once that no one could hurt me any more. It isn't true. You could—more than I could bear. If anything happened to you ..."

She tried pitifully to sound as though she were smiling.

"How stupid! I must have danced too fast."

She drank the water Madame Drouet had set before her. With her free hand she pushed back the page's fringe from a forehead damp with sweat. "Please—let us go home, Pascal."

Madame Drouet stood beside her. Over the bowed head her eyes questioned the Abbé's flushed and troubled face.

"My husband has sent for Chinot, Madame. The doctor is on his way."

"But I don't need him. I don't want to wait. Please, please, let us go home."

When Dr. Chinot brought his Vespa to a standstill, he found the Drouets and the Abbé waiting for him under the plane tree. The light from the Auberge door was on their faces. There was a curious rigidity about them as though they had been spellbound by some invisible disaster.

Madame Drouet said in a flat, colourless voice, "Your patient, Madame Guis, has gone home, Doctor. She apologized for troubling you."

"What happened?"

"She fainted."

The little shabby man mopped himself and laughed.

"Well, it's a stifling night. And, in fact, she has good reason."

The Abbé could not break free from Madame Drouet's silent, implacable interrogation. She said harshly, "Jean Barberis ran past here a while back. He shouted something about a ghost. I thought it was just his craziness."

The Abbé interrupted bitterly. "He must have recognized the fellow too. It's no ghost. Captain von Freytag has come back, the devil knows why. I suppose he reminded Nina Guis —well, as he reminds all of us—of what we'd hoped was forgotten."

"Captain von Freytag," Chinot echoed. He put his hand to his eyes as though shielding them from the light. "These Germans," he said, "are like vultures. They come back to pick the bones." He looked from one set face to the other. He questioned them almost defiantly. "Well, it's all of nine years ago. What can he do to us?"

# III

MADAME Royat stood up. Beads of sweat were caught in the hairs of an incipient moustache.

"Give me your arm, Emile. I feel faint too. It's this awful heat."

The orchestra was engaged to play till two o'clock, but already the villagers streamed down their tunnel-like streets as though a sudden mistral had arisen and they were particles of dust. They left behind them a grey, disillusioned squalor. A few foreigners remained to drink against a threatening hangover or to lean on the ramparts and watch the stars fade above the black-silhouetted mountains and to await the merciful breeze that would precede daybreak. For some reason unknown to them, the fête of St. Roche had foundered.

The solitary man with the dog asleep at his feet still sat at his table. His opaque white face under the light of a guttering lantern gleamed like a luminous mask. La Baronne, across the empty dance floor, filled her glass with the dregs of her third bottle. She was drunk but, to her companion's relief, singularly subdued. She said thickly, "He stayed with you, Mlle Milly. Doesn't he frighten you too?"

Mlle Milly tucked back a straggling grey strand of hair. It was a girlish, almost coquettish gesture.

"Oh, no. We were quite friends. He was so kind to my cats. You can see he loves animals. That's always a good sign, don't you think? Angele was a kitten at the time. But she may remember him. Cats have such wonderful memories. I hope he comes over and speaks to us. I have a little joke to share with him."

"Be sure that it's a German joke. There—he's looking us over too. He's wondering about us. He's not quite sure." She pulled herself, groaning with effort, to her feet. "One thinks of the Black Death," she said irrelevantly.

Clinging to her small guardian's arm, she navigated across the square and came to a teetering halt at von Freytag's table.

"Well, so you have come back, Herr Hauptmann."

He stood up at once, correctly, his heels together, the corners of his mouth lifting.

"*On revient toujours,* Madame la Baronne."

She patted his arm with a swollen hand.

"Always the cavalier."

Mlle Milly smiled shyly at him.

"If you are staying long enough, you must come to have tea with me, for old times' sake."

"I shall be staying long enough. I shall be delighted."

"My cats won't have forgotten you."

He put his thumb and forefinger to his left eye to adjust the missing monocle.

"I shall be sure to bring them a reminder."

At first expressionlessly, then with an ironical grimace, he watched the two grotesque figures melt into the shadows. Then he resumed his seat with the air of a man whose purpose is not yet accomplished and who can afford patience. He refilled his glass. He had been drinking, but not excessively or expensively. The orange lantern overhead burnt to dead fruit. His face caught the first reflection of the rising sun. He looked, Freddi thought dispassionately, like a forgotten corpse. Freddi strolled over and sat at his guest's table, his arms folded. It was a detached attitude, expressive of neither hostility nor friendliness.

"You didn't surprise me at all," he said. "I've been expecting you. But you might have chosen a less conspicuous occasion. You've been rather a blight on my party." He laughed. "But then tact was never German."

"We have a sense of drama," Ulrich retorted. "We like to make effective entrances."

"Eight years is a long time."

"It's longer in prison."

"I was surprised to hear of your release."

"Or shocked?"

"Merely surprised. After all, a life sentence . . ."

"My dear Waldkirch, the Military Tribunal was playing to the gallery. Since then, *pour épater les Américains,* who reckon cleanliness next to godliness and consequently us Germans as really very fine fellows, it has been discovered that I was grossly wronged. A cousin was at Paradis. The little shooting affair here was due to the excessive enthusiasm of a sergeant whom I had left in command. The worst they could say of me was that I had run away—which under the circumstances was commendable." He produced a silver cigarette case and offered it. Freddi said politely, "Thanks. I don't smoke."

"I remember. You have no vices."

"I have developed one—virtue. It has grown on me. I have a charming wife, two splendid boys. I am a blameless *père de famille.*" He added with light emphasis, "I intend to remain one."

"No doubt authority is complaisant?"

"Why not? My café is very popular. It encourages tourism. If the tourists and I carry on modest financial transactions under the counter, it is our affair. The French are a rational people. They tie us up in red tape with the assurance that we shall know how to untie it."

"So you have prospered?"

"I don't complain. You look well preserved yourself, Herr Hauptmann. One would have said that prison had agreed with you."

"I kept myself fit. I took daily exercises. I occupied my considerable leisure cultivating my memory." He looked around the half-deserted Place. "Really, I don't think I've forgotten anyone."

"No one, it seems, has forgotten you."

Ulrich von Freytag made an impatient gesture. They might have been playing a game of which he had now tired.

"What have you done with it?"

"Nothing. It is where we left it. As far as I am concerned, it can stay there. I don't propose to dig up the past—in any form. It would be dangerous. And I am under no necessity."

"I am. Urgent necessity."

"Then, my friend, you must proceed alone."

The two men stared at each other straightly. The increasing light had infused a faint colour in the German's cheeks. He looked, Freddi thought, less corpse-like, almost humanly angry. "You see," Freddi went on, "I am in a unique position. Having never pretended to be anything but what I am, you cannot denounce me. Everybody knows that I supply a need. I keep my nefarious bargains. I am a necessary cog in an over-complicated machine. As such I am accepted and respected."

Ulrich blew a complete ring of smoke into the quiet air. He watched it dissolve, his eyes narrowed.

"Is that all?"

"No—for old times' sake I suggest you leave well enough alone. Leave your Nibelungen Hoard to some adventurous schoolboy a century or so from now. Keep away from here. You will have Pascal Guis to deal with. He is a strange fellow. He has something—what the old Romans, no doubt, would have called 'virtue'. Old-fashioned and, from my point of view, quite inexplicable. But I am a realist. I respect power, even if I do not recognize its source. At present Guis is quiescent. But if he were roused . . ."

"A blind man!"

"He has a wife who isn't blind."

"I remember her very well. As you saw, she remembers me."

"You may have some hold on her, of course," Freddi admitted. "But she loves her husband. Under pressure she might be dangerous too."

"I think," Ulrich murmured, "she will be reasonable."

"Women," Freddi corrected sententiously, "are unpredictable." He appraised his companion with a naked curiosity. The man's clothes, he calculated, were those of a bankrupt who is trying to reassure his creditors. Freddi made the best of an unprofitable business. He picked up von Freytag's check. "Permit me—for this unique occasion. Now I must be on my way. The café is officially closed, and if I am not home by morning my wife worries. She insists that I am not so young any more and need my sleep."

Ulrich stretched out his white, manicured hands on either side of his empty glass. He seemed to consider them with satisfaction. But Freddi had an idea that he was disguising an unusual embarrassment.

"Must you go? I have been very much alone for a long time. Just now, when Mlle Milly invited me to tea, I was actually pleased. I always enjoyed her absurdity. I have enjoyed you too, Waldkirch. We have, I think, more than our precious loot, in common."

"Men do the same things from different motives," Freddi observed. "You and I have both killed people. When I was a youngster I killed an old peasant woman for a potato. I am sure you would kill an old peasant woman—but not for a potato."

"For more or less." The long delicate fingers crisped themselves like the claws of a cat. "I learned to kill very young," he murmured.

"Well, you Germans have always been in love with death. I happen to be in love with life—chiefly my own life, of course." He did not, as was his custom, offer to shake hands. "Please consider my advice, Herr Hauptmann."

"I shall consider it."

A minute later Ulrich heard a powerful car burst into exultant life. Headlights flashed in and out of the streets and flung a long bright streaming of gold on the mountainside. They vanished. In the strengthening daylight the stiffly erect figure at the café table had the desolate, tragic look of a man shipwrecked and left behind by a receding tide on a flotsam-littered shore.

He stood up. The little fuzzy dog who slept under the table

198

yawned and stretched herself. He took no notice of her. She trotted, patient and trustful, at his heels.

## IV

SHE lay, motionless as an effigy, in the huge bed in which a shadowy woman had given birth to the man beside her and then died. She felt that if she moved, an avalanche, poised to overwhelm her, might be set in motion. She was wide awake. Pascal slept, his naked body relaxed, his hand on her arm like that of a child that, groping in the dark, had found comfort. His tranquil breathing was the only sound to break the intense quiet that precedes daybreak. The light was beginning to fill the frame of the open window. In a few minutes a crystal-cool breeze would pour through from the mountains, breaking the feverish heat.

Her wide-open eyes were turned pitilessly on herself. Who was she? Sauvan had called her a rotten little tramp. Was it still the truth? Had it ever been the whole truth? If so, when had the rot started? In trivial childish thefts and lies (but all children stole and lied), in her hatred of a loveless old woman whose contempt of her had goaded her from one reckless folly to another? Was it inheritance? Her father had been a dull but brave and decent man. Even her slattern mother had refused to run away, had perhaps died for a cause in which she didn't even believe. But she herself had been in full flight all her life, dodging retribution, jumping from one mad expedient to another like a fugitive in a torrent, leaping from ice-floe to ice-floe, trying to save what mattered nothing to anyone else, so little even to herself. But Pascal had warned her, not knowing that he warned her: the time came when you had to turn in your tracks and face the pursuit of consequences. They were like the furies. They took no account of years of ardent love and unflagging, patient toil. They clung to your heels. They were inexorable. And if at last she did face them, and in the open, she would involve a man who already had endured too much, crush him with a guilt of which she was not even sure. If she forestalled Freytag's malice—? After all, he might not be malicious. His coming might be no more than a German's thick-skinned urge to return to places and people he had outraged. The Abbé had told her, "Whatever burden you carry—have the guts to carry it alone."

Pascal stirred faintly. His hand tightened on her arm.

"It's you, Nina?"

She tried to say lightly, "Who else should it be?"

"I don't know." She heard a drowsy, half-smothered laugh. "What other woman would sleep with a blind unsightly man . . ."

". . . who happens to be my whole life."

"You say such charming things, Madame." The merciful breeze had come at last. His arm closed over her body, drew her against him with a hungry urgency. "All the same, I shall pay you out for that abominable quarter of an hour. I was really in the dark—terrifyingly alone. You'd left me—I couldn't bear it."

She said with love's arrogant defiance of mortality, "I shall never leave you."

"Then everything's all right, forever."

He had meant to make love to her. Instead, like a tired boy he sank back into contented sleep. It was she who was alone.

## V

THOMAS Clerissy came out of the cypress avenue into the Guis courtyard. He caught the flash of a white face and a black shirt that vanished into the dark of the storehouse and called out, "Hi, there!" But there was no answer. Nor had he really expected one. The old woman had become a legendary will o' the wisp, flying crazily from all human contact. Well, most people were a little crazy, some more openly than others. Most people were hunted by their private furies—as for instance, that poor devil, Bernard, who last night had put a bullet through his brains.

Pascal and Nina were eating supper under the patio vine. Pascal recognized the Abbé's heavy tread. He pulled out a chair, showing his strong white teeth in a grin of welcome.

"You're just in time, Father. Grand'mère has made the bouillabaisse of her life. It's still warm. We've kept a plateful for you."

The Abbé sat down, sighing gustily. He dusted off his thick black boots with the usual lamentable handkerchief.

"It's indecent the way I always arrive on time. I set out with the best intentions. I say to myself, 'I will accept a cup of coffee—no more'. But then I catch a whiff of Grand'mère's cooking, and I begin to walk faster." He smiled at the woman across the table. Perhaps blindness might be a mercy. The man who loved her could not see how beautiful she was, but also he could not see the shadows under the fawn's eyes or that look of fear. He asked gently, "You are recovered, Nina?"

"Thank goodness—no," Pascal answered gaily. "She will not be recovered—not for six months. Can you believe it, Father? She did not tell me. She let this wild fellow dance her off her feet. She had to faint first and frighten the life out of him."

The Abbé asked silently, "Is that true?" And she nodded. But she continued to hold his eyes as though she were trying to warn him, to plead with him. He plunged a spoon into his plate. It would have been against his gastronomic principles to have eaten bouillabaisse quietly.

"That's great news. I've waited a long time for it."

"We'd almost lost hope." Pascal added slyly, "But we kept on trying. Now perhaps we shall have a son who will make the great Burgundians look to their vine leaves." He became grave. "Perhaps he will pay poor Christophe Guis my debt."

"What do you owe that fellow?" the Abbé asked sourly.

The black-shaded eyes turned directly to him. It was difficult to believe that behind their defence they were not alight and beautiful. The full and generous mouth was touched at the corners with a faintly teasing good-humour.

"Not life, anyhow. As you may have guessed, Father, I am not his son. He knew, as Grand'mère knows, which is one reason why she hates the sight of me. When they shot him, they must both have felt that I had done him a last outrage."

The Abbé looked at him with love.

"You have learned to be tolerant, Pascal."

"It's an easy lesson—when you're happy." He put out a confident hand and touched the woman's cheek. Touch, the Abbé thought, had not only become a second sight; it was another language. With it he spoke directly to her heart. He must have felt its heaviness. He said with gentle yet urgent assurance, "So very happy."

"I wish I were," Thomas Clerissy lamented. "I've left a hornet's nest behind me. Bernard has committed suicide.

Apparently he kept a service revolver handy. A man with no legs and some private demon gnawing at his vitals might reasonably take a short cut. But his poor frantic wife insists that he must have gone suddenly mad. Well, that's what I told Monsieur mon Curé, who was all for casting what remains of him into outer darkness. Sinner or no sinner, he's going to get a decent Christian burial." He rubbed his handkerchief over a hot and troubled face. "What is sin, anyway? I permit myself in my unorthodox moments to wonder. When we meet God finally, we may be surprised and annoyed to find that we have tormented ourselves and each other for a lot of shibboleths, that we shall be condemned—if indeed He condemns anyone—for trifles that have given us not a moment's concern: malicious gossip, a tin can tied to a cat's tail, a wretched calf slaughtered for our delectation with monstrous cruelty. I suspect indeed that cruelty is the only mortal sin, the father of all our venial sins and most of our miseries." He went off at a tangent, following a secret, harassing thought. "I was the last man, I believe, to talk to Bernard. He asked me if it were true that Captain von Freytag had come back."

Nina had risen abruptly. The Abbé prayed, "Whatever is the matter, please God, help her."

Pascal fished out a Gaulois from his shirt pocket.

"He was a pretty decent fellow, wasn't he?"

"We called it 'correct'."

"You must have known him, Nina."

She was halfway to the kitchen. She said with the steadiness of what might be resignation to disaster, "He and the Fouqué-Basdurs were old friends. He used to visit them. Yes —I knew him."

"Anyway, there he is," the Abbé said quickly. "As 'correct' as only a German can be who is engaged in trampling out someone's guts." He scraped his platter clean with a crust. "They gave him life imprisonment for the Paradis massacre and that little shooting affair outside our walls. But now we are such buddies it appears that it was all a mistake. He has been amnestied, no doubt with suitable apologies."

"Why has he come back?"

"The devil knows."

"He frightens you, Father. Why?"

The Abbé started as though he had been touched on a raw nerve.

"I'm not frightened. I'm disturbed. I thought our village was at peace, as much at peace as any community can be. I suppose it was just stagnation. Toss a stone into a stagnant pool and ugly things float to the surface. There's a stink—contamination in the air. The pool needs to be drained and cleansed."

"The job is obviously yours, Father."

"No. I'm too suspect. According to Lucien Sauvan's ready tongue, I'm in league with the devil—he means God. And God plays politics with capitalistic Big Shots. Either way I'm an Enemy of the People." He added disgustedly, "With a big 'P'."

"He's an eloquent fellow," Pascal observed. "Even at school he used to harangue us on some injustice that had been done us. I still listen to him sometimes." He laughed ruefully. "He almost convinces me that I shot myself in order to become a professional martyr in the cause of capitalism. Yet we fought on the same side. The leaders of our *Réseau Alliance* used to meet up with P.F.T.F. in the mountains to try and work out some form of collaboration. It never worked. I don't think Sauvan wanted it to work. He was always furious about something. Once he accused us of getting an unfair share of the R.A.F. air-drops. He hated me. He still does."

"He hates on principle," the Abbé observed. "He turns legitimate grievances to unreasonable greeds and uses them as tools. There's that national strike brewing, nicely timed to blow our summer prosperity to hell. Sauvan doesn't want prosperity. He wants misery to become intolerable. He will lead the revolt against it—harangue himself into Mayor Toussan's shoes. After that, who knows? He's a tentacle of a huge octopus. If we're not to be strangled by it, someone has got to lop him off."

"Who?"

"You're loved, my son. Our people will listen to you."

Pascal shifted his chair back and put up a defensive hand as though to ward off a dangerous approach.

"Let me be, Father. I've had my bellyful of fighting. I don't want power. I want Nina, and perhaps our children and the vineyards. Besides," he added triumphantly, "a lot of people hate me. I've been a trouble-maker in my time."

"You shall be again. They don't hate you. You make them

sore. They're little people who are ashamed of their little-
ness. They want someone to help them to be great."

"I'm not that someone."

"Help them, Pascal."

"To open old wounds?"

"If necessary. Let them bleed out their poison." The Abbé
pounded the table with an exasperated fist. "Don't imagine,
my son, that because you've fought and suffered that you're
absolved from fighting and suffering. We were not born to
be at peace, and happiness is something we glimpse rarely,
between storms." He calmed down to say with deliberate
emphasis, "If France is to be what God meant her to be—the
loveliest, happiest country on His earth, the heart and
fortress of our Western civilization, we French have got to
clean house. In every city, every town, every village, men
who love her and have courage and good-will have got to
form ranks to drive out the cheats, the political careerists, the
scroungers, the spiritual traitors. This is your acre. Plough
it, Pascal, God won't let you off."

Pascal grinned ruefully.

"Must we chase out our Freddi?"

The Abbé grinned back at him.

"Every community should be allowed to keep its pet rogue
—as a museum piece."

Nina walked with the Abbé to the verge of the great
cypresses.

"They should be thinned out," the Abbé grumbled.
"There are too many of them. They hem you in."

"They are a sort of rampart. I feel safe behind them."

"There are no ramparts. There's no safety either; there
never was—except in ourselves." He turned to consider her
in the fading light. He said gently, "Don't pretend to me at
any rate. You're frightened too."

"I suppose," she countered, "anyone who is completely
happy must be afraid."

He was not to be sidetracked.

"You ran away, after your fashion, when you recognized
that fellow. Is it possible that Pascal doesn't know?"

"That I was Victor's mistress?" She sounded almost gay.
"I'm not a fool, Father. In this viper's nest someone would
have felt it a duty to tell him. But I *had* told him."

"Then what remains?"

"Is this the confessional?"

"Perhaps. I'll do my confessing first. Pascal is my son."

She stood in her favourite attitude, that of someone very young, her hands locked behind her back. She smiled up at him, half affectionate, half mocking.

"Is that supposed to be your secret? I guessed. Pascal, I think, knows. He's very proud of his father. But he doesn't want to embarrass the good Abbé Clerissy. You and I," she went on gravely, "stand on the same ground. We would die for him."

"It would be better for him that we should live."

## VI

THOMAS Clerissy begged a ride to Nice in Freddi's long-nosed sports car. Freddi was always innocently delighted to do anyone a favour so long as it didn't cost too much, or at any rate not more than a possible quid pro quo justified. He had spent the day in close consultation with the café's bartender and manager. After a fête there was always a great deal of bookkeeping and even more of broken crockery.

"I have never understood," he said, "why people should have to break things when they're having a good time."

"Perhaps they're not happy," the Abbé suggested.

"Perhaps. But happiness, to me, seems extraordinarily simple. A good digestion, a co-operative bed-fellow, a roof over one's head, a first-class chef. What more is there? I have it all. I am happy. And I have no inclination to break anything."

"That's because you have no conscience," the Abbé explained to him. "You are such an outrageous fellow, Freddi, that you are almost a work of art."

Freddi chuckled contentedly.

"I'm not as good as I was," he said. "I have Roland and Antoine. Such delightful children. Would you believe it, I'm bringing them up to believe in God and pay their taxes? Sometimes I rub my eyes. But there it is. To disillusion them would break their father's heart. So you see, I have become vulnerable."

"I have a sneaking affection for you," the Abbé said. "I shouldn't like your heart to break."

"Then offer up a prayer for me," Freddi requested

solemnly. "If this goddamn strike develops, I may need it. The whole season may be washed up." He added, but without venom, "Damn the bastards!"

"They're bastards if they strike," the Abbé commented, "and fools and cowards if they don't. They're scandalously underpaid and foully housed in a country dripping with milk and honey and lousy with your plush clientèle, Freddi. It's a vicious circle. God knows who'll break it." He ruminated. "Perhaps one brave and honest man."

"That lets me out," Freddi said cheerfully.

He set Clerissy down outside a demure-faced apartment house in a residential side-street. He blinked up at it with a conspiratorial chuckle.

"Madame Maman too," he said, "has made her peace with virtue."

Rather laboriously and ignoring a self-operated elevator, which he distrusted, Clerissy climbed two flights of religiously dim stairs and rang the bell of one of four apartments. Its melodious tinkle was answered by an elderly woman who in a neat uniform was only to be recognized by imagination as one of Madame Rose-Thérèse's favourite girls. Redeemed too, she had followed Madame into an almost excessive respectability. The room into which she ushered Clerissy was mainly Victorian, cluttered with knick-knacks, small tables, and not very easy chairs. Only signed photographs of grateful clients and an out-cropping of faded dance favours testified to a deplorable career.

Madame herself swam out of her bedroom in a lush peignoir, kissed her son affectionately, and commanded his favourite apéritif. She had resigned herself to a comfortable plumpness, but it was still possible, in spite of a metallic black hair-dye and too much make-up, to recognize the remnants of a Madonna beauty. She knew the make-up was excessive, but in her profession one was apt to lose a sense of proportion. "But God and I are reconciled, Thomas," she had consoled him. "I attend Mass even on weekdays. I go to confession regularly. Unfortunately I have so little to confess that poor Father Hippolyte is bored to distraction. So you see, there's no need to be worried about me. I'm a brand snatched from the burning."

"But still smouldering," Thomas had grumbled.

She had found that richly funny.

Thomas had no illusions. She had adopted the narrow

path as the most agreeable to declining energies. She too had no illusions about him. People always wanted something of you. His weekly visits were a display of real affection. They were also a defiance of authority. Now, she realized, there was something else. She didn't hurry him. She allowed the apéritif to mellow his shyness, to make whatever he had come to ask easier.

"In your day," he said at last, "you must have known the Occupation forces pretty well. I wonder if a certain Captain von Freytag ever figured among your clients—if you remember him."

She had, in fact, a memory like an orderly address book. Figuratively she flipped over its pages.

"Captain Ulrich von Freytag. Yes, he came several times, until he picked up a little friend of his own, a certain Madame So-and-so whose husband was taken prisoner and has since returned. She has a shop on the rue Meyerbeer, and I understand they are very happy. Why not? Four years of virtuous widowhood are apt to wilt a woman's talent for love. Though I'm sure he is unaware of it, Monsieur So-and-so owes the gallant Captain a debt of gratitude."

The Abbé sighed. She still had the power to shock him. And she was so often right.

"I'm only concerned with von Freytag. Did you have any impression of him—any inside knowledge?"

She was outrageously amused.

"My dear child, a client has to undress in all senses of the word. My girls talked. I was one of them. They had complete confidence in me. As I remember, the Captain was something of a shock even to them. Clarisse—a charming girl, and more than usually intelligent—told me he was like a man tormented by some sort of dreadful thirst."

Clerissy stood up. He began to pace back and forth among the knick-knacks. He knocked over a small table and apologized to it nervously.

"A thirsty man and eight years of drought!"

"It all sounds a little mad, doesn't it? But then Germans are a little mad, don't you think? I suppose you can't psychoanalyse a whole nation, an you? It's a pity. You might turn up some amusing complexes. Well, anyhow the Captain was in the S.S. That of course made it impossible to complain."

"And his comrades?"

"He came alone."

"Well, he must have changed his methods with his uniform. In our village he appeared as a simple Wehrmacht captain, sincerely anxious to make friends. He was, I regret to say, successful."

She narrowed her dark, lovely eyes shrewdly.

"Then," she said, "he was up to something. He was up to no good."

"Now he has come back—as a harmless tourist afflicted with nostalgia. And the village is like an overturned antheap."

His mother refilled his glass.

"Sit down. Don't fidget. Did you think the war was over, my poor innocent? For the von Freytags at least it is never over. Fortunately, you and I are too old for all that nonsense. Keep away from that fellow. Leave him to the devil."

"I can't," Thomas said glumly. "I'm not sure enough that the devil claims his own."

"Well then, leave him to God," his mother suggested with good-natured malice. Then, because she recognized some dark distress in him, she asked, "My grandson—has it anything to do with him?"

"I don't know."

"Isn't he happy with that wench?"

"He's happy. But I'm frightened for him."

"That's quite stupid, Thomas. I've been happy all my life I've never been in the least frightened. I must come up some time and take another peek at him. La Baronne might introduce us." She chuckled comfortably. "And my darling puppy, Suzon?"

"Pascal loves her. But he doesn't need her any more. He has learned to see in the dark. It's just as well. Your puppy is growing old—like all of us."

Madame almost snorted.

"But I don't feel old at all. I don't intend to. I could still cut a caper or two, only I'm so damned lazy."

"Well, thank God for that!" Thomas said piously.

They both roared with laughter. But she could see that he was still unsatisfied. She asked seriously, "What is wrong with him, Thomas? Whether anyone disapproves or not, he is my grandson. I have a right to know."

"He is not content. Underneath happiness is an unquiet conscience—restlessness. He knows what you know, Maman. The war goes on."

"What do you want of a blind man who has done his fighting?"

"To forget his blindness and get back into the fight."

"For what?"

"Rocquedur—our Provence." He went scarlet to the roots of his black hair. "France!" He added angrily, "How low have we sunk that we should blush for loving her?"

## VII

THE bar of the Auberge des Alouettes should have been a crowded, pleasant place. When shrill winter winds hunted down the narrow streets, a log fire drew warm reflections from the polished woodwork. In the torrid summer heat it was cool and restful in the twilight under the oak rafters. But it was too often empty.

Madame Drouet sat at her desk and audited the month's accounts in careful, laborious long-hand. When the tax-assessor examined them he would find them accurate to the last centime. But the results deepened lines of anxiety on a worn face that, once pretty, had attained the distinction of endured and conquered suffering. How long, she wondered, could they hold out? If the once-vigorous stream of English and American flyers dried up altogether—not for long. How quickly people forgot! You had to have broken hands and what was known as a broken heart to keep your memory green.

Behind the polished oak bar, Richard Drouet measured out a "fine" for his one guest. He detested Lucien Sauvan, but there were times when his bitterness welcomed bitterness.

"So Victor de Fouqué-Basdur is coming home," Sauvan said. He held his glass to the shaded overhead light, appraising its gold with his hot, brilliant eyes. "He is bringing back what remains of a fortune stolen from the People. So he will be welcomed. You see, my friends, we have all been cheated. The Government has cheated you. What about these famous war damages? What have you received of them? A few sous, perhaps. The rest has gone to feed official rats skulking in a bureau of something or other. We're stupid. We betray ourselves. We should cut off a few heads, make a clean sweep.

You were brave. But surely you realize now that you sacrificed yourselves to a stinking corpse."

Madame Drouet, her head bent over her books, listened. It was one of this man's talents to sense where the shoe pinched, where an old wound, under pressure, could be made to ache again. She and Richard had expected to be welcomed, not as heroes, but at least as patriots. They had found their home in ruins. They had been ignored, overrun by so-called *Résistance* men and women who had never, like Louis and Claude Royat, risked so much as a hair, or treated as doubtful characters who had aided and abetted foreigners to the endangerment of their own people.

"The old Comte is trying to evict Mlle Milly," Sauvan went on, "so that the returning warrior may take up his ancestral residence. That, at least, may not be so easy. She's an obstinate old woman who knows her rights, and the people have a liking for her. They have not forgotten either that the Fouqué-Basdurs ate like pigs whilst they were starving. Even that fool Toussan has put his foot down." He laughed. "When I am mayor I shall put both feet down—on a lot of necks."

He tossed a thousand-franc note on the counter. Richard Drouet picked out the change from his cash-box. He muttered, "Captain von Freytag has come back too."

"So I observed. I am not surprised. He had good friends here. Whether they will be glad to see him is another matter. A lot of them must be sleeping badly—at Mas Guis, for instance."

Madame Drouet jerked a splash of ink on a neatly figured column.

"The Guis should be left in peace. They are good people."

"Good? Well, that's a matter of taste, isn't it?" He emptied his glass. "As for yourselves—well, I don't envy you. You are caught between the hammer and the anvil. Take the advice of a friend. Come down on the side of the hammer. The anvil is worn out. Another blow or two and it will split wide open." He raised a clenched fist. "Good night, Comrades. Think it over."

He merged, soft-footed as a panther, into the street shadows.

Drouet washed and polished the empty glass.

"So we are being threatened again."

"Someone is always threatening us." Raymonde Drouet

ruffled her soft blond-white hair. "Now it is the bank. We are in arrears again. We shall have to ask them to have patience, unless . . ."

She left the sentence hanging. Perhaps it was true that they had suffered to no purpose. She picked out from among her papers a letter from America that they had left unanswered, pretending to each other that they had forgotten it. She remembered, with a rueful smile, its writer—a gangling American youngster whose haircut, which he had called a crew-cut, had made it necessary to keep him in dangerous hiding till it had become normal. His letter, typed on good paper, stamped with some unpronounceable address in the Middle West, invited them to take over the management of his father's hotel, which, as he boasted proudly, was the last word: air-conditioning, bathrooms, television and radio in every room. The boy owed his life to them. Wouldn't they let him pay some of his debt? Their first reaction had been of shock and recoil. At their age to try and throw down fresh roots? Seek friends among an alien people? Leave their dust in alien soil? Leave France? She thought of France in all its beloved aspects and made a grimace of pain. The last bitterness was to have to hate what you loved most.

She glanced over her respectful head at her husband's

The night silence was broken by footsteps on the paved terrace under the plane tree. They stared at each other, motionless and appalled. They had heard those steps before, regular, mechanical, relentless. They were imprinted on their flesh.

Richard Drouet switched on a light over the doorway. It fell on an opaque-grey face. Ulrich von Freytag bowed. He had taken off his hat as though to facilitate recognition. In his right hand he carried a cheap new suitcase. A fuzzy little dog, waving a fantastically plumed tail, panted at his heels.

"Good evening, Monsieur and Madame Drouet."

They were motionless as wax figures. "You remember me? I remember you with pleasure—and regret. I would like to renew our acquaintance under happier circumstances, to spend a few nights under your hospitable roof. I was assured you would have room for me."

"No," Richard Drouet said softly, between his teeth. "No —never."

"Come now—we can't, any of us, afford old grudges. What

is past is past." He went over to the citations, white smudges on the dark wall, and adjusted the invisible monocle. They could hear his mocking, unspoken comment. "Well, so what did citations do for you?" He turned to say gravely, "You should be very proud. Actually engraved. The real signatures —unless they too were engraved wholesale. You deserve better. You did more than your duty. I did mine, too, as a soldier. It was often painful to me. A so-called friend of yours made it unavoidable."

"If I knew . . ." Richard Drouet blurted out.

"I could tell you her name."

"No," Madame Drouet interrupted sharply. "We don't want to know. Not now. It is too late."

Ulrich shrugged.

"As you please. I was merely pointing out that I was not the real enemy. I am not now."

The sweat glistened on Richard Drouet's face. He looked like a man in the throes of a violent physical sickness. Madame Drouet closed her account book. She stood up and held out a broken, deformed hand. Ulrich took it and bowed over it.

"We Germans admire courage where we find it."

She glanced over his respectful head at her husband's ashen face. She said coolly, "We are hotel keepers. We do not choose our guests. Certainly we have room for you. Permit me to lead the way."

He woke to the early morning sunlight pouring through the open window onto the huge Provençal bed. The room was simply furnished. But at least there was a wash-basin with running water. In the old Auberge, as Ulrich remembered, a little maid had stumbled up the steep stairs with tall cans of hot water for the guests. Willy-nilly, war brought progress. It cleaned the ground of a lot of outworn clutter in the way of things, people and ideas. "We Germans," he thought, "are benefactors."

He yawned, stretched, pushed Mitzi off his feet, and strolled over to the window. It was set curiously at an angle so that it overlooked both the Place de l'Eglise and the steeply descending rue des Princes. From where he stood he could see Mlle Milly's studio window and two tiger cats, like Egyptian statuettes, sunning themselves on either end of the sill. The thought of that comical old Englishwoman amused and faintly pleased him. She had been his friend. He had enjoyed inviting her to tea in her own living room, which she had kept so scrupulously clean for him. (He remembered the evening when, returning unexpectedly, he had caught her with the rug by the hearth, rolled up. He had protested politely against her domestic attentions. But she had been quite indignant. "After all, Captain, you are my guest.") He had enjoyed her chatter. It was like floating on a woolly cloud, shot through from time to time with the shrewdness of a practical if misguided and doomed race. Her cheerful assumption that it would scramble out from under the wheels of the juggernaut had amused him in much the same measure as he had been exasperated by the red-faced, obsequious soldiers who like hungry dogs snuffled round the village for friendly scraps to be thrown them by people whom, at his orders, they would have shot down without a qualm. Mlle Milly's crazy fearlessness had been curiously restful. He had found himself talking to her as he talked to no one. She had been an attentive listener.

"You poor boy!" she had said once, to his complete astonishment.

And then, when he had wanted a real woman, there had been always Mitzi, willing, humble—and hungry.

The corners of his mouth lifted in amusement. Well, after all those years, there she still was for him.

In prison he had kept his bodily fitness by a severe self-discipline. He had retained his sanity by a day-by-day retailing to himself of every moment of his life. He had recalled, registered against a future, possible liberation, the names of people and places—the streets of Paris, Nice and Rocquedur, the men and women who one way or another had served his purpose—as for instance, Madame Royat with her deceptively good-humoured, upturned nose and bright, hard eyes, and her timid, bewildered husband, Emile, whose vegetable and fruit and flower stalls still painted bright colours on the silver-grey of the Place de l'Eglise. Strange how many women, themselves expendable, regarded men as mere means to an end. When the end had been obtained, they devoured them. Emile Royat had provided Madame with sons and then, his mission accomplished, had been devoured.

"I realize your distress, Madame," Ulrich had said on that far-off summer day. "I have no doubt your boys are entirely innocent. But we have to protect ourselves against the disloyal action on the part of wrongheaded people. Personally I regret the necessity for hostages. I would be glad to help you—if you would help me."

She had stared at him across the counter, alert and wary.

"My Captain, I would do anything."

"Well, show me what you can do."

He had waited, nibbling a stale *cœur sucré*, which he had picked up from her counter. She had wriggled like a vixen caught in a trap. He saw her glance furtively through the open door which led to her husband's stall with its few wilted lettuces. Monsieur Emile sat on his low stool, huddled in despair.

"You must believe me, my Captain." She had spoken in a whisper. "My poor Emile has been wickedly misled. It is not his fault. It is just his foolishness."

"Madame, we are tolerant of mere foolishness."

"It is those Drouets—those foreign traitors."

When they had arrested Emile, she had howled like a banshee. An admirable performance. Ulrich had kept his bargain. Her precious Louis and Claude had come back in good shape, positively as heroes. The Germans, they had declared, were not the demons of allied propaganda. On the contrary, they were very decent fellows with whom one could come to terms. And why not? To live, one had to use good sense.

Ulrich smiled faintly at their memory.

The French were a queer people. They valued their material possessions more than their lives, and much more than that, an amorphous entity, France. That grim old baker, Antoine Barberis, had pretended to Ulrich—and perhaps, more successfully, to himself, that he was heartbroken for the breadless plight of his neighbours. Actually all that he cared about was his bread. All that he wanted of life was to plunge his great heavy hands into a fat pile of dough, thrust brushwood into his flaming furnace, and draw out of his oven's maw the shapely golden loaves that had been the Barberis pride for generations.

"What can I do, my Captain? To make bread, I must have flour."

He had had his flour.

Ulrich wondered what had become of that gangling,

fanatical son of his—whether Jean Barberis had survived Buchenwald, and in what shape.

There was that clever P.F.T.F. fellow.

On the night of St. Roche's fête, Ulrich had recognized him and had been, he was sure, recognized. Sauvan had manifested complete indifference. So that it was probable he did not know what Ulrich knew concerning that affair outside St. Martin's. The realization might shake him. He might even become amenable and useful. Since Freddi's odd and exasperating defection, Ulrich needed an amenable and useful man. If what Freddi had whimsically christened the Nibelungen Hoard was still intact—two suitcases crammed with various currencies and the jewels with which a family named Eichtersheimer had paid for a safe-conduct to Switzerland (actually they had travelled to Auschwitz in a cattle-truck)—it would be too much for a man no longer young to unearth and transport down a path that had been worn out of the mountain-face by goats. Lucien Sauvan, no doubt, was still shrewd and cynical enough to resume an old if unacknowledged collaboration.

Ulrich leaned his elbows on the window sill. How familiar, unchanged and unchangeable it all seemed, how deceptively peaceful the morning sunshine, the still cool and tranquilly shifting shadows. The villagers came and went across the Place. They passed each other furtively, without greeting. Perhaps they felt him there, watching them, like a god with thunderbolts in either hand, able to shatter their shabby little lives and to rebuild his own life on their ruins. He luxuriated in a superb well-being.

A cracked old bell broke the still sleepy silence. Monsieur l'Abbé hurried out of the presbytery, across the Place, and vanished into the church's ancient twilight. At one time he had been a disturbing element. He believed in God, and such men, as Gauleiter Bach had said, had the irrational power of madmen. They believed in miracles, and sometimes that belief invoked them. Ulrich had suspected him of more and worse than faith. But his name had not been on the Drouets' list of the *Réseau Alliance,* and in any case he was not the type to respond to pressure. He would have sweated out Bach's most ingenious methods with the constancy of the saints he served. It had seemed wiser to let him stew in his religious juice, to watch his congregation melt away from him, his shabby church become shabbier and more desolate.

Probably by now the faithful, reassured that no sacrifice was expected of them, had drifted back into the fold. Anyhow, the Abbé had grown stout, elderly and probably quiescent and virtuous. If Freddi's gossip had any substance, he had not always been virtuous. He had been what he would now call, no doubt, an adulterer. He had a son. So he too was vulnerable.

Ulrich shifted his position as though in sudden physical discomfort. The smoothly flowing tide of memory foamed up against a barrier, recoiled, carrying him with it into the backwater of a bleak anonymous room where he faced a prisoner, a ragged, unshaven, beautiful young man who was helpless and yet, as Ulrich had recognized, menacing. On either side of him had stood monolithic S.S. men, inflexible as ramrods, their gloved hands pressed to the seams of their black riding-breeches. They were the élite, Ulrich's own men. For once he had felt impatient with them, as though for this event they too were to prove inadequate.

His eyes and the prisoner's clear, grey, girlishly shaded eyes had met. It was a brief yet mortal encounter. Ulrich von Freytag, the modern, completely rational man, stripped of all the childish superstitions which hampered men in their ceaseless quest for power over one another, had, for the first time, felt unsure—so unsure that he had left the foreseen event to take its course. By his inaction he had permitted the prisoner to escape into a black prison of his own.

Into that prison Bach and his men had followed him. They had brought to bear on his flesh refinements of their craft of which even Ulrich had not dreamed. He had sat through the proceedings, devoured by curiosity, a feverish thirst, a sense that his own security was incredibly at stake. If the prisoner had screamed once, had even whimpered, Ulrich would have been rid of him. But except for that heavy agonized breathing, he had maintained silence.

In prison Ulrich had requested the Spandau doctor for an opiate which would enable him to sleep, to escape not pity or regret, but an obsessive phantom.

Well, now he had found and faced it. It had been reduced to the dimensions of a happy man, dancing with a pretty woman. A happy man could be broken. He could be made to

pay for those nightmares in which Captain Ulrich von Freytag had had to question the earth on which he stood.

The church bell had clanged for the last time. He could
hear the drone of an old organ and thin childish voices. For
hundreds of years, he reflected sardonically, a non-existent
deity had had to endure that tuneless adoration. He stretched
himself like a man released from some physical constriction.
He was hungry. Madame Drouet, he remembered, was a
superb cook. Seated under the plane tree over morning coffee
and delicious croissants it would be pleasant to force her to
stand humbly beside him, menu in hand, and take his orders.
Leisurely he began to dress.


# VIII

BLACK ominous storm clouds emerged suddenly from behind
the mountains and canopied the village with their shadow.
Men and women walked hurriedly to their work. The storm
might break at any minute. They did not stop to speak to one
another. Madame Royat no longer nodded a condescending
"good day" to Madame Drouet as she passed the Auberge.
She avoided an encounter that seemed to frighten her like a
hostile ghost. Her husband had muttered to himself, "What
does that devil want? Why has he come back?" A rage, deep
buried under his timorous quiet, exploded. "He knows who
turned me in. I'll get it out of him, if I have to wring his
neck."
"Why can't you forget, Emile?"
He had turned on her like a madman who had feigned
sanity too long.
"Easy for you to talk! What did you suffer? What do you
know of hell?"
She winced away from him, her fox's eyes hard and bright
with terror. That night he went over to the Auberge alone,
without a word to her. He was drinking his third "fine" with
the Drouets when Ulrich von Freytag passed through the
shadow of the plane tree on his way to his room. Emile Royat
spat on the clean stones. Madame Drouet's face was a mask,
expressing nothing.
Ulrich stopped dead by the three of them. He said in his

perfect French, "Why do you insult me? I did not insult you when I had the power. It is true I arrested you. Your own people left me no choice. You had your traitors." He held out his hand frankly. "Now that we have enemies in common, we should be friends."

"My quarrel is not with you," Emile stammered. He accepted the outstretched hand because he was a simple fellow and taken aback by a manly forthrightness. "Do me a favour—if you are a friend. Tell me who turned me in." He gestured toward the two Drouets seated like passionless puppets on either side of him. "These people and I have a debt to settle."

"After all these years?" Ulrich shrugged. "It would be better, surely, to forget."

"You've been in prison, Captain," Royat said. "Have you forgotten? Haven't you a score to settle?"

"I am a reasonable man," Ulrich said. "I pay back when and what I can. If it's too expensive, I reconcile myself. The debt is cancelled. Why not do the same?"

"Because the damned thing eats my guts." Royat beat the table with a frenzied fist. He shouted, "Just tell me. I'll settle with whoever it was."

Ulrich looked from one face to the other. If they had asked him to sit with them it would, perhaps, have made a difference. He knew they never would. He was beset by the violent temptation to throw a name into the old man's convulsed face—to turn rage to sick horror. But he held back. He was savouring power again. It must not be expended wastefully.

"I did not come here to make trouble," he said. "You must give me time to think—and to remember."

He made them a formal little bow. Frozen into immobility, they listened to his ascending footsteps, their firm and measured tread. Emile Royat tossed down the last of his drink. His scowl fixed itself on Madame Drouet's hands. He had never really noticed them before. She had a trick of moving them very quickly, almost surreptitiously. Now she spread them out on the table, in all their piteousness.

Royat ground his teeth.

"Are we supposed to forget things like that?"

"People do forget. Other people." She raised her washed-out eyes to the lighted bedroom window overhead. "We and they have become allies, Monsieur Royat. Didn't you know?

218

One of these days we are going to fight side by side." She smiled faintly, terribly. "Perhaps."

It is not a light task to be God's representative on earth and to have to carry the guilt and suffering of His creatures. Madame Royat's whisper seeped through the grill of the confessional box like a tainted breath. Thomas Clerissy found himself shrinking from it, covering his face with his hands.

"Father—they were my sons. I who had given birth to them loved them as he couldn't. He had no right to endanger them. Besides," she added venomously, "I was not the only one. I could tell you of other . . ."

"Be silent!" he interrupted sternly. "You have only one concern—to seek forgiveness—" (he was going to say "of your country, of France," but he knew he would be speaking to a long-established deafness) "of the man you so abominably betrayed."

"He would kill me."

He sighed.

"That would be too easy for you."

"Give me a penance, Father."

"So that you can feel absolved, cleansed?" He told her with cold scorn, "Your penance is to remember what you have done every day of your life, year after year, each time the cock crows."

"Can I come to Communion, Father?"

He said bitterly, "You have been coming all these years."

He knew she would come again. In time she would mend her conscience. She would forget that it had been a torn and dirty rag.

She had said that there had been others. Clerissy had tried not to know. It was like covering up a stinking cesspool and pretending that it wasn't there. The stench pursued you. He came out of the confessional sweating nausea. He glanced up at the grotesque, bleeding Christ nailed forever to his crucifix. "Father, forgive them. They know not what they do." Ah, but they had known how to save their skins, which mattered to them more than honour. It was a long time since "honour" had been a part of the civilized code. No one spoke of it any more. What can it profit a man if he lose his life for it?

219

His wrath tasted like gall. To allay its bitterness, he remembered to play his old spiritual trick. Marie Royat's "I am" because his "I am". He saw through her hard acquisitive eyes what she had seen of life. Not much to warm the heart. She came of a dark, grim people to whom "love" meant little more than a need of the flesh to be briefly, brutally satisfied. To her, marriage had been a contract between two little, anxiously contriving partners to be dissolved only by death, which itself would be accepted as part of the formal ritual of living. But she had said truly, "I love my sons," as Thomas Clerissy might say "I love my son." He thought, "If I could, I would have suffered for him. Perhaps if I had had less to lose, I too would have allowed someone else to have suffered in his stead."

After all, there was no need, he thought, for forgiveness, but for the understanding of the intolerable burden of loneliness and confusion under which most men stumbled. He had been lucky. He had never been alone. He thought, "I was too rough with her." He would stroll over to her dim little shop and munch one of her *cœurs sucrés*. It would be a simple communion that she would understand. Finally he would give her a pat on the shoulder. "We must forgive ourselves and trust in God to have compassion."

Probably God was only a fading superstition to her, but she would feel safer.

He came out into the furnace heat of mid-day. At the far end of the Place he could see Emile Royat hobbling between banks of vegetables and fruit and bright shining flowers. It might have been better if he had never come back to them with his corroding doubts and hatreds.

"Good day, Monsieur l'Abbé."

The little green Volkswagen had pulled to a halt beside him. The stone-grey eyes stared down at him. But the long mouth smiled. "You remember me, perhaps?"

"Yes, I remember you, Captain von Freytag."

"Let us forget titles. This is another world we live in."

Clerissy put his big peasant hand on the car's window ledge.

"Why have you come back?"

"I have old friends here. I hoped you might be one of them —that you would remember that I had done my best to make a hard business easier."

"I am not judging what you did. I am asking you to go away from here—back to wherever you came from. Leave our people in peace."

The man stroked the head of the little dog beside him. Its amber eyes blinked up at him in adoration. The Abbé found his own eyes riveted, fascinated, on that white caressing hand. The man asked softly, "Are they at peace? Are ghosts so easily exorcised?"

"Have you no conscience—no pity?"

"I have a conscience. All men have consciences, Monsieur l'Abbé. But they serve different gods. As to pity—frankly I have always considered it contemptible."

Thomas Clerissy stood back with a gesture of dismissal.

"You may need it yet."

"Never. I have never insulted an enemy by offering it. I shall never ask for it." He asked politely, "Could I drive you wherever you are going?"

The Abbé threw back his head with a big, releasing laugh. "You Germans," he said, "are the most comical of all God's comical children."

This time he had struck home. The opaque-white face flushed crimson. Ulrich von Freytag slipped roughly into gear.

"It's not wise, Monsieur l'Abbé," he said, "to laugh at us."


IX

THE black pall of cloud continued to hang unbroken over the village. The people looked up at it and cursed it. They even prayed to it. But no rain came. The forests were tinder-dry, and the vines heavy with fruit withering to premature sweetness. At night the narrow streets brimmed over with a stagnant, evil-smelling heat. Since the threat of a national strike persisted, tourists had temporarily fallen off, and the Café des Artistes closed early, so that Lucien Sauvan could talk uninterrupted to men who could not sleep and who, after he had driven back to his headquarters at Nice, stood silent and sullen by the ramparts. Here and there a cigarette glowed in the dark like an inflamed and angry eye.

In the big low-ceilinged bedroom of the Mas, Nina's naked

body waited with stoic patience for the brief relief of daybreak. The heavy scent of lavender suffocated her. Her nerves
ached under the ceaseless chatter of frogs and the whirr of
the cicadas. Only the nightingales were at last silent. The
time for love was long since over.

The man beside her kept so still that she thought he
slept. But then she knew he was aware of her—that in his
double darkness he was anxious to the edge of fear. He
stretched out a seeking hand and laid it gently on her breast.

"It's bad, isn't it, beloved? I'm such a rough, tough fellow.
I could sleep like a baby, even in hell. Shall I send you up to
St. Martin? It's cool there; you could sleep."

"Away from you? I shouldn't sleep at all. It's nothing. I
had an ugly dream. I was afraid to sleep again."

"I could go with you. The place could run itself for a few
days. We're not so poor. All these years you've taken care of
me. Now it's my turn."

He lifted himself on his elbow. Downstairs he had heard a
dog's growl, at first tentative and then vehemently protesting.
There were scuffling, furtive footsteps and Grand'mère
Guis's hushed urgent command: "Be quiet! Be quiet!"
Pascal was used to her night prowlings. But it was not usual
for Suzon to growl at her. Even now it seemed that she was
not satisfied. Distrust rumbled in the old throat.

"Grand'mère's talking to herself. Did someone answer? I'd
best go down and see." He laughed softly. "At least I can see
in the dark."

She clung to him.

"No, please, it's no one. She's always talking to someone
who isn't there. I'm frightened, Pascal. It was such a hideous
dream. Love me, my darling. I want to be lost and safe in
you."

He gathered her in his arms. In that deeply shared passion
the sound of voices was submerged. When at last they lay
lulled in exhaustion and content, the Mas had sunk back
into its night silence.

Grand'mère Guis stood pressed back against the mountain
flank. It was as though she were trying to hide herself in its
blood-brown surface. Her ears were still sharp. They followed those surreptitious but unhurried footfalls as they
receded into the tunnel of the cypress trees. But in her dis-
tracted mind the man was still standing at the foot of the old

track that wound upwards to the cave where the boy Pascal
had escaped the loneliness of his childhood and where, as a
man, he had sought an illusionary safety. Its entrance, with
the years, had become a tangle of thorn and broom, man-
high and impenetrable.

He had flashed a light on her face. A scream had gathered
in her throat. With an outstretched hand he choked it to a
moan.

"Be quiet, old woman! Tell that damned dog to be quiet."

He terrified but did not astonish her. She had always
known that he would come back. She had been living in wait
for him. His voice kept its soft, dead level. "Well,
Grand'mère, how have things gone with you? Does he know?
Have you confessed to him? Has he forgiven you? If not, it
must be hard for you to live with him."

She made a little whimpering sound, and he snapped off
the light. "But perhaps he doesn't know. I imagine that he is
a man not easily suspicious. Ought I to tell him? Would he
kill you, do you think? Or would you kill yourself?"

She went on whimpering very softly—an animal hopelessly
trapped. "Well, why make trouble, Grand'mère? I don't
want much of you. Just have these bushes cut away for me.
I want to be able to collect what belongs to me, without fuss
and interference. I can give you stuff to quiet that brute;
harmless stuff, of course."

His shadow had been a denser fragment of the night. He
had put up his hand to his face to wipe away the sweat, and
by the flash of his wrist-watch she saw his eyes. "In a week
there will be a full moon to work by. A week should be time
enough for you. No one need know. You can finish your life
in peace."

She could have told him that peace would never come
again, that she was a poor crazy old woman hunted by
spectres. But he would not have cared. He was a devil. When
she was dead she would find him in hell, waiting for her.

"You won't fail me, will you, Grand'mère?"

The shadow had shifted, melted into other shadows. Now
the footfalls had faded into total silence. It seemed to her that
even the familiar sounds of the night were silenced. She
began to claw frantically at the thorns—a trapped animal,
briefly escaped, seeking the safety of its lair. They lacerated
her withered old hands. They mocked her into gasping
defeat, so that she crumpled up, a dirty heap of rags,

mumbling for mercy against the arid, unresponsive earth.

They ate at daybreak so that they could work before the great heat set in. It was not usual for Grand'mère to stand and watch them. She ate alone. Now, mouthing silently, she stared at Nina over Pascal's head, as though trying to communicate some secret. He ate and drank, seemingly unconcerned. But Nina in her own terror was not deceived. For the first time in their life together, he was enduring the full burden of his blindness. He was aware of some event with which, since it was unseen and strange to him, he could not contend. He looked up suddenly.

"What's wrong, Grand'mère? Come here."

She came at once to him with the submissiveness of a guilty child. He took her claw, streaked with dried blood, and held it to his face. He had smelt blood too often. "You shouldn't wander about at night. You've hurt yourself."

She muttered, "It's nothing. I fell into those bushes by the goat track. They tore at me. They should be cut down. They're wicked."

"If you leave them alone, they won't hurt you."

But she persisted stubbornly, almost with frenzy. "They should be cut down. Christophe would want them to be cut down. You should do what my son wants."

He let her go and sat with his hands on either side of his cup, his head bowed, attentive, Nina thought in panic, to something unseen.

"You're right, Grand'mère. The track is an old friend. One shouldn't neglect old friends. I'll tell some of the men to clear it for you—you and Christophe. The thorns won't scratch you any more. Perhaps you will sleep better."

Nina followed the old woman into the small bleak bedroom where she hid herself. She closed the door and stood with her back against it.

"Who was here last night?"

The sharp black eyes peered at her out of the shrunken skull, hostile and defiant.

"He came."

"What did he want?"

"He wanted the path cleaned."

"Why?"

"He says—up there—there's something that belongs to him."

224

"He must not come again."

The lacerated hands were clawing at each other in sudden fury.

"You've no right to tell me who shall come here. This place belonged to Christophe. It belongs to me. You and Pascal are thieves and trespassers. Pascal murdered my son."

Nina interrupted coldly. "No one must hurt Pascal again."

Then she saw that the scarecrow huddled on the unmade truckle bed was trying to cry. Her face was distorted with the effort, like the face of a terrible, old, brokenhearted child. But no tears came. No tears could ever come. Nina sat beside her and gathered the skeleton body in strong, compassionate arms.

"Poor Grand'mère—poor all of us."

# X

THE Place de l'Eglise was half stifling twilight, half the white-hot blaze of mid-day, and empty except for that stiff, motionless figure with its back to Mlle Milly's house, as though waiting to keep a rendezvous.

He was hatless and wore a white shirt open at the neck. For one startled moment Nina saw him as a man set up against a wall for execution. He was so rigid. He seemed so utterly alone. His white face had the blank, almost somnambulant look of a man who has accepted death. But a little dog panted at his feet. Dogs do not go to executions.

As Nina came up to him, he raised his hand as though to touch a high-crowned cap in greeting.

"I was calling on an old friend. Mlle Milly is not at home. The English refuse to acknowledge temperatures. I waited. I had an idea that you would come. I'm glad to have this opportunity, Nina."

She said coldly, her head up, "I am Madame Guis."

"So I have heard. My belated congratulations. I am partly responsible for your happiness. It was ungrateful, surely, for you to faint at sight of me." He looked her over with dispassionate interest. "May I say that you are as charming as ever? Few women wear slacks well. You have the figure for them. You work hard, don't you? Perhaps too hard. You look a little tired. Or perhaps you don't sleep too well."

"I heard you last night."

"I apologize. It was that dog. And Grand'mère rather lost her head. I intended merely to reconnoitre, not to disturb you."

"What do you want?"

"I tried to explain to the old lady. Like many of our soldiers, I had collected a few trifles that I was unable to take with me. That cave of yours offered a safe place. Too safe. It has become inaccessible. I realized that your husband might not be co-operative."

"He would have you arrested."

"So I foresaw. Hence my caution. But, as I told Grand'-mère, the sooner I have recovered my possessions, the sooner I shall be gone. I need a clear field. You might perhaps suggest a little holiday in the mountains; the heat is quite intolerable."

"I shan't suggest it."

"You would be wise."

"That's a threat, isn't it?"

"Is it a threat to remind you of a bargain?" He added with light malice, "Of which, I fancy, Monsieur Guis has remained ignorant?"

"If I did help you," she said, "you wouldn't go. You wouldn't be satisfied. You want something else. What is it?"

She saw something in his face that she had never seen before—a break in its iron defences, a fleeting look of perplexity.

"You may be right, Nina. How clever you are! For one thing, I should like to meet your husband. It's an odd whim, isn't it? But then even the most reasonable of us have our oddities. Du reste—" he rocked negligently on his heels, "I really don't know exactly. Perhaps few of us know exactly what we want. Of late I have been in doubt myself." He smiled and shrugged. "Doubt is not natural to me. It must be resolved."

"Has it ever occurred to you that someone—someone not like that Bernard might kill you?"

"You, for instance? Well, yes—I realize you have that sort of courage. But to what purpose? You would be guillotined, or, if they don't guillotine women in this chivalrous country, put away for a long time. It would be hard on Monsieur Guis. I shouldn't be precipitate, if I were you."

He waited a moment. She was aware that his cynicism covered an uneasiness more profound even than her own.

Then he saluted again. "I shall give myself the pleasure of calling on you both, Madame. You will introduce me to your husband as a German officer who was also a gentleman of good-will."

He walked away from her with a curious broken stride, his dog at his heels. She wondered if he was on his way to the chateau where an old man decayed behind his decaying walls. She thought bitterly that the two of them would have memories and perhaps hopes to share.

The sweat ran ice-cold down her face and body. She was suddenly convinced that from behind the shutters of the tall houses she was being watched. The watchers snickered to one another that she had danced and laughed with the man who had just left her. Their own dubious past would not soften their bitterness against her. She was an alien. Though she worked the soil as they did, it was not her soil. They could betray it; that was their right, not hers. It was true that they had begun to forget her past, as they had begun to forget their own. But Ulrich von Freytag had shaken the dust out of their eyes and ears. Old memories and old hatreds and distrusts stalked among them.

She almost ran up the church steps and thrust open the padded doors, as men and women through the centuries had fled to seek sanctuary. But sanctuary, with God, had ceased to be respected. On the night of the Liberation, the people had hounded the wretched Félix Millo to the steps of the high altar. They had smashed his face to pulp before they'd hanged him. You could still see the old bloodstains. The Abbé had preserved them in memory, as he said, of Cain.

Inside, the overpowering heat gave way to a dank chill. The age-old shadows under the stark arches were faintly irradiated by the guttering candles at St. Roche's feet. It was a long time since the saint had been so well remembered. Surreptitious fear had crept to this place in surreptitious supplication.

Nina knelt on one of the high-backed stools, but not to pray. If God existed, He was an enemy. To have prayed to Him in her despair would have seemed to her an ultimate cowardice. Yet here in this dark place which had sheltered so much grief and fear and hope she felt less alone. Here for a moment was home.

Thomas Clerissy came down from the altar, which he had been dusting vigorously. He thrust the cloth in his soutane pocket, where he would forget it or use at some future time as a handkerchief. He had seen Nina. He plumped himself down beside her with a gusty sigh, and the chair creaked under him. He was not aware, for she had been there several hours, that La Baronne with her frowsy head on a pillar-base was sleeping off a record-breaking hangover.

"You make me think, Nina," he said, "of an unloved waif standing on the edge of a nice party to which you were not invited, hungry, sulky and envious. It's sad. Because you are loved, and you really are invited."

"By whom?"

"All the angels and archangels."

"Are you one of them?"

He chuckled.

"I hope to be. I should have mentioned your chief Host."

"If that means God, I'd better be honest with you. I pretend in order to be with Pascal. But I don't believe in Him. If I did, I shouldn't like Him. A God who charges a brave man's sight for admission to His Holy of Holies is beyond my comprehension. What's more," she added with despairing insolence, "I suspect He is beyond yours too."

"If I were able to comprehend Him," Clerissy said comfortably, "I should be unable to believe in Him. If He were as comprehensible—shall I say?—as relativity, He would be ridiculous. He did once try to explain Himself to us in simple terms, and all He got out of it was a crucifixion." He glanced at her sidewise. "Why do you come here?"

"To get my breath. It's a sort of respite."

"From what? Pursuit?"

"I suppose so."

"Who pursues you?"

"Myself—the past of me."

"As represented by that poor devil, Freytag? God knows why or when he became a devil. Or it is possible that he too is hounded? What can he do to you, Nina? I've seen Pascal unhappy and uneasy for the first time in all these years. He is my son. I have a right to know."

"You sound as though you loved him more than I do. You don't—you can't. Even the love of a rotten, cowardly woman is more than the love of one man for another."

"It should be. No doubt it is. I don't pretend that I could

228

replace you. I am asking you to help me. Go on. You've confessed a lot of nonsense to me from time to time. I've absolved you for trivialities. Now I want the truth."

"It will be a long confession."

"I have learned patience."

She rose from her kneeling position to sit beside him. Now they were two shadows, huddled close to each other. The man was silent. The woman's voice was no more than a murmur. But it stirred the sleeper by the pillar to a fuzzy listening. She pulled herself up cautiously on her elbow. Her head felt as though it were being pounded by a trip-hammer. But she had sharp ears.

The murmur died to an exhausted silence. Thomas Clerissy groaned and shifted his big bulk.

"I don't see how my old women can sleep on these damned chairs. They must have posteriors of iron." He laid his hand on Nina's knee. He said gently, "My poor child!"

"I'm not sorry for the poor child. She has made a disastrous mess of herself. She doesn't even know who or what she is—an irresponsible coward, who set out—perhaps—to betray the only human being she had ever truly loved. She doesn't know. She never will know."

"I have often thought," Clerissy said with one of his seeming irrelevances, "that Peter, every time he heard a cock crow, must have winced. But he made quite a good thing of himself. Well, cocks still crow at sunrise to remind us of our betrayals of each other and ourselves. But we can still dust ourselves off and stand up like men."

"I'm not a Peter. I'm a terribly frightened woman—frightened, this time, not for myself."

"You could tell Pascal. He has been a hunted, frightened man. He would understand what fear can do to the best of us."

"Yes, if he could see me—perhaps. But he can only hear me. He would hear me say, 'When I came to you that first time I was a German spy. When I went up to the village that night, for all I shall ever know of myself, I was still a spy.' No!" She spoke with a sudden vehemence that made La Baronne shudder. "He has suffered enough unkindness. It would be easier for me to die."

"Indeed much easier," he agreed, "and too damn silly." He brooded, his arms folded over his chest. "Of course it would be sensible if highly unmoral to let the fellow take his loot and get out."

"He wouldn't go. He wouldn't be satisfied. There's something else. There's something he wants to destroy, I don't know what or why."

"Well, he has destroyed Rocquedur's peace, such as it was. He has kicked over an ant-heap, and the ants are scurrying about in a mad panic. Old sores are breaking out. They stink. I don't know myself what should be done." He stood up and took her arm and helped her to her feet. "I shall ask God," he said with simplicity.

The two shadows passed into the sacristy. A door creaked and closed softly. La Baronne heaved up her flabby bulk so that her back rested against the pillar. She twisted her fat decomposing face into successive expressions of disgust and nausea. Her mouth felt coated with foulness. Of all awful hangovers, this was the worst. She'd have to cadge a hair of that familiar dog from someone—perhaps from that German swine, for old times' sake and because she, at least, having scraped the bottom of existence, feared no one.

## XI

It had been another terrible day—no sun, but a nerve-fraying, relentless mistral. Now the wind had died down, leaving a dry tension. To the north another black mass of storm advanced slowly but relentlessly across the flat livid surface of the sky.

Pascal and Nina and Jean Barberis worked side by side along the terraces. No one knew what went on in Jean Barberis's shattered mind. He rarely spoke. But he understood the vines. He guided the older man with tenderness. Pascal himself had become expert. His hands, Nina thought, were also his eyes. They saw when a vine should be cut back. They could gauge the quality of their fruit. They could graft new shoots. He could find his way, if need be, alone. Old Suzon drowsed away her life on the patio, loving him without remorse.

Something was wrong with Jean Barberis. He had retreated into some black contemplation. Not even Pascal could bring him back among them.

By dusk they had cleaned out the last weed. They had worked their way to where the lavender sent up a grey-mauve mist of sweetness. Pascal stood between the tufted bouquets, smiling down at them.

"I smell a good crop, Nina."

But she was watching the sky. She saw in that implacable advance of cloud the forewarning of another peril. She said anxiously, "We should go in. There's a bad storm coming." As she spoke, a jagged stroke of lightning severed the black mass with a roar which seemed to roll round the whole horizon, breaking at last against the mountains.

"It's too late for hail," Pascal said reassuringly. "We need rain. The trees are dry as tinder."

"You should cut some of them down. The Abbé has often warned us."

He laughed, his arm over her shoulder.

"Poor devils like us? How should we pay for labour? For years I've been trying to persuade timber merchants that they needed timber. Maybe I'm to blame. I hate to destroy things —even bad things. I'm not sure how bad they are. And sometimes I've a crazy notion that trees cry when they are cut down." He pinched her ear. "Are you laughing at me, Madame?"

"I'm loving you."

"You'd better love me—though God knows why."

"He knows I have good reason."

"You say such charming things, Madame."

Grand'mère Guis had set out bread and cheese and coffee. Like Jean Barberis, once her task was accomplished, she vanished. It was as though some poor damned ghost had waited on them. Nina could hear her, at the rear of the Mas, scratching feebly at what remained of the bushes on the old path. Her skeleton hands were torn by them. "Let her do what she wants," Pascal had said. "She does no harm."

She did what she had to do.

It was night under the great vine. The thunder was now almost overhead, ripping the sky to shreds. Only a little reluctant rain fell. A few drops broke through. One of them fell on Pascal's cheek. He rubbed it away, grinning shyly.

"One would think I was crying."

"Haven't you ever cried?"

"Of course. Often. Mostly because I was afraid."

"Of what?"

231

"Of being alone—of being hurt. I used to try and imagine pain—the kind of pain those old martyrs suffered—and to wonder how they had endured it. I knew I couldn't. I knew I'd run away."

"But you didn't."

"Oh, yes, I did, as far as I could get." He was eating with a tranquillity that did not deceive her. For some reason, he was uneasy, intently waiting as though for some invisible, inevitable event. "Then it seemed that I had crossed a sort of frontier. I was beyond pursuit. My body was something I had left behind me, an old rag that they could tear to pieces and not touch me. I was rather sorry for it—for those men too. It all seemed so stupid and useless. But at least I knew I would never run away again." She was shocked by his sudden pallor, the draining out of his vigorous life. "Only from the fear of losing you."

"You'll never lose me."

Vain promise. She looked past him. How long had the man been standing there? Because he was embedded in her conscience, she could have believed that the Mas had become his habitat, that he merely emerged from some secret place to remind her that now he had an inalienable part in their life. Against a briefly illuminated dark, he loomed up monstrously. She stood up to switch on an overhead light that would reduce him to the size and danger of a man. But the electric current had been cut off. He remained monstrous.

Pascal asked, "Who's there?"

Ulrich von Freytag came forward without embarrassment. The comical fuzzy little dog trotted at his heels, and Suzon, asleep at Pascal's feet, awoke to growl ominously.

"I'm sorry. My little Mitzi is a gentle creature. Neither of us intended to disturb you. In the dark I took the wrong turning—the old road from the valley, a very bad road, if I may say so. Would you allow me to shelter here till the worst is over?"

"Of course. Our Suzon is jealous. But she is old and has only her growl left. Please sit down. If you are hungry, help yourself."

"Thank you, I'm not hungry. But the smell of your coffee tempts me. If you permit, Madame?" He took her cup and filled it and raised it to her in audacious mocking salutation. The light had come on again. It showed her a strained grey face, a stiffly smiling mouth under blank eyes.

"My name is Ulrich Freytag. In the days when we still flourished our titles, it was von Freytag. I know, of course, who you are, Monsieur Guis—a man beloved and respected in these regions."

Pascal sat in his favourite attitude, his broken hands on the table, his dark head bent in attentive listening.

"I know your name."

"I was in command here during the Occupation. I hope also that you know that I did my best to make a harsh situation bearable, and that I have been exonerated of the excesses of a subordinate. We were both soldiers, so in a sense we are comrades. At least I hope you will accept me as such."

He held out his hand across the table. Nina made an involuntary movement of interception. The thing was abominable—intolerable. But she was too late. Pascal had, in his own way, perceived the gesture and accepted it. Ulrich held the broken fingers in his white hand.

"Did we ever meet?" Pascal asked. The broken fingers had great strength. They held Ulrich's hand when he would have withdrawn it. He might have been trying, with that physical contact, to see what was invisible.

"I think not. You, as I understand, fought in the *Résistance.*"

"Until I was caught. I don't know why I'm so sure that I have met you somewhere. I seem to know your voice."

"It's unlikely. I was a simple captain in the Wehrmacht. I had no part in the handling of prisoners—for which I thank God."

He sounded forthright. He smiled up at the woman standing between them. It was as though he said, "You see, I can put on a good show—when I choose."

She was goaded by her horror of him to a reckless challenge. "Why have you come back?"

Pascal shook his head.

"That's no concern of ours, Nina. It's all a long time ago. We have to forget—and forgive each other."

"What have I to forgive you?" Ulrich asked.

He sounded almost angry.

The thunder had died away beyond the mountains. The rain whispered on the vine leaves overhead, like a fourth presence.

Ulrich did not know why he had asked that absurd

question. The heat and storm had rubbed his nerves raw. He had spent the afternoon tormenting the little brown partridge, prowling round her absurd "Mille Choses", frightening her sick and faint. To appease him she had agreed to invite him to meet Marcel as an old friend who had been kind to her. Meantime he had helped himself to the contents of her till, her assistant gaping at him in horrified bewilderment. The whole business was not only profitable, it had been amusing. But the habit of torment was like a chronic thirst; it could not be slaked. He had reached a point of exasperation when he wanted to slap that pretty, terrified face, tear the pretty clothes from that plump body, and inflict on it grotesque pain and humiliation. He was still sick with frustration when he had chosen the old road to the Mas. Now, strangely, it was ebbing out of him, leaving him cold and hollow.

"Why should I forgive you?" he asked again.

"It's hard to say," Pascal answered. "I used to be an artist, and artists are apt to feel things that they can only put on canvas. Words are not their medium." He smiled charmingly, without bitterness. "You see, I have lost my medium. I can only say—forgive me too."

"You tortured him," Nina said. "Isn't that enough? Leave him alone."

Ulrich frowned up at her. His opaque-grey face glistened with sweat.

"This is between us," he said sharply.

It was as though he had warned her, "This man and I have an account to settle." He went on with amiable calm. "Well, then, I do forgive you, Monsieur Guis, for whatever you may have done to me. As to the reason for my return—well, I have friends here, good friends, not just the Fouqué-Basdurs, who were our natural if not respected allies, but the simple, honest people who understood that I only did my duty. For those who, like yourself, made it difficult, I had a soldier's respect. I still have. I had hoped that we might be reconciled."

An excellent, manly little speech. But he was not smiling any more. He was wrestling with the temptation to throw truth in this man's face—to tear the black glasses from those unimaginable eyes, to force them to see this woman for what she had been—his creature, his paid and bonded creature. He swallowed down the temptation like a flood of nausea. Some queer mental trick had taken him back to a bleak, white-washed room. He was looking straight into eyes that had been alive and beautiful, reliving the shock of an inexplicable encounter, almost that of love. He remembered how, subsequently, he had reeled out of the place like a man drunk and damned.

It was, no doubt, the aftermath of those lost years. Ostensibly he had kept himself intact and had held with relentless stoicism to his standards. But something within him, it seemed, had weakened and momentarily betrayed him.

He stood up. He said thickly, "It is not raining any more. I'll be on my way—with thanks."

"You were welcome." Pascal added gravely, "I still feel that we have met before."


## XII

GEORGES ROBERT and his five companions picked their *boules* out of the dust and followed Lucien Sauvan to the café table. The storm had only intensified the breathless, nerve-racking heat. They were tired, sweaty, on the verge of exasperated argument. But Sauvan at least was good for one round of drinks. Also they had acquired the habit of obeying him. Freddi, in immaculate white sharkskin, nicely balanced between formality and informality, nodded a good-natured greeting. It was too early for his expensive guests. Until their arrival, Sauvan or the devil himself could play host. The national strike that, at the height of the tourist season, threatened an already unhappy, dislocated country with ruin and perhaps revolution, would not seriously affect the Café des Artistes. Indeed, whatever catastrophe overtook whatever social system, Freddi would emerge unshaken. Any social system would have to have its Freddi Waldkirch, if only to circumvent its absurdities.

Georges was grateful for the beer he could not afford. He tried not to think of his dying wife and sickly baby. It was of no use to think about them. He did all that a man could do, and it was not enough. Covertly he kicked off his worn espadrilles to allow his swollen feet to cool off a little. He listened to Sauvan with a dull respect. Other men perched themselves on the ramparts, their arms folded over their brown, naked chests, their faces wary but attentive. They did not like or trust Sauvan; they did not like or trust even themselves. But they hated sullenly the rich people who presently would drive up in their big, shining cars to spend on one meal the wages of a week. At any cost they wanted to kick in those greedy teeth and put a fist in those complacent faces. They listened to Sauvan's promises of a better world with cynicism, but the word "comrade" was his gift to their helplessness and loneliness. It gave them not only a sense of dignity but of marching somewhere and not alone.

"The strike is only the opening round," Sauvan said. "But be prepared. Anything may come of it. You think that because *Messieurs les policiers* have guns in their racks that you can't shoot them too. But we have our guns. When the moment comes, I shall put them in your hands. You have only to see to it that this first round is won." He patted Georges on a bowed shoulder. "Then, my friend, you can feed your wife caviar out of those shop-windows."

Thomas Clerissy, billowing in and out of the tables, loomed over them like a big, black bull.

"Well, how are you getting along with the new god?" he asked good-humouredly. "How are his miracles coming?"

"Take yourself off to your old women," Sauvan told him. "When they're gone, you'll have no one left."

"I shall have God and myself."

"We won't leave you even that much."

Clerissy chuckled.

"We're tough, we two," he said. "We've been eliminated over and over again for centuries. We resurrect." He made them a fatherly sign of blessing, as though, whether they liked it or not, they were his sons, and made his way to a rampart table where a man and woman sat facing a brazen sunset. The men scowled after him, but with respect. He wasn't afraid of them. He'd always been good for a fight, against that Basdur curé and even his Bishop. His burly, good-tempered courage made them sulkily uneasy.

"We'll see what a firing squad will do for him," Sauvan said. He tossed a handful of tattered notes on the table. "I shall be back," he told them.

He strode out of the Grand' Place and down the Petite, past the dimly lighted Auberge des Alouettes, into the Place de l'Eglise. Hearing footsteps behind him, he stopped to light a cigarette and wait.

"Monsieur Sauvan . . ."

Lucien squinted over the little hot flame.

"My Captain . . ."

"I should like to chat with you."

"About what?"

"What we have in common?"

"What have we in common?"

"Ideas. A way of life. Enemies. Friends."

The opaque-white face looked amused. Sauvan smiled back warily.

"We fought each other."

"Oh, from time to time. Not too seriously. And there were co-operative interludes. You remember, I'm sure, that little affair outside St. Martin."

The match had gone out. Sauvan blew a spiralling cloud of smoke into the dark. He gave himself time to seem indifferent.

"You knew about that?"

"We were well informed. Also farsighted. We foresaw against whom you would, eventually, use those guns."

"Who else knows?" he asked, seemingly casual. "Pascal Guis, for instance?"

"I should suppose not. At least—I have not told him. Fortunately for you."

"I'm not afraid of blind men."

"This blind man might be dangerous."

"In what way dangerous—to me, or anyone?"

The two men walked on slowly side by side.

"I have often wondered. But I know the danger is there. My S.S. comrades broke his hands with their revolver butts. He seemed unaware of them, or to regard them as rather unhappy children. A man like that is incalculable." He hesitated, and then added almost to himself, "I remember that once he smiled."

"He seems to have impressed you," Sauvan observed curiously.

"Power of that sort is impressive."

"All the same, we shall eliminate him."

"We should have said 'liquidate'. Different terms—the same technique. But liquidation in the crude sense is not enough. Men can be killed but not destroyed. It is more important that Pascal Guis should be destroyed. I am something of an expert in destruction. I can usually gauge a man's capacity to survive. Some men, like Pascal Guis, can stand up to incredible physical pain but will crack under a moral hurt —as, for instance, betrayal by someone deeply trusted."

"I don't know what you are talking about."

"Of course not. You know probably that Madame Guis was Victor de Fouqué-Basdur's mistress. It's no secret. It's forgiven if not forgotten. But I am the only one who knows that she was our agent whom I planted on Pascal Guis after his release. The Allies intervened, otherwise she would certainly have betrayed him and what we had left of his *Réseau Alliance*. As it was," he laughed, "she married him instead."

"It's all a long time ago. Have you proof?"

"The Fouqué-Basdurs, father and son, would corroborate me. *Du reste,* if challenged, I don't think she would deny it. She has not his stamina. I suspect that she is close to her limits of endurance."

"You are very astute, my Captain. Are there many like you —where you come from?"

"Quite a few. In an unobtrusive way, we are getting together. New slogans, of course, new songs, new flags. We don't sing the 'Horst Wessel' any more. We are not so crude. If necessary we shall make friends with your friends across the border."

"For what have you come back?"

Ulrich von Freytag did not answer immediately. He seemed to meditate over a vital question.

"To rebuild my life."

"Is that all?"

"For money. We need money. I need it. I suspect you need it too."

"Do you know where it can be found?"

"Here and there. Under certain conditions I am prepared to tell you more exactly—even to share with you."

Sauvan ground out his cigarette. He said lightly, "In the world to come I'm afraid you will prove a deviationist, my Captain. We may have to eliminate you too."

"Or vice versa," Ulrich said with amusement.

They walked on more quickly, like men who after some fumbling have found the road to their destination. They passed the bakery against whose red glare old Barberis was blacked out in massive shadow, down the steep steps to the rue des Princes, under the great oak-beam from which, for three days, a body had dangled, swaying gently with the wind.

The street was narrow and unlighted except for a lantern over a locked and studded door in a high wall. Sauvan patted it almost affectionately.

"Monsieur le Comte has discovered that after all I'm a fine fellow," he said. "I have promised when I'm mayor in this rat's nest to toss out Mlle Milly and all that parasitic foreign trash. The old man is almost senile, but he still has influence."

Ulrich laughed.

"So we do have friends in common."

The street wound back deviously to the Grand' Place. The sunset had died to a feverish glow. Night was falling. The gay lanterns had come to life, throwing their colours on the pretty tables. A loudspeaker tossed a lively fox-trot to the languid dancers. Pascal and Nina Guis and the Abbé still sat at their table by the ramparts. Freddi knew that later they would eat inexpensively with the Drouets, but he did not hurry them to make room for the big spenders. He had an unexplained feeling for those three, almost an affection.

"Take your time, my friends; others can wait."

Sauvan touched his companion's arm.

"A charming sight! Married and still happy."

"Do you think so? Perhaps she's glad he's blind. He doesn't see that she hasn't slept well. Perhaps his happiness frightens her. She knows what I can do to it."

"Well—why the delay?"

"It is a matter of timing. One should not hurry over a good meal."

## XIII

ONE of Freddi's means to a successful survival was his genuine love of pleasure, even of other people's pleasure. It made him aware of, if not necessarily responsible for, their distress. The tables of the Café des Artistes were crowded, but his guests were not happy. The majority of them were too exhausted by the torrid heat to dance or even to enjoy their food. They drank out of a sort of defiance of their own uneasiness and of the sullen resentment that encircled them. For if it was true that a deadly paralysis was creeping over the whole country, that from tonight on no train would leave its siding, no engine leave its shed, it was also true that there was plenty of *essence* to carry the big cars from one well-stocked restaurant to another, and that trucks would travel through the night so that prime meats would arrive in time from Lyons. All this Georges Robert, leaning against the ramparts, knew, for though he had no letters to deliver he had bicycled down to Basdur to pick up Lucien Sauvan's last orders from his Nice headquarters. "Wait. But be ready to take over." Take over what? And how? Little Georges Robert didn't bother his head with such questions. He was thinking of his wife and baby, for whom the new heaven on earth, just beyond this present confusion and wretchedness, would come too late. He was kindly and easygoing. But he was ready, as Sauvan wanted him to be, to take some anonymous throat between his hands and squeeze the guilty breath out of it.

Freddi Waldkirch had had experience of such states of mind. They were dangerous. But he knew also that with a little skill a mob on the verge of rampage could be diverted. Definitely he did not intend that the Café des Artistes, his darling enterprise, should suffer broken crockery, broken heads, or even worse.

He made his suave, smiling way to the inconspicuous side table. He bowed with formal courtesy.

"Madame Guis, we remember how charmingly you sing. Help us over a touch of *cafard*."

She said almost roughly, "I don't sing any more." But then she looked at the man opposite her. In her imagination the smiling mouth, still young in its capacity for love and happiness, illuminated the eyes behind their dark defences, so that she saw them as she had first seen them—their shining recognition of a miracle.

"I haven't forgotten, Nina," he said softly. "But please remind me."

So he too had gone back over the years. He was asking her to relive that vital moment with him. She had no choice. He heard the frou-frou of her peasant skirts as she passed him. The breath of her warm body, lavender scented, fanned his face. He heard the applause and then the grateful silence. He could see her standing alone on the empty dance floor, her hands clasped behind her, her face lifted dreamily to the lights and bright with them.

"Is it absurd or wonderful to be still so terribly in love?" he asked.

The Abbé grunted. "A rhetorical question, my son. You know it's wonderful."

That husky, well-remembered voice—

*Auprès de ma blonde*
*Qu'il fait bon dormir*

She sang with innocence. When you loved a woman, of course it was good to sleep with her. It was also good, if you loved a man, to sleep with him. This was simple experience shared alike by the hungry and the surfeited, even by people who hated each other so that for the moment they hated each other less. She sang "La Seine qui coule-coule", and Georges Robert, to whom the Var was the only river in the world, felt that the Seine belonged to him too and that he loved it as the great city through which it flowed loved it. For just so long as she sang he forgot his wife and baby, his swollen veins and feet, and his bewildered wretchedness.

Freddi knew that clients should rise a little hungry from the finest meal. He went out on to the circle, cutting short the applause, and kissed Nina's hand. "Thank you, Madame. You have done us good." At the same time he waved to the overhead loudspeaker. To a slow waltz a few dancers, suddenly revived, drifted on to the dance floor. A man stood in Nina's path back to her table.

"May I request the pleasure, Madame?"

But it was not a request.

Pascal said, "She sang '*Sur le pont*' the first time I saw her, in that ghastly little Left Bank *boîte*. She played her own accompaniment, so casually that you would have thought she didn't give a damn for any of us. Perhaps that was part of her charm. Then she and I looked at each other—full in the eyes, as one does so rarely, and then we both cared. It was like a lightning flash. It flamed up again on that road south. We found each other here. Father, do you believe such things can happen?"

"Since they do happen," the Abbé retorted drily, "I am bound to believe in them."

Pascal pushed up his dark glasses and rubbed his eyes. Sometimes they ached. He went on rather hurriedly, "She isn't happy. Perhaps if I could see her, I wouldn't know, I wouldn't be so aware. She has always withheld something.

Whatever it is, it has widened between us like a rift in the earth. It frightens me. I have never felt so blind."

"We all withhold something from each other," the Abbé told him. "We can't help ourselves. It's one of the tragic facts of our human make-up, one to which we never reconcile ourselves."

"What do I withhold from her?"

"Your knowledge of her—of her unhappiness."

Pascal shrugged.

"I have to wait. One mustn't ask for what is being withheld. Perhaps I've expected too much. After all, ours is no life for a lovely woman, still young, so full of the joy of things: just hard work, poverty and a blind man."

"Whom she loves."

"But perhaps love isn't enough." He asked, frowning with uneasiness, "Why doesn't she come back?"

"She is dancing with that German fellow."

"But she shouldn't. The last time she danced she fainted."

The Abbé pulled him gently back into his place.

"Leave her alone. My future grandson comes of sturdy stock. A waltz won't discourage him."

Pascal said softly, mockingly, "So at last you acknowledge me."

"I've always acknowledged you in my heart. If mine was a sin, I'm proud of it."

"I have always wanted to ask you—did you love my mother very much?"

"I'm no judge. She was my first and last love. We were both young, both lonely. We made each other happy in the short time we were given. I've almost forgotten what she looked like, except that you have her eyes."

"I had." He added rather shyly, "I'm proud of you, too. Even when I was a little boy I liked to call you 'Father'."

Two shadows scuffled past. Thomas Clerissy, on the verge of tears, clutched at the diversion.

"Madame Royat and her luckless Emile. She drags him everywhere with her. It's as though she can't rest and doesn't dare let him out of her sight. There's talk that she's getting a little queer. She goes round hinting that she knows more about her neighbours than is good for them."

"What is she doing now?"

"Who? Nina? Still dancing. I don't think she wants to.

But that German is a persistent fellow. He goes after what he wants."

"What does he want?"

"I don't know. I know what he has done. He has disturbed a number of our respectably buried dead. It's not a pretty sight."

"I thought him harmless, even friendly."

"Germans are never harmless, least of all when they are friendly. And this is no time to pile more trouble on our plate. Sauvan is making the worst of a bad business. Our poor Toussan has visions of himself swinging from that beam. An undernourished simpleton like Georges Robert would undoubtedly knot the noose without question. He believes in Sauvan as humbly and devoutly as his ancestors believed in St. Roche. After all, wasn't he a hero, a great patriot?"

"He was decorated," Pascal agreed drily.

"Decorations! Pah! They have become the hallmark of scoundrels. Not that I should call any man a scoundrel. Who am I to judge? I prefer to call Sauvan a clever beggar—mounted on a red horse that when its time comes will throw him and break his neck—but not before other necks are broken. Our poor people! It's up to you, Pascal; open their eyes in time."

"I can't even open my own," Pascal interrupted good-humouredly. "Who am I to lead the blind?"

"A beloved man, the salt of God's loveliest earth. My son, do you want our people to tear out each other's throats again and wreck what little they have?" He chuckled ruefully. "Do you want even Freddi to be strung up?"

"He won't be—ever. He'll organize a grand fête in honour of the survivor!"

"You won't be one of them. It is one of our national illusions that individuals can stand on the sidelines and watch other individuals slide into chaos. You'll slide with us, you and Nina and the Domaine and my grandchildren." He mopped a hot, red face. "Name of God—I've a right to my posterity."

"Would your Bishop see eye to eye with you?" Pascal asked slyly.

"Monseigneur never sees eye to eye with me. Fortunately he has almost forgotten me. And don't try to sidetrack me. You have your duty."

"I had peace and happiness."

"There isn't any peace." He put a Gaulois in Pascal's mouth and held a match to it. "As to happiness, as I have told you before, it is not our business."

"I wish she would come back," Pascal muttered. "I don't know why I should be so afraid."

Ulrich von Freytag had been a good dancer. He still danced correctly, but with the stiffness of an automaton. Nina tried to hold herself away from the hard, compact body. He was too strong for her, and she guessed that it amused him to force her reluctance. In uniform he had had a compelling masculinity, the charm of a sinister perfection. Now there was a stale odour about his immaculate cleanliness—perhaps of the prison whence he came.

"So Madame Grand'mère has had the track cleared for me," he murmured. "How wise of her! I must make her an appropriate thank-offering. What would she like best? Monsieur Pascal's head on a charger?"

"I've warned you: no one is going to hurt him—not again."

"How fierce that sounds! I'm not as frightened as I should be. I'm giving orders, Nina. You and Monsieur Pascal are going to take that little vacation in the mountains. It would do you both good. At least it would save you a lot of trouble. One night would be enough."

"We're not going."

"Remember, *il faut reculer pour mieux sauter*—or sometimes just to hold one's ground."

"I'm not retreating." She raised tired eyes to his. "Not any more."

"How English you still are! So stubborn! So stupid!" He smiled down at her. His eyes, when he was dead, would not be emptier. "At least be sensible enough to see to it that Monsieur Guis sleeps well."

Thomas Clerissy walked between them, Pascal's hand on his arm. He felt like a link in a chain that was wearing thin and that under sudden pressure might break and cast these two into a tragic separateness. He was their father and their priest and bound helpless by his priesthood.

They strolled down the narrow, twisting rue des Princes and along the grim chateau walls. Pascal had paused for a moment to run his hands over a locked and studded door.

244

"It feels like a prison."

"An old prisoner has locked himself in," the Abbé said, "with his hates and beliefs and illusions that may become realities again. He still believes that we are his recalcitrant serfs who should be brought to heel. He is waiting for others to reinforce him—a mixed pack who after they have hunted us down will doubtless tear out each other's throats. Meantime we shall have lost our little freedoms, justly, since we have not cared enough to fight for them."

"He's goading me, Nina," Pascal said ruefully. "And all I want is to be at peace."

"Peace!" the Abbé snorted.

They climbed the steep, worn steps to the Place de l'Eglise. The bakery door, at the corner, was like that of a small inferno. Barberis hadn't shaved. His heavy, flat-featured face had a look of bafflement and fear. The Abbé greeted him.

"Good evening, my friend."

The man grunted, clenching and unclenching his hands.

"Jean has gone," he said. "My son has been gone two days."

Involuntarily Clerissy drew Pascal closer to him.

"What have you done to him?"

"Me? I have done nothing. What could I have done? I'm his father. Why should he run away from me? The boy's half-witted. Is that my fault? Who is going to deliver my bread for me?"

"Have you told the police?"

The brown, animal eyes seemed to recede, out of reach, in the shelter of the black brows.

"I don't like the police. They stick their noses into matters that do not concern them. I thought that you, Monsieur l'Abbé . . ."

"What can I do? Ask St. Anthony to intervene? Are you on good terms with saints?"

"That's not funny, Monsieur l'Abbé."

"I did not think it was," Clerissy retorted equably.

The three of them walked on into the Place de l'Eglise.

"His bread," Clerissy observed, "is his life. Nothing else has ever mattered to him. Now he is afraid for it again."

At the far end of the Place, Emile Royat's stalls slept under their shrouds. Overhead, in Mlle Milly's studio, La Baronne had started out on one of her great nights. The big window stood open and spilled out light and a cacophony of raucous

245

voices. Two cats sat on the sill, their backs turned disdainfully on the uproar and weaving shadows.

"This afternoon she sold one of her most atrocious paintings," Clerissy said. "Tomorrow I shall have to convince the gendarmerie at Basdur that an artist has a right to temperamental celebrations."

As though she had heard him, La Baronne loomed up, a massive silhouette against the golden background.

"Join us you three! Father, we need your blessing."

"You will need someone sober to keep you out of jail," he flung back at her. "You are about to create another scandal, my daughter. At least abstain from throwing certain things at the innocent. And God forgive you."

She flung up her fat arms in a huge gesture, half comical, half tragic.

"He doesn't have to forgive me or any damned one of us. He needs to be forgiven. Perhaps if He apologizes to me like a gentleman, I will forgive Him."

"Blasphemous old harridan!" the Abbé muttered unhappily.

Under the cypress trees was such dense night that they were both blind. Pascal, who knew by memory every rut and stone, held her close to him, guiding and half supporting her. Her breath came brokenly. With bewilderment and fear, he could feel her utter exhaustion. He stopped at last.

"I'm a boastful fellow. I bragged once that I had become invulnerable. It's not true. Nina, you could break my heart." He asked, "Why are you unhappy?"

"I'm afraid, Pascal. I've been too happy." She tried to laugh. "I'm afraid the gods may be jealous."

"But I've been happy too. So we're both in trouble."

"I've so much to be forgiven. When I wake at night I remember how much. I wonder if you remember . . ."

"I remember how blessed I am."

"Poor Pascal! Who lost so much."

"And gained so much."

"Do you trust me?"

"You know." He turned to her and laid his hands on her shoulders. She could feel the uneven pressure of those broken fingers. "You know."

"But you don't know me—not the whole truth of me. Perhaps one doesn't really know anyone—not even oneself."

246

"Do you love me?"

She answered, after a moment, with the simplicity of an absolute affirmation. "Yes. I've always loved you. I shall always love you. Nothing else is really true."

She heard him sigh faintly. But then he kissed her on the mouth.

"That's all the truth I need—all, at least, that I have a right to ask."

After Sauvan had left him, Ulrich von Freytag had stood for a while on the fringe of the café lights, watching. Now he turned and elbowed his way through the sullen crowd of spectators. They broke before him as though to avoid touching him. It was only a few steps back to the rue des Princes and the studded door. Ulrich knocked three times and then, after a pause, twice. He wondered if a half senile old man would hear and remember.

In the profound silence he heard slow, shuffling footsteps. The door groaned protestingly on its rusty hinges. In the faint light thrown by a lantern on the flagged pathway, the two men considered each other with unsmiling curiosity.

The Comte de Fouqué-Basdur held out a swollen, unsteady hand.

"I was hoping you would visit a lonely old man, Captain. It is a pleasure to meet a gentleman again."

## XIV

Jean Barberis had left no trace. Not even to Pascal, whom he had seemed to love, had he sent an explanation. There were black rumours that he had been killed—or had at last, out of some deep-buried despair, destroyed himself.

Single-handed, Nina piled baskets of stripped lavender into the two-wheeled cart and harnessed Annette, their donkey, between the shafts. With Pascal beside her she toiled in silence up the hot-shadowed, dusty road, through the village gateway, to the Place de l'Eglise. There she left Pascal to sit on the church steps and wait for her. He would smoke a Gaulois and exchange greetings with men and women who of late had become preoccupied and silent. It was as though they asked secret questions of one another—and of themselves. And received no answer.

Mlle Milly peered out of her window and called out, "Good day, Monsieur Pascal!" and he waved in the direction of her voice. He loved the queer old woman. They had been comrades-in-arms in a time which, as he looked back on it, seemed one of peace and deep content. She had been a rather casual, happy-go-lucky fighter of what she called amateur status. But then, as she had explained cheerfully, she came of a race of amateurs who never took serious things seriously, were always blundering on the verge of disaster, and then at the last moment, inconsequentially, wandered off in a new direction.

In the dark Pascal could see what the light might have hidden from him. He could see, between himself and Nina, a third anonymous presence. It was drawing her away from him. One day he would stretch out his hand, and she would not be there. Old agonies, griefs and frustrations rolled down on him from the past, submerging him. She was leaving him newly blind, desolate and defenceless.

Well, as Clerissy said, men were not born to happiness. They were born to loneliness. Only they wouldn't believe it. They sought stubbornly for some perfect union with another heart and mind. Like spoilt children they whimpered because a fairy tale would not come true.

Pascal took off his glasses and covered his eyes with his hands, shielding them from the black sunlight. She should have faith enough to trust him with his share of her burden, even the burden of guilt or her dying love for him. But he could not ask for what she did not want to give. He could only wait.

Ulrich von Freytag perched himself on the sill of Mlle Milly's window, dislodging a black cat which spat at him. From this vantage point he could watch the man on the church steps opposite. Something of the old supremacy, the physical well-being which power over other men had always given him, eased his unaccountable disquiet and tension. Behind him the absurd old woman bustled around in dusty confusion, preparing the tea which he had always loathed but accepted as her peculiar manifestation of her friendship. She had seemed really glad to welcome him. Her faded blue eyes had twinkled with an almost girlish gaiety.

"I knew you would come back, Captain," she chattered in her appalling French. "We have so much to tell each other."

"Prison life is not rich in incident," he said drily. "There is an uneventfulness which makes for boredom. I amused myself by remembering my friends here."

"I hope I was one of them."

"My favourite."

"You had so many."

"Many more than you'd think. Most of them would be glad to be forgotten. I shall remind them." He had always been impelled to boast to her. Now he was under some other compulsion. It was as though he were confronting the man seated, apparently secure and at peace, in the sunlight opposite him, with his insecurity, the absurdity of his faiths. "Would you believe, for instance, that Madame Royat helped me to track down the Drouets or that Barberis turned in that wretched son of his for a few sacks of flour? Or that Madame Guis . . ."

"No," Mlle Milly interrupted firmly. "I shouldn't believe it, even if it were true. Nina and Pascal are my friends."

"Is Lucien Sauvan a friend?"

"Certainly not. I'd believe anything of him. I'd like to. My nephew, Peter, would have called him a twerp—though perhaps by now twerps are out of date."

"But a good fighter who knew what he was fighting for. Do you remember that famous air-drop outside St. Martin? Sauvan and his P.F.T.F. sat on the mountainside and watched us mop up Pascal Guis and his outfit. They wanted guns and supplies for themselves. They got them. We offered no objection. The more often these people cut each other's throats, the better for us—then and now."

She covered her silver teapot with something absurd and woolly that, as he remembered, she called a "cosy".

"How clever you Germans are! You plan so far ahead, don't you? Not like us English who just scramble from one day to another, hoping for the best. Sauvan should have been shot. But then so many people should have been shot who weren't—me, for instance."

"Why? By whom?"

"You."

He was amused.

"Never. Why should I? You were a delightful hostess."

"You were such a nice guest. You used to tell me such interesting things. I can't say that I made much of them myself. But London seemed able to piece them together."

He slid off the window sill, stiff, alert.

"London? I don't understand."

"Of course not. You never gave me a thought." She put the teapot on an oil stove to draw. Why it had to draw he had never known. He had only drunk the stuff to please her. With a conspiratorial twinkle, she rolled back an ancient rug and pried up a loose board. "I've kept it there, as a memento. I thought, 'One day, if the Captain comes back, it will amuse him'."

He stood over the aperture, narrow as a child's grave. As a pall, the ancient transmitter had acquired a thick grey coat of dust.

"God in heaven!" he said softly. "So it was you—in this house—in my very room."

"I knew you'd laugh. I used to laugh—especially at the name they gave me, 'Hedgehog'. And I am not in the least prickly—do you think?"

"I trusted you," he cried out in bitter disbelief, like a betrayed child. "You owed your life to me—you and your damned cats."

"We were so grateful. All except Kiki, who never really liked you. Sometimes I did feel that it wasn't quite cricket. But of course when my nephew—he landed at night at St. Christophe's from a submarine—suggested that I do my bit, I couldn't refuse, could I? After all, it was for my country, just as you were fighting us for yours."

She looked up. He was standing over her. She saw his face.

One cry escaped her, a short, piercing cry of a trapped bird.

Pascal heard it. He had heard the cry of fear too often. He lurched to his feet, blundering across the square, bruising his hands against the wall opposite. He groped over its surface for the open door and stumbled up the narrow steps that even with seeing eyes would have been treacherous. At their head he stopped for a moment, breathless and uncertain. Then a man's body hurled itself against his. For a moment they clipped each other in a panting embrace out of whose rage emerged a strange awareness of each other's flesh and blood. Then Pascal felt his assailant's clasp relax. He was thrust aside. He heard fugitive, stumbling footsteps. They faded into an aghast silence.

"You know," Mlle Milly gasped, "he was really angry. I think for a moment he wanted to kill me. He actually had me by the throat. It was my fault. I ought to have remembered that Germans can't laugh—I mean, not at themselves." She was becoming calm and cheerful again. "There, now! He never drank his tea. You must drink it for him, Monsieur Pascal, whilst I get my breath." She took his hand and led him to the window. He felt that in spite of herself she was still trembling. "I shouldn't have screamed like that. You might have hurt yourself on those awful stairs. What has an old woman to be afraid of anyhow? Why, you're trembling too!"

"I was afraid I wouldn't reach you—not in time. I've never felt blindness as I did then."

"Well, you see it's all right now. I daresay it was just my imagination. One forgets how strange Germans are, so difficult to understand. Say nothing, Monsieur Pascal. The poor fellow is ashamed already."

He sat where Ulrich had sat, in the sunlight, his torn hands about the scalding tea cup, his face bent down to the Place, listening for Nina's return to him with an anxiety which was the aftermath of a near death. For Mlle Milly had not reassured him. Something hidden and deadly had rushed out into the open. He had felt its hot breath on his face. It had embraced him with hatred but also, as he had felt in that strange moment of contact, with fear and despair. Mlle Milly's tinkling voice only brushed his hearing.

"They boast so, don't they? Perhaps they're really frightened people. The Captain used to boast to me, because I pretended to believe him, about winning the war and supermen running the universe. Such nonsense, I used to think. I daresay all his talk about the people here is just more nonsense. He said he'd never forgotten them. He wants to make them afraid of him again, poor souls. I expect they are. No one is quite innocent. Whenever I see a policeman I always feel I've been doing something I shouldn't. And really I'm very law-abiding. But as to that Lucien Sauvan, I could believe anything the Captain said."

Pascal turned to her sharply.

"What did he say?"

Nina drew Annette to a halt.

"I've brought the lavender, Madame Bernard. It's the best crop we've ever had."

The woman sewing at a little muslin bag did not immediately look up. She sat in the shade of the tall grey shambling house, and beside her was an empty chair, a blanket over the

seat, covering the thighs of a ghost. When she at last acknowledged Nina her eyes were stony.

"You're very kind, Madame Guis. I shall not be working
for you much longer. You must find someone else."

A tiny widow's pension and money from the sale of lavender to the tourists were all she had. Nina said compassionately, "But one has to live."

"Does one? Perhaps living is a bad habit that one should
have the good sense to break."

Nina unloaded her baskets and carried them into a dim
passageway. When she came back, Madame Bernard had laid
her work aside. With a worn hand she drew the blanket a
little higher. Late afternoon shadows deepened about her
and her ghost. A cripple felt the faintest chill. "He was all I
had," she muttered.

There was no answer to a despair so absolute. Nina
thought, "In her place I wouldn't want to live." Perhaps it
would be better for her too if, like this woman, she would
let go her hold on the loveliness of life, be gone whilst it was
still lovely. She said, "We have to go on. We seem to have no
choice."

"That's not true. He had a choice. He chose to leave me."
Her stare focused itself on Nina's face. For a moment it
blazed, "Do you know why?"

"I suppose he suffered too much."

"Because he had denounced Pierre to that German. But he
had every right. It was his official duty, wasn't it, to denounce
a man fighting against the government? But he had always
loved and wanted me. So he wasn't sure. The doubt ate him
like a cancer. He thought if I knew what he had done to
Pierre I would hate him too."

"Who told you?"

"A good neighbour, Madame Royat." A dry, ugly little
laugh. "She wanted, she said, to help me. She said if I knew
the truth I would grieve less."

"Who told her?"

"I don't know. She said I could ask the German himself."
Her hands clenched themselves to fists. She said violently,
"My God, didn't Pierre know that I wouldn't have cared if
he had denounced Christ Himself?"

It was of no use to tell her that perhaps the dead man had
found escape in death, not from her contempt but from his
own. That, Nina knew, could happen. What you were, what

you had done, could become an intolerable burden. In the end it was your own judgment that condemned you. Madame Bernard was an uncomplicated peasant; she would not have understood.

Nina took the donkey's bridle and went on her way. She was very tired. She knew who had betrayed the luckless, bewildered cripple and who, inevitably, would betray her. Pascal, too, would be destroyed. He was not, it seemed, fitted for survival. A man of good-will and compassion and love had fought and suffered for virtues that were now only stinking rubble. It was Ulrich von Freytag, ruthlessly in love with death and power, without conscience and so without guilt, who was the true inheritor of the new world.

She passed the Auberge des Alouettes. She had been tempted to stop for a while, to get her breath, to rest from secret flight. But the terrace under the plane tree was empty, the shadowy bar deserted. She loved the Drouets, but she could not open a tormented heart to people who had been tormented beyond the reach of torment. They were like stone images that had the power to move, to be generous and kindly, to seem alive. They might have survived the bloody past, but in the dusty present they had both died.

The tranquil Place de l'Eglise, the deserted church steps—their emptiness overwhelmed her with a fear beyond all reason. He had gone. She had lost him. She began to run like someone suddenly demented. The cart rattled its old bones; the donkey's hoofs beat out a staccato rhythm on the worn cobbles.

Emile Royat, hobbling between his stalls of fruit and vegetables and flowers, stopped to watch her. What was the matter with the woman—what was the matter with everyone? It was like the time when they knew that old Papa Petain had been fooled and that the Germans were coming anyway. Everybody had run to cover, hiding food and money, hiding from one another. Emile had been so ashamed of them that he had to do something, risk his own neck, just to get straight with himself. He had never told Marie, whose hen's head was full of nothing but worry about Louis and Claude and what would become of those miraculous young men. She'd had nightmares and had muttered in her sleep. Now she had begun to mutter again. What right had she to nightmares? Emile thought bitterly. Life hadn't been too easy for her, but she hadn't watched oily smoke go up through the chimney of an incinerator, wondering when it would be your turn.

He humped his heavy shoulders. How rotten things were! They stank to heaven. Everybody playing for his own hand, nobody giving a damn for his neighbour, let alone the next village, Provence, least of all France. Now there was this crazy strike, chasing foreigners and their money out of the country that was like a raped woman, struggling up out of the bloody mess. Well, he thought, measuring out a cautious kilo of tomatoes, he'd done his part, and much good it had done him or anyone else. To hell with everything. Let the bloody Russians and their French pals take over. Better to lick a Russian boot than have your mouth stuffed with French dust.

"Pascal! Pascal!"

Nina heard Mlle Milly's birdlike reassuring voice. She looked up and saw him seated on her window sill. He wasn't smiling. His face was stern and closed. She had a sudden horrible illusion of a puppet—a tragic puppet perched up there in the stage-like framework of the window, not flesh and blood but a figure of sad, implacable retribution.

Mlle Milly peered out beside him.

"We're having a real cup of tea. Come up and join us, Madame Nina."

She heard herself laugh. The frightful illusion had vanished. She saw that the strain had gone from Pascal's face. He was smiling now, his wide and thankful smile.

"I thought you'd never come," he called down to her.

So, after all, he had been waiting for her. Perhaps he had been frightened too.


## XV

MARCEL was usually so gentle and eager to please her in every way. But now he was sullen and stubborn. She'd had hard work to persuade him to wear his best blue suit. He hadn't wanted to accept the German's invitation. He detested Germans. He'd had his bellyful of them. Besides, everything was in a turmoil: the Nice station crowded as it had been at the outbreak of war, swarming with refugees who pushed and fought each other and asked stupid questions about trains to

Paris, Lyons, wherever they came from. And not a wheel turning. Some of them camped in the waiting-rooms or on the street kerbs, like people who had given up the struggle and were just waiting for the garbage trucks to carry them off. Their holiday money was gone; they hadn't even enough to buy milk for their wailing children. (Anyhow there wasn't any milk—or not for them.) The lush hotels strained at their seams, but the cheap ones had emptied overnight as though locusts had swept through them. Consulates and tourist agents were besieged, and tempers frayed to the breaking-point of violence. Now Marcel came to think of it, he was on strike himself. The *Bureau de Poste et Télégraphe* was closed tighter than a drum. Who cared that he didn't want to go on strike, that he was disgusted with the whole business? Nobody cared what he thought or wanted.

Anyhow it was no time to go gallivanting with some damn German.

"For my sake!" she had pleaded, "because he was so kind to me when I was frightened and alone."

His small, insignificant face had gone white with temper. "How kind?"

She had flung her arms round him, giggling.

"Darling—how sweet! To be jealous after all these years!"

He had been only partly mollified. Now he sat on the rear seat of the Volkswagen, scowling morosely at their two backs. The seats were narrow. He saw how close her plump body was pressed against the stranger's. Marcel could have sworn that he was not quite a stranger, that he had seen the fellow somewhere before. But then, he thought, all Germans had something in common: those horrible flat heads, those thin sensual mouths, those sharp, hard eyes, those tough, insensitive hides, those impeccable manners that suddenly gave way.

Captain von Freytag had insisted on shaking hands.

"I seem to know you already, Monsieur Passano. It is not surprising. Your wife talked of no one else. She left me no peace. I had to try and find out what had become of you. I wasn't lucky. After all, I was an insignificant captain. My colonel reproached me for wasting my time on a French prisoner."

"You were very kind," Marcel had muttered with stiff, dry lips. "We are very grateful."

"I was glad to do what I could. It grieved me that we should be enemies. Well, all that is *tempi passati*. We're allies now. In the next war we shall fight shoulder to shoulder."

"We don't want any war," Marcel had growled ungraciously. "All we want is to be left in peace."

"Peace is decay," the German had stated dogmatically. "Only the dead are at peace."

It was of no use arguing with him. Thank heaven, seated where he was Marcel didn't have to try. He was free to brood over his troubles. Everybody had troubles. Brother Hippolyte, whose position as Captain in the Nice gendarmerie was Marcel's pride, was being harassed to death, preparing to cope with disorder—hunt down some crazy fellow who was hiding in the mountains and fled, howling, at the sight of a uniform. And there was Nice itself, where everything had been so gay and carefree, looking like a bedraggled prostitute. What a world! Wouldn't you think men would have enough sense to get together and tidy up the mess? Acts of God, about which you could do nothing, were surely bad enough.

The car swung into the Valley of the Var, already in twilight. Where did this suave bastard get his car and his money? But then all Germans, it seemed, had money. They might have lost the war, but whilst an honest Frenchman could rot in his tracks, they could afford to trample over the countryside like a herd of pigs. Well, who cared? They weren't the only ones. Cars and motor-cycles screeched past them on their way to fresh air and a good time. There were always plenty of people who knew how to scrounge what they wanted out of disaster.

Freddi Waldkirch, incontestably, was one of them. He wouldn't be caught short by a mere strike. In case the electric light failed, he had set coloured candles on the tables. His refrigerators bulged.

"Anything you fancy, my Captain," he said, order pad in hand. His brown, warm eyes speculated over the sullen, anxious-looking little husband and his wife—quite a pretty woman still, though a trifle too plump and not so young, dressed with the inexpensive chic of a shrewd bourgeoise. She and Freddi and even Marcel were good friends of his. On several occasions Freddi had steered custom to "Mille Choses", and enjoyed an apéritif at the apartment on the Boulevard du Cimiez. It would never have occurred to him to reveal by so much as a twinkle how much he knew of the little woman's war-time past. Unless it offered dividends, he was too good-natured to stir up trouble.

He consulted Ulrich with the seriousness of a good host.

"Might I suggest truites aux amandes? A filet mignon to follow?"

And champagne, of course. Mitzi stared at the gold-topped bottle as though it were a bomb that might blow her to pieces at any moment. That afternoon Ulrich had strolled into "Mille Choses" with his casual air of owning the whole place and her.

"I'm afraid it's going to be an expensive party, Mitzi."

He had emptied her cash-box with the cool confidence of a pimp, indifferent to her loathing. All the same, she could not resist the "truites aux amandes", which were delicious, or the music, or the dancers in their gay summer clothes and who didn't seem to have a care in the world.

Marcel danced with her between the "truites" and the "filet". He held her firmly to his meagre body and felt a fine, dominating fellow. She melted against him in adoration. After all, they loved each other. Everything would be all right. He kissed her ear. He was beginning to thaw out, to enjoy himself. Sheer well-being subdued his uneasiness. Even when Captain von Freytag cut in, he gave way good-humouredly. A host had his rights. But when he got back to his table he refilled his glass and tossed down the unfamiliar contents at a gulp. He had an urgent need to be drunk. He was careful not to watch the dancers. He turned his small, white, sweating face to the valley beneath him, already night-filled.

Ulrich bent his cheek to hers. He murmured, "You see how easy it is for us all to be friends."

"Because he doesn't know."

"He doesn't even suspect. He never needs to—if you're a wise, nice little Mitzi."

She gaped up at him, wide-eyed with misery.

"But it can't go on. He's beginning to ask questions—about the money. I've always paid our rent."

"Oh, well, you've been a little extravagant. Business hasn't been so good. A night of love will straighten things out. I might settle for a night of love myself."

He could almost have pitied her. Wretched little brown partridge, winged and fluttering.

"You're horrible—horrible. You always were. You never loved me. You only wanted to torment me."

"Hungry little Mitzi! You only wanted to eat."

In his presbytery study Thomas Clerissy could hear the music like a sardonic background to his anger. He paced up and down the shabby room, his fists plunged in his soutane pockets, in and out of the lamplight. The two Drouets sat stiffly, like effigies, on the hard chairs against the wall. He was not sure that they were even listening. Name of God, he'd make them listen.

"My Bishop has reproved me for the hundredth time," he rumbled. "He says that my Curé and that old dodderer, the Comte de Fouqué-Basdur, have complained that I interfere in matters that are not my business. I have explained respectfully that since God made me a Frenchman, France is my business. The loveliest, richest, most heaven-blest country on the earth is dying—falling apart like a stinking corpse. Why? Because people like you have deserted her. You've thrown her to the wolves. You two are shaking her great dust off your feet—you're running away. Pascal stands aloof, cultivating his vineyards."

He stopped to shake a fist in their faces. As though he had actually struck them, blood flowed into their grey cheeks. A fire like that of rekindling embers glowed in eyes that had been implacably indifferent. The effigies had been called to life. "Well, Monsieur and Madame Drouet, you are not going to America. Maybe you'll starve. Maybe you'll be despised and rejected to your days' end. But, name of God, you'll die where you belong, not like uprooted vines."

He was too angry to hear the door open, but he became aware that the Drouets' gaze had shifted. He turned sharply on his heel and recognized the scarecrow figure teetering against the passage light. He strode up to it and took it by the shoulders and shook it. "You damned son of a damned baker—where have you been?"

"In the hills." Jean Barberis' voice had the thin quality of an exhausted child's. "One is safe in the hills. But then I ran back—almost all the way. Sauvan and his men are marching here. Hundreds of men. Some of them are armed. They're very angry. They make jokes about hanging people—people like you, Monsieur l'Abbé. I heard them. I ran alongside them, among the trees. You should run away too, Monsieur l'Abbé. I can show you where to hide."

"Hide? Run? Damn it—I never ran. It's too late to begin

now." He pushed Jean Barberis aside with such violence that he stumbled into Richard Drouet's arms, and snatched up his beret from where it lay nested in a disorderly pile of papers. Without it he would have felt naked. "Name of God, this time Pascal is coming out of his corner fighting, or I'll repudiate him. I'll deny I ever begot him. I'll curse the day he was born."

He stormed into the passageway where the old Vespa leaned against the wall in dusty neglect, and wheeled it out onto the Place. This time the old rattletrap was going to do its job or he'd kick the guts out of it. To his amazement—but he recognized the hand of God—at the first kick the rusty creature sputtered into noisy life.

Lucien Sauvan marched at the head of two hundred men up the main road from the valley. He had not slept except in snatches for a week. He had sat in on every Party meeting. He had threatened and pleaded. He had finally prevailed, over the timidity of cowards. The hour for direct action had struck. The fruit was ripe for picking. He was impervious to fatigue and hunger. Power fed him. Power flared through his lean, hard body. It was for this he had lived dangerously and patiently through the barren years.

He had warned his father and mother of his coming. They would see, at last, with fear and respect, that he was a great man who held their little wretched lives in his hands. They might even plead with him humbly to be allowed to live.

His men carried lanterns and red flags, and at intervals they broke into the "Internationale", their voices hoarse with the dust that swirled up from under their shuffling feet. Though a brazen sun had gone down behind the mountains, the heat was at its worst—stagnant and feverish. The men did not know why Comrade Sauvan had imposed this gruelling, crazy march on them. He had insisted that the waverers of this mountain rat's nest should be scared into solidarity. With the exception of Georges Robert, they were Niçois. What went on in a village which few of them had ever seen and some had never heard of, seemed to them a grossly inadequate reason for this torment. They were becoming conditioned to unquestioning obedience, but also they were exasperated by days of idleness. At home their wives would reproach them, and there would be vicious quarrels and even blows. They were hungry and thirsty, but no food or drink would be waiting for them. Someone was responsible for their misery. Someone had damn well got to pay for it.

Beside a smooth plane of rock, Sauvan called a halt. Robert held up a lantern for him, and with the facility of practice he painted its surface with a rough hammer and sickle and underneath the words, "Yanks, go home!" There were scattered cheers and angry laughter. Georges Robert himself didn't understand why Americans should be sent home. They seemed a kindly, decent people. Tourists staying at the Auberges des Alouettes actually tipped him when he brought them letters—something no Frenchman would have done. They seemed to realize that it was tough on a fellow with swollen veins to ride up that long, steep road in all weathers. They even asked after his sick wife. Georges felt in his heart that he should have stayed at home with her. She was failing fast, Dr. Chinot said, and her hollow eyes had been full of sad reproach. He had tried to explain what had seemed so clear when Sauvan explained it. He had been promoted. He was Sauvan's liaison officer. To show obedience and solidarity, he had to march at Sauvan's heels. But now nothing was clear to him. He was too tired and footsore even to think.

Swinging through the gateway that led into an upward-winding, cobbled street, the men closed ranks and marched briskly in step. Their singing became louder and defiant. Now at last they would come to grips with something—put their fists in some bastard's face.

Freddi Waldkirch heard them and shrugged resignedly. Now there'd be a fight, broken crockery, and broken heads—about which he cared less. The loudspeaker swept into a waltz which played an ironic counterpoint to the slow-paced, almost religious singing. (It was odd, he reflected, that revolutionaries out for blood should have chosen a German Weihnacht's *Lied* for their theme-song.) The dancers hesitated, glancing uneasily over their shoulders at the frieze of dark, angry faces, raised fists, red flags swaying in the lantern lights.

Lucien Sauvan strode into the bright circle. His nerves thrilled to see how the dancers slunk away from him to their corners. They had recognized their master. Somewhere in the encircling crowd his mother and father would be watching too.

"Clear out, canaille," he ordered, "or we'll chase you out!

There'll be no more feasting whilst the masses starve. I give you just five minutes. Someone send for Mayor Toussan. I am taking office from him. If he values his neck, he'd better hurry."

Pascal put the Abbé's hand gently aside. He did not need to be led. His hearing led him. He crossed the empty dance floor and came to a halt within a few feet of where Sauvan waited for him. In the absolute, sudden quiet the two men, confronting each other, seemed alone.

"The Mayor is ill. He has asked me to represent him. What do you want here, Sauvan?"

Ulrich von Freytag had called him potentially dangerous. Sauvan reflected that he did not look dangerous—a stocky, unheroic figure in his faded workman's clothes, his black, grey-flecked head thrown back, not arrogantly, but as though in attentive listening to things unseen. The scar that ran from his right temple to his jaw stood out on the bronzed flesh like a white painted line. He adjusted his dark glasses. A blind, helpless man. (Ulrich, watching him from his table, put his hand to his throat as to a collar whose constriction irked him. Here, out in the open, was the force with which, sooner or later, he would have to reckon, master, destroy, and then, perhaps, forget.)

Sauvan said loudly (for his mother was a little deaf; she might not hear him), "I have come to clean this place of filthy corruption. I am taking over authority."

"In whose name?" Pascal asked.

"The People's."

"We are the people of Rocquedur. We are our own authority."

"As to that—we shall see. I've no business with you, Guis. Keep out of this. Get back to your collaborationist whore."

A blunder—a bad blunder. He knew it instantly but too late. He was not apt to blunder. Something had confused him and broken the line of his purpose. The very quiet of the man confronting him, his immobility under a stupid, vicious insult was an indecipherable danger, baffling and even frightening. It imposed an uneasy silence on the mob at Sauvan's heels. An espadrille scuffing the dust sounded like the first rustle of storm.

"That was ill-advised, Sauvan," Pascal said. His resonant, calm voice carried over the sea of faces to the last listener. "I was prepared to forget. You force me to remember and to remind others who were guilty with you. I recall a night in January, 1943, when you and your men watched from the hills of St. Martin whilst my men of the *Résistance* were ambushed and slaughtered. You neither warned us nor came to our aid. You stole the guns that had been dropped for us and that we needed desperately."

"I fought with them," Sauvan flung in.

"But not for France. You are not fighting for her now, but for her disruption. You are turning Frenchmen against Frenchmen. You are using their griefs and disillusionment for your own purpose—to serve an alien interest. That is why we here in Rocquedur will have no part of you."

Sauvan stared about him, furiously seeking. But his mother and father had not come. They had stayed away from their son's triumph. So much the worse for them. When his time came, he would have no pity. As to that damned German— you could trust a German to betray an ally when it suited him. So much the worse for him too.

"You are a liar, Guis. Luckily for you that you are also blind."

"My blindness gives me the right to call you to account. Two days later I was arrested. You may know who betrayed me, Sauvan."

Ulrich led Mitzi back to the table. He refilled Marcel's glass. The absurd little fellow was already very drunk.

"You French," Freytag said, good-humouredly, "always pick on the wrong traitor." But he noticed that his hand shook.

Marcel pushed the glass away from him. His meagre body was racked with impotent hatreds—hatred of himself, of his weak acceptance of a detested hospitality, hatred of Sauvan and the dupes herded at his heels. It was as though he and they, hating each other, had united to lay France open to the enemy's derision. It was not for this that a little official in the *Poste et Télégraphe* had worn a uniform and fought and suffered. Violently he stood up, screaming into the face opposite. "Long live France!" He felt Francine's hand clasp his—her pride in him. "Long live France!" he repeated with hysterical exultation.

Someone laughed sardonically as at an old shop-worn battle cry. But Pascal turned swiftly in Marcel's direction. He raised a hand in salutation. And there was no more laughter.

"She shall," he said, "we shall see to it that she does. We are going to clean house—first here in Rocquedur, then everywhere. We have been selfish, corrupt and cowardly. We have failed ourselves and one another. But from tonight our failures are buried. Here and now we begin again." He added with passion, "I at least have been blind too long."

A stone, like a vicious bird, flew over the heads of the crowd and struck Pascal's glasses so that they fell and broke with a small tinkle that sounded loud and ominous in the aghast silence. Pascal put his hands to his face and then dropped them with a gesture of courteous apology for an unsightliness. (But there were many who remembered his eyes as they had been.) Voices, like sparks of a forest fire, leapt out of the dark, died down and rekindled. Freddi Waldkirch had heard that sound too often in his life. A dangerous unity had come to Rocquedur. Its people were closing ranks. This blind man was their man. These intruders would be wise to keep their hands off him. Old griefs, old angers, even old guilts merged in a common rejection of a shameful past.

Freddi slipped out into the open circle, not hurrying for fear that a hasty move might unleash violence, and touched Sauvan on the arm.

"We are all friends here, Sauvan—peaceful people. We don't want trouble. If I were you, I'd get out of here fast."

Sauvan turned furiously on the men behind him. One false move had led to another. What undisciplined fool had thrown that stone? A time would come when he would have the power to shoot a man for less. But that time was not now. He happened to look straight into Georges Robert's face. Its bewilderment, its idiotic grief warned him that for the moment power had gone out of him. His little army, exhausted, on hostile ground, wavered, began to fall back, to disintegrate. He knew his men and secretly, deeply despised them. They would desert him, run to save their skins because though they had bitter resentments they had no faith in him or in themselves. That silly cry, "Long live France!" might even have wakened old, childish memories, old loyalties. Well, a skirmish might be lost. A good leader must know how to retreat. But he would come back. He would live to strike again—more surely. As he stumbled down the dark street, jostled by blundering, panic-stricken shadows, he heard, chasing at his heels, the most deadly of all pursuits—a savage, scornful laughter.

Ulrich von Freytag looked up from his hands, clenched and strained white on the littered table. The strong threads that they had held had somehow broken. A force that he had believed subdued and helpless had risen and was closing in on him. He felt its hot breath on his neck. He had recognized its threat in that drunken fool's hysterical outburst, flung in his face like an insult. He saw it incredulously in Mitzi's wide open eyes, fixed on him as though they saw him for the first time. He recognized a desperate but absolute resolution.

He was no longer safe here.

Freddi's sense of timing was infallible. With affection, he put his arm over Pascal's shoulder and led him back to the table where Nina and Thomas Clerissy waited for him. Then he turned to his guests, smiling and urbane.

"You see, ladies and gentlemen, we have a native-born leader in our midst—a true Provençal, a brave and honest Frenchman. Now it is for his good wife to help us forget a stupid unpleasantness. Madame Nina, sing for us the songs we love. I beg of you."

She rose, helplessly obedient. She looked down for a moment, at the beloved face, streaked with dust and sweat, at the unprotected eyes. For once he showed no awareness of her. There was no response to the brief, questioning touch of her hand on his. It was as though with her frantic appeal against the Abbé's challenge—"Don't go with him, Pascal. These people are terrible. They might kill you. You are all I have"—her old secret betrayal had come out into the open. Almost roughly he had pushed her away from him. Like an abandoned, desperate child, she had followed in the dust of the Abbé's Vespa with its double burden. Now, as she passed him, Pascal withdrew a little, as though to make way for her. But it was a deeper withdrawal.

She sang *"La Seine qui coule"* listlessly knowing that he did not hear her.

They walked through the black tunnel of trees, hand in hand, because the man was blind and it was their custom. But actually he walked, impetuously, a little ahead of her. Ground down by fear, exhaustion and the intolerable heat, she had to take little stumbling runs to keep up with him.

"Pascal—I'm sorry. I shouldn't have tried to hold you back. I lost my head. I was so frightened for you."

"You shouldn't have followed me."

264

"I couldn't let you go alone."

"I had to go alone. My father called me an embusqué—a First World War name for the eternal shirker. He was right. I pretended that the war was over—or that it was no concern of mine. I had skulked behind the Domaine, my debt to Christophe, you, even my blindness."

"There's still the Domaine and me," she pleaded humbly. "We still belong to you."

"The Domaine never belonged to me. And no one belongs to any one." He added gently, with compassion, "People love one another, but they can cease to love one another. Or they may have to take different roads. It's no one's fault."

She declared, panic-stricken but defiant, "I might die. I couldn't help that. But so long as I live I should love you and go with you."

"You don't know where I'm going."

"Do you?"

"Not yet. But I shall find out. Up to now I've made a mess of things. I haven't grown poor Christophe's famous wine. I haven't painted André's pictures for him. But at least I can stand up again for what we both loved, I can find other men to stand up with me." He added with a short angry laugh, "The Sauvans and the Basdurs and the Freytags are going to have a stiff fight on their hands."

She thought bitterly, "But I shall break your heart first."

She asked, "Have you always known what Sauvan had done to you?"

"Not till Mlle Milly told me."

"Who told her?"

"That German fellow. During the Occupation he confided in her. He thought she was his harmless, half-witted friend— perhaps his only friend. When he found out how she had fooled him, he tried to kill her."

Her voice sank to a dry whisper. "What else did he tell her?"

"I don't know." He repeated sombrely, "I don't know."

She was pressed close to him. The fever-heat of her body flowed into his. He could feel her heart beat. But in all that mattered she was a long way off.

He remembered that his schoolmaster, young Monsieur Boutton, had taught his class that once upon a time the moon had been part of the earth. Then, in some horrific cataclysm, it had been torn loose, flung into space, and since then had to keep its course in eternal solitude. He remembered how, one night, as a boy he had sat outside his cave, his arms locked about his knees, and watched the sad white face sink below the horizon, his heart aching with pity and understanding for its loneliness.

It could happen to a man that some one who had been part of him could be torn out of his life.

What happened to him then?

He could feel the hopeless exhaustion of the woman beside him. He shortened his stride and put his arm about her, steadying her. He wanted to tell her, "I've never loved you more." But he would not add to the burden under which she staggered.

Men feared loneliness. They fled it. They bartered their freedom and their integrity for release from it. Only when they accepted it as their destiny could they attain God and their full stature.

It came to him in a flash of illumination that he too could go on alone.

They came out of the trees into the silver-painted courtyard of the Mas. The barn-door stood open. In the light of the full moon Nina saw a shadow hanging from the rafters. It swayed gently, rhythmically, as though only a short while ago it had been dancing and now was coming slowly to rest.

A hot-faced, flustered, but revived Mayor Toussan drove down in his baby Renault, bringing Dr. Chinot and two Basdur gendarmes with him. They stood around the living-room table on which the body, fragile and withered as a last year's leaf, lay stretched out in implacable serenity. In life Grand'-mère Guis had had no substance. Now she dominated the living by her austere enigma.

"She has been dead only a short time," Chinot said. "Who would have thought she would have had the strength and knowledge to tie a noose like that? She must have died at once. You see—the neck is broken." He mopped a white, sweating face. "Well, she has escaped."

"From what?" the Mayor demanded resentfully. "She had had her troubles, like the rest of us. But they were over."

"No, she was hunted by them," Pascal said. "There was nothing I could do to help her." He groped for one of the old

266

claws and held it between his hands. "Perhaps if life had been easier for her, she would have been kind. She took care of my first puppy—my first Suzon. She knew it was all I had." He bent and kissed the sunken cheek. It was as though he reassured her. "I have not forgotten."

Nina stood in the doorway, apart from the five men. She thought, "I'm hunted too. I've been on the run all my life. Now I'm caught. I'm going to be pulled down and destroyed —and he with me." If only she could give this suffering man his child, and then escape, as Grand'mère Guis had done! But as the Abbé had said, death was too easy.

She crossed the patio on which the moon at its zenith poured a white-hot tide. At the foot of the old goat track, cleared now of its tangled overgrowth and which twisted up the Baue like a scar, she came on something black and stiff and contorted. Suzon's body was still warm to Nina's hand. Death had come to her not with the peace of old age but by way of some prolonged and awful suffering.

## XVI

THE funeral cortège wound its way down from the church, through the narrow street and under the archway, to the cemetery where centuries of dead sprawled over the mountainside. It was a tiny coffin, but the four men in their stiff black suits sweated under it. In those feverish, burning days, the dead had to be hurried to their graves. Even those who, like Grand'mère Guis, had sinfully thrown down the gift of life had to be absolved and blessed. Monseigneur and Monsieur le Curé of Basdur could gnash their ecclesiastical teeth over it. The Abbé Clerissy marched resolutely behind the coffin, his strong hands locked in prayer, and behind him men and women to whom Grand'mère Guis had been dead for a long time. But now they remembered that she had been young. Their own deaths stalked at their shuffling, dusty heels.

Ulrich von Freytag watched the procession from the ramparts. He was furious and badly shaken. Mlle Milly had betrayed him. She had laughed at him. And he could not endure laughter. She had not even bothered to complain against him as her assailant. He could imagine that she had said "Poor boy!" as though he had been a badly brought-up child. That wretched old Grand'mère Guis! Even Mitzi had escaped him.

Last night he had persuaded Freddi to return his two guests befuddled and exhausted to Nice, and before the moon waned had made his way swiftly and silently down the cypress avenue to the darkly sleeping Mas. As he foresaw, no menacing growl threatened him. His order had been obeyed—old watchdog poisoned into silence. For all that, he had been aware in all his exasperated nerves of some attentive presence. Instinctively, against all caution, he had switched on his flashlight and through the door opening out onto the patio had seen her lying there, stretched out, in wait for him. He had seen death so often. To inflict it had been life to him. It was still incredible to him that he should have turned and fled. Something perhaps too taut in him had snapped.

Only yesterday he had been the secret master of this place. Even to the Drouets he had represented the power which had reduced them to disillusioned impotence. He had cracked his whip, and a man had shot himself. Madame Royat scampered hither and thither like a panic-stricken hen from the butcher's knife. Pascal Guis he could have destroyed too, maiming the man's heart as experts had maimed his body. He had not done so. When he had collided with Pascal on Mlle Milly's stairs, when for a moment he and this man had held each other in that strange, almost fraternal embrace, the time had been ripe for seizing. He had not seized it. The man was formidable. Ulrich's will to destruction had been flung back in confusion.

Or was it Mlle Milly's laughter? It was not wise to laugh at him.

Freddi Waldkirch strolled out of his bar to stand casually at Ulrich's elbow.

"Well, you've had your fun with us, my Captain," he said pleasantly. "You've dug up a lot of decaying bones and made a nasty stench. But what you never seem to realize is that there comes a moment when the meanest of us has to take a stand and fight. If I were you, I should get going."

"I shall go when I've got what I came for."

Freddi shrugged.

"You can have my share of it."

268

He drove the Volkswagen to Nice and, as was his custom, parked it outside the Casino and strolled without haste down the rue Meyerbeer to "Mille Choses". The shop was shuttered. A hastily scrawled note explained: "Closed for the duration of the strike." From there he drove to the house on the Boulevard du Cimiez. Marcel opened the apartment door to him. He was collarless, and unshaven, and unsmiling. He did not stand aside.

"Francine isn't here," he said. "I don't know where she is." He went on rapidly like a man released from fear by fear itself. "I don't know what you were to her, or what you've done to her. But in future keep out of her way and mine. I don't like Germans. I don't like you. You—you make me sick."

The two men stared at each other. "Little rat!" Ulrich thought contemptuously. He could put his foot on the wretched creature's neck and squelch the life out of it. But then it would be finished. The rat would be dead and beyond torment. In any case he had more immediate business.

"You are not grateful, Monsieur," he said equably, "and I think that you're unwise."

He turned away. The door slammed at his back. The little self-service elevator carried him down to the lobby. Outside the swing doors he took up an impatient watch. Sooner or later the little brown partridge would fly home. One way or another he would make a last use of her.

The mistral, suddenly aroused, lashed black clouds over the white city. It drained the brilliant colours from a sea that, flecked with angry tongues of foam, had become livid and ominous. It swept the streets and boulevards with burning dust. It stung Francine Passano's face to tears—an ashen, sick, desperate face. It seemed to her that she had walked for hours. Her short legs shook under her. Her heart beat a tattoo all over her plump body that was racked with a burning, aching fever. All night she had lain at Marcel's side in a half-delirious wakefulness and stared up into a grey, murderous face. It had recognized her resolution, her defiance. The winged, brown partridge, fluttering in its tracks, had turned, at last, to fight.

But there was no real fight in her—only a simple, humble need to be done with lies, to hide somewhere from Marcel's grief, to die in some hole—forgotten and forgetting.

Someone put a hand on her arm. Someone said urgently, compassionately, "Madame is ill." Then darkness—as though the merciful earth had closed over her.

Ulrich waited. Night fell, and the wind blew maddeningly, but the brown partridge did not come. Instead Marcel stormed out through the swing doors and, recognizing the man in the house-shadow, went up to him and took him by his lapels and shook him in despairing fury.

"She's ill—desperately ill. They've taken her to the hospital. If she dies, I know it will be you who have killed her. And I shall kill you."

"You're suffering from a stupid illusion," Ulrich said. "I am a friend. I have my car here. You are in haste, naturally. Permit me to drive you."

The little man spat in his face.

## XVII

IT was one of Thomas Clerissy's private, reprehensible beliefs that the conception of atonement and divine forgiveness were purely human. God Himself was above them and indifferent to them. Men sought His forgiveness because they could not forgive themselves. They invented childish acts of atonement to quiet their consciences. Guilt and remorse, unforgiven and unresolved, stalked the streets of Rocquedur. They crept into the old church, lit candles at St. Roche and prayed for the miracle of release.

Dr. Chinot came to confession.

"Do you believe?" Clerissy asked him.

The man muttered, "I must, Father. Otherwise life doesn't make sense. We carry burdens that are too heavy for us." In the dark Clerissy heard that he was crying. "Father—I am a coward."

"We are all cowards, in some degree, at some time or another."

"I have broken an oath—the only big thing in my little life." It came then with a gasp, a groan of long-suppressed agony. "I refused to go to the help of a dying man—an escaped airman. I was afraid. I'd worked so hard for what I had. I had too much to lose."

"What more could you have lost than you have lost?" Clerissy could have asked him. But he said gently, "All that is in the past. You have carried your burden for a long time. Why bring it to me now?"

"I had forgotten—almost like an old nightmare. But it is alive again. It has come back."

"It never left you. Evil is within ourselves. You have seen it take shape. You have had to face it in the open." He went on after a moment. "You have confessed. I can give you a penance and the Church's absolution. Your own absolution you can only earn with every dedicated hour of your life." (Not orthodox, of course. But he was not orthodox. He knew that only the heaviest truth could bring ease to the man kneeling in the stifling dark.) "It's a long hard road, my son. But every night that you rouse yourself from exhausted sleep to bring comfort to the sick and dying, you will have passed a milestone."

Afterwards, when he came out, sweating and sad of heart, into the merciless heat, he found Chinot waiting for him. The pale eyes were red-rimmed. But the man had acquired a humble dignity.

"Father, look in on La Baronne. She hasn't far to go. Every organ in her body is rotted. She has led a terrible life. But I think she has harmed no one but herself."

"Her church and mine have been at dagger's point for centuries." Clerissy mopped himself and chuckled. "I will try to steal a convert."

## XVIII

LA BARONNE gave a farewell party to her two best and oldest friends. She regretted that it had to be a relatively sober one. Madame Rose-Thérèse sat at the open window, an opulent matriarch, serious but not sad. Even the jolliest life had come to an end. It was of no use making a fuss about it. She knew that La Baronne would have detested tears.

Mlle Milly bustled about assiduously, trying to bring order where no order had ever been, and from her studio couch on which her huge swollen body lay sprawled, La Baronne watched her with affectionate amusement. For two days she had not bothered to undress. The mistral's feverish breath had overturned an easel, scattered paints and brushes, the left-overs of awful meals, and a milk bottle that dribbled stale milk onto a Persian rug. She had never cared about such messy details; she didn't care now. She had come to the end of a mad but amusing journey. And a good thing too. All that was left her was her love for the men and women who had helped her to occasional oblivion, for the close-fisted peasants who had given her refuge and tolerated her with understanding, for Madame Rose-Thérèse, who had made such a success of an abominable life, for this comical little Englishwoman, who was crazy too, though differently.

"You have never been a whore, Mlle Milly," she said thickly. "You should have been. Whoredom is like prison: it broadens the understanding."

"I was never tempted," Mlle Milly admitted modestly. "To tell the truth, no one tried to tempt me. Not even the Captain. He was almost too respectful."

La Baronne turned her head on its greasy pillow to wink at Madame Rose-Thérèse. Her hair at the roots was the grey of decaying dust. Madame Rose-Thérèse winked discreetly back at her.

"Are you still friends?"

"No indeed. He's very angry with me. And I'm angry with him too. I used to think he was a nice fellow. Of course he may have been badly brought up. Perhaps if he had been to Eton or even Harrow . . . Anyhow, he's cruel. Do you know why he came back here?"

"He told me, '*On revient toujours à ses premiers amours.*' I supposed you were one of them."

"Just to frighten people."

The sick woman lifted her swollen lids to stare.

"What people?"

"Little people. He even gave me their names—just to make me realize what he could do to them. You'd be shocked to know how many of them had worked with him against each other."

"I shouldn't be shocked at all. They were frightened. Fear does things to you—especially if you haven't much to lose. They tried to hold onto what little they had." She roused herself to difficult clarity. "First and last one should hold onto oneself. One should keep oneself intact at any cost."

Mlle Milly desisted in her efforts to brush dust from one place to another. She stood absent-mindedly anchoring a strayed wisp of her grey hair.

"I think I know what you mean. 'To yourself be true', as Shakespeare said. That's why I've stayed English in spite of those temptations dear Gilbert and Sullivan used to sing about. If I wasn't English, I wouldn't be anybody."

The bloodshot eyes rested on her with amused curiosity.

"You've strayed a long way from your roots."

"Not really. We English take our roots with us. I remember what that lovely young poet Rupert Brooke said—something about his grave, wherever it was, being forever England. A lot of people thought it very conceited of him. But I understood. My grave will be like that, even in that awful cemetery."

La Baronne's eyes had closed again. Mlle Milly patted one of the swollen hands in affectionate reassurance and made an admonitory gesture at Madame Rose-Thérèse, who shook her head and remained obstinately seated. But Mlle Milly had no choice. Down below she had heard indignant feline clamour. She tiptoed from the room.

With the closing of the door the old woman dragged herself to her feet. It was like heaving up a huge, bloated bundle that might fall apart at any moment. She staggered, wheezed and groaned. From a battered oak chest she picked out something that was wrapped in a clean napkin. She unwrapped it tenderly and held it out in the palm of a shaking hand. It was delicate and vicious looking. The short barrel gleamed like silver.

"It belonged to my father," she explained. "He was a soldier—among other things. He gave me this just before they killed him—as a last resort."

Madame Rose-Thérèse shook her head.

"Don't, my dear friend. Never take unnecessary risks. There just might be something in all this religious nonsense. You might find yourself in hell."

"I should feel perfectly at home. But I wasn't thinking of myself, but of a last act of good-will to friends."

Someone tapped at the door, and she slid the revolver under her pillow. Clerissy saw only a dreadful wreck of a woman, teetering aimlessly. He greeted Madame Rose-Thérèse with a "Good day, Maman", and wondered why her imperturbable well-being always acted on him like a reassurance that in the long run everything would work out well for everybody.

"Good day, Madame la Baronne. Dr. Chinot gave me bad

273

news of you. As a friend and neighbour, what can I do for you?"

She brushed soiled clothes off a chair to make room for him. She produced a bottle and a dirty glass. He did not refuse it. He sat down, his big powerful body gratefully at ease, his brown eyes thoughtful and compassionate.

"A last stirrup-cup, Abbé. There's not much you can do. I'm on my way to my reward—I hope a nice quiet sleep. If I find myself, as your mother suggests, among flames and demons I shall only shrug. *Plus ça change, plus c'est la même chose.*"

Clerissy sipped delicately.

"It is only a question of time," he said, "before Monseigneur gives me a valedictory kick. Among my many nonconformities is a refusal to believe that God is a sadist. I believe He is incapable of bestialities. They are born, in my opinion, of our fantastic urge to torment one another and ourselves."

"Well, do you believe in Heaven—in the resurrection of the body?" She spread out her barrel-shaped arms, displaying her dreadfulness with a sort of arrogance. "Of this?"

"Of what you really are."

"A drunken, useless old bitch . . ."

"A good, lovely girl . . ."

". . . who once killed a man for a rouble and has slept with the scum of the earth for the sake of a bed."

"I can believe anything. I have sinned myself."

She fell back on her couch with a good-humoured laugh that shook the folds of a creased and dirty neck.

"Your sin walks our streets, Father. It has your voice, your stride, your guts. It has a woman's eyes."

"She and I," the Abbé said, "sinfully but God knows not wickedly brought a brave good man into the world."

She flung at him with sudden bitterness, "To suffer in the worst of all hells—to be a blind artist who will never paint his pictures."

"He may still paint them—after another fashion. One day you will be proud, Maman, of our mayor, our deputy, perhaps France's first blind premier, who will see what must be done to save her."

She chuckled.

"In which case I shall lay illegitimate claim to him. I adore great men. And he will need a rich old grandmother."

"He will walk into the Chamber of Deputies on his own feet."

"Who will lead him?"

"He will not be led." He set down his empty glass and stood up and stretched his shoulders so that the seams of his old soutane creaked in protest. "Well, it's a rough, lonely voyage for him and all of us. It's comforting to know that we shall all sail into the same port." He went over to the sweating, gasping woman and blessed her and then bent down and kissed her on each raddled cheek. "Au revoir, Madame la Grande-Duchesse."

## XIX

The mistral died down suddenly. It left the stale airlessness of an empty and forgotten room. A serried army of dense, sable clouds advanced inexorably from the west. When its ranks were split by a white-hot, twisted sword, a ball of fire throbbed and kindled and spread out greedy devouring tentacles. From the Rocquedur ramparts Mayor Toussan and a huddle of men and women watched anxiously. The mayor counted the thunderclaps aloud.

"Five miles—four miles. It's bad. The wind is rising. God grant," he added piously, "that it blows away from us."

Ulrich von Freytag ran down the narrow stairs from his room. In his pockets were what money he had left, his passport, and a few bare necessities. Not even the Drouets must guess that he was in full flight. He found them standing together under the plane tree as though they were in wait for him. Something, he recognized, had happend to those two. They had been dead. Now they were alive and watchful. Also they were indifferent to him, almost unaware of him, as though he had lost substance. They did not even hate him. He had a momentary, dangerous impulse to throw himself on their understanding of pursuit and fear. He choked it down.

"I shall not be back for supper. Good night."

They did not answer.

He walked fast, keeping to the deepest shadow. When lightning struck and filled the street with a brief lurid glare he stopped instinctively, his face to the wall. Yet no one watched for him. The street was empty. There were no lights in the windows. A shutter banged in a gust of wind. And he started violently. But there was no pursuit. He scarcely knew from what he fled. The thunder drowned his footfalls.

All the same he was afraid and angry with himself. Through eight years of impotence and humiliation he had kept his pride and will intact with an irrational yet fixed purpose. He would somehow, some day, come back to the place. The recovery of the Eichtersheimer ransom money was one goal. It was not the main one. He had thought of the village as of a woman whom he had ruthlessly possessed and who had finally driven him out with derisive laughter. She would be beaten for it. He would inflict wounds and watch them fester. There was to be no more laughter.

But Mlle Milly had laughed at him.

He knew now that his thirst for death and suffering had disastrously dominated reason and caution. The village, at first stricken and cringing, had turned on him like a mauled and savage animal. Or perhaps he was exaggerating. His nerves had rotted. Only by a desperate reassertion of his will could he control his legs from running, his mind from headlong, irrational panic.

Something shuffled softly at his heels. He turned with a stifled gasp. The little dog stopped too, a humble shadow at his feet. He had shut her in his room, hoping to fool her. But she had not been fooled. He could feel her honey-coloured eyes blinking up at him with loving triumph. "You see, you can't leave me behind." And he could hear her panting.

"Get back, Mitzi! Damn you—go home!"

If the stupid brute persisted he would have to kill her too. Where he was going he would have to be, finally, alone. He almost hated her. He almost loved her.

He controlled himself with an effort. One thing at a time. First, he had to have money. Nina Guis, if she valued her own safety, would have to save him. That damnable old woman! It had not occurred to him that he might frighten her literally to death. He must not make the same mistake again. What had Freddi said? That there was a point at which the worst coward had to stand and fight.

"Mitzi—you little fool—go back!"

He kicked at her savagely. She withdrew out of reach. She knew that he would not go without her. He was only pretending to be angry.

276

He passed through the gateway and took the dirt road under the cypress trees to the Mas. Even in his excitement he was aware of a pale, persisting glow that illuminated the dust and of a mounting heat that poured sweat down his face and flanks. When an obese figure lurched out from among the black tree trunks in front of him, he made a short, barking sound of sheer terror.

"Good evening, my Captain."

The drunken old Russian bitch! He had to control himself. After all, they had been friends. She had eaten at his table, befuddled herself with his wine. She had no scruples and no fear of man or God or devil. She might be useful.

"A bad night, Madame la Baronne."

"A disturbing night. I don't mind lightning. Thunder gets on my nerves. I was restless. Permit me to walk a little way with you."

"I am in a hurry."

"Pascal won't run away. Will you?"

"What?"

"Run away."

He stopped to stare at her. The bloody glow illuminated her amused and dreadful face. They might have been two characters caught in the spotlight of some violent, senseless melodrama.

"Suppose I do?"

"It's stupid to run away. I've tried it. You end up where you started—with yourself."

"You and I come of a generation of the hunters and the hunted," he told her. "We should help each other."

"To escape?" she asked. She waddled beside him, horribly panting. "Your little dog—so faithful. They say animals are good judges of people. There must be some virtue in you, Captain von Freytag. Deep buried. But she has smelled it out."

"I feed her," he said scornfully.

"You must have more confidence in yourself. You Germans lack confidence. You plan too much. When you come up against imponderables, you fall apart. Now you are planning to escape, but the imponderables are like the furies. They stick to your heels."

"Is this a lecture?"

"Merely a last word."

"In that case I'll say good night."

277

He walked on fast. He was almost running when the sharp clear sound overtook him, almost in the same instant that a blow caught him on the thigh. It was at first painless, but it brought him down. He crouched in a swirl of dust, furious and bewildered. His hand, lifted to the lurid, brightening light, was black with blood.

"The bitch," he whispered. "The damned, crazy bitch!"

He shifted his position to look back at her and curse her. What he saw brought him with a scream, briefly to his knees. The whole world, it seemed, had exploded in red, billowing, smoking fury. The cypress trees had become torches that passed their flame from one to the other. They were marching down on him. But he could not stand. He could only drag himself, like a maimed animal, through the hot dust. He had only one purpose left, as imperative as the instinct for survival—to reach Pascal Guis, to keep with him a final predestined rendezvous.

## XX

SOMETHING small but ominous had happened.

At a sudden rending thunderclap, immediately overhead, the little donkey, Annette, usually docile and imperturbable, had kicked her stable-door to splinters and bolted into the night.

"Animals can smell danger," Pascal had said.

Nina prepared a *piperade* for supper in the low-ceilinged kitchen that had been an old haunted woman's refuge. Here, perhaps, she had been trapped by a final horror of herself.

Thunder crackled overhead. It tore the sullen quiet like calico and rolled over the valley to crash against the mountains. Lightning must have struck the Basdur electric plant. The overhead bulb faded and went black. But there was no following darkness. Instead a red, luminous tide flooded about her and threw on the naked wall a terrifying simulacrum of herself.

She fled from it to the man standing in the patio, sightlessly on guard. He put his arm about her as though to reassure her against catastrophe. In a moment the opaque dark had become an evil carnival of monstrous lights that breathed and throbbed and spread swiftly to merge in a closing molten semicircle. The roofs and ramparts of Rocquedur were silhouetted above them like a backdrop of a witches' sabbath.

There had been other forest fires. They were the dread of the Provençal summer. Nina had watched them flower and then—their wicked growth cut down by resolute men—die out. This was different. This was a wild, rampaging beast out of all control.

Pascal asked quietly, "Where are they?"

"Everywhere."

"It's the wind." He lifted his face, scenting the hot, acrid breath, measuring it. "Against wind and fire and drought, one can do nothing. Have they reached the vines?"

"Not yet."

"Poor Christophe! He loved his vineyards." He drew her closer. "You're crying. Why? We shall be safe."

"You'll have lost everything."

"I shall have you."

She asked falteringly, "And if I were lost?"

"I should go on somehow."

She withdrew from him with a tired gesture of total resignation.

"So it's I who have lost you."

"No, I meant . . ." He was stammering a little in search of some absolute truth. "Just that if you had to leave me—if—if you wanted to, I know now that I could find my own way. We have to—all of us."

With disaster closing in on them, they could talk of what concerned them more than life. It had brought them through years of groping to this reckoning with each other. She imagined that the blank eyes really saw her for the first time and that they were lighted with compassion. He had opened a locked door. He had set her free. He had lifted from her conscience the burden of his vulnerability.

"So what I am—what I have done—doesn't matter any more."

"It matters to you. Not to me. You are what you are to me. Even you can't change that." His hands fastened on her shoulders. He shook her lightly, with a rueful impatience. "All right, if you must—tell me what you've done—what you think you are."

"It's rather late."

"Not too late."

"Did you never suspect?"

"I knew the Germans wouldn't let you come to a dangerous fellow like me—except on their own terms—I suppose Captain von Freytag's terms."

She said in bitter self-contempt, "All my life I've made terms with someone—just to stay alive and safe. When I found you, it was too late. I'd fallen into my own trap. I'd made terms just once too often."

"I guessed that too."

"Yet you accepted me."

"I loved you." He added, "I love you."

"Didn't you realize that on the night when you sent me for Chinot, I might go instead to Freytag?"

"But you didn't."

"I never had the chance. So I shall never know. You will never know for sure. Even if we come out of this alive, you will always wonder . . ."

He said with simple humility, "I shall always wonder at your love." He caught her to him almost angrily. "My stupid woman! Even when I made love to you, you held fear of yourself and me between us like a drawn sword. You could have trusted me . . ."

"To understand treachery?"

"Where I have been one learns to understand that too."

"I tried to tell you, often. It was too hard. I couldn't hurt you. I couldn't bear to lose you. Now it's been simple." She asked childishly, "Is it because it's all over—that we're going to die?"

"We're not going to die." He had the high-hearted serenity of a runner who, stripped for the race, knows that he can win. "Madame forgets that I am an old hand at escape. I've not forgotten."

From the heart of a sinister explosion, a high column of flame was tossed up like an exultant banner rallying an army to a final assault. They heard amid the crackling laughter of burning vines and cypress trees, a human scream of pain and fear. A man dragged himself into the fire-lit patio. Behind him was a black trail of blood and a panting, limping little dog.

Thomas Clerissy raced down the narrow, glowing street. At his heels flooded the men of Rocquedur. They carried spades, axes and any weapon that in their horror and panic they could lay hands on. But outside the gateway, they recoiled, scorched and blinded. The cypress avenue had become a seething, billowing road of flame.

Thomas Clerissy fell on his knees.

They knelt behind him—his people, who for years had been estranged from him and from one another, to whom God had been no more than a hostile superstition.

Ulrich had cried out in German and then fainted, sprawled out almost at Pascal's feet. He and Nina lifted and carried him into the protection of the living room. There he recovered consciousness and, by a convulsive effort, as though in repudiation of his appeal to them, he wrenched himself free and dragged his body like a tattered rag to a chair by the table, where he sat huddled, his head sunk between his shoulders, his eyes colourless in the flushed, agony-distorted face. One leg hung from his body like the broken branch of a tree. The slowly draining blood made a dark pool about him. The dog sniffed at it, doubtful and uneasy. He tried to kick her away from him.

"Damn the little tramp! I couldn't shake her off." He drew a shuddering breath. "That Russian whore shot me—God knows why. She must have been drunk. She couldn't shoot straight. It's my thigh—shattered. I can't stand."

He drank greedily from the glass of wine that Nina held to his mouth, staring up at her over the rim with a cold and calculating malice. "Even you, my dear Nina, can't cheat your way out of this mess." He saw her glance at the man who stood apart from them both, and in a flash of furious understanding, dashed the glass out of her hand. "Of course. Stupid of me. What irony that Grand'mère Guis should have prepared a get-away for you both, and at my orders! Did you know, Guis, that she took my orders?"

Pascal roused himself from contemplation of disaster to say equably, "I knew that she was terribly afraid of someone."

"Of you—not me. She had betrayed you to us. Did you know that too?"

"Her son had been killed on my account. It was natural for her to hate me."

"She loved you," Nina interrupted. She came to the defence of a tragic, defenceless ghost. "Hating you broke her heart."

Ulrich jerked his head at her.

"You don't have much luck with women, Guis. If Nina had

had the chance she'd have sold you out too—you and what we and Sauvan had left of your precious *Alliance*. She wasn't only Victor Basdur's mistress, she was my spy."

His last weapon—somehow blunted and useless.

Pascal shrugged. He said, rather wearily, "You're like a dog yourself, Freytag, digging up an old bone. It's very old. No marrow to it. You would have done better to forget it."

"That means—doesn't it—that she's conveniently confessed in time."

"In a way, I've always known."

"And understood? Well, anyone can understand a pretty woman trying to save herself from Buchenwald or a firing squad. But you must have an immense tolerance." He leaned across the table as if trying to come to grips with this remote, preoccupied man. He ground out, ironically between clenched teeth, "Do you understand everyone, Guis—even the men who broke your hands?"

"Not at the time." He lifted his head, frowning at some persistent but elusive memory. "I did wonder about one of them. An officer. I thought, 'He knows what I'm up to.' But he didn't try to stop me. I didn't know why . . ."

"Perhaps it amused me to make Bach look like a fool. Or it was something else. I don't know either."

"I recognized your voice. I couldn't remember where I had heard it."

"I sat at your bedside. I urged you to talk. I hoped you would refuse. I wanted to see what we could make of you."

Nina laid her hand on his shoulder. She touched him without shrinking. It was he who shrank from her.

"If you would let me, I could perhaps stop the bleeding."

"Keep your hands off me! Get out of here! Climb to the top of the Baue. You should have a superb view of the Domaine, Guis and Ulrich von Freytag burning up together." He added in bloody, sweating triumph, "You can describe it to him, Nina."

But the triumph, obscure but vital to him, faded, lost colour, became confused. He couldn't hold it.

"No," Pascal said. He turned in the woman's direction, and to Ulrich's inflamed fancy, the blind eyes challenged her. He fancied that she answered with a silent, resolute affirmative. "Whatever chance we have, we take together."

"Whatever chance you have, I refuse to share it with you."

He shook her hand from his shoulder. "Keep out of this, Nina. This is between us two."

She withdrew at once as though in acquiescence to an inevitability and stood aloof from the two men who, as the unearthly light which played on their faces through the open door, died down for a deceptive moment, became grey phantoms. She was now a spectator to a conflict, long impending, on whose outcome something indefinable but more significant than their or her own survival depended. Even death, racing to destroy them, would have to wait.

Pascal felt his way to the table. He stood so close to the wounded man that they could have touched each other.

"Yes," he agreed, "it has always been between us two."

"Well, at last I shall have finished with you." Ulrich coughed with the acrid smoke that was beginning to veil them from each other. He rubbed his hand over his face, leaving it a bloody mask. "After all, you'll have lost out to me, my dear Guis. In compensation, I'll leave you my Jew's ransom, buried up there in that cave of yours. I'd have shared it with you, if you'd been a reasonable man. But for that crazy Russian, I'd be safe on my way with it." His sardonic grin became a grimace of pain and disintegration. "Your Nina would have helped me. She has always helped the right people. Now she can help you." The sweat ran down his cheeks, suddenly sunken and old, mingled with blood and trickled into the corners of his mouth. He licked it and an expression of startled, almost innocent remembrance, crossed his face. "Well, what are you waiting for? Even your time is running out."

Pascal stretched out his hands.

"They're not much. But I'm strong. Nina knows the track almost as well as I do. If you'll help me, I'll try to carry you."

Freytag flung at him in furious outrage, "Never."

"You'll have to let me try—or we stay here."

Ulrich met Nina's eyes, dark with tragic acceptance of this man's costly victory. He imagined the three of them on that dire ascent. His arms would be about Pascal's neck. He could kill again—for the last time. There'd be an end to conflict— to derisive laughter. Silence and oblivion.

Nina exclaimed almost angrily, "You couldn't do it, Pascal. It's beyond any man's strength. You can't perform miracles."

"Can't he?" Ulrich choked down a high-pitched, vicious laugh. "You don't know him. He's some sort of a damned

283

saint. That great oaf, Bach, had his measure. He told me, 'Don't lock horns with saints. You can tear them apart; you can bury then ten feet deep, but they destroy you in the end.' Only I didn't believe him."

"You can believe that I shall do my best."

"Not at my cost. God in heaven, leave me alone! All right then, listen." The table shook under his clenched fist. Every bloody item was a drumbeat. "I was there when they broke your hands. I watched them light your body with their cigarette ends. I smelled your flesh burn. I was curious to see how much you could endure before you broke. I was an officer at Paradis. I ordered the execution of those hostages." At the woman's exclamation of horror, he turned on her exultantly, "Ah, that shocks you! Now perhaps you can persuade this stubborn fool that it is his saint's duty to wash his hands of me."

It was incredible to her that she should ever have feared this broken and defeated man, or that she should have seen in Pascal, serving a seemingly futile virtue, his predestined victim. She said with cold horror, "You must be mad, Ulrich."

He nodded a sly acquiescence.

"Perhaps. I may have counted too much on death. You can't kill imponderables. That Russian hellion warned me that you couldn't." Now he was talking fast, stumbling over his words. "That fellow who broke your hands—that young Standartenführer—you never saw him. But you lurched against him and apologized. That frightened them. They were not easily frightened. They lost their heads. They beat you into insensibility. They didn't dare to kill you. Your death might have exploded under their feet. The Standarten-führer fainted. The next day, Bach broke him. He shot himself. As for me, if you had so much as whimpered, I should have been quit of you. I could have forgiven you. Now save your skins. I shall have settled our account."

Pascal turned his face to the fiery doorway. He said impatiently, "We are wasting time."

"Listen to me, Guis—" Freytag wrung his hands in furious appeal—"you have everything to live for—a woman who loves you—who's still beautiful. You can take my word for it, more beautiful than when you saw her last. You could rebuild this place with what I am leaving you—replant your vineyards."

"You have nothing to leave me, Freytag."

"Ach! How inevitable you are! The outmoded man of honour with his moral clichés!" He twisted his body so that he confronted the aloof woman. "What about you, Nina? Do you want to die for no sane reason? They say burning isn't too pleasant. You've a child coming. You know the three of us have no real chance. There are no miracles."

She was not looking at him, but at Pascal's waiting, attentive face. This time she would not fail. She said simply, with finality, "We're staying together."

"You see," Pascal shrugged, "she's my sort of stubborn fool."

Freytag groaned—not now from pain. He had asked for pity and thereby breached the walls of his own defences. The impotence of those eight lost years, humiliation at the hands of despised men, had culminated in this final disintegration. And pity—the kind of pity that would have enabled him to stand up and meet death on his own terms was being denied him.

The thickening, suffocating smoke dissolved like a veil over a child's dream. He saw a little boy riding a fat pony down the green allées of a familiar Wildpark. The pony must have stumbled, for now the boy was lying on the grass, the pony nuzzling him in affectionate concern. "You should learn to hold on to me with your knees, Ulrich." They laughed together. They were friends and allies in a strange and dangerous world. Then suddenly the pony wasn't fat any more. She was just a heap of bloody nothing. Her blood was on his mouth. He tasted its sweetness, wondering and intoxicated. Her brown eyes that had watched him, broke and emptied.

So life was nothing. Death was a man's superb, climactic gesture of its dismissal.

He was losing strength, becoming more terribly confused. As in dreams, one vision melted into another. Now the boy stood in a sombre gallery and looked up into the hard, unsmiling faces of men in brilliant uniforms. They stared down at him from their gilded frames. They said, "You have lost everything we won. We have no place for you among us." His father put a stern hand on his shoulder. "A Freytag never cries. You should have shot yourself—as I have done." Then he too vanished, or rather he became a golden-brown partridge, winged and fluttering for its life, a little dog with laughing, amber eyes.

He came out of the fog of semi-consciousness to the sound of his own voice. He wondered in sick shame if he had betrayed himself.

"Have I been talking, Guis?"

"A little. It's all right. Nothing that you should mind my hearing—about a pony, some tiresome old soldiers . . ."

Ulrich's groping hand found Mitzi's head pressed against his knee. The flickering firelight and the intense heat frightened her so that she trembled. He dug his fingers convulsively into her tousled mongrel hair.

"I don't want her to suffer. She's been a faithful little tramp."

"I had a dog too. I loved her. She was killed horribly."

"I killed her. I gave Grand'mère that poison. She didn't know. Perhaps that's why the old witch hanged herself." He demanded, "Isn't that enough? What more justification do you need?"

Pascal did not answer directly. He looked down at his fists, clenched-white, as though he saw them.

"She'd have no chance," he said. "It's an ugly path. She'd fall or be lost. We'd not forgive ourselves. I have a revolver. Nina will find it for you."

"No, Pascal," she cried out in aghast protest. "He's mad and dangerous."

"I keep one chamber loaded—the second. Captain von Freytag can choose how he will use it."

The two men heard, like a soft accompaniment to the roar of wind and flame, her quick footfalls overhead; the opening of a cupboard; hurrying, searching sounds.

Freytag bent down. He said softly, "In the ear, Mitzi. If one has a steady hand, it's instantaneous. I know." He looked up. His eyes narrowed to colourless slits of light. He might have been contemplating an ironic jest. "Bach did not tell me that saints could be such clever devils—too clever. You are taking a great risk."

"Am I?"

The livid face became tragic in its disintegration.

"I have never pleaded with anyone before. I am asking you —have the decency to leave me."

"I can't."

"In God's name, why not?"

Pascal rubbed his eyes. The heat and smoke had started up an old pain. But he was smiling faintly. "I think, perhaps, because as Mlle Milly would say, it isn't cricket to leave a wounded man."

"You talk like a damned schoolboy." He buried his face in his arms. The cracked, harsh sound of a man crying shook Pascal. He pleaded in his turn, "Don't, Freytag. You are a brave man. You're not afraid."

But Ulrich von Freytag cried not out of any fear, but out of indefinable, irreparable loss, a final irreparable defeat.

"You have no right to do this to me." He forced himself to sit upright. He laid his open hands on the table in a gesture of exhausted resignation. His eyes closed for a moment. The long, strange mouth was locked at the corners in the sardonic smile of the dead. His face, ashen and bloodstreaked, was that of a man inwardly crucified. "You should not inflict this on me. It is intolerable. What have I done to you? We never really touched you. You were too much for us. You made our powers and disciplines ridiculous. You destroyed that Standartenführer. Now you are destroying me." His pale, delirious eyes widened on a final truth, "When we are both dead, you will survive."

"You're raving, Freytag. I do what I must—my best. If it is not good enough . . ." He stretched out a groping, fraternal hand, "I shall not forget that, for a moment, you were compassionate."

"Never—never. Don't touch me. Leave me alone, Guis." The frantic repudiation broke. Pascal heard a murmured *"Leb wohl,* Mitzi!" His outstretched hand was taken for a moment in a brief, passionate clasp, then furiously flung aside. He heard a crash, the harsh, agonized breathing of a despairing, hunted man dragging himself to a last sanctuary. He cried out, "Freytag! Ulrich!"

There was no answer.

Nina stopped short on the lurid threshold. The old revolver in her hand had become useless. Pascal stood alone by a chair that had been violently overturned. A black trail led from it to the open door, across the patio, into the smoking, flaming night.

"Pascal, he's gone."

"He had to go." He stooped as though in search of something small and forlorn and helpless. "His dog, Nina—he really worried about his dog."

"She's gone too," she said in pity and wonder. "She must have gone with him."

A grey and guilty dawn.

They stood close together on the rock ledge outside the cave where they had taken shelter for the night. A furious, hungry sea of fire had licked the mountain in search of them. It had not reached them. Only its sparks, like vicious spray, had stung their faces. At last the clouds had burst open with an icy, smothering deluge. It had saved Rocquedur. It had left nothing of the Domaine but smouldering ruin, dead vines, the ashes of the Mas, a still sullenly glowing bed of lavender.

Nina thought, "We're free. We can begin again."

A big, familiar voice, hoarse with fear, reached them through the coiling and uncoiling wreaths of smoke. Pascal waved and shouted back with an exultant reassurance. "We're safe, Father—together."

They held each other's hands. But she withdrew a little to look at him. She saw him neither as the radiant boy whose passionate recognition had answered hers, nor as the patient Provençal peasant toiling for that great harvest that he would never see and with whom she had lived these years of a deceptive peace. She saw him as the soldier, unshaven, ragged and bloody, who had stood upright and alone on that long road of defeat.

The undefeated man.